EARLY PRAISE FOR *SAV*

A tale of missed opportunities, co~~~ ~~~ ~~~-
derstandings leading to disaster, He~~~ ~~~~y's *Saving Phoebe Murrow*
is a compelling first rate domestic drama, a book to set on the shelf
alongside Sue Miller's *The Good Mother*. Insightful, gripping,
in the end thrilling. Most highly recommended.

— Wayne Johnson,
author of *The Devil You Know*

When people talk about the fragility of adolescence, when they talk
about social media and cyberbullying, when they talk about suicide
among teenagers, they will talk about Herta Feely's novel,
Saving Phoebe Murrow.

— Louise Farmer Smith,
author of *One Hundred Years of Marriage*

Saving Phoebe Murrow is a believable, gripping, heart-wrenching novel about how reality can be tragically manipulated in this age of social
media. The wealthy, high-powered political milieu of Phoebe's parents
echoes the social jostling of the teens. Phoebe's anguish as she tries to
fit into the private-school social world is palpable. The intentions –
good and otherwise – of a panoply of characters
coalesce to a dramatic climax.

— Jyotsna Sreenivasan,
author of *And Laughter Fell From the Sky*

Herta Feely deftly evokes the uncertain and fraught world of teenagers and their parents. In her novel, she confidently navigates this
world with brio, candor, and a rigorously grounded and, at times,
humorous style that immediately grabs the reader.

— Sandra Hunter,
author of *Losing Touch*

In her debut novel, *Saving Phoebe Murrow*, Herta Feely masterfully
draws us into a domestic world of petty hurts that morph into pain…
Mothers and daughters beware!

— Ellen Bryson,
author of *The Transformation of Bartholomew Fortuno*

HERTA FEELY is a writer and full-time editor. Her short stories and memoir have been published in anthologies and literary journals, including *The Sun, Lullwater Review, The Griffin, Provincetown Arts,* and *Big Muddy.* In the wake of the James Frey scandal, Feely edited and published the anthology, *Confessions: Fact or Fiction?* She was awarded the James Jones First Novel Fellowship and an Artist in Literature Fellowship from the DC Commission on the Arts and Humanities for *The Trials of Serra Blue.* She has also received an award from American Independent Writers for best published personal essay for a piece on immigration. In *Saving Phoebe Murrow,* Feely continues her commitment to activism on behalf of children. A graduate of UC Berkeley and Johns Hopkins University, Feely is the co-founder of Safe Kids Worldwide, an organization dedicated to saving children from unintentional injuries, the leading killer of children in the United States. She lives in Washington, DC, with her husband and cats. (www.hertafeely.com)

Saving Phoebe Murrow

· • · • · • ·

Saving Phoebe Murrow

a novel

WITHDRAWN

Herta Feely

Upper Hand
PRESS

ISBN 978-0-9964395-6-5

Published in the United States by
Upper Hand Press
www.upperhandpress.com
and in the United Kingdom by Twenty7 Books
www.twenty7books.co.uk

Upper Hand
PRESS

P. O. Box 91179
Bexley, Ohio 43209
USA

Interior design by Columbus Publishing Lab, Zanesville, Ohio

For the three points of light in my life:
Jim, Max and Jack

In memory
of
Megan Meier

· ● · ● · ● ·

Part One
Conflict

Chapter One

Monday, November 10, 2008

At the end of the day, as Isabel stepped through the large glass doors of her law office, a strange thing happened. Outside in the cold, she suddenly felt trapped in a bright cone of light. As if some alien spaceship were training its eye on her.

Uneasily, she gazed into the dark November sky. There was the culprit. A smiling gibbous moon. Or was it smirking, maybe even mocking her? Yes, she thought, that would be more appropriate. Work had become insanely busy, though in its own strange way that kept her mind from dwelling on her recent topsy-turvy personal life.

Which included that awful teen party at Sandy Littleton's, an event that had ruined the weekend. Phoebe drunk, and when Isabel brought her home, Ron found their daughter's wobbly walk vaguely amusing. In front of Phoebe, they'd kept a united front. But later, in the bedroom, Ron told Isabel she was being too harsh on their daughter.

"She's thirteen, Ron."

"Almost fourteen," he'd said.

She really couldn't understand Ron's blasé attitude toward the drinking that Sandy had allowed, encouraged even, nor could she understand Phoebe's recent obsession with some boy named Shane. They'd met on Facebook, of all places, and he'd promised to show up at the party, then hadn't. Ron had attributed Phoebe's drinking to her disappointment over this no show, as if that made it okay. Not okay, definitely not.

Nor did she like the fact that Phoebe had never actually met this character Shane, that all of her communication with him had been online. Who was he anyway? Again, Ron thought it was no big deal! "That's the way kids communicate these days," he'd said.

In the end, Isabel had caved, and Phoebe had received little more than a slap on the wrist. Mostly because she feared the possibility of the 9th grade kids teasing and taunting her as so many classmates had the previous year. Now, she was eager to get home to find out how Phoebe's school day had gone. She hoped there had been no fallout from the Saturday night fiasco, though of course Phoebe didn't know what she had done. Kids could be incredibly cruel.

Isabel strode hurriedly to the underground garage. The wind, gusting up Pennsylvania Avenue, tossed stray bits of paper into the air, bouncing them about inside tiny swirling tornadoes. She flipped up the collar of her raincoat.

Traffic seemed unusually heavy, though rush hour congestion in DC was routine, and cars were backed up as far down Pennsylvania as Isabel could see. As she inched along in her BMW, she mused on the few recent signs of behavior that Ron, her husband of sixteen years, had exhibited only once before. It had been two presidential campaigns ago, to be precise, after he'd been on the road for several weeks covering John McCain's bid for the GOP nomination. In early 2000. At home, Ron had turned sour, testy, distant. She'd attributed his mood to work. He'd wanted to be on George Bush's campaign trail, in the company of the sudden darling of the Republicans and his attendant court of megawatt reporters. Traipsing after McCain, Ron saw himself as nothing more than second string. She'd tried to soothe him, and he'd come around, at least a little.

But then she discovered the true source of his discontent. One night she picked up the phone to call her mother and stumbled on Ron speaking with a woman in an unmistakably amorous tone. Making plans. Her insides had grown watery. Their relationship suffered a blow. She'd been on the verge of calling it quits. If not for five-year-old Phoebe and their infant son, Jackson, she might have. No, she would have. She wouldn't suffer another betrayal. She'd made that clear. And Isabel was a woman of her word. Actions had consequences.

· ● · ● · ● ·

When Phoebe entered her Cleveland Park home, an elegant Victorian where she'd lived her entire short life, she could feel the void of human vibration. She hated coming home to an empty house. It depressed her. "Hagrid," she called out. "Where are you, kitty?" At least their housekeeper, Milly, had left the light on in the foyer.

She'd had a tough day. Shortly before lunch, her once best

friend Jessie had hissed accusingly, "Your mother called the cops on my parents, do you know that?" Followed by: "Do you get what a b-i-t-c-h she is?" Phoebe had stared at her mutely. Had her mother done that? It was true on Saturday there'd been drinking at Jessie's party, but afterward Phoebe had been with her mother and she hadn't heard her make such a call. It would completely suck if she had. So embarrassing. Not to mention that her relationship with Jessie had been on the precipice of a thaw.

Phoebe switched on all the lights in her path – "Hagrid, here kitty, kitty!" – and stopped in the kitchen. If Milly had been home, she would have offered her some cookies and milk, and they could have had a chat. She loved their housekeeper Milly, her reassuring grandmotherly manner. But it was probably best that she not have cookies. No, cookies were the enemy. Had her mother been home, which she rarely was at this time of day, she'd probably have given her carrots.

Phoebe rummaged through the fridge, found a couple of plastic-wrapped cheese sticks, grabbed those along with a small bottle of carrot juice and trudged up to the third-floor, her heavy backpack weighing her down. As she ascended, one thought brightened her mood. At last she'd be able to talk to Shane. Well, sort of talk. On Facebook.

She'd finally be able to ask him the question that had plagued her since Saturday night. Why hadn't he shown up at Jessie's party? He'd promised, and she'd waited. And waited. Then, on Sunday, because she'd been caught drinking, she was denied use of her computer, her phone, basically all forms of communication, and she hadn't been able to contact him.

Now, at last, she'd discover what had happened, and even more importantly she'd remind him of her birthday party, only five days away. She and Skyla were turning 14 and they'd invited the entire ninth grade, plus Shane, who lived...well, she didn't know exactly where he lived, but his handsome Facebook visage hovered in her mind. That mischievous dimpled smile that separated him from all the other boys she knew. Even Noah.

In her room, Phoebe flopped onto her bed, burrowing her back into a mad pile of pillows and favorite stuffed animals; she flipped on her computer, then logged onto Facebook. It had taken some doing, but her mother had finally agreed to let her invite Shane even though he went to Walter J High, a public school about twenty minutes away in Bethesda, and was only a Facebook friend. Phoebe knew she'd mostly agreed because there, at the party, her mother could oversee their encounter.

Still, excitement and relief descended on her at the thought that, finally, she'd meet the real live sophomore boy who'd picked her and *friended* her. Who said he really liked her and was "dying to hook up" with her. Whom she'd set her sights on after several weeks of private chats on Facebook. He was the single bright spot in an otherwise bleak Monday.

Her eyes darted to her private messages on the lower right-hand side of her Facebook page. Five awaited her. And, yes!, one from Shane.

Eyes affixed to the screen, she read, *I don't want to see you. Ever.* Her hopeful smile faded into a frown. *Ever?*

Phoebe read the message a second and third time. What was Shane talking about? Her stomach dipped. She checked for the little green dot that indicated he was available to chat, but it wasn't lit. She stared at his name in the right-hand column of her Home page and prayed he would log on. Her mouth felt dry. *I don't want to see you. Ever.* "*Ever?*" Why was he saying that? What had she done? And her birthday party only a few days away.

Phoebe's glance zigzagged across the room, her attic hideaway, landing first on her childhood saddle and riding gear, then on her Victorian dollhouse with the hidden box cutter, and, finally, on the wall to her right, where the lime green and purple bulletin board hung chock full of photos and memories. She'd pinned Shane's Facebook photo in the middle of all the other memorabilia. He had gorgeous wavy hair and green eyes that blazed with self-confidence.

The green dot popped on next to his name. Her fingers typed as fast as they could: *Why are you saying that? You're joking, right?*

She held her breath.

Not joking.

A tiny gasp escaped her lips. *Shane, what are you talking about?* Again, she waited.

Your mother called the police on Jessie's parents…you tattled about the booze at the party. And then the Littletons got arrested.

I did not tattle, she thought briefly, but that was replaced by the bitter realization that Jessie may have been right: her mother *had* called the police. Had she? Panicked, Phoebe wrote: *I didn't say anything to my mom, I swear.*

So why'd she go inside the Littletons?

I don't know, I guess she was looking for me.

That's so lame.

Her thoughts swirled as she wrote. *You weren't even at the party, so how do you know all that stuff?*

No response. She waited, barely breathing, then his reply appeared. *Don't you worry how I know. I just do.*

She was hardly paying attention to these strange words; she could only think how much she wanted to see him, talk to him, get him to kiss her, to understand this was all a terrible mistake. What should she say? Finally, she wrote: *Why didn't you come to Jessie's? You promised.*

I didn't because I heard you've been messing around with Dylan. What? *Who told you that?*

Instead of private messages, his response now appeared on her Facebook Wall, where everyone could see what he was saying: *I don't tell on my friends.*

She wrote back a private message: *It has to be Jessie, but if it is, she's lying.*

Again he posted his message on her Wall: *You're calling Jessie a liar?*

And now, to defend herself, Phoebe switched to making her responses public too: *No, I meant if she said that about me, she's not telling the truth. Why don't you believe me?*

Again, several moments passed before an answer appeared: *I don't trust you. I heard you said Jessie was fat and no boy wants her, especially Dylan. That's bitchy. Nobody likes bitchy girls.*

Tears sprang to Phoebe's eyes. Why was he making things up? *That's not true,* she wrote. *I never said that!! Please let's talk. On the phone?* In the four weeks they'd been communicating, she'd never heard his voice. All their exchanges had happened right here, on Facebook. He'd suggested that hearing the sound of one another's voices would be a wonderful surprise when they finally met. And to save it for that special day.

But then this from Shane: *I get it, your mom hates Mrs. Littleton, so you hate Jessie.*

She stared at the words. *That's sooo not true. I swear,* she wrote. Though in fact she knew her mother didn't care for Jessie, and probably not Mrs. Littleton either. This was happening because of her mother. All because of her mother. She glanced at the dollhouse. Through the blur of tears, she saw Shane's green dot disappear.

Her gaze fixed on his name. If only she had his cell number. She began rubbing her arms, her fingers absently running over scars and recently healed wounds. "No, no," she muttered softly. She typed a private message: *Shane, please believe me. I didn't say anything. Whoever told you I did was lying.*

She waited for him to respond, her breath catching. Her eyes flicked to the box cutter's hiding place and lingered there for several moments before returning to Shane's photo. He was the cutest boy who'd ever friended her, and a year and a half older than she. His dimpled smile grinned at her from the bulletin board. He looked amazingly like the guy in *Twilight,* though without the ghostly pallor. Why didn't he believe her? Why would he believe Jessie? Had someone else said something? Yet, who could that be? Skyla? How could things get so messed up? Phoebe saw her dream of Shane as her boyfriend slip away.

Why had her mother called the police on Saturday night? This was all her fault. About to retrieve the blade from the dollhouse, she snatched her cell phone instead and angrily tapped her mother's number.

· ● · ● · ● ·

Isabel's iPhone released its symphonic chime. Without taking her eyes off the road, she grabbed the phone. "Hello?"

A frantic voice shouted into her ear: "Mawm, you've ruined everything! You called the police on the Littletons! How could you? Now Shane thinks I lied and he won't see me. Ever!"

Phoebe's attack caught her by surprise. "Calm down. What are you talking about?" Isabel said, although her daughter was right. She *had* called the police. She'd felt duty-bound. Irresponsible parents feeding young teens alcohol! But how had this ridiculous Shane found out?

Phoebe's response came in the form of loud panicked sobs.

"Phoebe? Sweetheart, talk to me." Isabel kept her voice even despite the sudden onslaught of guilt. "Exactly what did he say?"

Between sniffles, she managed, "That he couldn't trust me because obviously I must have told you about the drinking. And you know that's not true! And then he claimed that I said Jessie's fat and no boy would ever like her."

"Did you? No, I mean –" Isabel cast around for the appropriate thing to say. "Phoebe, darling, are you there? I know you wouldn't say that. Where did he get such an idea?"

"Mom, what difference does it make? I like him and now he says he won't see me! Not at my birthday party! Not ever!"

Isabel recognized the panic in Phoebe's voice. For the past year, she'd been flying into emotional overdrive at the drop of a hat, but she was also sensitive, overly sensitive. For an instant, Isabel saw the wounds on her daughter's arms, self-inflicted cuts that made her want to cry. The whole thing actually did sound like a mess. But how had it happened? This guy was only a Facebook friend. "Honey, I'll be home in ten minutes. I'll make you some hot chocolate and we'll sort this out. Okay?" She knew it might take her as long as half an hour, but she'd get there and calm her daughter down.

Why wasn't Ron home yet, she suddenly wondered. He'd be there shortly, she reassured herself, unless some assignment had delayed him. She'd call him.

"This is horrible," Phoebe moaned.

"It's going to be all right," Isabel said soothingly. "Just get off Facebook, okay?"

Once home, she'd explain the truth to Phoebe. She would explain how sometimes you have to make difficult choices, stand up for your beliefs, and that you can't worry about what other people think. Is that what she'd tell her? And then there was this mysterious Shane character; she'd been wary about him, apparently for good reason. Who was he to treat her daughter this way? Maybe now, for once, Ron would listen to her. That's when she remembered he hadn't called her all day.

She waited for Phoebe to say something, but there was silence on the other end. "Phoebe, honey, talk to me." She had to keep her on the phone. Then she heard her weeping miserably. "Phoebe, sweetheart, I'm sure he'll see you. It's just a misunderstanding." The sounds of distress suddenly grew distant then stopped.

"Phoebe?"

She glanced at the phone and saw that Phoebe had disconnected the call.

The latticework of cuts on the inside of Phoebe's pale arm, and many more on her thigh, swirled into Isabel's mind as she finally reached 22nd Street and sped north, aiming for the entrance to Rock Creek Parkway near Dupont Circle. She had to get home, but traffic in the nation's capital – oh hell, the light was turning red. She stepped on the gas.

Seconds later, a siren wailed behind her.

The furious lights of a police car blinked in Isabel's rearview mirror. "Oh, God, not now." She looked for a place to stop on the one-way street, hoping the siren was intended for someone else.

But the vehicle stopped behind her. "Damn it," Isabel moaned. In her side mirror, she watched the policeman's eyes sweep the length of her new convertible BMW, probably making a judgment about her. He sauntered up to the window in that idiotic, languid way some cops have of showing off their authority. If ever she needed to exhibit self-control, now was that time.

She rolled down the window, drew on her lawyerly restraint and explained to the man an abbreviated version of what had just transpired on the telephone with her daughter. Surely he'd understand her need to hurry. Seeing his bemused expression, his complete lack of interest, she went on to describe Phoebe's high-strung personality, and then against her better judgment and sense of privacy told him of her tendency to cut herself when under extreme emotional distress.

But he just stared at her. "You ran a red light, lady," he said, "I need to see your license and registration."

Isabel fished through her purse, finally managing to locate the documents. "Please, officer, I'm telling you the truth."

He took the items from her, glanced at them, said, "Be right back," and strolled to his vehicle. She watched him retreat in her mirror. She picked up her cell phone and tried Phoebe again. After five rings Phoebe's voicemail switched on.

"Hi," her sweet young voice said. "You know what to do...so do it."

Isabel felt the same alien anxiety she'd experienced earlier. *I have to get home.* With one more backward glance at the police car, she cut the lights, put the BMW into gear and eased into traffic. She drove toward the P Street entrance of Rock Creek Parkway, only a couple of blocks away. Never in her entire life had she done anything like this.

As the smiling gibbous moon shone overhead, she kept looking in the rearview mirror, but saw no sign of the police. Her foot pressed harder on the gas, one eye fixed on the odometer. She could kick herself for what she'd done on Saturday night. Calling 911 had been spur of the moment. She always said you shouldn't act in the heat of anger. Still she'd been right to do it. *Damn that Sandy!* Now she had to explain it all to Phoebe. She tapped their home number and waited for someone to answer. Despite two more calls to Phoebe, plus one to Ron, no one picked up. *Damn it!*

· ● · ● · ● ·

Phoebe fought back her tears. She was struggling to make sense of the fact that her mother *had* called the cops. Now she knew for certain that Jessie and Shane had been right. But Shane had also accused her of having been complicit in Mr. and Mrs. Littleton's arrest. *Why can't you just admit it,* he'd said. And yet there was nothing to admit, she hadn't told her mother! Worst of all, he was no longer interested in meeting her and he WASN'T coming to her party! She'd NEVER get to know him. She'd never be a "10" in his eyes! And now everyone would HATE her for what her mother had done.

She fetched the box cutter and began marching around the room. What could she say? How could she defend herself? She ran her thumb across the blade's sharp edge, then returned to her computer on the bed and laid the box cutter beside it. She would announce that she was sorry, very sorry, but she couldn't be held responsible for her mother.

Before she typed a single word, there in broad daylight, posted on her Facebook Wall, she saw that all sorts of people were slamming her. Messages from girls *and* boys, some she hardly knew. A couple she didn't know at all. *What a loser. Glad you're not my "friend."* Several accused her of tattling to her mother about the drinking and called her mother "sick" for calling the police.

Oh, please, not again, Phoebe thought, she couldn't take another year like the last one. She just couldn't, and this was definitely worse.

How low! You are such a piece of trash!

Phoebe gaped at the words then defended herself once more, saying that she absolutely did not say anything to her mom about drinking at the Littleton's party. At once a post appeared from Vanessa, a former Woodmont school friend of hers who she hadn't seen since the summer: *Your mom did that? If I were you, I'd leave home or...slash my wrists! Get it?*

Somewhere in the distance the phone rang, but Phoebe refused to answer it, certain it was her mother. What could she possibly say that would make a difference? The damage had been done.

The words on the screen became a grating noise in Phoebe's head. She closed her eyes and covered her ears. This can't be happening. Make it stop. Please! And where was her friend Emma? She knew she could count on her. But the slights and insults kept coming.

Her hand flew to her mouth when she read: *The world would be better off without you.* She might have expected something this cruel from Skyla or some of the others, but not Shane. No, not Shane.

· • · • · • ·

Isabel maneuvered the car along the curves of Rock Creek Parkway. She pressed harder on the gas pedal, allowing the speedometer to climb well past the speed limit. Half an eye on the road, she kept the other on her iPhone. "Hell's bells," she said aloud, fumbling with the icons, touching the wrong one, banging "end," then striking another. Finally, she tapped Ron's name again and listened to the phone's endless ring.

"Damn it," she said viciously, "answer the fucking phone."

A feeling of dread lodged itself in Isabel's gut, and a sense of foreboding and darkness galloped through her mind. One moment it was the certainty that something bad had happened to Phoebe, and in the next the irrevocable fact that only minutes earlier she'd escaped the policeman, who couldn't be far behind.

She looked into the rearview mirror every few seconds, knowing that when he or another cop caught up to her there'd be hell to pay. How would she talk her way out of this? Could she be disbarred? She only knew that she had to get home and make sure Phoebe hadn't resorted to anything drastic. Anything, God forbid, irreversible. Then she remembered something she'd read on the Internet about cutting: *the worst thing of all about self-injury is that it is strongly connected to later suicide attempts and death by suicide.* No, no, no, she told herself. NO!

Concentrating, watching the car lap up the road, she chased the thought from her mind.

Once more, she tried the home number. But no one answered. The gibbous moon continued to stare down at her with its mocking smile.

Chapter Two

Two months earlier, Monday, September 8, 2008

There was something tragic about fall, Isabel thought, as she stared out the bay windows of her kitchen and saw a leaf flutter to the ground. She was in the midst of setting the table for breakfast, but in that instant, in Isabel's mind, the entire maple tree's foliage crumbled and fell. Though not often, because she didn't allow herself to wallow, Isabel felt a deep staggering melancholy. Today was such a day. The children back to school. The relaxation and joys of summer vacation over. Back to an intense schedule. Autumn death and winter ahead.

A pair of cardinals, chirping and flitting about, rescued her.

"Phoebe, Jackson, time for breakfast!"

·●·●·●·

"Mirror, mirror, on the wall, who's the fairest of them all?" Phoebe said.

With only a few minutes left before she had to catch the bus to her new school, she stared at her reflection in the mirror. Her fat freckled cheeks had slimmed over the course of the summer, or was that her imagination? No, she'd trimmed a few pounds off her weight and she'd gained at least an inch or two in height. She tilted her head and gazed at her eyes, almost amber in color – yes, they were still one of her most attractive features, something she and her mother agreed on. Phoebe batted her eyelashes, which matched her strawberry blonde hair, and tried on a smile. Then, turning sideways and drawing in a deep breath, she compared her body's shape to the magazine photos she'd taped to the mirror's frame, one of Emma Stone and the other of a skinny model from *Teen Vogue*.

Though her figure looked more slender than her pudgy eighth-grade self last year, she knew she wasn't the fairest of them all, but was she even in the game? Making faces at herself, she dashed on pink lip gloss, then grabbed her lime green monogrammed book bag and ran out the door, yelling good-bye to her mother.

"But you didn't even have breakfast! Don't you want me to give you a ride on your first day of high school?" Her mother's shout reached her as she crossed the recently mown lawn of her family's three-story home that stood in the shadow of the National Cathedral. "I'm good," she yelled back. She walked several blocks to the bus stop on Wisconsin Avenue and found a spot on the bench to await the bus's arrival.

Today was no day to have breakfast, not on her first day as

a freshman at Georgetown Academy. Ever since last year she'd vowed to lose weight and leave the ugly duckling years of middle school behind. She could still hear the hideous insults Skyla Van-Dorn had thrown at her after grabbing her thermal lunch bag last spring and dumping its contents onto the cafeteria table. For everyone to see! Two sandwiches slathered with peanut butter and jelly, a container of yogurt, a banana, an apple, a Snickers bar and two Oreos. The girls around her had pointed at the pile of food and laughed. "Gee, Phoebe, eat much!"

Her visiting great aunt Marta had packed the lunch, and even Phoebe was appalled. What had she been thinking? But Phoebe knew. Growing up in Hungary after the war, great aunt Marta had often gone to bed suffering hunger pains. And then Skyla captured the attention of a few boys wandering by with their trays, and they'd joined in the hazing. Even Noah, who she had a crush on, hadn't defended her. Though he did avert his eyes.

Phoebe had wanted to die. Instead, her face had flushed red, even brighter than her hair, and tears sprang to her eyes. She rushed from the table and headed to the girls' bathroom. In the last stall, she sank to a crouch on the floor and sobbed. She was sick of being humiliated, sick of being the brunt of jokes and teasing; Skyla had picked on her so often she'd lost count.

That's when she found a paper clip in her pocket, and without thinking, untwisted it until one end jutted out like a tiny dagger. She'd taken the weapon and run the sharp metal across the inside of her thigh, pushing it hard until droplets of blood surfaced. Then she'd stabbed herself. She'd done it again and again. What had surprised her the most was the sensation of relief that had flooded her body. The way the ragged cuts absorbed her sadness. She'd let out a deep breath of air, then torn off some toilet paper and dabbed at the blood, watching the scarlet color spread onto the tissue. That was the first time she'd resorted to what Dr. Sharma called self-injury.

· ● · ● · ● ·

Isabel stepped out onto the veranda that wrapped around the front of their house hoping to catch sight of Phoebe, but she'd missed her. Her shoulders drooped a little. She took in several deep breaths of air, then a final long exhalation. She straightened, her hands on her hips.

Was it really true, only four more years before her darling girl headed off to some university? The words Vassar, Columbia, Brown, and Stanford cycled through her mind. They were all possibilities, though the thought that Phoebe might live all the way across the country left her breathless. Then again leaving the East Coast for a place like Stanford might be a good thing. Especially after last year's horror.

She glanced at her watch, its single diamond glinting in the early morning light. A few more minutes before she had to leave for work. She lowered herself into one of the wicker chairs and closed her eyes. Her mother had taught her the value of prayer, and though Isabel didn't place much stock in God, she did aim, each day, to be grateful for something.

Today she expressed gratitude for the fact that *mean* girl Skyla VanDorn would not be attending Georgetown Academy. It didn't seem altogether right that she'd wished for this last school year, and then rejoiced when she'd heard the girl didn't get in, and now felt so happy that it was the case. No, her gratitude usually followed more positive lines of thought. But once she'd discovered the perfidy of Phoebe's grade school best friend – Skyla's attacks had been nothing less than vicious – she couldn't help herself. Since there was so little she could do to protect her daughter, not having Skyla at the same school felt like a step in the right direction. The other steps, as she knew all too well, involved building Phoebe's self-esteem and ability to defend herself. And they'd been working on that all summer long. Hopefully the sessions with her therapist, Dr. Sharma, had helped, as well as the talks she'd had off and on with Phoebe.

Isabel opened her eyes. They landed on something lying beneath one of the bushes on the lawn. She craned her neck to see what it was. Then she stood and ran lightly down the steps to get a closer look. It was a brightly plumed goldfinch. Bloodied and mangled. "Oh, Hagrid, how could you?" She couldn't help adding, "Please, God, protect my girl."

· ● · ● · ● ·

Fifteen minutes later, with a mix of trepidation, hope, and excitement, Phoebe joined a stream of students walking up the main drive of the leafy, manicured campus. The school, formerly a mansion, sat amid an entire residential block of Georgetown, all of it walled off from the prying eyes of neighbors and passersby. The red brick walls – some overgrown with ivy and moss, while others showed years of decay – had been constructed by the original eccentric and exceedingly private owner a couple of centuries earlier.

The school's carved wooden doors stood wide open and seemed friendly, as if beckoning students, new and old, inside. Also welcoming them was the recently installed headmistress, Miss Kendall, who seemed young compared to Phoebe's former principal. This woman seemed approachable. Though Phoebe hoped there'd be no reason to approach her. Not like at Woodmont, where visits to the principal had been too frequent. All had included Skyla. The principal always wanted them to resolve "their issues," but they weren't her issues, she thought, and anyway, Skyla was so good at faking it.

As Phoebe was about to pass by her, Miss Kendall said, "Hello." Phoebe came to a halt and greeted her in a small voice. "Hi, Miss Kendall."

"Phoebe Murrow, right?" The headmistress's mouth and eyes smiled. Phoebe nodded. "Welcome aboard," the woman added.

"Thank you," Phoebe said, impressed Miss Kendall knew her name, and moved inside, hoping to find someone she knew.

"Hey, Phoebe!"

Phoebe glanced around in search of the familiar voice. Jessie! Their eyes locked. Friendly, smiling Jessie. New at Woodmont last year, she'd been Phoebe's lifesaver, rescuing her on more than one occasion from the wicked Skyla. Now Phoebe ran to her, her book bag sliding off her shoulder as they embraced, clutching each other for a solid minute. As if they were long lost sisters. Then Jessie latched onto Phoebe's arm and together they continued into the large central foyer called the Great Hall.

They caught up on the last few weeks while each had been away. First, Phoebe had visited her uncle on Martha's Vineyard, then she'd visited her paternal grandfather on Cape Cod. His wife, her Nana Helen, had died shortly after she'd taught Phoebe how to sew a few years earlier, the two memories intertwined, making her both weepy and wistful at times.

Jessie spoke animatedly about her family's trip to the Jersey shore as Emma, their tall, dark-haired friend, joined them. In her skinny black jeans, simple white t-shirt, and assemblage of silver studs and hoops, Emma affected a Goth look. In contrast to Jessie, and now the budding Phoebe, Emma was all angles, flat-chested and narrow-hipped.

"Group hug," Emma said. The three threw their arms around each other for a lengthy, laughter-laced embrace. Though Phoebe's friendship with Emma was recent, she admired this artistic, free-spirited girl. For at least ten minutes, they chattered and giggled, and talked over each other in a stream of gaiety and delight. All the while, Emma snapped a few shots with her new iPhone, capturing this milestone event for later scrutiny.

At once, though, Phoebe stopped, her forehead wrinkling. It couldn't be. But yes, there it was, across the Great Hall. A ponytail. Skyla's ponytail. About twenty feet away. The blonde-haired girl, squeezed inside a knot of tittering girls, turned slightly to reveal the set of mesmerizing emerald eyes Phoebe had come to fear and loathe.

Dr. Sharma had suggested that "without the head of the snake," Skyla's minions would be rendered powerless. Phoebe had counted on it. Now she groaned.

"What?" Jessie said, glancing around, trying to follow Phoebe's gaze.

"Look. Would you look?" The color had drained from her face.

In tandem, Emma and Jessie located the source of their friend's distress. Emma's fingers intertwined Phoebe's and gave them a squeeze.

"Aw, geez," Jessie said, releasing a slight whistle. "What the hell's *she* doing here?" Then going into typical Jessie rescue mode, she instructed, "Act like you haven't seen her. Just keep walking. She's nothing. You're twice as pretty. Honest!" As if that were Phoebe's chief concern.

It seemed as if Skyla had heard Jessie's remark, because the pink-clad girl turned toward them, her eyes dismissing Jessie and Emma and zeroing in on Phoebe. She gave her a long appraising look, then turned away and continued on, several girls trailing in her wake like minnows.

The morning's excitement vanished. In its place, a lump the size of a small fist lodged itself in Phoebe's throat. She simply couldn't survive another year like the previous one, no matter what her mother said. ("Don't let her get to you, honey, you're stronger than that.") *No, I'm not*, she wanted to shout. *I'm not!* And Dr. Sharma's instructions vanished. Clutching Jessie's arm and Emma's fingers, she moved forward, staring vacantly as last year's disasters flashed before her, one by one.

· ● · ● · ● ·

Mother and daughter arrived home at nearly the same time. Isabel had left work a little early to make this day a memorable one. When Phoebe entered the kitchen, Isabel could hardly contain herself. "How was the first day of high school, sweetie?"

Phoebe's eyes slid across Isabel's face and stopped somewhere beyond her left shoulder. She slipped into a kitchen chair and propped her elbows on the table, her head heavy in her hands. Then her chin trembled and Isabel was certain she was about to break into tears. She stared at her daughter, trying to decide what to say or do. What could have happened?

She crossed the room and ran her hand over Phoebe's hair and across her shoulders, saying nothing. A few moments later, Phoebe wiped her eyes with her sleeve and finally told her mother about Skyla. In the process, her eyes darted about, as if frantic to

find shelter. "I can't do it, Mom, I can't go back to that school."
She sounded forlorn, like a child someone had abandoned in the
woods. Like the fairy tale Gretel.

As she looked at her, Isabel's morning gratitude turned to dust.

Chapter Three

For the rest of that first week of school, Isabel pumped up her daughter. "It'll be okay. It will. You're not a little girl anymore. You can handle this. You can."

And each day Phoebe told herself that eighth grade belonged to the past, as her mother and Dr. Sharma directed. "I can handle it." She mouthed the words, as she looked herself up and down in the mirror, selecting just the right clothes and the right amount of make-up, wearing her reddish-blonde hair in a long smooth curve that ended about two inches below her shoulders. Isabel would enter her room, smile at her and tell her what a smart girl she was.

Nevertheless, each day when Phoebe stepped through the doors of the school, she couldn't help peering around skittishly, just waiting for Skyla VanDorn to pounce and again make life miserable. At least, as her mother had observed, they didn't share a single class.

On those occasions when Phoebe couldn't avoid Skyla's gaze, usually across an acre of students, it seemed that Skyla directed a fabulously friendly smile at her. No matter how hard she tried, Phoebe couldn't help glancing over her shoulder in search of the real recipient of that winning expression. But it seemed the waves and smiles were meant for her.

No way she would trust that, though. No way would she fall into one of Skyla's malicious traps. "No way," Jessie and Emma would say, buttressing their friend and peppering her with silly jokes about stupid Skyla.

Then on Friday, at the end of the second week of school, it happened.

In the morning, just before school started, Phoebe was hanging out with Jess, and she noticed that Skyla had again spotted her in the Great Hall. Surrounded by her usual clique, Skyla beelined toward them. Though of average height, Phoebe's nemesis seemed tall, very tall, and her stride purposeful. Her blonde-streaked ponytail flipped maniacally from side to side as she pushed closer to Phoebe and Jessie. No fewer than five girls shadowed her like bodyguards, maneuvering their way between clusters of students.

Phoebe grasped Jessie's arm. "Oh, my gosh, here she comes," she said in a breathy whisper, her hard-won courage all but failing her.

"It'll be okay," Jessie said softly, her eyes tracking Skyla's dogged movement toward them. "You're fine. Just be cool."

A few seconds later, Skyla wore a triumphant grin as her assured walk ended and she stood before them. "Isn't this sooo exciting?" she gushed at Phoebe.

"What?" Phoebe said, her brow furrowed in confusion.

"Four grades of boys to choose from! Not just one like last

year. Isn't that sooo awesome? Every day I can hardly wait for lunch. My friend Kevin says that's where they check you out." She arched her eyebrows dramatically. "At lunch in the cafeteria."

Phoebe's palms grew sweaty and her throat constricted, making it almost impossible to talk. "I thought you were, uh, going to— uh—" she groped for the end of the sentence. To another school, she wanted to say.

"So who's Kevin?" Jessie said, intervening smoothly.

"He's a sophomore. Very awesome dude." Turning back to Phoebe, Skyla said, "Don't you just love the salad bar, Feebs?" Feebs was Phoebe's nickname from grade school.

At the mention of food, Phoebe's stomach twisted painfully and the urge to flee grew. But Skyla's entourage had formed a tight circle around the girls, giggling and chattering and nodding, making escape impossible. "Yeah, it's great," Phoebe managed, dreading what Skyla would say next, wishing she would leave.

Skyla cocked her head, and Phoebe took a step back, afraid of her penetrating eyes, as if in a single glance they could decipher her every thought and fear. "Look," Skyla said, leaning in confidentially and lowering her voice, "could we like maybe leave all that crap behind, you know, from last year? And sit together at lunch?" Her eyebrows rose half an inch.

Phoebe studied her face, searching for the familiar hint of sarcasm, but Skyla's expression seemed genuine. And the warmth of her voice lingered, enveloping Phoebe like a down blanket. Despite their tortured past, Phoebe could feel herself wanting to believe Skyla. For a moment, she hovered between two worlds. One in which she imagined herself smiling and walking away and another in which she let bygones be bygones. The chasm between the two seemed vast. Then, avoiding Jessie's intense stare, Phoebe said,

"Yeah, sure. Sounds good."

"Okay, deal," Skyla said and lifted her palm for a high five. Phoebe smacked it. As if she'd completed her mission, Skyla said, "Let's go," to her troupe and tilted her head toward the door just as the school buzzer bleated. Like a flock of butterflies, Skyla and her friends fluttered away, whispering and laughing.

Phoebe began to move with them until she felt Jessie's arm jerk her back.

Phoebe stopped. "What?"

"Exactly, what the hell was that?"

"I guess she wants to be friends."

"Seriously? She calls you 'Feebs' once, invites you to lunch, and you trust her? After what she did to you all last year?!"

"Maybe she's changed."

Jessie heaved an exasperated sigh. "Murrow, you've got a lot to learn."

Chapter Four

Friday, September 26, 2008

Often the simple things in life made Sandy happy. And Fridays were one of them. Today, though, as she rummaged through her gargantuan closet, a touch of anxiety bubbled up. Generally, Sandy experienced little nervousness, but the task at hand, selecting the appropriate dress for the evening's ninth grade parents' party, prompted perfect rings of sweat to blossom on her t-shirt.

One part of her looked forward to the event, while another wished that this Friday marked nothing more than the beginning of a casual weekend, a time when she'd no longer be alone in the oversized house Bill had built for her. On Fridays, she looked forward to doing things with Jessie – chatting, shopping, goofing around – and with Bill – dinner out, a movie, a round of golf with a few friends. The latter ranked right up there as one of her favorite activities, though she hadn't managed to get any of the women at Jessie's middle school to join her. She assumed it was because they belonged to the wrong club. The Woodmont moms, and now the ones at Georgetown Academy, belonged either to the Chevy Chase Club or to Congressional. She and Bill belonged to Kenwood.

In Towson, some thirty miles north of DC, where Sandy grew up, she'd joined her high school golf team after her stepfather had taken her to a public course. She'd had such a good time with Les that she wanted to replicate the experience. Plus, the golf team gave her as much time away from home as she wanted. Her mother definitely hadn't missed her. Immersed in the sport, she could imagine another kind of life than the one she'd gotten stuck with.

Now, standing in her closet, she longed for a simple night of duck pins with Bill at their club; she longed for that hushed moment when her ball glided down the lane – her body bending and twisting to influence the ball's trajectory – and then the clattering noise, the nanoseconds of suspense, her breath held, awaiting the outcome. How many pins had her ball knocked over? When she got a strike, she often squealed or shrieked, all eyes turning toward her. And she basked in the glow of their attention.

But tonight there'd be no bowling. No, she and Bill would be mingling with the parents of all the ninth grade students at the Thomas's ritzy home in historic Georgetown. A mansion, Jessie'd called it. Though Sandy could hardly wait to see the inside, meeting the new parents gave her heartburn.

She knew that most, if not all, these folks would have advanced degrees, but especially law degrees. In fact, she'd memorized a line of Sandra Day O'Connor's to get a laugh at cocktail parties: "There's no shortage of lawyers in Washington. In fact, there may be more lawyers than people." If necessary, she'd quickly refer to her as the first woman on the Supreme Court who'd recently stepped down. But there her knowledge ended. And, the fact remained these people were smart with a capital S, while Sandy had barely eked out a diploma from a college in Baltimore, not known for its brilliant students.

All those degrees brought on long moments of suffering, especially when they trotted out the latest in domestic and foreign affairs, and references to concepts she couldn't care less about and often had never heard of. While she longed to penetrate the women's cliques, she felt more comfortable around the men. Despite their highbrow talk, she knew they were vulnerable to her charms. She giggled. *Highbrow.* Not part of her vocabulary, though on occasion she'd drop it and other such words into conversations. Sandy's instinct to fit in kept her sharp.

She pulled a red, low-cut, jersey dress out of the closet. Held it before her in the full-length mirror. It had possibilities. Though maybe a little too bright. She knew this crowd of women tended to wear black to evening gatherings. Like going to a funeral, she thought. She tossed the red dress onto her bed and picked up the phone. She'd call Isabel and find out what *she* was wearing. Perhaps this was the kind of call that would help her connect with Phoebe's mom. She was impossibly busy and never had time for her.

As the phone rang, she glanced at her watch. Isabel had once asked her not to call during business hours, except maybe at lunchtime or in case of an emergency with the girls. Sandy had felt the "request" to be rude and unfriendly, but now it made her nervous to be calling. Still, it was close to noon, so maybe that qualified as lunchtime.

"Hello? Isabel Winthrop here."

Her officious greeting made Sandy hesitate before launching

in. "Hey, it's me, Sandy, hope this isn't a bad time? How are ya?"

After a slight hesitation, Isabel answered, "I'm fine. What can I do for you?"

Sandy cringed at her businesslike tone. And she didn't sound fine. Not really. "Well, I was just wondering what you're planning to wear tonight? To the parents' party, I mean. I figured you'd know what's appropriate, you being a room parent and all? One of the hosts, you know?" Sandy's nerves were getting the better of her.

"It was on the invitation, wasn't it? Business attire, I think we said, since some people will be going there straight from work."

Was that a dig? Sandy wondered, since she worked from home, selling a product that didn't impress Isabel in the slightest. "Well, yeah, I just thought—" she let the sentence trail off. She didn't have the courage to ask exactly what constituted business attire? Why couldn't Isabel be a little more helpful? After all, Jessie was one of her daughter's best friends. Had rescued her more than once from that awful Skyla. Shouldn't that count for something?

"Oh, gee, Sandy, a call's coming in. I've gotta run. Business. Would you excuse me?"

"Sure. See you tonight." Sandy hung up. She twisted a lock of her tinted blond hair around her index finger. *Guess I set myself up for that one*, she thought. She was glad, though, that she'd heard a telephone ringing in the background. At least Isabel hadn't lied.

Sandy had made a few acquaintances last year, but now their daughters were attending another school. Back to square one. She'd tried Emma's mother, Lorraine, but she was just plain strange. Practically an outcast. Isabel seemed her best bet, and yet the coldness of Isabel's voice still echoed in her mind. For the life of her, Sandy couldn't understand why she was so drawn to that woman. Maybe it was her sophistication, the ease with which she traveled through various social circles that Sandy envied. Wanted. Isabel could help her break in. If only she would. She owed her, didn't she?

In the next instant she wondered if changing her name to Sandra would make a difference.

· ● · ● · ● ·

That third Friday of school went well enough. Maybe too well. Phoebe had found most of her classes to her liking, especially English, where she not only fell in love with Ms. Dickinson, who had laughingly claimed to be a distant relation to Emily Dickinson, but also discovered she shared the class with Noah, her middle school crush. At the end of the first week, he'd come up to her after class and in a playful way asked her to trade. "Your notes in English for my help in Algebra?"

Somehow she'd managed to keep her cool. "Sure, Noah. That'd be great." And graced him with a sweet smile.

They'd spoken a little more each day, before and sometimes after class. Today, as he ran his hand through the thick weave of his short rust-colored hair, his neck turned a splotchy pink, and she wondered what was up. Then he asked her to join him, Dylan and several other guys in Adams Morgan after school, an invitation that excited her.

"Can Jessie and Emma come?"

"Definitely. Meet you at Five Guys on Columbia Road, okay?"

The thought of this made her tingly and nervous. No way would her mom allow her to go to a neighborhood as sketchy as Adams Morgan, she knew this without even asking. But she had to go, didn't she? She couldn't say, Oh, my mom won't let me. Then other thoughts trooped through her head, questions her mother would in-variably ask: Exactly what is it you're planning to do there? Who are you going with? Why Adams Morgan? In other words, the third degree.

Well, why not? she told herself.

At lunch, she searched the room for Jessie; she'd know the answers to these questions. Then she heard a shout. "Over here, Feebs." It was Skyla. She took one more look around for Jessie, then, not spotting her, took her tray over to the table where Skyla and a few of her friends sat. Skyla scooted over and patted a place beside her.

Phoebe had sat with Skyla more than once since the previous Friday. It surprised her how easily she slipped into conversation with her former archenemy, much as they had before all the drama began at the end of sixth grade. The one topic she avoided, though, was mention of Noah and Adams Morgan, until Skyla asked, "So, who do you want to go to the fall dance with?"

"Fall dance?"

"Yeah, it's in a few weeks, you know, a mixer. Kevin told me."

Wary of sharing such confidential information, she said, "I guess...uh, I don't know."

"Come on, there's gotta be someone." Skyla gave her a sly, wide-eyed look. "What's the big secret?"

"No secret."

"Okay, well then?"

"Maybe Noah?" Phoebe said tentatively, recalling his hair, sev-eral shades darker than her own, something that seemed meaningful.

"Yeah, he's cute, in a dweebie way." She grinned, her magnifi-cent pink lips stretching across her fabulously white teeth.

Phoebe smiled. "I'm a little bit of a dweeb too, Skyla." She shook her head. "No, you're not. Look at you." She stared pointedly at Phoebe's chest. "You lost weight and gained it in all the right places. *Now* you look fantastic."

These words jarred Phoebe, but before she could fully consider them she felt someone's eyes on her; and when she glanced up, she saw Jessie staring at her in dismay. "Hey, you're late, where've you been?" Phoebe asked.

"Stupid teacher kept me after class," Jessie said in a disgruntled tone as she perused the crowded table. "Guess I'll look for another spot. You seen Emma?"

"She got switched to next shift. Come here, Jess." Phoebe tried to squeeze over but to no avail.

"Over there, Jessie," Skyla said, motioning for two of the girls at the other end to make room. When they didn't, she said, "Hey, guys, move. Okay?" Reluctantly, Jessie sat down.

"Everybody happy?" Skyla chirped before turning back to Phoebe. "You know who I want to go with?"

"No, who?" Phoebe said, trying to make eye contact with Jessie.

"Max. He's a sophomore. Made Varsity football. Pretty cool, huh?"

"Yeah, that's cool all right," Phoebe said, planning to move to the other end of the table as soon as someone left. But Skyla chattered on, making escape impossible.

At once, Skyla lowered her voice. Eyes wide, she said, "What do you think about a joint birthday party, Feebs? Sweet fourteen?" She batted her lustrous eyelashes in dramatic fashion. "Just like the old days?"

Phoebe wanted to correct her, sweet sixteen, not fourteen, but confined herself to, "Okay, sure," recalling their tenth and eleventh birthday parties. They'd been fun – delightful, really – and she yearned for the uncomplicated normalcy of those days.

"Maybe we can have it at the club?" Skyla went on, referring to the Chevy Chase Club, where Phoebe's parents were members and Skyla's had once hoped to join. Phoebe's eyes traveled to the end of the table worried Jessie might hear, but she was chatting with Daisy.

"Yeah, maybe," Phoebe said. "I'll have to check with my mom."

After lunch, and out of earshot of Skyla, Jessie said, "Your new best friend, huh?"

"Yeah," Phoebe said and they both laughed, though she detected a hint of jealousy. She imagined if she claimed that she and Skyla had both matured, her comment might be met with Jessie's crossed arms and a skeptical look.

So there was no way she would tell her about Skyla's suggestion of a joint birthday party. In her mind she was already making excuses: Well, our birthdays are only a week apart in November. It'll be fun, don't you think? And, really, I think Skyla *has* changed.

Now she hugged Jessie and whispered Noah's invitation into her ear. Minutes later, a plan was in place to deflect Phoebe's mother's questions.

Chapter Five

With the parents' party in mind, Isabel left her law office early so she could spend a relaxing hour getting her nails done. Work had left her frazzled. Though she often enjoyed running into friends at Aqua, today she just longed for some peace and quiet.

About to enter the neighborhood salon, Isabel heard the chime of her cell phone. She didn't much feel like talking, and prayed it wasn't one of her law partners, or a needy client. Rummaging through her purse, she finally located the phone and saw that it was Phoebe.

"Hi, honey, where are you?" she said automatically.

"Just leaving school."

"Did you have a good day?" she asked.

"Yes. But I was wondering if, uh—"

Isabel grew alert. "Wondering what, honey?" Phoebe sounded as if she were about to stretch the truth. Isabel knew that lying came with the tricky territory of adolescence, but still, she didn't think deception should be tolerated. She had enough of that with her clients. She reminded herself to be patient; after all, Phoebe hadn't lied yet.

"Well...don't say no, okay, Mommy?"

"Okay, no—I mean I won't automatically say no. But listen, honey, I have a nail appointment, so can we just get to the point?" "Yeah, well, we're going to this thrift shop—"

"Thrift shop?" she said. The very words annoyed her as her mind conjured up the pile of smelly used clothing in Phoebe's room. "Who's we?"

"Jessie, Emma, and a few other kids."

Isabel heaved a sigh. "Which thrift shop, honey?"

"Second Chance, and maybe another one."

"Another one?" Isabel asked. "And where is that?"

"It's over in," pause, "uh, Adams Morgan."

Aha, Isabel thought, with some relief. Even when Phoebe knew she might object, she told the truth, and Isabel truly appreciated this in her daughter. So she felt a tiny bit bad when she said, "No, honey, I'm sorry, but you're *not* going to a thrift store in Adams Morgan."

"But Mom—"

"You know that's not a safe neighborhood. Too many things can—" she hesitated, *go wrong,* she thought, but then supplied what she hoped would be just the right solution. "There are plenty of secondhand shops in Georgetown. I'm okay with that. Go ahead, hang out in Georgetown with your friends. Anyway, don't forget you have to be home by six to babysit your brother. The ninth grade parents' party – it's tonight. Remember?"

"But Maawwm—"

"I'm counting on you to make a good decision here. No Adams Morgan. Listen, I'm about to be late, but you can reach me if anything comes up, okay?"

"All right, bye." The call ended abruptly.

Isabel stared at the phone. She had the urge to call back – had Phoebe really heard her say no to Adams Morgan? – but she stopped herself.

As she stepped inside Aqua, Isabel was thinking that more than anything she wanted to crack the code on teen behavior. In lighter moments, she knew she'd be worth a fortune if she did. It was ironic, actually, since she'd broken the code on dealing with white-collar criminals long ago. Sure they were liars, but most of them wanted to tell the truth, to someone. They wanted to brag about what they'd achieved, how they'd pulled the wool over the eyes of unsuspecting colleagues or board members or whomever, and tell her how they'd managed to defraud them, how their schemes had worked, how they'd gotten away with murder. Well, until they'd gotten caught. But getting a thirteen-year-old to talk, to tell you what's on her mind, that was like trying to break into Fort Knox. Heck, Fort Knox would be a breeze by comparison.

Over the past couple of years, Isabel had learned that raising children required a delicate balance. Too much intervention and you ended up with rebellion, not enough and who knew what might happen?

But Adams Morgan? Not a good idea. Again tempted to call Phoebe back, her finger hovered over the send button until she heard the receptionist clear his throat. She looked up. With little more than two hours to go, how much trouble could Phoebe get into?

· ● · ● · ● ·

Afraid her mother might hear the rumbling of the bus, Phoebe quickly ended the call and switched the phone to vibrate, then stuffed it deep into one of several pockets she'd sewn onto her jeans jacket. She gave Emma and Jessie a thumbs-up. The alibi had worked. Well, sort of. At times like this Phoebe wished she could be more like Jessie, who had no qualms about lying to her mother, though Mrs. Littleton was so lax Phoebe couldn't imagine why she'd have to.

"Five Guys is that way," Jessie said, pointing down the street. Jessie amazed Phoebe; she seemed to know everything: innocent lies to tell your mom, the location of Five Guys in Adams Morgan, *how to get Noah to invite her to the fall dance.* When she'd pondered this after lunch, Jessie had said, "Just kiss him and see what happens. I bet he'll ask you."

Now she could hardly wait to meet not only Noah and Dylan, but also Nick and Sam. She had wondered a bit about why Noah would be hanging out with Nick and Sam, who were part of the fast crowd, while Noah had always been known as more of a geek. Well, whatever the reason, going to this Five Guys and not the one in Georgetown had caused her anxiety over the course of the day. Emma had shed light on the subject – Sam lived in Adams Morgan – but this had only sent Phoebe's mind spinning.

"What do you think we're going to do?" she now asked again, feeling her stomach tighten at the thought of kissing Noah, and what that might lead to. She wasn't ready for anything more yet, though she knew the same might not be true for Jessie or Emma. Nick and Emma had gone out a few times over the summer, and she'd admitted to him having *finger-fucked* her, which sounded gross to Phoebe, who'd hardly even kissed a boy. And she knew that it had been no big deal for Jessie and Emma to hook up with guys at the movies, and at a few parties.

"Who knows? And who cares. I just want to be with Dylan," Jessie said.

They talked a little about the possibility of the guys inviting them to the fall dance, though they agreed that might be awkward for Sam, since there were only three girls and four guys. For some unspoken reason Emma smiled mysteriously, then brushed off Phoebe and Jessie's demands to know what she knew, and insisted on taking a few photos to commemorate the afternoon.

"Right over there," she said, pointing at a colorful window display of balloons, paper plates and napkins, which reminded Phoebe of the joint birthday party she'd agreed to. Maybe she ought to break the news to her friends now. Then, instead of mentioning it, she begged Emma not to post the photos on Facebook. "My mom'll go ballistic if she finds out I was here."

"Yeah, yeah," Emma said, and they all burst into laughter. Emma, with her Modigliani-like curtain of hair, dark smoldering eyes, and nose, brow and ear piercings, wrote poetry and endlessly aimed her phone or camera at events surrounding her, often posting them on Facebook and YouTube. Her Facebook profile claimed she aspired to record their teen lives much the way Edward S. Curtis had chronicled Native Americans. Though hopefully "we're not a dying breed," she'd written.

The three girls arrived at the glass doors of the fast-food restaurant, and after a quick glance at their reflections and some last minute primping, they stepped inside. The guys were crowded around a table in a back corner, where they seemed to be in the midst of a heated exchange. At the sight of the girls, they fell back in their chairs and waved them over.

· ● · ● · ● ·

"You have appointment?" the young man with bronzed spiky hair asked Isabel as she approached him. He was Vietnamese, like all the petite, dark-haired women in the shop.

"Yes, yes," she said and aimed at her name in the appointment book. "Mani-pedi with Thuy." As she searched the long narrow room, she heard him say, "Pick a color, please."

Isabel nodded, finally spotting Thuy toward the back finishing up with another client. They exchanged a small wave. On occasion, Isabel brought Phoebe with her, treating her to a pedicure or manicure, and the two of them would sit on adjacent chairs and chat. In the shop, she now saw several such mother-daughter couples and a pang of envy stirred her. How long had it been since she was last here with Feebs?

As she stood before the rows of nail polish, she tried to decide on her mood and match it with a color. She tended toward shades of pink, but today she felt like something different. It may have sounded silly, but whenever she left the shop, armored with perfect nails, she felt ready to battle the complexities of the world, of which there were plenty.

A few hours earlier, a local DC politician, accused of misusing campaign funds, had shown up at her office. Most likely, news accounts were accurate; the guy was guilty. A charming man, really, she could understand the voters electing him, but now he was in trouble and he'd turned to her. She hadn't said no, but her client list was full. Could she manage the case by passing it on to one of the new associates and overseeing her?

The real problem was managing the success of her firm, something she occasionally felt Ron envied. He'd grown unhappy with his AP reporter's job and aspired to more, perhaps in part because he was a descendant of the famous Edward R. Murrow. Never mind that she brought in nearly three times the income he did, which didn't matter to her in the slightest, but on occasion she detected it bothered him.

Relationships were fragile, she knew, and small fractures could develop into deep ruptures. Perhaps she ought to pay more attention, encourage him to move on. That's when she remembered that she'd forgotten to call him to remind him of the evening's event. First, though, she needed to pick a color.

As she scanned the shelves, her eyes briefly rested on a row of polish worn by so many girls these days – turquoise, metallic blue, lime green, violet, yellow, puce, purple, black. For a fraction of a second, she toyed with the idea of painting her nails one of these rather exotic, youthful shades, until the vision of Jessie's and Emma's nails, invariably bedecked in black or blue, flashed through her mind.

She didn't really approve of these girls: Emma with her piercings and morbidly pale skin, and Jessie who exuded a kind of wild girl aura. They seemed to be on the fast track to trouble – Jessie overtly boy crazy, and Emma part of the "stoner" crowd, according to her friend Jane. Add to that the matter of drinking, which apparently Sandy had allowed at a party over the summer. Emma's mother she didn't know. She'd never attended a single Woodmont event. All these things, and more, made her uncomfortable. Perhaps Phoebe would find a new set of friends now that she was a freshman. Friends Phoebe would have for life, just as she had.

"Hello, Eesa-bell?" Thuy's lilting voice called out, startling her.

"Be right there," Isabel said, examining a bottle with the name Key Largo. The name itself lifted her mood as she recalled a trip to Key West with Phoebe. They'd romped on the beach and built sandcastles. Phoebe's five-, seven- and ten-year-old selves would be forever imprinted on Isabel's heart, but what about this new, almost-fourteen-year-old version?

What plagued Isabel now was how to keep her daughter safe. Especially after last year. Which again made her want to call Phoebe. "Oh, heck," she muttered softly and dug the phone out of her purse. She tapped Phoebe's name. The phone began to ring.

What should she say? Just checking on you, honey? You're not going to Adams Morgan, are you? Trust between mother and daughter was essential, and she so wanted to trust her. I do, she told herself. With a click she ended the call.

Stowing her litany of concerns, she grabbed the tiny bottle, ready to be transported, ready for Thuy's special form of magic, a pedicure followed by a manicure.

· ● · ● · ● ·

The guys squeezed the girls between them, Jessie making sure to grab a seat beside Dylan. "What were you guys talking about?" she asked, sniffing as though something was up.

Even now Phoebe noticed the guys telegraphing each other. Nick studied each girl in turn before saying, "Nothin'."

The volume at the table rose all at once. "Come on, that's not fair!" Jessie said, insisting they tell. Phoebe could see Jessie had gotten it in her head they were about to ask them to the dance, but the guys merely spoke in cryptic three-, four-, and five-word sentences. "It's nothing, honest," "You don't wanna know," "Come on, change the subject."

Jessie stood up. "You guys are jerks, you know that?" She looked as if she were about to leave. Now that they were here, Phoebe was reluctant to go. Was she really serious? Emma stood up and took out her iPhone and aimed it at the group.

"Okay, okay, keep your cool," Sam said. "Put that thing away, Emma." He scratched his close-cropped hair, a little like Will Smith's, as if trying to figure out what to say. One more glance at his three friends and it was clear they weren't in agreement, about something.

"Nick and I are gonna score some weed," he blurted in a hushed but triumphant tone. Then glancing at Nick, who gave him a nod, he added, "They live just up the street."

The tumblers in Phoebe's head suddenly clicked into place. Now she understood why they were meeting in Adams Morgan. Sam lived nearby, the dope was here, and after Nick and Sam "scored," they'd probably want them to go to Sam's to smoke. But what about Noah, this didn't seem typical. Seated next to him made it hard for her to see his expression.

Nick leaned over and whispered something into Emma's ear.

A faint smile curled the edges of her slender lips. "It's like this, girlfriends," Emma said, pausing to cast her calm gaze on Phoebe and Jessie, "do you want some?"

Phoebe's heart beat fast, like a rabbit's she'd once held at Easter. Her first impulse was to glance around to make sure no one else at Five Guys had heard. Unlike Emma and Jessie, Phoebe's illicit adventures had been limited to a few sips of beer, which she hadn't liked. No weed, ever. Her parents were very clear on the subject. She watched Jessie to see what she would do, but she and Emma were silently communing across the table.

Something vibrated in her pocket. She pulled out the phone; it was her mother. A riot of thoughts flashed through her head. Did she know she wasn't in Georgetown? Could she hear their conversation? Of course not. But she recalled her mother once saying, "There's no point in lying, I'll just find out anyway. Mothers always do."

She shoved the phone back into her jacket just as Dylan asked, "You guys hungry?" She wondered if she'd missed something, because everyone acted as if there'd never been any mention of drugs. She watched Dylan brush his long surfer-blonde hair out of his eyes and tuck it behind his ear. "Let's get some fries and Cokes, okay?" he said.

A flurry of responses ensued, mostly on the order of who wanted what. Meantime, Noah reached for Phoebe's hand beneath the table and said in a low voice, "I want you to know this wasn't my idea, so it's cool...you don't have to do anything you don't want to."

But Phoebe wasn't so sure that was true. "What about you? What do you want to do?"

Before Noah could answer, Jessie's voice rose above the din: "I'll just have a diet Coke."

"Me too," Phoebe said, trying to achieve the same relaxed attitude of the others.

At once she felt Dylan's hand graze the top of her thigh and rest there. As casually as possible, she brushed it away, hoping that neither Jessie nor Noah had noticed.

"Supposedly the weed's awesome," Dylan said to her. "You should try some."

She wanted to shake her head and also tell him that she liked Noah, and didn't he know that Jessie liked him? In any case, she definitely didn't want to go to Sam's to smoke.

Suddenly everyone but Noah was laughing.

"You look like you just saw a ghost, Phoebe!" Nick said. She joined in the laughter, knowing it was in good fun, but wondered how they could be so cavalier. Her mother, and maybe even her father, would kill her if they found out. Didn't their parents care?

Chapter Six

Aqua buzzed with the chatter of clients and manicurists, and several TV sets were on, though the sound was off. The TV nearest to Isabel flickered with silent images of the *Dr. Phil* show. Captions scrolled across the screen. The talk show host sat there with two girls, about Phoebe's age or maybe a little older, and two sets of adults who appeared to be their parents. Dr. Phil wore his usual serious expression as he spoke to the parents.

Isabel read the subtitles. "So when did you first notice something was wrong?" Dr. Phil asked.

"After things had already gone pretty far," one mother said. The other mother agreed, saying she'd had no idea. Isabel wondered what they were referring to, though she'd felt similarly shocked when she'd learned of Phoebe's "self-injury," the label Dr. Sharma had applied to Phoebe's cutting.

"It's a way of coping with emotional pain by inflicting physical pain on one's self," she had explained. For a time Isabel couldn't understand why her beautiful girl had done this. She could hardly look at Phoebe's wounds and scars without bursting into tears, and Isabel was not prone to hysterical crying.

She still experienced bouts of guilt when the memory picked at her, sure that her busy schedule had caused her to miss signs of trouble between Phoebe and Skyla. Ron had insinuated as much. Though of course he hadn't noticed either. If she'd had an inkling of the depth of the problem, she would have intervened. Or at least handled things differently.

Isabel knew that some of her friends found it surprising, contradictory even, that while she felt obligated to manage many aspects of Phoebe's life, she tended to stay out of "girl dramas," believing it best they resolve their own differences. It was what her mother had taught her. How else would they grow up? But it was painful when she recalled that Phoebe, attempting to uphold her philosophy, had refrained from revealing the severity of Skyla's lengthy torment. Now Isabel prayed that the cutting had been an aberrant episode, as Phoebe insisted. And as Dr. Sharma claimed was possible.

But she wouldn't make that same mistake twice. She'd be watching Phoebe and urging her to talk about what went on at school. If only she would. After the initial revelation about Skyla attending Georgetown, and a week of seeking her advice, Phoebe had resorted to saying, "It's no big deal, Mom, really." She just hoped Phoebe would have the courage to keep the girl at arms' length.

Girls, she thought, and shook her head a little as she watched the two on TV exchange furtive glances. What *had* they done? She wished she'd tuned in to the beginning of the show.

As Thuy rubbed her calves with cream, Isabel released a long muted groan. The memory of Ron massaging her feet slithered into her mind. In the early days, he'd often whispered how sexy her feet were, and she used to tease him with her toes. Maybe tonight, she thought. We could use a little sex. Her mouth tilted into a crooked smile, but her eyes returned to the TV. She watched Dr. Phil's lips and read the delayed, sometimes misspelled subtitles.

"So, young ladies, from now on you're going to stay out of trouble? Right?" She could hear his trademark inflections in her head. "Because what you were doing almost got you killed, didn't it?" The girls nodded dumbly. "And you know that's not what you want?" Nod, nod. "And, in the future, you're going to be more careful? You're not going to do that *ever* again?" They continued nodding, though not very convincingly. "Right?" he demanded.

Their hesitant answers and embarrassed little smiles made Isabel certain they were disingenuous. What had they been discussing? Drugs flitted through Isabel's mind. She assessed the girls more carefully. Were those circles under their eyes? She couldn't help thinking how many more dangers and temptations existed for children as they grew older. And it seemed far worse today than during her own youth.

· ● · ● · ● ·

Thankfully, the *Dr. Phil* show had neared its end and was followed by a Jenny Craig ad, which reminded Isabel of the high-protein weight-loss drink, something called *Slenderella*, that Sandy had tried to sell to her on several occasions. She'd figured it was Sandy's roundabout way of trying to befriend her, though she'd been tempted to ask if she thought she was overweight, which at

120 pounds and a height of 5'7" was hardly one of Isabel's concerns.

She'd be the first to admit, though, that she had resisted Sandy's pursuit of friendship. Isabel would like to say that, as with most things, she'd given the matter considerable thought. For example, she could make the case that she and Sandy had little in common outside of their daughters, and to build a relationship based on that – when who knew how long their children's friendship would last – seemed pointless, especially when her free time was so precious.

Likewise, Isabel could say that she objected to the woman's laissez-faire parenting. *Kids will be kids,* was Sandy's incantation no matter the transgression. And then there was her mindless, gossipy chit-chat. Isabel detested women's tendency to gossip and rarely indulged. She made no apologies for it, and once or twice when she'd cut her off she knew Sandy had felt rejected. All of these facts would contribute to Isabel's rational examination of why she did not reciprocate Sandy's attempts at friendship.

But the real truth was that each encounter with Sandy triggered an inexplicable revulsion, as if somewhere deep inside of her she sensed that Sandy could not be trusted. That, at her core, the woman was sly and cagey, and around men an unapologetic flirt. Yes, this was, most likely, woman's intuition at work. And yet she chided herself for this automatic response, because her mother had taught her not only about the Golden Rule, but also that all people contain goodness, one only has to know where to look.

As these thoughts cycled through her mind, Isabel remembered Sandy's earlier call and realized she'd missed an opportunity to cut her some slack and also to advise her, because when it came to attire, Sandy often looked like she'd just stepped out of a Victoria's Secret catalog, so inappropriate for the Georgetown crowd.

Every item of clothing clung to her body – a shapely one, she had to admit, even if her breasts had been surgically upholstered – a birthday gift from her husband Bill. At least that was the rumor. Isabel only hoped that tonight Ron wouldn't make a fool of himself, the way some men did. The same held true for Sandy.

Thuy gathered Isabel's things and moved her to the manicure table. As Isabel glanced around, nearly every chair and workstation was occupied, making the place feel overcrowded.

The noise of an ululating phone was silenced when a teen-age girl a few chairs away answered it. Several heads turned as the girl began speaking – too loudly. She roared with laughter then suddenly dropped her voice to a whisper. The room seemed to grow quieter too. Isabel listened more intently. "You think you can me get some?" the girl asked. "I'll pay you back." The implication seemed all too obvious.

Isabel's thoughts traveled between Phoebe, the TV, which again featured a commercial, and Thuy, whose soft, quiet features belied the strength in her hands. She rubbed Isabel's forearms, then her palms and each finger. Isabel closed her eyes and tried to relax. She needed to spend more time getting to know Phoebe's friends and their parents, even if one of them was Sandy. She'd start by being friendlier, that evening, and released a long exhalation of air.

"You have long week?" Thuy asked in a low voice. Isabel nodded. Much too long, she thought, when suddenly she noticed a local news commentator's head appear on the TV screen. He wore an earnest, worried expression as he spoke.

The words "Breaking News" popped up behind him. His mouth moved rapidly, though in silence, and for some reason subtitles now failed to crawl across the screen. Isabel's brow wrinkled. What was he saying? Anything could have happened. Anything from those exploding sewer lids in Georgetown, to a drive-by shooting (she thought of the DC sniper of a few years ago), to another act of Al Qaeda terrorism. Why on earth didn't they turn up the volume?

The image on the screen flipped to a low-income neighborhood. At the bottom it said, "Adams Morgan." She caught sight of several police cars outside a crumbling apartment building. What the hell's going on, she wondered. But the announcer's face returned, mouthing the words, "...breaking news story. Back in a minute."

The news had made her restless. As Thuy deftly lacquered the nails of her left hand, Isabel wished the manicure were finished. She wanted to be home to sit in her clean house (thank you, Milly) and have a glass of Chardonnay. She again tried to relax, inhaled the familiar scent of polish, but another uncomfortable thought about Phoebe niggled its way into her brain. What if she'd gone to Adams Morgan after all?

The teenager in the salon had finally stopped speaking into her cell. In repose, this girl had a pouty lower lip, and an angry slant to her eyebrows. Not very pretty, Isabel thought. Instantly she chided herself. What did that matter? She was someone's daughter. Isabel rarely wondered what other adults thought of Phoebe. Even after she cut herself, she'd always taken for granted that Phoebe was wonderful, smart, reliable, and kind. And very pretty, even if she had inherited Ron's short, slightly stubby fingers.

She considered this as Thuy brushed sunrise onto her long nails, which accentuated her shapely slender fingers, fingers someone had once referred to as perfect.

Actually, she'd always thought that Phoebe was perfect, or nearly so, until a little over a year ago, when she'd begun accumulating used clothing. Disgusting smelly men's pants, coats, and shirts, women's dresses, and even old petticoats and tattered jeans. God only knew where she found them. Surely she hadn't been going to shops in Adams Morgan all along?

One day – when was it? – Phoebe had told her she wanted to design clothes. A skill she'd learned from Ron's mother. With her chubby, nail-bitten fingers, Phoebe began tearing these hideous clothes apart, then sewed the dark swatches of fabric together, layering them into skirts and assembling them into misshapen jackets.

At first, Isabel had objected. She wanted to steer Phoebe toward a sensible profession. But all at once, passionate, determined, and headstrong, Phoebe had insisted fashion was her future. Isabel believed it to be a cutthroat, low-paying industry, and hoped her own mother was right when she'd called it a phase Phoebe was bound to outgrow.

On the TV, the commercial concluded and the same neighborhood featured earlier reappeared. Isabel leaned toward the screen. A crowd of people had gathered behind Cynthia Chan, the female reporter at the scene, microphone in hand. Police cars stood in the background. The reporter was saying something, her mouth moving exaggeratedly. Still without subtitles, Isabel could only guess at the content. Her eyes drifted to the cluster of people surrounding the woman, mostly Latinos, though whites were among them, and a few African Americans.

A girl standing further back near a policeman caught Isabel's eye. A fair-haired white girl, wearing a jean jacket that looked like one of Phoebe's creations!

Isabel's distance from the TV made it impossible to discern the girl's features. She tugged her hand away from Thuy and jumped out of her chair, awkwardly threading her way toward the TV set in her paper flip-flops. She called out for the volume to be turned up. As she drew near, the camera angle shifted and the policeman and the girl disappeared.

Isabel gazed emptily at the screen. The image switched back to the anchorman, whose mouth shaped the words, "Thank you, Cynthia."

Isabel turned around to find people staring at her. She felt the need to say something, but the words caught in her throat. "I just thought the girl looked—" She stopped; her eyes scanned the clientele. They looked like jurors, hanging on her every syllable, their own thoughts in limbo. Normally she took this in stride, but now their stares unnerved her. Finally, she met their gaze, and groping for a word, added, "Familiar. She looked familiar."

Chapter Seven

Heading home, Isabel pressed the button to turn the car radio on and again noticed the botched polish on her index finger. She'd nicked it in her rush to leave the salon. How annoying. Now, she'd have to live with this imperfection for an entire evening. Thuy would gladly have fixed it, but after her outburst, Isabel had felt too embarrassed and all she'd wanted was out.

She switched to a news channel, hoping to find out about events in Adams Morgan, and praying there was no connection to Phoebe, who shouldn't have been there, in any case, and who hadn't answered when she'd called. Eventually, the announcer had stated that a drug ring had been infiltrated, a dozen people arrested. They provided the names of the leaders, part of a local Latino gang, several of whom had connections to drug kingpins in Mexico and Central America. There was no mention of Phoebe or her friends. Thank God!

Isabel shook her head, partly at herself, and also because she was glad the police had been successful. She knew, however, that for every apprehended criminal, there were dozens more who roamed free. Until recently, it hadn't bothered her how often she defended guilty clients. Everyone had the right to a defense. But lately it galled her that she spent more time on her clients than with her family, and that so many got off virtually scot-free.

The ride home calmed Isabel. She reproached herself for jumping to a conclusion, which in law school she'd been taught to avoid. Witnesses did it all the time. They put the wrong two and two together to arrive at incorrect assumptions.

Having seen the words "Adams Morgan," she'd thought of Phoebe and assumed she'd been talking to the policeman, possibly that he was arresting her. She tried to summon the TV image to review what the girl had been wearing and what she'd looked like. After careful consideration she decided the girl appeared similar to but had not been Phoebe. To be absolutely certain, she'd simply ask her when she came home. Of course she'd have to phrase the question just so, but then she spent her life doing that.

Isabel arrived home a few minutes past five. Maybe a little early to have a drink, but after such a harrowing manicure she breezed through the clean rooms and headed straight for the wine fridge in the kitchen. She pulled out a bottle of Sonoma-Cutrer Chardonnay. The cork made a lovely popping sound, and the golden liquid gurgled as it filled the glass.

On the way to the solarium, she picked up her worn leather briefcase in the hallway; maybe she'd review some briefs for a case going to trial in a few weeks. The large glassed-in room was her favorite. At least a dozen orchids were in full bloom, not only Phalaenopsis, but other rarer breeds, too. And in assorted colors.

Curled up in the peacock chair, she was almost instantly greeted by Hagrid, who jumped on her lap and began to purr as Isabel stroked his thick black fur. She took a few sips of wine, stared outside at the brilliant display of fall in the backyard – two maples seemed aflame and a gingko's gold leaves shimmered in the slight breeze – then closed her eyes. "Ahhh," she said, finally relaxing and enjoying the quiet moment. It was 5:20.

Instead of the legal brief, though, she picked up the latest copy of Phoebe's *Seventeen*, which had arrived in the mail. It was yet one more way to get a handle on her daughter's teenage mind, and something they could talk about.

One by one she flipped the pages, taking in the teen fashions, admiring some, disparaging others. She examined the emaciated models – their toothpick legs, the dark bruises under some of their eyes – and wondered about their lives. She'd read about heroin addiction. Though Phoebe's collage of teen idols included a couple such photos, from what she gathered Phoebe had no desire to be one of them. She had chosen the images for the clothing they wore. Among them was a short gathered skirt, which actually resembled an item Phoebe had copied and sewn. At times, Isabel felt a grudging admiration for her skill.

She took another sip of wine then thought she heard movement at the front door. She suspected it was Phoebe and realized she'd given little thought to what she would say to her daughter. Her mind raced to find the right phrases and words. The doorbell rang and an alarmed Hagrid dug his claws into her thigh before scampering off.

"Ouch!" Isabel said in a half whisper.

Fully expecting to see Phoebe when she opened the door, it

startled her to see Jackson. "Oh, it's you," she said, "hi, honey." Be-hind him a silver SUV tooted its horn. Though normally she might have taken a minute to chat with her friend Kat, now Isabel just waved and shouted, "Thank you."

"Bye," came the response. The vehicle sped off.

"Did you forget your key, honey?" Isabel ushered Jackson inside.

He shook his head and looked at her sheepishly. "I saw your car in the driveway."

She ran her fingers through his brown mop, a virtual replica of Ron's. "You rascal you," she said, "too lazy to get your key out, huh?" In the kitchen she offered her ten-year-old son a snack. After a few minutes of rather distractedly asking him about his day and getting short monosyllabic answers, she conveniently allowed him to play his new video game.

She ran through several scenarios of what to say to Phoebe, expecting her at any moment. When she saw that it was nearly six, she grew worried. She should have been home by now. Only then did the specter of something actually having happened to her daughter return. What if Phoebe had been arrested? Police swoop in, arrest everyone in sight. Guilty or not. Had that girl talking to the policeman been Phoebe after all?

No, she couldn't have been arrested. The police would have called. She'll be here any minute. Reluctantly, she turned to a news channel on the kitchen's small flat-screen TV, the same channel she'd watched at Aqua.

As the news anchors appeared, Isabel found herself white-knuckling the counter, afraid of what she might see and hear, but her anxiety turned out to be pointless because a few min-utes later Phoebe strolled through the door. Isabel was so relieved to see her daughter that she ran over to give her a hug.

"Hi, Mom," Phoebe said, shrugging her off after a two-second embrace and dropping her backpack on the floor. She continued toward the Sub-Zero, where she heaved open the massive door and stared inside.

A peculiar smell in Phoebe's hair registered in Isabel's mind, but this bad habit of her daughter's – leaving the fridge open and allowing the cold air to escape, the waste of energy, et cetera – distracted her. She was about to reprimand her, then remembered her mission and bit her tongue. "How was your afternoon, honey?"

"Oh, fine," Phoebe said, keeping her eyes trained on the refrigerator shelves. She pulled out a bottle of carrot juice and poured herself a glass. It was part of the healthy diet regimen Phoebe had adopted over the summer.

In as level a tone as she could muster, Isabel asked, "Where'd you go?"

"Where do you think we went, Mom?" Phoebe said, a slight rise in the pitch of her voice.

Isabel blanched. "Georgetown?" she said, making every effort to imbue the word with a neutrality she didn't feel.

"Checked out a few shops, had a soda, took the bus home. Oh joy, exciting life. And now I get to babysit!" She released a long exasperated sigh.

Under normal circumstances Phoebe's attitude might threaten Isabel's patience, but now only happiness surged through her. Phoebe hadn't been in Adams Morgan. All that worrying for nothing. She poured a little more wine, took a sip and invited Phoebe to come sit with her in the solarium and chat.

Just then the sound of an incoming text caught Phoebe's attention.

Isabel watched her daughter's thumbs fly across the tiny

keyboard.

"I've been going through the new issue of *Seventeen*, honey, and thought maybe we'd go shopping tomorrow. You could use a few things, right?"

"Yeah, maybe. But I promised Emma I'd go with her to take some photographs for a project she's working on."

"What project?"

"Some thing on homeless people."

The thought of this set off all sorts of alarms, but Isabel suppressed both a groan and her safety lecture. Really, though, was this an appropriate activity for young teenage girls?

Phoebe sucked down the carrot juice and rummaged through the cupboard where snacks were kept. "Hey, guess what? A few guys I know are going to start a band. I think they might ask me to design their outfits." She turned and looked at her mother. "Cool, huh?" Hagrid rubbed his black fur against her leg and she squatted down to pet the cat.

"Oh, that is cool," Isabel agreed.

"I've got some stuff to do before I babysit, so is it okay if I go to my room?"

"Sure, Phoebe," Isabel said, wishing she could have spent a few more minutes with her daughter. She pulled out some leftovers for Jackson and Phoebe's dinner, then went upstairs to choose an outfit, half wondering what Sandy might show up in. As an alum of Georgetown Academy and a room parent for Phoebe's class, Isabel thought people might look to her for insight into the school, and she wanted to look her best. Not that she didn't "dress for success" every day of her working life. But this was different. And now that Phoebe was home, safe and sound, her attitude toward finding just the right outfit had improved considerably.

Glancing at herself in the closet mirror she thought about doing her hair in a French braid. That's when the smell in Phoebe's hair returned to her. She'd mention it to Ron.

Chapter Eight

But Isabel did not tell Ron about the smell in Phoebe's hair, nor did she relay her worries about Adams Morgan, or anything else that might ruin the semi-romantic evening she'd planned in her mind. She clasped her husband's hand on the short ride, which ended as Ron pulled into the circular drive of the stately Georgetown home of Amanda and JP Thomas, Dylan's parents. Several young Latino men were stationed there to park people's cars, and almost instantly Isabel's door swung open with one of the valets helping her out.

She was slightly awestruck by the 1875 stone and brick three-story mansion. She'd never been inside and was curious to see how Amanda had decorated it. She'd heard it was exquisite. But then they had loads of money. Amanda, and JP, came from considerable wealth. They were among Washington's social elite, the coveted A-list.

As Ron circled the car and joined Isabel, he asked, "What's the dad do?"

"The dad? I thought you knew?" she said.

He gave her a look. "I don't track the career of every socialite's husband, honey."

"Oh, didn't I tell you?" Isabel realized she'd only mentioned Amanda's name. "Her husband's JP Thomas, that high-profile guy at Treasury, under Clinton; he went there after quite a career on Wall Street, then stayed on under *W*—" she scowled slightly as she said "W."

"Now he's working on the Obama campaign."

"That's whose house this is?" Suddenly Ron exuded enthusiasm. They climbed the wide steps to the front door. There, he stopped. "You mean they actually named their son Dylan?" When she looked slightly puzzled, he added, "You know, as in Dylan Thomas? Christ, that takes balls."

The thought made Isabel smile. She linked her arm inside his and pecked him on the cheek. "Let's not stay too late tonight, okay?" she whispered.

"No problem there, Iz." He dropped his hand and gave her buttocks a squeeze. "It's your room parent debut, so you call the shots."

"Honey, it's so much more than that. We're doing it to get to know the parents of Phoebe's friends; so take notes. Mental notes. We'll compare at the end of the night."

"Count on it," he said and laughed again.

She rolled her eyes. "Men!" Then with a sly look, she added, "What if I told you a couple of members of Congress will probably be here? Several diplomats too, not to mention power players in the presidential campaign. They all have kids in Phoebe's grade."

He shot her a lopsided grin. "As if I care about that sort of thing!"

"Right," she said.

"Okay, spill it. Who's coming?"

Before she could say another word, a man dressed in a butler's tuxedo opened the door and led them into a two-story foyer with twin spiral staircases and a massive crystal chandelier. Sprays of light danced on the marble floor, the pale silk-lined walls and the high-domed ceiling. It had a magical Gatsby-like effect, and made her carefree and giddy.

The classically designed house had quite a history of previous famous owners. Just then Amanda descended the marble steps to the massive entryway. The tall beauty, whose clothes reflected a comfortable elegance, wore black silk chiffon pants and a white taffeta high-collared shirt wound tightly about her slender waist. Ferragamo ballet slippers on her feet.

Isabel could tell she was one of those rare women destined to do everything with grace and aplomb, whether decorating, throwing a party, or designing a wardrobe, something Isabel envied, though she wondered how she was at raising four sons. Surely the woman had hoped for a girl. Dylan was the second youngest. If she had to guess, Isabel put her age at forty-plus. Doubtful she would try for another.

"Welcome, welcome," Amanda said, greeting several guests at once and reaching for their hands. She folded her own around each one in succession and those she seemed to know she leaned in for an air kiss. "So good to see you."

Isabel introduced herself and Ron. Amanda leaned back a bit as if to fully take them in, then said, "Phoebe's parents, right? And you're my room parent partner, Isabel?" To which Isabel nodded. Lifting her manicured brow and shaking her head, Amanda added, "Quite a day the kids had."

Her statement puzzled Isabel, but not wanting to appear uninformed, she merely smiled and said, "How's Dylan enjoying school?"

"Oh, it's not school I'm worried about. It's the rest of life these kids have to navigate that concerns me." Amanda laughed lightly. "I suppose they'll muddle through. The way we all do."

Yet again, Amanda's words surprised Isabel. How difficult could life be with their obvious wealth, and the privileges and advantages that came with it? Ron jumped in, saying, "That's the truth isn't it? We all muddle through."

Isabel caught him admiring their hostess, her swept back hair and graceful neck that reminded her a little of Audrey Hepburn's. Isabel was, by nature, rather confident. Still, like many women, she wasn't immune to the occasional twinge of jealousy and she noted Ron's reaction.

Amanda called to one of the waiters carrying a tray of drinks and motioned him over. "Help yourselves," she said. "Enjoy the evening." Turning to Isabel, who chose a glass of white wine, she added, "Maybe we'll have a chance to chat about this room parent thing. Right now, I'm afraid, duty calls. I'll be stationed here for the next half hour or so. There's plenty of food. Don't be shy. I'm counting on you to encourage the others."

With that she turned to the next guests and welcomed them, saying something fresh and new. As if she had an endless list of phrases handy for occasions such as this. Of course, she does, Isabel told herself. She probably spends half her life entertaining. Though she envied Amanda's effortless grace, this was a task Isabel did not covet. She and Ron received plenty of invitations, but constant socializing was not her cup of tea.

"What on earth was she talking about?" Isabel asked Ron, then sipped the wine.

"What do you mean?"

"You know for a supposedly observant reporter you can be awfully obtuse."

"Thank you," he said, with a small bow.

"I'm referring to her comment about what a day the kids had, as if something happened."

"Maybe something did."

Adams Morgan and the drug arrest she'd seen on TV coiled back into her mind. About to say something, she stopped herself. As far as she knew Phoebe hadn't gone to Adams Morgan and the arrest had absolutely nothing to do with their daughter. So why would she even mention it? If she did, it would only elicit a typical Ron response, of the "stop worrying" variety, so she said nothing. She took another sip of her wine. "Mmm, delicious. I wonder what it is."

"I could go for a beer or a scotch. You mind if I get myself one?"

"No, go ahead. But come back. I want you to meet some of the parents with me, okay?"

He nodded and trotted off. She spotted a few of the VIP guests, but before she could make her way over to them, Skyla's mother, Liz, waved at her. She wanted to pretend she hadn't seen her, but that would be rude. They hadn't spoken much since all the unpleasantness between Skyla and Phoebe. Several people's heads turned as Isabel passed. Though Isabel knew she was a good-looking woman, she felt an uncomfortable undercurrent of something.

After bussing one another's cheeks, Liz asked how Phoebe liked Georgetown. "What's not to like," Isabel said, "but thanks for asking. She seems to be adjusting pretty well. Surprisingly well, in fact. And Skyla?" Though tempted to ask how the heck she'd gotten in, Isabel refrained.

"She's in love with the place. Especially the fact that there are *four* grades of boys. Can you believe that?" She arched her brow and released a boisterous laugh.

"Kids!" Isabel said with a tight smile, already wondering how to extricate herself.

"I told her, 'you'd better hit the books, kiddo; this isn't Woodmont.'" She laughed again.

"You're right about that," Isabel said and glanced around in search of Ron.

"By the way, Skyla mentioned something about a joint birthday party. Wouldn't that be fun?" Liz said, her eyes wide with anticipation.

For the second time this evening, Isabel tried hard not to appear surprised. "Hmm, a joint party?" Why hadn't Phoebe said a word?

"Oh, yes. Skyla came home today, all excited, even mentioned having it at the Chevy Chase Club, so I'm guessing that was Phoebe's idea."

"Really? I guess Phoebe forgot to mention it. She came home a little late and I was getting ready. For this," she said. "Oh, shoot, will you forgive me, I see a couple of people I need to catch up with. Room parent duty, you know. Get to know the new parents."

"Sure, but let's catch up soon, okay?" Liz said, clutching Isabel's wrist. "It's been too long. Have a glass of wine and make plans for the kids' party?"

Isabel slowly retracted her arm. "Sure. I'll touch base with Phoebe. Call me?" Perhaps this was Liz's version of an olive branch, but she'd put the ball in Liz's court. After all, she only worked part-time, some cupcake venture, a business that seemed at best half-serious.

"I'll do that," Liz said cheerfully and waltzed off.

Isabel imagined that getting together might not just be about patching things up or even the girls' party. Inevitably, talk would turn to Liz and Steve launching a second bid to join the Club, which didn't particularly bother her, but now it seemed they'd be hosting a birthday party there too. That baffled her. Was Phoebe really ready to trust Skyla? More to the point, was she? She wasn't sure. Actually no, but maybe meeting up with Liz wasn't such a bad idea. And perhaps Phoebe should invite Skyla, so she could get a sense of the girl.

As she made her way through the clusters of people, and occasionally waved or said "hello," she ran into Ron. "Oh, there you are. Thank God." She was about to mention her encounter with Liz when she noticed the distressed look on his face.

"Listen, I have to tell you something," he said, his voice a hoarse whisper, "and you're not going to like it. A few kids were—" he hesitated as if hunting for the right word, "—caught smoking marijuana at some guy's house in Adams Morgan today." He grew circumspect. "I think Phoebe might know something about it."

The afternoon came flooding back. Isabel placed a hand on Ron's arm to steady herself. "What exactly would she know?" she managed.

"Well," he said slowly, "I think she was there, along with Jessie and Emma and a few boys. The only name I recognized was Dylan's."

Isabel grappled with the news. So that's what Amanda had meant, and that's why people had been looking at her. They knew. Unlike me, she thought, whose daughter had actually been there. She couldn't bring herself to believe that Phoebe too had been smoking – but how had she acted so normal? And now she recalled the smell! That's what it was. She wasn't sure which hit her harder: the actual news of Phoebe's friends smoking marijuana or her daughter's flawless fabrication. No wonder she hadn't said a word about Skyla or a party.

She shifted her stance to face Ron and the plum-colored wall behind him. She didn't want people to see her distraught expression, or anything else for that matter. "What happened? What do you know?"

"Apparently they were at a boy's home in Adams Morgan, an apartment, and the boy's mother barged in on them. Pretty stupid."

She nodded emptily. Already she could imagine the gossip that must be circulating. She only hoped that it wouldn't be taken up at school. If it was, people would believe that Isabel, as an alum, room parent, and donor, not to mention potential future board member, would shield Phoebe from any unpleasant aftermath. Though from Isabel's perspective, the exact opposite was true. Along with her status came the expectation that she be a role model; Phoebe would have to suffer the consequences of this idiotic event. "Oh, lord," she moaned.

Ron stared at her. "What?"

"You do realize what this means, don't you?"

"What?" he said again.

"Dammit, I should have told you earlier."

"You're not making sense."

Just then a parent she should have recognized, but whose name she couldn't recall, stopped by and said hello. Isabel pasted on a smile and greeted him. She glanced down in the hope that he would keep going, and after a brief exchange with Ron he did.

"I was afraid you'd tell me I was being ridiculous," she said and proceeded to describe her conversation with Phoebe, about going to a thrift store with Jessie and Emma, and then what she'd seen on TV while at Aqua. "My intuition told me something was up but I didn't want to believe she'd disobey me." She turned slightly to see if anyone was watching them.

Ron held her hand. "You do realize the drug bust in Adams Morgan and the kids getting caught smoking aren't linked. Not in any way. The two things are entirely coincidental."

Isabel gave him an alien look. As if, now, he weren't making any sense. Then, "Yes, of course, but you can't believe what a perfect little liar she was when she came home. Seemed so happy. Like nothing had happened. Christ!" She took a long drink of wine.

"Iz, don't go jumping to conclusions."

She looked at him pointedly. "Ron, don't be stupid, Phoebe lied. She withheld the truth. And what if she was smoking too?" Isabel's face crumbled. The thought made her want to weep.

"So she smoked once," Ron said in a firm tone and held her elbow tightly, "maybe."

Isabel shook his hand loose. "I also just found out that she's planning a birthday party with Skyla." She watched his face cloud over. As if having a party with her former tormentor was worse than her lying or possibly smoking.

"You're sure?"

"Got it straight from Liz; she was all excited about having it at the *Club*!" She released a long sigh. "We should get home and deal with this."

He shook his head. "No, Iz, we need to stay. What will people think if we leave? Especially since you're expected to be here." He gave her a sympathetic look.

"Oh, Ron, I—" she yammered softly. "I don't know." As strong as Isabel was most of the time, certain events had a way of undoing her.

"If Amanda can host this after what happened, then of course you can stay," he said and took a half-step back. "If people ask, just say that you don't know all the details yet, like everyone else here. Give them your 'innocent 'til proven guilty' spiel. You're a lawyer.

Just say it's been a trying day, like Amanda."

He smiled at her. "Look, hon, it's not like Phoebe robbed a bank or something. In fact, we don't know for sure she was there, whether she smoked or not, or if she even knew that some of the kids were planning to smoke. So remember that. Act like she's innocent, which she probably is." He drained what little was left of his scotch. "Come on, I'll get you another drink."

They began to circulate and things didn't go as badly as Isabel had anticipated; she found the wine bolstered her confidence, and the years of lawyerly training allowed her to steer conversations. Isabel's feelings toward Phoebe, however, remained mixed and confused. And when she came face to face with Sandy, the thought occurred to her that this had all been Jessie and Emma's fault. They'd probably convinced Phoebe to accompany them.

"You're not letting them get to you, are you?" Sandy asked.

"Get to me? Who?"

Sandy tilted her head, as though examining Isabel's face to see if she was serious. "You know, everybody here. About the big deal."

Squaring her shoulders and narrowing her eyes, Isabel asked, "Exactly what do you know?"

Sandy drew closer and adopted a confidential whisper. "Well, the girls and a few boys were over at Sam's and his mom walked in on them. Right in the middle of everything. Caught them red-handed. So people are talking about that ... and our girls."

"Are they talking about *our* daughters? And what is it *they're* saying?"

"Well, no one's said anything specific, not to me. But you know how people are. They're thinking it." She arched her brow then moved even closer to Isabel, who couldn't help but notice her cleavage-revealing garb. A fur-trimmed ivory cashmere sweater.

Isabel took a half-step back. "So let's just keep it that way, " she said with a meager smile. "They can think all they want. But I dare them to talk about my daughter." Though she'd promised to be nicer to Sandy, she simply couldn't.

"I getcha and I'm with ya," Sandy said with a half-cocked grin.

Isabel inched away. "I'm sorry, will you excuse me? I promised Amanda I'd meet up with her. Room parent stuff, you know." She smiled dismissively.

"Sure, no problem." Sandy's grin had turned into a frown. "I'll let you know if I hear anything," she managed.

"I'll do the same," Isabel said before she turned and left. Only later would she reproach herself for not having pried out the details of the girls' day that Sandy seemed to possess.

Chapter Nine

Sandy took in a deep breath before heading into the adjacent room for a drink. She certainly needed one. She couldn't believe what a snobby bitch Isabel had been. Wedging her way into the crush of people surrounding the bar, she glanced around for Bill but instead spied Ron at the front of the crowd and edged toward him. She brushed up against several men along the way, smiling coyly as she squeezed by.

More than once Les had commented on her resemblance to Marilyn, and Sandy wondered what the star must have felt. So beautiful and sexy, and yet so lonely and sad. On occasion she could relate to her sense of abandonment, and at other times she felt plain sorry for her. Mostly, though, given Marilyn's fame, the words "what a waste" would flit through her mind.

Sidling up behind Ron, she said in a low breathy tone, "I hate to ask, but would you mind getting me a glass of champagne?"

· ● · ● · ● ·

Ron glanced over his shoulder. The attractive woman seemed familiar, surely he'd seen her somewhere, but he drew a blank.

"Sandy Littleton, Jessie's mom," she explained as if reading his thoughts. With a beguiling dimpled smile, the woman added, "And Bill's wife, among other things." Then she actually winked at him like some 1950s starlet.

Now he recalled who she was, though he knew her mostly from snippets of conversation with Isabel. Her shameless flirtation fit Isabel's description. He smiled back at her. "Sure, sure. No problem." With the Phoebe mess foremost in his mind, her upbeat attitude felt like a temporary reprieve. He couldn't help welcoming her attention either. At the bar he ordered another Dewar's on the rocks for himself and a glass of champagne for Sandy.

When he handed her the fluted glass, she said, "Come on, let's get out of here," and gave his hand a tug as if she planned to flee the party. He half-wished he could go with her. Reluctantly, he said, "'Fraid I have to stay. Isabel's one of the room parents."

Her brows knitted together in a little frown, then another smile bloomed onto her plush red lips. "Silly, I just meant let's find a quiet place to drink."

"Oh, of course," he said, the heat of embarrassment pinking his cheeks. As he trailed behind her, his mind flipped into gear, convinced that he was entitled to enjoy her company – they were here to meet other parents, after all – but also that he might be able to glean some valuable information about Adams Morgan. Perhaps she knew something from Jessie. He hoped, though, that they wouldn't run into Isabel before he could do a little digging. Surely she'd disapprove.

Several rooms later, they entered a parlor devoid of people but filled with an astonishing array of original artwork, including a John Singer Sargent and an Andrew Wyeth. Ron ogled them. A baby grand piano stood at one end before an ornately curtained window.

"How about this?" she said, and drew him to a moss green velvet sofa. As they sat down, she purred, "I've been trying to get a word with you all night, Ron Murphy," and laughed lightly.

"First of all, I don't believe you, and second, it's Murrow, not Murphy," he corrected her with an indulgent smile.

"Oh dear, I'm sorry." She turned to face him, her knee touching his thigh as her mouth drew into another dimpled smile. "Really, Ron...Murphy, Murrow, does it matter?"

He smiled. "I wouldn't say that to everyone here. You know how people are in Washington. Names *are* important." He kept his voice low, not wanting to embarrass her.

"Oh, brother, don't remind me," she said. "What a bunch of stuffed shirts, if you ask me. Now you're not like that, are ya, Ron?"

"Maybe just a little." He smiled at her again and she giggled.

"So, how about Isabel? Are names important to her?" Without waiting for an answer, she added, "I get the feeling she doesn't like me."

"No," Ron said quickly. "I mean...yes. What I mean is, of course she likes you."

"Now, Ron, I wasn't born yesterday," she said with a laugh, and gave his bicep a good squeeze. "Ooh, feel that," she said.

Watching her eyes dance, Ron knew what she knew: on occasion men loved to be teased and complimented. Though grinning stupidly as if to tell her he wasn't immune, he also agreed with Isabel and felt a tad sorry for her husband.

When a few people wandered in, Ron slid several inches away from her.

· ● · ● · ● ·

It was understandable that people weren't saying much about the afternoon's event to her, so Isabel decided to find out what they were saying to each other. She drew Jane, one of her dearest friends since high school, to an out of the way spot to talk. Jane was also a Georgetown alum and the mother of a boy Phoebe had played with as a toddler. Isabel trusted her. "What have you heard?" she asked.

Jane gazed at her. "Honestly, not much, but then people know we're friends. If they have any sense, though, they're not saying anything. They should know better; it could just as easily have been one of their kids.'"

Isabel gave a resigned little shrug, hoping her friend was right. "I don't know what to think." She paused. "Tell me the truth, do *you* think Phoebe was smoking?"

"Who can say?" she said. "At that age they have to spread their wings; they experiment, do what their peers do; you know that." Jane's deep-set blue eyes probed her gently. "We've all been there. Even you were an imperfect teen once," she teased.

"I suppose," Isabel said, a hint of a smile lighting her up, "but my Phoebe's always been such a good girl." She could hear the slight whine in her voice. Stop it, she told herself.

"What if she did smoke? It's not the end of the world."

"But we can't condone it, can we?"

"No one's saying you should. But wait to hear her version of things. You need to talk to her." Jane had a way of calming her. Of being truthful and at the same time providing a sane perspective.

"I know. You're right. It's just that," her gaze strayed off, "there's that dangerous edge between—" A moment ago, she hadn't noticed anyone in the room behind Jane. Now Sandy sat on the couch, not two fingers' width from Ron, wearing a sexy grin.

"Between?" Jane said.

"Between—" she'd lost track of what she was saying. She held Jane's eyes in the hope that her friend wouldn't turn around. Then she remembered. "Oh, yes, between trying something once and then wanting to do it again." A dozen examples crossed Isabel's mind.

"Well, yes, I know what you mean, but I wouldn't worry about that with Phoebe—"

"No, maybe not," Isabel said, "but what about the other two, Emma and Jessica? Should I just let Phoebe remain friends with them? You've heard stuff and so have I." She shrugged her eyes meaningfully.

Jane ran a thoughtful finger through her hair. "That's a tough one. Let me sleep on it."

Isabel glanced off again at Ron and saw Sandy laughing and talking animatedly. She forced her attentions back to Jane, praying she wouldn't see what a spectacle Ron was making of himself. "Feebs had a tough year last year; this one can't be the same."

"I understand, but it won't be. I'm sure of it."

"I hope you're right. Still, I'm dreading the fallout. You know the whole thing will mushroom before it dies down. I wonder if we'll have to meet with Alison Kendall. Oh, God, the whole thing's making me incredibly tired." Isabel knew that just as with news cycles, some other event would have to take center stage before this one disappeared from the lips of gossipy parents. She wondered what that might be. "Oh, gosh, here I am going on and on." She paused then told her friend to go enjoy herself.

"Call me if you want to talk," Jane said.

"You know I will," she said, and reached out to squeeze her hand. "You're the best, Janie. Thanks."

"Thanks, nothin', how many times have you been there for me, Iz?"

Isabel decided the time had come to go home. She strolled with Jane into another room before circling back to collect her husband.

·●·●·●·

At once Sandy saw Isabel stride toward them. She felt Ron tense up and scoot further away from her. In the next instant, Isabel was hovering over them.

"We were just talking about you," Sandy said, looking at her with faux innocence.

"Oh, really?" Isabel's lips pressed into a tight smile.

Sandy watched a series of emotions ripple across Isabel's face and imagined she was dying to know what had been said.

"Hate to break this up, but we need to get going, Ron," Isabel said, her gaze fixed on him. She drew in a deep breath.

Before Ron could answer, Sandy's laughter curled into the air. "Oh, Isabel, the fun's just starting."

"That may be, but the fun will just have to go on without us."

Ron looked at her awkwardly.

Isabel's jaw tightened. "Phoebe is expecting us."

"She's a big girl," Sandy interjected. "She can wait a little, can't she?"

"No. She can't. I promised." Her words were clipped. "Anyway, I don't know about the two of you, but I had a long day at the office. I'm beat." She stared at Sandy.

Drawing her legs out from under her, Sandy slid off the couch and stood up. "Well, all right then," she said, a smile reaching across her face. "Nice talking to you, Ron. Murphy." She threw him a tantalizing grin. "And you too, Isabel." She gazed about the room, pretending to be undecided about where to go next.

Ron continued to sit on the sofa as Isabel made an about-face and left.

Sandy watched her go as Ron levered himself off the couch. Sandy couldn't resist. She gave him a peck on the cheek, leaving behind a scarlet stain, and with a rueful smile she wished him luck. *You'll need it*, she thought, wondering how Isabel had landed such a catch. Those tousled looks of his reminded her of the Kennedys; he had their boyish enthusiasm and a certain familiar charm too.

As her eyes followed the movement of his tight ass, she thought she might hear from old Ron again. She wasn't sure he'd noticed, but she'd tucked her business card into his pocket.

· ● · ● · ● ·

Isabel glanced over her shoulder to make sure Ron was coming. She knew she was hopeless at masking her feelings in situations like this. But then why should she? She shot a final icy stare at Sandy. How old *was* she when she'd had Jessie anyway? She barely looked over 30. A high school pregnancy, maybe? The woman had social climber written all over her. All those pies she was forever dropping off at people's homes the minute they sniffled. No one really joked about it, but they smiled, as if tolerating a child.

The image, though, that crept into Isabel's mind was of ivy sucking the life out of sturdy oaks. No, she didn't trust Sandy. Not for a minute. And what the hell was that Murphy thing all about?

Chapter Ten

Darkness enveloped them on the ride home. For a time, Isabel sat without a word. She didn't take what happened between Ron and Sandy lightly, but she'd mull it over before broaching the subject. It wasn't the same as eight years ago, but it felt uncomfortably close.

As Ron turned onto their street, she broke the silence. "We'll need to question Phoebe when we get home."

Ron turned to look at her, perhaps trying to gauge whether or not she was still angry with him. "I don't know, Iz," he said. "Can't it wait till morning? It's practically midnight."

"Morning? We need to get to her before she hears word got out at the parents' party and has time to make up more lies," Isabel said with a disgruntled look. "How she thought this would stay quiet is beyond me. These kids' sense of invulnerability really does make them stupid. Not to mention a menace to themselves. So what do you suggest?" Now she was placating him. There was no way she'd wait until morning to confront their daughter.

"What are you going to say?" he asked.

"I'm going to ask her why she lied. Plain and simple."

"Will you let me take the lead?" he asked.

"I'd be delighted."

At home, the scent of desiccating leaves permeated the night air. Climbing the stairs to their wrap-around veranda, Isabel took in several breaths and composed herself. This was not how the evening was supposed to go. As for Phoebe, she told herself she wasn't angry with her, or even terribly upset over the fact of her disobedience; no, the nub of her distress revolved around Phoebe's lying and the fear of what smoking marijuana might lead to. If this now, then what next? How could she adequately protect Phoebe from the evils of the world? This thought terrified her.

And, in truth, she felt a stew of emotions reminding her of something she couldn't quite put her finger on. It hovered just beneath the surface.

They reached the front door and Isabel's thoughts ricocheted back to the present. What to say to Phoebe? She knew she had to be careful, because she routinely made mincemeat of lying witnesses, just as her father had taught her. Another breath. Come to think of it, in her own teen years he hadn't spared her, regardless of the infraction. No, he'd been judge and jury, blunt and to the point. Meting out sentences without room for appeal.

"Okay, you ready?" Ron said, glancing at her sideways.

"You know the answer to that, so why ask." Her tone was curt. "And you might want to wipe that lipstick off your cheek."

"Oh, Iz," he said, giving her lifeless hand a squeeze. He rubbed his face with the back of his hand and unlocked the door.

They found Phoebe and Jackson lying on the couch in the den – Phoebe half-asleep, her eyes affixed to the TV screen, while Jackson snored lightly. It was a sweet scene and softened Isabel's frame of mind. She felt a sudden impulse to hug her daughter as she had earlier, but the desire evaporated when she remembered the ease with which Phoebe had lied.

"I'm going to get myself a glass of water. You want anything?" she said to Ron.

"Sure, I could use one, thanks."

Phoebe lifted herself off the couch as if to leave, but Ron stopped her. "We need to speak with you a minute, honey." His voice was gentle, yet commanding and firm.

Isabel turned to see Phoebe glancing warily at him, but then sitting back down and saying nothing. She hurried off to the kitchen, poured two glasses of Perrier, returned with them and took her place in one of their recently purchased Osvaldo Borsani arm chairs.

"Okay, Feebs," Ron began, his steepled fingers touching his lips. "We heard some disturbing news at the parents' party tonight and want to ask you about it. Okay?"

Phoebe's eyes grew wide at Ron's pronouncement. She tucked her bare legs under her bottom and folded her arms around her torso as if curling inside a protective shell. She glanced at Isabel, then rested her eyes on Ron. "What did you hear, Daddy?" she asked softly.

Dropping his hands into his lap, he spoke with notable calm. "We heard that a group of kids got caught smoking marijuana today, and that you were there. We'd like you to tell us what happened."

They both watched Phoebe squirm a bit and waited for her response. She looked like every delinquent at the moment of capture. Surprised, afraid and desperate for a way out.

"Just tell the truth, Feebs," he urged, reading her hesitation.

"I know what you're thinking, Mom," she said, turning to Isabel, "that I lied. And now I'm going to get into trouble. But what was I supposed to do, tell on my friends? And then you'd ground me and probably call the kids' parents and tell them." She began to cry. "I know that's what you'd do."

Though jarred by the accuracy of Phoebe's response, Isabel's expression remained neutral as she gazed at her daughter. "Come on, Phoebe. Tell us what happened. We wouldn't be having this conversation if you'd just told me the truth in the first place."

Phoebe peered at Isabel with the confidence of a mouse about to be dropped into a snake pit. "Well, we were in Adams Morgan," she began slowly. "I know you told me not to go there, Mom, but that's where everybody else wanted to go. And anyway how was I supposed to know what was going to happen?"

Both Isabel and Ron stared at their daughter, attempting to assess if this was true.

She sniffed and began again. "We just had a soda at Five Guys and then Sam invited us over to his house. Well, apartment, actually. There, a few kids decided to smoke, uh, you know," she said, obviously avoiding the word marijuana, "and it felt too awkward to leave, so I stayed. Then Sam's mom came home and started yelling at us. Of course, we all left, and I went to Second Chance, like I told you." She looked sharply at Isabel, then turned to Ron. "I feel really bad for Sam. I hope he's not in big trouble?"

Isabel saw that Phoebe hoped to appeal to Ron's soft side, and she wasn't about to let her get away with it. *Maybe you should worry more about yourself,* Isabel wanted to say. Aloud, she said, "Okay, let's back up a second." Phoebe had conveniently left out some details. "So you're saying you had no idea anyone planned to smoke?"

Phoebe looked momentarily confused. "Well, a couple of guys said they had a surprise for us at Sam's apartment, but we didn't know what it would be."

Isabel noted Phoebe's confusion and figured she was telling only partial truths. Whenever she thought a witness was lying, she always circled back and rephrased questions. Now, too, she intended to find out the truth. She was about to ask about the "surprise" again, when Phoebe, who was staring into her lap, added, "That's when Jessie, Emma and I went to the bathroom to figure out what to do, and I guess we made a bad decision."

Ron stepped in. "Yes, you did, honey."

"I'm really tired, Daddy, can I go to sleep now?"

Isabel looked at Ron with surprise. She could tell he was about to release her when they hadn't even gotten to the most important question. "Not yet, Phoebe," Isabel said. Hoping to explore the depths of her daughter's psyche, she looked at her very directly. "Did you partake? And what about Jessie and Emma?" Other than Dylan, she didn't know the boys well and so did not ask about them.

"*Partake*, Mom?" Phoebe said, looking at her with disbelief, "No, of course not." Then she paused, and with an indignant twist of her mouth, added, "Anyway, you'd kill me if you found out that I did! And yes, Jessie and Emma had a puff. One."

Annoyed at herself for sounding like such a dinosaur, Isabel tried to regain the upper hand. "And you're telling me the truth now? Because I plan to follow up with Sam's mom."

Phoebe's face fell. "Please don't call her. That's so embarrassing."

Even Ron, his mouth slanted into a deep frown, seemed to be signaling alarm at the suggestion.

"Am I in trouble?" Phoebe said.

"What do you think?" Isabel asked. She felt the tightness in her jaw. She took in a breath, exhaled, and tried to relax.

"Yes?" Phoebe whispered.

Before Isabel could respond, Ron said, "What do *you* think your consequences should be, Phoebe?"

"That's a euphemism, isn't it, Dad? You mean punishment, right?"

"All right, call it a punishment."

Phoebe thought a moment. "Dad, I'm sorry. But I don't really get what I did that's so wrong."

"You don't get what you did wrong, young lady?" Isabel blurted out. "Is that what you just said?" Isabel heard the shrillness in her voice and knew she couldn't let her anger cloud her judgment and behavior. She dialed it down. "Honestly, Phoebe, you think it's okay to lie to me? Not just once but several times."

Phoebe shrank back.

Isabel scrutinized her face. "Even now I'm not sure that you're telling us the *whole* truth. You really had no idea they were going to smoke pot?" she asked.

"No," Phoebe said, though this time her "no" sounded less than convincing.

"No?" Isabel glared at her. "You lied to me and you intentionally misled me, Phoebe." She ignored Ron's beseeching look to ease up and went on. "Tell me how I'm supposed to trust you after this? How will I know if you're telling the truth?"

Phoebe began to cry.

Though Isabel had a moment when she wished desperately that punishment wasn't necessary, in the end, not only did she tell Phoebe she was grounded for several weeks, but also that she was absolutely not allowed to hang around with Jessie and Emma.

They were clearly a bad influence.

"Weeks? How many?"

"Four," Isabel said.

At this, Phoebe burst into loud sobs, accused her mother of hating her and ruining her life, and ran out of the room and up two flights of stairs. The loud crash of her bedroom door punctuated the evening's discussion and sent a resounding shudder through the house that awakened Jackson.

"What's going on, Mom?" he asked sleepily.

Isabel ran her hand through his tousled hair. "Nothing, honey. Why don't you go brush your teeth and get in bed. Daddy'll tuck you in." Avoiding Ron's frustrated and angry stare, she tried to smile reassuringly at her son.

Chapter Eleven

Saturday, September 27, 2008

The next morning the Winthrop-Murrow house contained an aura of discontent. Everyone but Jackson seemed grumpy and out of sorts.

Following in the footsteps of her father, Isabel got Phoebe up early – though did nine o'clock really qualify as early? No, when Isabel had had "a lapse in judgment," as her mother called it, being woken by her father at seven on a Saturday was *de rigueur*.

Isabel had breakfast waiting for her daughter and hoped that the two of them could spend a little time further discussing the previous day's events. She hoped to explain to Phoebe that she wanted the best for her, something her father had never bothered with. She wanted her to know that teenagers were notorious for being incapable of seeing the consequences of their actions, which is why so many teens drove recklessly and sometimes were killed. They placed loyalty to their peers above telling their parents the truth. So now, did Phoebe understand that simply going along with her friends wasn't always the right thing to do? And not telling your parents the truth only compounded the problem?

"Oh, is that so?" Phoebe said after Isabel had finished her little speech. She picked at a piece of cantaloupe on her plate.

Her daughter's answer rattled her. She didn't recall being that sardonic with her father. No, she hadn't dared. We're too easy on these kids, she thought.

"It wasn't Jessie and Emma's fault, so I don't get why you don't want me to see them?"

"Because they used even poorer judgment than you. Smoking marijuana is illegal, in case you've forgotten."

Isabel suddenly recalled her own mother saying that examining someone's parents told you reams about the child. If Jessie was a reflection of her permissive mother, nothing more needed to be said. She had to get Phoebe away from her.

"I just don't think Jessie's a good influence," Isabel said. "I don't want you hanging around with girls like that."

Phoebe stared at her a long moment, before saying, "Would Jessie's mom tell her not to see me? No way, Mom! No way! You are *so* weird. Do you get that?" Phoebe shoved the plate of food away and ran up the stairs.

Isabel didn't have the heart or energy to follow her. Nor did she know how to keep Phoebe from actually continuing her friendship with Jessie and Emma. After a few minutes, an idea occurred to her. She found Ron in his study and after she made the suggestion he looked at her much as Phoebe had. "You mean you want *me* to tell Jessie's father that we think the girls shouldn't see each other?"

"Of course not. Maybe you can just casually drop the hint that they should cool it for a while. See what he thinks. But if he disagrees, push him." She watched him closely. "I know what you're capable of in the persuasion department."

"That's nuts, Iz."

"You have a better idea?"

He shook his head, though the look on his face suggested otherwise.

"Then what are you waiting for?" She handed him the school directory. "Under 'L' for Littleton, though I guess you knew that," she said. She took a step back, about to leave.

"Oh, Christ, Iz. Do I have to?"

She met his question with silence, then pivoted and left his study. In the hallway, she heard him release a weary sigh. Though normally this might have engendered a sympathetic response, just then her heart felt closed toward him. He would do as she'd asked if for no better reason than being grateful she'd said nothing more about Sandy. And there were times, this being one of them, that Isabel fought for the safety and well-being of her kids, even if it meant alienating Ron.

· ● · ● · ● ·

Hunched against the chill wind, Ron scurried across the empty street to the Silver Dollar, a retro diner in Bethesda, known for its 1950s style breakfasts. Eggs, bacon, hash browns, OJ, and unlimited refills of coffee in thick old-fashioned mugs. Though he'd accepted his assignment without complaint – well, almost – he did not relish this breakfast with Bill. It had been awkward just calling him. He'd even felt vaguely faggy doing it and had hoped Bill couldn't make it.

His breath blew out in plumes. About to step inside the diner, he recalled his encounter with Sandy and the hard-on he'd had in the middle of the night. Another gust of wind reached down his neck and shook him out of his reverie.

Just before heading out, Ron had Googled Bill's company, and read enough to know how successful it was. Apparently, Littleton Construction was responsible for converting entire Bethesda neighborhoods from 1950s and '60s tract houses into monstrous six- and seven-thousand-square-foot, energy-sucking homes. Of course it also meant that Bill provided handily for his wife, which stirred a bit of envy in him.

Inside the diner he spotted Bill in a corner booth. Prepared not to like him, Ron was surprised by his friendliness and how quickly the guy drove to the bottom line of their meeting. Ron imagined this was a sign of his considerable success, or perhaps that he didn't suffer fools gladly (and what was this but a fool's errand?), or that someone in construction might be busy even on weekends. A man on the rise.

"So – I guess this whole thing with Sam's mom sucks," Bill said.

"What do you mean?"

"You know, her bustin' in on the kids. Another half hour and she wouldn't have caught 'em." He must have noticed Ron's slightly startled look, because he added, "I mean I did worse when I was in high school. And look at me, I turned out all right." His face broke into a grin.

Unsure how to respond, Ron said, "Yeah, I know what you mean."

"You were a wild ass too?"

"Well, not exactly." He took a sip of coffee, trying to figure out how to maneuver the conversation toward what needed to be said. Outside, a gust of wind scattered a few leaves; a stray piece of paper tumbled into the street. A man hurried by, his collar turned up. Ron's eyes still on the passerby, he said, "So, you think it's okay for the kids to smoke pot?"

"Hell, that stuff should be legal. Way too much money spent on law enforcement over something not much different than drinking booze."

"I agree with you there. But for now it's still illegal—"

Bill seemed fidgety. He played with a straw the waitress had left. Dipped it into the water then sucked it into his mouth. "So what'd you want to tell me?"

Ron stared at him, trying to summon the words he needed, but lost his nerve. "We grounded Phoebe. What about you guys?"

"Yeah, we can't come right out and say smokin's okay so we're keeping Jess close to home this weekend."

"Oh?" A weekend, that's it, Ron thought, then added, "Phoebe's grounded for the next few weeks." He hesitated to say a full month.

Bill's brow arched in surprise. "Lockin' her up, huh?"

"Sort of. She lied to Isabel. That doesn't sit well with her." After Phoebe's outburst the previous night, he and Isabel had argued for the better part of an hour about the whole situation. He thought she'd meted out too harsh a punishment, but he couldn't believe the tap on the wrist Jessie'd gotten. Wait till Isabel heard. It would confirm all her worst fears about Sandy and Bill, though maybe, he hoped, she'd also realize that four weeks was far too long.

Bill's fingers tapped the Formica table. "Sure wish you could still have a smoke now and then. Cigarettes, I mean." He chuckled. "Typical Jess, she told Sandy everything. Came clean. Sandy thought she should reward her for that."

"Jesus, really? Izzy thinks if ever there's a time to pull the reins in, this is it. Before they get into worse trouble."

Bill tilted his head, as if scrutinizing Ron, who suddenly felt as if Bill understood the entire complexity of his relationship with Isabel. That his attractive, accomplished wife might on occasion be difficult, that she had strong feelings about child-rearing and that sometimes this was a bone of contention between them. Along with a host of other things. Like this assignment she'd foisted on him.

Two plates of food clattered onto the table. "Any more coffee, gents?" the waitress asked.

They both nodded. "Please," Ron added. He dug into his food and again tried to think of how to broach the sensitive subject he was obligated to communicate. Maybe he would simply *forget* to mention the idea of Phoebe and Jessie "cooling it." Iz would never know. The eggs tasted great and the bacon was cooked to crispy perfection. Ron hated limp bacon.

Now as he watched Bill eat heartily, he couldn't help wondering what Sandy was like in the sack. How often they had sex. Probably more frequently than he and Iz, which never seemed enough. Where did twice a week fall on the Richter scale of sex among married couples? And, really, once a week was more like it. He wondered if things would be different if he made more money, or at least was a star reporter. Time to get serious about another job, he suddenly thought, as he continued to observe Bill, who chewed his food loudly. He returned to the task at hand. How could he get to the point? Why had his shrewd interviewing skills suddenly abandoned him?

"What do you think the girls should do?" Ron asked. He recognized the vagueness of his question as soon as it exited his mouth so he tried framing it another way. "I mean in terms of hanging out with each other?"

Bill's eyes narrowed. "What do you mean?"

Ron waved at the waitress, hoping to catch her attention, then drained what was left of his coffee. She stopped by and he extended the cup in her direction. "Thanks." Turning back to Bill, he said, "I mean, look, Isabel thinks maybe they should cool it a while." Oh, God, had he just said that? Actually blamed Isabel? "Well, you know, not hang out."

Bill stared at Ron. "You're kidding, right? They're best friends."

Ron felt like he was in quicksand. "I'm with you, Bill. It's crazy. Guess she thinks they're not a good influence on each other. For now. A month apart and I'm sure this'll blow over. Everything'll get back to normal."

Bill leaned back against the leatherette booth, tapping his fingers in rhythm to a Buddy Holly tune playing on the jukebox. "Can't say this'll go over real well at home; imagine Sandy'll be a little pissed off." He speared the hash browns, then, half-grinning, he added, "Your wife, she a control freak?"

Ron felt that way at times, but now came to her defense. "She's just overly protective. Phoebe had a rough time last year and Isabel doesn't want a repeat." He explained the circumstances briefly, but stopped short of revealing that she'd begun cutting herself.

"Jessie wasn't part of that teasing shit, you know."

Ron was surprised he knew about it at all. "I figured, but thanks for telling me. Phoebe tried to keep the whole thing a secret, but eventually we found out. It was pretty awful. Poor kid." Ron pushed his last piece of bacon around on the plate. His appetite had diminished.

"Look, maybe just skip telling Sandy the thing about Phoebe

and Jessie. I don't think it's a good idea." He knew he was going out on a limb and would probably pay for it later. "I like your daughter; I'd like to get to know her better. Phoebe thinks very highly of her, and right now she needs her friends."

"They all do."

The two men concluded their meeting with small talk. With his regular acquaintances, he'd turn to politics, the presidential election and the like, but with Bill he brought up the Redskins, how they'd do in the coming season, whether Rex Grossman would be the starting quarterback, which players were benched for this reason or that and their chances against other teams. Could this be the year?

Before they left, they traded cell phone numbers, agreeing to stay in touch, though Ron knew it was unlikely. He was just glad the encounter was over. Now he had to return home and face whatever disaster was brewing there. At least he had time to figure out what he'd tell Isabel.

Chapter Twelve

While Ron was out, Isabel made the call; after three rings someone answered.

In response Isabel introduced herself as Phoebe's mom. She assumed the husky voice on the other end belonged to Emma's mother, Lorraine Blau, but felt obliged to ask.

"Yes, I'm her mother, how can I help you?"

"Well, I'm calling about yesterday's incident in Adams Morgan. Are you aware of what happened?"

"I think I know the basics. Emma mentioned it."

She had? So why hadn't Phoebe told *her*? Isabel felt out of breath and unsure what to say next. "I guess I wondered what your thoughts were—"

"I don't talk about other people's children; that's their problem. I have enough problems of my own."

Her response took Isabel aback. "Of course not, I didn't intend to talk about anyone's children but our own. Emma is a friend of Phoebe's and they were together...I guess I just wondered if you thought they were moving down the wrong path." Isabel felt awkward, a rarity in her dealings with adults, and wondered about this woman, about her modus operandi. And how unfriendly she was. She couldn't just come out and say, I hear your daughter was smoking pot, could she? No, she wouldn't compromise Emma or Phoebe that way.

"I don't really see that Emma was involved. Was Phoebe?" Lorraine asked.

"Well, they were with Sam when his mother came home and discovered the kids smoking marijuana." There, she'd said it without accusing anyone specifically.

"Yes, well, I'm sure lots of people do lots of things when you're not around them that you have no control over. I don't really see how that affects our daughters."

This conversation wasn't going at all the way Isabel had expected. But now that she thought about it, how had she expected it to go? "I guess I'm hoping this wasn't an indication that the girls were also smoking marijuana."

Lorraine gave a derisive laugh. "I don't know whether Emma was or wasn't, but there's little I can do about the choices she makes each day after she leaves the house."

Now Isabel really had no idea what to say or how to proceed, although she wanted to tell her that she thought she was wrong. There are things a parent can do, in fact is obligated to do to keep her child on the right path. "I am pretty certain Phoebe doesn't smoke or drink – we don't allow it – but I guess I wanted to hear what you thought. Based on what you've said, I assume Emma isn't grounded or receiving any sort of restrictions?"

"That's right. She told me she was taking photos of homeless people for some school project; so I don't really see any reason to ground her."

Isabel wanted to press her and ask if she thought it was all right for Emma to continue hanging around with these boys, but what was the point. Her overall attitude made it pretty clear what her answer would be, and the whole thing made Isabel more certain of the importance of separating Phoebe from Emma and Jessie. No wonder Emma looked the way she did. It sounded as though she received no oversight. Or limits of any kind.

"Well, thanks for your time, Lorraine. Please feel free to call me anytime."

"You bet."

Without a goodbye, the phone clicked in Isabel's ear. She stood there staring at the receiver for several seconds before hanging up. Wait till she told Ron about this.

· ● · ● · ● ·

Phoebe spent Saturday morning in self-imposed exile in her third floor lair. Without computer or cell phone, she imagined herself isolated and falsely imprisoned, like the Count of Monte Cristo, the character in the novel she was reading for English. For a time, she lay on her bed studying the sloped sky-blue ceiling, crisscrossed with white-painted rafters and clouds. She also toyed with the box cutter she'd retrieved from her dollhouse. Repeatedly, she ran her thumb across the blade, testing its sharp edge, tempted to use it.

Last night, while watching TV with her brother, she'd pictured herself dancing with Noah at their first Upper School social event.

Before the fateful climb up the stairs in Sam's building, he'd invited her to go with him. She'd fairly melted, thrill upon thrill coursing through her. Now there would be no dance because it fell during her four-week punishment, and she'd only see Noah in class, so there'd be no after school jaunts. These thoughts plunged her into despair.

It plagued her too that she couldn't talk to Jessie, to make sure she wasn't still mad about Dylan having put his hand on her leg. She'd apologized, because Jessie *had* noticed, explaining that she hadn't known what to do, and Emma had made peace between them, but last night she'd only gotten a couple of texts from Jessie, one of them saying she'd told her mom about smoking pot. Which had freaked Phoebe out. Why had she? Was that how word had leaked out? Because as they'd scurried out, Sam had sworn he'd keep his mother from calling the other parents.

She wished she'd told her mother about the dance, but in the stress of it all she'd forgotten. Maybe if she told her mother how sorry she was, she'd relent for that one night, though it was doubtful. She didn't know which was worse, being grounded and not going to the dance or insisting she not see Jessie or Emma. Her best friends. She recalled how she'd shrieked at her mother earlier and knew that hadn't helped matters.

Phoebe wasn't a vengeful child, but sometimes she felt her mother was terribly unfair, and now she wanted to get back at her. One way was to give her the silent treatment. To lock her out of her life. After arriving in her room, Phoebe had propped a chair against the door and couldn't wait for her mother to check on her and find the door locked. It would send her mother into a panic, jumping to conclusions. But what Phoebe really wanted was to make the ache go away, to have her mother say, "You can go to the dance, honey."

She examined the sharp edge of the box cutter and once again ran it lightly over her thumb. She hadn't used it in several months. Throughout the summer, she'd seen Dr. Sharma and had promised she wouldn't. She liked Dr. Sharma and felt slightly guilty as she pushed up the sleeve of her J. Crew waffle shirt. She moved the blade just above the crook of her arm. She pressed, but stopped short of drawing blood. I shouldn't, she thought. Then Noah's image sprang into her mind and tears welled up. Her life sucked.

She held her breath, and pushing a little harder, pulled the blade across an inch of skin near the inside of her elbow. It made a superficial cut. The sensation she was waiting for pulsed through her. One more little cut and then another. Blood popped to the surface. Briefly closing her eyes, twin sensations washed over her – stinging pain mingled with relief.

I'm sorry, Dr. Sharma.

She watched the blood collect, then begin to run down the side of her arm. She allowed one drop to fall onto a white section of her quilt, and watched the stain spread before grabbing a Kleenex and blotting her arm with it. If her mother discovered the blood she'd probably freak out and that gave Phoebe a bit of satisfaction. Of course, she'd deny having cut herself, though it would be easy enough to discover the truth.

Truth, she thought, and lies. It was true, she shouldn't have lied, but it wasn't a big lie. It hadn't hurt anyone. Why didn't her mother understand?

Sounds wafted into her room from downstairs. The drone of a Saturday morning cartoon, the churn of the washing machine on the floor beneath her, her mother's voice on the phone, and the random opening and closing of doors. She liked these sounds and for a few minutes she closed her eyes, resting. Daydreaming about Noah. "Oh, Noah," she said with a sigh.

Then she cast her gaze outside, where tree branches waved in the gusting wind. Two trees' branches intertwined. That image reminded her of the dance, the dance she wouldn't be attending, and that thought again reduced her to tears.

· ● · ● · ● ·

A knock on the door and Phoebe stopped her daydreaming. She'd imagined an elaborate scene in which Noah had brought her flowers and was whisking her off to the fall dance.

"Who's there?" She glanced down at the raw wounds on her arm and lowered her sleeve. A moment of regret – as if her entire childhood had just been lost – passed through her.

"It's me, Phoebe," her father said. "Can I talk to you a minute, honey?"

She removed the chair from the door, then opened it and peered out at her father.

"May I come in?"

She shrugged her shoulders. "Sure."

When he entered, she saw his eyes travel to her dollhouse, to the miniature people strewn on the floor, and she felt a blush rising to her throat, something that rarely happened with her father. She wanted to explain, justify, joke about it. "Mom treats me like a little kid, so what d'you expect?" But of course there was no point, so she sat on her bed cross-legged and waited for her father to speak.

He told her about his meeting with Jessie's father, explaining that he thought Bill Littleton was a nice man and that both of them believed their daughters hadn't used the best judgment in the world, but trusted they would do better in the future.

"Thanks, but is that it, Dad?" she said in a weary tone.

"Come on, Feebs, this isn't the end of the world. Before you know it, things'll be back on track." He explained, more or less, what he'd told Bill.

"Dad, Mom grounded me for a month, I'm not supposed to talk to my friends, *and* she took away my computer and my cell! She might as well just kill me!" She flounced back against her pillow. "I thought she didn't believe in capital punishment!"

With a smile, he said, "Okay, Miss Drama Queen, a little down time is hardly capital punishment." He regarded her for a moment. "How about I check with Mom to see if you can have your phone or your computer, and maybe if you talk to her and apologize she'll let you off on probation after a couple of weeks of good behavior? How about that?"

Phoebe's mouth turned up into a smile. She felt as if he'd just thrown her a lifeline. She hugged him tightly, and then with amber eyes wide, she said, "You really think she'll go for it?"

"I do, Princess. But don't tell her about our little conversation, okay?"

"I won't. I promise. And I promise to be good."

"I know you will."

Then, her gaze shifting to her lap, she said, "Daddy, there's one more thing."

"What's that, honey?"

"This guy, Noah, invited me to a dance. It's in three weeks. Can I go? Please? I beg you."

He bit his lip and looked at her expectant face. "I don't want to get your hopes up, but I'll try. And you'll try too?"

She nodded vigorously.

· ● · ● · ● ·

In the solarium, Ron found Isabel surrounded by documents, working at her computer. Chopin played on the radio. He seated himself on an ottoman a few feet from her. He'd lied to Isabel earlier about his exchange with Bill, but he figured as long as she didn't talk to Sandy she'd never know. Now he felt more at ease.

"Listen, I've been thinking." He waited for her to set aside her work and look up. Once she lifted her eyes, he continued. "I think it's not helpful to cut Phoebe off from her friends. She needs them, especially at a time like this."

"I don't want her talking to those girls. Not right now. It won't kill her." She paused. "Why can't you agree with me? Just once?"

He ignored her question. "She'll see them on Monday anyway, or are you planning to home school her?"

"Ha, ha, very funny," she said, continuing to eye him coolly.

"Look, what I'm trying to say is that we don't want her to get so stressed out that she—" he hesitated, again drawing her eye to his before adding, "—that she starts cutting herself again, right?"

There was momentary silence, as Isabel's eyes took on a pained expression. "Oh, God, don't say that. You don't think—" the remaining words refused to cross the threshold of her lips.

"If you handle this right, Phoebe will see you as her ally, not her enemy. The last thing you want is for her to feel like a martyr."

Isabel looked forlorn as she thought about what he said. "We're hostage to her self-destructive habit. It's not fair, Ron. It just isn't. We need to get her away from those kids, don't you see?"

"By *those kids* are you including Dylan?" he asked.

She pursed her lips refusing to answer, fully aware that if Amanda invited Phoebe over she would likely let her go, and that indeed this qualified as a contradiction and a double standard. But then Amanda was not Sandy. She thought about telling Ron this, but not after what happened last night. At least not yet. It was Liz and the suggestion of a joint birthday party that suddenly rose to mind. Maybe that was it. The answer to this vexing situation.

She looked at him blankly when he said, "So what do you think? We give her back the phone or her computer?"

"What?"

He repeated his suggestion of returning one or the other to Phoebe in order to avoid further alienating their daughter. To keep her from cutting. But Isabel was already up and halfway through the arched doorway before he could say anything about Noah and the dance.

· ● · ● · ● ·

As she mounted the stairs to Phoebe's room, she tried to think of what to say. She knocked, but Phoebe didn't respond. For a moment, terror engulfed her as she imagined her daughter lying in a pool of blood. She almost burst into the room, but knocked louder, this time getting a feeble reply. "Who's there?"

"It's me, honey. Can I come in? I want to tell you something. It'll only take a sec'."

Though Phoebe didn't invite her in, Isabel turned the knob and slowly opened the door. Peering into the room, she saw Phoebe on her bed staring at the ceiling. She went and sat on the edge of the bed still formulating what to say. "Look, honey, I've thought about it some more and I think it's okay for you to have your phone. Or your computer. You decide."

"Both," Phoebe said flatly, continuing to stare up at the scattered, white-painted clouds.

"Both, huh?" Isabel said, trying to figure out how to respond.

Her gaze dropped to the quilt as her hand ran absently over the textured fabric. Only inches from her fingers sat a dark reddish spot. She took in a sharp breath. Fresh blood? She stared at Phoebe's arms, wishing her eyes could pierce the sleeves of her shirt. "Okay, maybe. But you have to talk to me a minute, Phoebe, and then you can have your gadgets. You probably have some homework to do anyway, right?"

"Right."

This was more painful than she'd anticipated. Maybe she should have said, When you feel you can discuss this with me, let me know and then you can have your stuff back. It was often like that. In hindsight, the words came to her, but in the moment she needed them they simply went missing. She wanted desperately to ask Phoebe about the stain.

"Maybe I should come back in a little while?"

"I thought you wanted to talk," Phoebe said.

Isabel launched into an explanation about being in a tough situation because of her status at the school. "It means that I have to be a role model, Phoebe, and I imagine you don't care about that, but people need to know you won't get special dispensation just because you're my daughter. Do you see?"

"Not really, since I didn't do anything wrong."

"It's guilt by association, Phoebe. People will assume you were smoking even if you weren't."

"Yeah, and by punishing me you're making them think it's true."

"You know you have restrictions because you lied."

"But they don't know that, and anyway I'm sorry about that, Mom."

Isabel grew flustered. What Phoebe was saying bore a certain logic. She shifted gears. "Look, sweetie, maybe we can start planning a birthday party. Skyla's mom came up to me last night and said you two were planning to have one together. Is that right?" Phoebe nodded. Well, at least that had been true.

"So what do you think about that?" Isabel thought she detected a flicker of interest, but all Phoebe said was, "Maybe."

Isabel began outlining plans for the party until she saw that Phoebe wasn't listening. "What's the matter?"

"I don't really care about the birthday party. Anyway, it was all Skyla's idea, having it at the Club and whatnot."

She could see there was something else on her daughter's mind. "What *do* you care about? What is it?"

"I want to go to the fall dance." The next three words brightened Phoebe's countenance. "Noah asked me."

"Oh, why didn't you tell me?" The news took Isabel aback. She could see how much this meant to her daughter, and she couldn't fail but notice the schoolgirl crush in her eyes. She felt herself caving in, about to tell her daughter she could go, when she remembered words her own father had spoken on more than one occasion. "What's punishment without pain? No, you wouldn't learn a thing." Later, he'd told her that the best lessons are often as painful for the parent as for the child. And that's what she faced now. She had to be strong. She had to create clear boundaries and consequences. This was no time to waffle.

"I'm sorry, honey, I wish I could say yes, but you got yourself into this mess. You shouldn't have lied. Now you have to suffer the consequences."

"But, Mom, I'm sorry."

"I know you are." It truly made her ache to see the bitter disappointment in Phoebe's eyes, but what could she do?

· ● · ● · ● ·

Late afternoon, when Ron entered the kitchen, Isabel was chopping vegetables for the evening meal. Without looking up, she said, "You acted like an ass last night, you know that don't you?"

Her abrupt pronouncement startled him. "What?"

She continued to focus her attention on the red pepper she was carving into neat thin strips. "Don't play innocent. You know what I'm talking about."

"I do?"

"Damn it, Ron," she said in a plaintive voice, "Sandy Littleton was practically coiled around your neck, and you just sat there grinning like you'd won the fucking lottery."

Believing the best defense was a good offense, Ron said, "Oh, for God's sakes, Izzy, what did you want me to do, tell her to back off, my wife'll get jealous? How can you be upset about *her*?"

"*Her*?"

He knew that he didn't want to get into this discussion with Isabel; such exchanges never went well. Anyway, didn't Isabel know Sandy wasn't the kind of woman he'd ever get serious about? If nothing else, how could he ever trust her? But that was the least of it. No, she was little more than late night fantasy material.

"Well?"

He took in a deep breath. "Come on, let's drop it. What's for dinner?"

She hesitated, as if trying to decide whether she wanted to drop it or not. "Salad and a steak."

He headed to the table where the *Washington Post* lay. A week ago, he'd reached out to a colleague there, but he'd heard nothing. For a time he'd aspired to be as famous a White House reporter for

AP as Helen Thomas was for UPI, but he doubted that would happen. No, he hoped for a break at the *Post*. But he knew that hoping wasn't enough. He picked up the paper. "Hey, d'you see this?" He pointed at a headline in the middle of the page. "Housewife Sandy Littleton bests Cleveland Park lawyer." He laughed.

Isabel stifled a giggle. "You, you—" she stopped cutting and looked up at him from under her sweep of dark hair. "I guess I'll just have to deal with slutty women hanging all over my husband." Then pointing the sharp knife at him, she added, "Just don't test me, Ron Murrow, you know I'm not to be toyed with."

That, undoubtedly, is true, he thought, recalling the brief affair he'd had two election cycles ago. He rolled up the paper and swatted her on the butt with it. "When's dinner going to be ready, sweetheart?"

"Shortly after you throw the steak on the grill, *honey*."

When Ron looked over his shoulder he caught Isabel staring at his ass. Her eyes sparkled. He still knew how to turn her on.

"All right then. One big fat steak coming up." He pulled the meat and a bottle of Stella out of the fridge, giving Isabel a peck on the cheek as he passed her.

Outside on the deck, he turned on the grill and took a slug of beer, marveling that he'd survived the Sandy incident unscathed. The temperature had risen throughout the day, and while it was far from balmy, it was a glorious late September dusk. Surveying their landscaped garden, he thought that he and Isabel had created a beautiful home; they had great kids, teenage years aside, and had established a reasonably happy life together.

Of course Isabel's income helped. It only bothered him some that he made less; what bothered him more was that elusive Pulitzer, he seemed as far from earning it now as when his reporting career began. And he was sure that's what counted for Isabel. For that to happen, though, he figured he needed to start putting out feelers to top-tier papers besides the *Post* –the *New York Times*, maybe the *Wall Street Journal*. Maybe he could even switch to being an on-air reporter. CNN. He'd do it on Monday, he promised himself.

Ron took another long hit of beer, then breathed in the fall air. His mind wandered as he stared into the yard, at the Japanese maple and the nearby cherub fountain that Isabel had given him as a joke gift.

The water pulsed rhythmically out of the statue's small, un-circumcised penis. It captured his attention. A teasing, taunting, bare-breasted Sandy rose genie-like from the mist. In her papery whisper he heard her say, *Fuck me, Ron Murphy*, and then laughing gaily. He felt his cock stiffen. He closed his eyes and for the second time that day saw himself burying his head between her breasts, then licking her nipples while she sucked him off.

Isabel's voice wafted outside. He took a moment to clear his head. He knew the consequences. No, he told himself, no point in risking everything over another stupid affair.

Chapter Thirteen

Monday, September 29, 2008

On Monday morning, the pit in Phoebe's stomach felt like a heavy stone, something that threatened to send her to the bathroom. The sensation grew as she entered the school building, her steps slow and leaden, like moving through sludge in a nightmare. She considered skipping first period with Noah. How could she face him? She dreaded telling him she couldn't go.

On the long walk through the Great Hall, she hoped people weren't talking about her. Jessie would say, "Who cares?" But that wasn't how Phoebe felt. She didn't want them saying things about her, especially things that weren't true. Maybe she'd talk to Skyla at lunch. She seemed to know everything that everybody said. Even as the thought flashed into her mind, Skyla's sun-streaked ponytail swung past her eyes, practically striking her in the face.

"Ooh, you bad girl, you will sooo have to tell me about it at lunch. Usual spot? I'm supposed to meet Mr. Dunn, you know, the one who looks like Brad Pitt, for extra help, and I'm way late...see you?" Skyla left Phoebe nodding as she swirled away in a cloud of pink. Pink jeans, pink tank top, pink sweater with pink pearl buttons, pink scrunchy, and somehow, amazingly, it all worked.

The encounter gave Phoebe a slight boost until she saw Noah at his desk. They exchanged a shy greeting just as Ms. Dickinson demanded their attention. About halfway through class she managed to pass him a note that said, *Need to talk to you.*

Her heart hammered in her ears as he walked beside her. How could she go through with this? "It's about what happened on Friday," she began. "My parents are pretty mad. They're so ridiculous."

"Mine are pretty uptight too."

She felt some relief on hearing this and explained how she'd spent much of the weekend locked in her room, overdramatizing her punishment. Then, her eyes cast down, afraid to meet his, she said, "I'm sorry. But, part of what's happening, is like, well, my mother grounded me, and that means I can't go to the dance." She looked up at him with a miserable expression, her eyes searching his.

"Oh," he said. His cheeks puffed out and he released a long stream of air. "Yeah, that sucks. Wow. Parents can be so stupid. Well, don't worry about it."

"I'm sorry," Phoebe said.

The buzzer sounded for their next class and they parted ways.

On the verge of tears, Phoebe bit her lip and whispered "bye" as she headed off to the bathroom.

· ● · ● · ● ·

Sitting in bed with a tray on her lap, Sandy swiped her finger through the thick chocolate icing of the cupcake she'd saved from the parents' party and stuck it in her mouth. "Mmm," she said, and gave her finger another lick.

They weren't as good as anything Mrs. Eddinger had baked, but not bad. Mrs. E, as Sandy came to call her, had been her kindly neighbor back in Towson. She'd introduced Sandy to fine European pastries – Linzer tortes, Napoleons, all manner of chocolate confections. She'd encouraged Sandy and treated her like a daughter when her own mother hadn't. Often played checkers and cards with her.

She would have been proud of me, Sandy now thought, recalling several women who'd appreciated her efforts at spreading good cheer and goodwill as Mrs. E had taught her. Starting last year when Jessie entered Woodmont, Sandy had often brought food to those felled by the flu, delivered cookies to her daughter's friends on their birthdays, and had even cleaned someone's bathroom after hearing of the poor woman's reaction to chemo treatments. She'd done all these things hoping to be more accepted and included by Isabel and some of the other mothers at Woodmont.

But the thought that had been gaining ground all morning, well, it was related to the cupcake. If Liz VanDorn could promote her baked goods at the parents' party (the sign had read: "courtesy of Liz VanDorn's Cupcake Shoppe), she could see no reason why she shouldn't send a note to all the moms and introduce them to *Slenderella*. This might even endear her to them.

A short while later, in front of the computer, her bright pink fingernail clicked against her tooth in a steady beat as she scoured her mind for something witty to write. But as the minutes passed, she got nowhere. Finally, annoyed with herself, she said, "Keep it simple, stupid." Her motto after her mother had kicked her out. And with that arrived a brilliant idea. I'll give them a discount, she thought.

Her fingers went to work writing out an email, then she began the laborious task of typing each parent's email address. When she finally got to Winthrop, though, she frowned. She still couldn't believe what Bill had told her – that Isabel wanted Phoebe to stop seeing Jess. As if what had happened was all Jessie's fault!

"Screw her," she said aloud, and considered not including her in the email. Then she recalled Isabel's face when she'd found her and Ron sitting together on the velvet couch. Her eyes glinted at the memory. Clicking into a new tab, she thought she'd see if she could find Ron on Facebook.

· ● · ● · ● ·

A pink origami heron was taped to Phoebe's locker. It was a few minutes before her final class of the day, which she shared with Jessie. She hadn't seen her friend all day and couldn't help wondering if Jessie was avoiding her. She unfolded the paper bird, which she figured was none other than the work of dear Emma, of whom she was growing increasingly fond.

twitchy ponytail...eyes like frozen fire
you'd better look both ways...beware desire

She puzzled over it, then Emma appeared. "Hey, what's this?" Phoebe said, waving the pink paper.

"It just came to me over lunch, thought you'd like it."

"I do," she said with a smile, "but you're not like trying to send me a message, are you?"

"I just worry about you, little seamstress," Emma said, returning her smile. She leaned against the adjacent locker. "With

Skyla I do think you need to be careful though." Emma wore a very short tight skirt and black tights with high-top sneakers, one of them propped against the locker door. "D'you know your mom called my house on Saturday?"

Phoebe slumped slightly and shook her head. "I'm sorry, Emma. She's such a pain." As those words left her mouth, Phoebe glanced over her shoulder, hoping no one had overheard her.

"Yeah, she wondered if we'd smoked weed." Emma's long black bangs hooded her deep blue eyes.

"I didn't get you into trouble, did I? My mom asked if you guys had smoked and I couldn't lie."

"Nah, Lorraine doesn't care," Emma said. "I told her about it when I came home on Friday." Like Jessie, Emma sometimes referred to her mother by her first name.

"You did?"

"Yeah, nothing bothers her. At least nothing I do."

"Oh, I wish my mom was cool like that."

Emma's eyes darted off thoughtfully. "Cool, huh?"

"Yeah, I mean the fact that she didn't get all worked up about Friday, lets you go wherever you want. Lets you do just about any-thing. My mom'd kill me."

After a brief silence, Emma said, "You're wrong about that."

"About what?"

"That I have a cool mom." She leaned over and pulled her camera out of her backpack.

"She's not cool?"

"Nope. She, like basically doesn't give a shit. There's a difference."

"Oh." Phoebe's eyes drifted to Emma's piercings. From eye-brow to nose to ear. Reassessing. Readjusting her thoughts to fit this new information.

Emma turned her camera toward a cluster of students down the hall, adjusted the lens, took a shot. Wheeling back toward Phoebe, she aimed the camera at her. "Click," she said.

Phoebe thrust her hands in front of her face. "Oh, Emma, please don't, I look awful."

Emma shook her head. "No, you don't, you're so pretty, even now, when you're feeling all fucked up and sad." She did a little jig, which made Phoebe laugh. "You've got us, okay?" Just then the bell rang for next period.

"Okay. Guess I'd better get going," Phoebe said, avoiding Emma's heartfelt stare.

"Yeah, me too." Emma was turning away, when she stopped and embraced her friend. "Sorry you got grounded, Feebs. It sucks."

On the way to biology Phoebe wondered which was worse, a mom who cared about every little thing or a mom who couldn't care less. In the short time she'd known Emma, she'd never met her mother, though she'd heard stories. Now she wanted to meet her.

· ● · ● · ● · ·

The difficult and irritating weekend came speeding back to Ron when he returned to the office after a White House briefing. Now he could add Gil Rosenblum, his contact at the *Washington Post*, to his list of annoyances. A short two-sentence email congealed Ron's disappointment. Gil was sorry they hadn't gotten back to him sooner, but they were in the midst of making some important changes and he'd be in touch soon.

A polite brush-off at best. Ron sat fiddling with a pencil, twisting it from finger to finger, then tapping the eraser on his desk. Now he had no choice but to set up lunches with his friends at the

New York Times and the *Wall Street Journal*. One of the problems, though, was that each of these reporters covered the White House, Ron's beat. He'd have to convince them he could make the leap to another area. But which one? He could go back to covering Congress, though he really yearned for a broader canvas. Lately, at AP, he'd been coasting, so what clips would he use to show off his talent? He could point to his online following, maybe. What he really wanted was to dig back into investigative journalism, as he'd been trained at Columbia's graduate journalism school.

He picked up the phone, then put it back down. He turned to his computer and half-heartedly tapped out a couple of emails, not citing the specific reason for an invitation to a beer after work. For old-times sake he suggested meeting at The Monocle, a stone's throw from the Capitol.

As he scrolled through the rest of his inbox, he noticed an email from Sandy Littleton.

· ● · ● · ● ·

Phoebe dashed into her biology class just as it began. "Sorry," she mouthed to the teacher. When she sat down, Jessie whispered, "Where've you been all day?" and Phoebe gave her a discomfited look. Apparently, she wasn't mad at her.

Throughout class, she toyed with the idea of talking with Jessie about her stupid, crazy mother, but something held her back. During lab, in which she and Jessie were partners, Phoebe reported that she had told Noah she couldn't go to the dance and that she was major bummed.

"Oh, man, that's awful. Maybe your mom will change her mind?"

Phoebe shook her head. She almost said, *You know her,* but

again held back.

Jessie patted Phoebe's shoulder. "I heard Sam won't be going either; in fact he said his mom might pull him out of Georgetown." Jessie didn't wait for a response. "I'm hoping Dylan'll ask me, but if he doesn't, Emma and I are going without guys. She doesn't care and neither do I. I asked my mom if I could have a party afterward and she said yes. So work on your mom. At least then you can spend the night with me and Emma."

Phoebe looked at her blankly. Even if her mother let her go to the dance, which she wouldn't, she'd never let her spend the night at Jessie's.

"So what's up with that?" she said, as if Phoebe's thoughts were transparent.

Gazing at the plants they were supposed to classify, Phoebe tried to come up with a reasonable answer. She didn't do well in situations like this. Her thoughts grew into a kaleidoscopic jumble. Too many things to consider. She shook her head. "I know I won't be able to go, and if I could I'd have to be home before the clock strikes midnight! If not sooner."

Jessie laughed. "That's it," she said. "We just need to get you some glass slippers and a pumpkin coach!" The two giggled. Phoebe had felt sad all day and now, finally, the clouds seemed to lift a bit. "Have you met Emma's mom?"

"What made you think of that?" Jessie asked.

"She said her mom doesn't care what she does, and all mine does is worry. Isn't there some in-between?" She watched Jessie chew the inside of her cheek.

"Parents are weird," she finally said. "I overheard my parents say your mom doesn't want you to hang out with me. Is that true?" Her face fell. "Why doesn't she like me, Feebs?"

Phoebe drew in a sharp breath. "It's not you, Jess. It's...it's complicated." Her eyes grew watery. She held her hand out beneath the table. Jessie twined her fingers around Phoebe's the way they'd done nearly every day of their second semester of eighth grade. "Best buds for life!" they whispered.

Chapter Fourteen

Wednesday, October 8, 2008

A week and a half after the parents' party, despite all the self-talk, Isabel couldn't help dreading the meeting with the Academy's headmistress, one she prayed wouldn't include Jessie and Emma's mothers. Adams Morgan had come to this. She knew it would; Ron had been wrong.

On the morning of the appointment with Alison Kendall, Isabel was in the midst of a quick check of her personal e-mails, when one from Sandy appeared. She was in no mood to read anything from *her,* but the subject line itself was enough to grab her attention: *Slenderella: Special Discount for my friends.* On opening it, Isabel saw that Sandy had sent the email to every ninth-grade mother at Georgetown Academy.

She scanned the body of the text, in which Sandy touted the virtues of her "very own special high-protein weight-loss drink," replete with a few grammatical and punctuation errors.

Hey, it was so great meeting you all the other night.

*Just wondered if you ever heard of **Slenderella**?*

*Its the new hi-protein weight loss drink I represent! Twice a day and you'll be slim for the holidays that are just around the corner. And if you're like me and hate to exercise, well **Slenderella** is the right stuff!! Really, I can attest to that.*

So don't let a couple pounds get between you and your favorite ball gown! (Get it? Like Cinderella!! ☺ Don't want you stuck at home, while everybody else is having all the fun!)

If you order by the middle of October, <u>as my friend you'll get a 20% discount</u>. Click here: www.slenderella.com for more info, or call me at home. xoxox, Sandy

Isabel was appalled to think what impression this would make on the ninth-grade moms, especially on the spouses of diplomats – the elegant woman from Ethiopia, for example. And the very slender one from Denmark. Other people, too, like Members of Congress who considered their personal e-mails a very private thing. But she also saw it for what it was: yet one more attempt at breaking into the clubby culture of DC private school moms.

Had it not been for Sandy's flirtatious coziness with Ron, and the kids' getting caught smoking, well, Isabel might have called her and suggested this wasn't the way to make friends, at least not among the women of Georgetown Academy. As it was, she clicked the print icon and made two copies, relishing the idea of showing the item to Ron.

The email renewed Isabel's vow to keep the girls apart. Nothing good could come of hanging around with the daughter of someone so lacking in judgment. It occurred to her to have a word with Alison Kendall about it; perhaps that could change the outcome of the meeting, the thought of which made her stomach flutter slightly. Stuck at the back of her mind was the possibility that Alison might ask her and Amanda to step down as room parents, an embarrassing blow to say the least.

Isabel's fingers were poised above the keyboard as she contemplated how to respond. *Remove my name from your list,* she typed, hesitated for a moment as the memory of Sandy on the sofa beside Ron coiled back into her mind, then added, *slut.* Isabel knew the dangers of writing such things, even in jest, and clicked the delete bar four times, removing the word "slut," then typing in "please" before striking the "send" button.

Isabel briefly reviewed her calendar. Nothing but meetings. One with the man who'd misused campaign funds. Oh, joy, she thought, borrowing one of Phoebe's expressions. But the appointment with Alison weighed on her. She prayed she could turn it into an opportunity to let the headmistress know what sort of parents she and Ron were – the responsible good kind. On her way out the door she grabbed the extra copy of Sandy's e-mail.

· ● · ● · ● ·

Afraid she might be late, Isabel sped breathlessly into the reception area of the headmistress's office and greeted Ms. Kendall's secretary, Mrs. Watson. The prim elderly woman looked up and acknowledged her. "Why don't you have a seat? I'll let her know you're both here," she said politely.

Both? Isabel glanced around. There in a corner chair, watching her like a predatory feline, sat Miss Slenderella herself. Even

though she thought Sandy might be invited, the sight of her startled her. As usual she was dressed in a shape-hugging outfit. Her
skin-tight pale green sweater simultaneously lifted and revealed
her breasts. And though she was sitting down, if her pants fit any
tighter she might just faint from lack of oxygen. How could she wear
such an outfit to a meeting with the headmistress? She seemed to
lack not only good judgment, but also common sense.

"Hello, Sandy. How are you?"

"Just fine and dandy," she retorted coolly. "And you?"

"Perfect," Isabel said with only a hint of sarcasm, and a faint smile.

Isabel had intended to ignore Sandy without appearing to,
but her plan was foiled when Sandy asked, "Could we talk a minute
before we go in?"

Isabel hoped her dislike wasn't apparent and seated herself a little nervously in a leather wing chair perpendicular to Sandy's. A small,
round, highly glossed mahogany table occupied the space between
them. Several beautifully designed Academy magazines lay there,
waiting for someone to browse through. "What's on your mind?"

"Well, I might as well come straight out with it. No point
in—" she fixed Isabel with a hardened stare, "—pussyfooting
around. Can you explain why you don't want Phoebe hanging
out with Jess? I mean, she didn't do anything wrong, no different
than your daughter."

Of course there were a million reasons, she wanted to say,
not the least of which was that Phoebe had admitted both Jessie
and Emma had smoked, but what could she say without betray-
ing Phoebe's confidence? She straightened her back. "Well, I'm not
sure exactly who did what on Friday, so without getting into all
that, I just think it's better they all take a break from each other,
don't you agree?" Using her courtroom skills, Isabel hoped to con-

fuse Sandy, but she just shook her head.

"Maybe you'd better spell it out for me."

"Well," Isabel said, leaning in toward Sandy and lowering her voice, "I don't know who was smoking and who wasn't, but from my standpoint, and Ron's," she added pointedly, "they were moving down a path that could lead to trouble, big trouble, and Phoebe's never been in trouble like that before."

Sandy's eyes narrowed. "Well, neither has Jessie, so why do you think she's a bad influence?"

"I didn't say that and I don't mean that." Though of course she meant exactly that. Isabel paused for a moment, evaluating what to say next. "Look, I'm not trying to incriminate Jessie, it's just that, what if the situation had been slightly different and they'd gotten caught by the police instead of Sam's mother?" She noticed Mrs. Watson stopped typing.

"Incriminate Jessie?" Sandy asked, looking annoyed. "Could you just speak plain English?"

For heaven's sake, this woman didn't know the meaning of incriminate? Cop shows had to be a staple of her TV diet. "You mean you want me to define incriminate?"

"Of course not," Sandy said sharply, a flash of fury in her eyes.

Before Isabel could further clarify, the door to Alison Kendall's office popped open and the straitlaced headmistress stepped into the reception area. "Won't you come in?"

Isabel got up hurriedly, and with several long strides made it into Alison's conservatively appointed office ahead of Sandy.

Alison invited Isabel and Sandy to sit at the small antique conference table in her office. Nearby, Isabel noticed two straight-backed chairs opposite her desk and understood the politics of seating. For stern lectures and disciplinary measures, she imagined students sitting there, and for more relaxed, informal situations, she would seat them here in the upholstered chairs. Likewise with parents. She prayed this was the case today.

"I had hoped Emma's mother could join us, but she had a conflict, so it's just the three of us. I'm having a separate meeting with the mothers of the boys."

After her conversation with Lorraine, it didn't surprise Isabel that she was a no-show, though she did find it interesting she was speaking to Amanda and the other boys' mothers separately. Perhaps smaller groups were more manageable.

"Would you two like some coffee?" Alison asked, interrupting Isabel's thoughts.

They both nodded. "I'll take two sugars and some cream if you have it," Sandy said with an eager-to-please smile.

Two sugars? Isabel thought of the *Slenderella* ad as she said, "I'll have mine black, thank you."

"I won't keep you long," Alison said, "I'm sure you're both busy. I just wanted to touch base on this issue with the mothers of the girls closest to—" she hesitated, obviously choosing her words carefully, "—to the incident last Friday. Because it happened off campus, it's really beyond the purview of the school, but since it involved seven of our eighty freshman students, I thought I'd try to understand if you think we have a larger problem?"

Alison's approach surprised Isabel. And relieved her, at least for now.

Noting Sandy's perplexed expression, Isabel took the opportunity to speak up. "First, I assume by problem you mean drugs?" She waited for Alison to nod before continuing. "That's a good question. From my perspective, though, it's too soon to say. I'm simply unfamiliar with many of the students. However, I can say with relative certainty that, prior to Friday, Phoebe had never been around drugs, or alcohol for that matter," her gaze briefly settled on Sandy, "and we're taking steps to make sure it stays that way."

Alison then turned to Sandy, who still seemed at a loss for words, and asked if she would like to add anything. Isabel had never seen her so reluctant to speak and had a hunch that formal settings intimidated her. Somehow this was vaguely pleasing.

Sandy finally managed to utter, "Jessie's always been a good girl," then paused, as if gathering her thoughts. "I think kids just get into trouble sometimes, but they're not bad kids." She ended the sentence with a small shrug.

"No one's suggesting they are," Alison said. "I just hoped you might be candid with me. Do you think we have a problem, Mrs. Littleton?"

"Please call me Sandy. Well, as Isabel said, it's a little soon to tell, but I hope not."

A sense of smugness wrapped itself around Isabel. If this was the best she could do to articulate her thoughts, how could she possibly communicate important life lessons to her daughter? And what sort of influence did that make Jessie?

Alison Kendall spent a moment staring out the window. Isabel followed her gaze to the boxwood hedges, the two stately evergreens, an ancient oak blazing with color, and towers of gray-white cumulus clouds that would have been the envy of any Hollywood director. A typical fall day in Washington. She could almost taste its crispness.

"Can you share the girls' explanations about what happened?" Alison said.

Isabel turned abruptly. Suddenly she felt like one of the parents on the *Dr. Phil* show. His prodding not dissimilar from Alison's probing. Calming herself with a deep inhalation, Isabel decided the truth, up to a point, was probably best. "Well, according to Phoebe they went to meet several boys at Five Guys for a soda in Adams Morgan. After that, she was planning to go to a secondhand shop." She inspected Alison's face, but could discern neither belief nor disbelief. "Phoebe has this thing about used clothing stores. She buys clothes and then refashions them."

"Hmm, how interesting. I'll have to ask her about that. I'm all thumbs when it comes to sewing." She took a sip of coffee before adding, "So how did they end up at Sam's, if you don't mind me asking?"

Again, Isabel was quick to answer. "I don't want to incriminate anyone, and obviously I'm relying on Phoebe's version, but she said the boys mentioned going to Sam's, and once there someone pulled out some marijuana and the kids smoked it. She insisted that she did not smoke, but she also felt she couldn't just leave. I imagine that after last year – she had a difficult time at Woodmont," she said, briefly looking off, "well, she didn't want to be the oddball."

Isabel again searched Alison's face, but as before she observed only neutrality.

"Is there anything you'd like to add?" she asked Sandy.

"Well, you know, they're fourteen, or most of them are, and I think the boy-girl thing is kicking in, if you know what I mean," she said, her demeanor slightly more comfortable than before. "They went with the boys maybe hoping they'd ask them to the fall dance."

"I see," Alison said with a faint smile. She waited a moment, perhaps to see if either of them had anything more to say, then added, "Well, I imagine this is a bit personal, but I wonder what steps, as you mentioned earlier, Isabel, you've taken to handle this?" She looked at Isabel, then Sandy without saying more.

Isabel felt thrown off guard; clearly the headmistress had

lulled them into feeling relaxed and now this zinger. But she rose to the occasion. In fact, she relished the opportunity to illustrate the difference between her method of parenting and Sandy's. When Ron had returned after his meeting with Bill, he'd tried to shame her by describing the Littleton's light-handed approach to discipline. Now she could tell him about this.

In a matter of a few sentences, each woman described the punishment she'd meted out to her daughter: Phoebe's four weeks of being grounded; Jessie's a single weekend. As much as she tried, Isabel could not detect a bias in Alison one way or the other. What was she thinking?

"On our end, I've met with Phoebe, Jessica and Emma, and we're taking steps to provide more drug-related education and counseling to the class. We've also made it clear that we observe a zero-tolerance policy for drug use. I don't know if you're aware that Sam's mother has withdrawn him from our school?"

Both Sandy and Isabel shook their heads, though Isabel thought it for the best and made a mental note to ask Phoebe about meeting with Alison.

Alison glanced at her watch and asked if they'd stay in touch with her.

Afraid her chance would disappear Isabel spoke up, asking for a private moment. She cast an apologetic look at Sandy, then said, "Good to see you."

"Yeah, you too," Sandy said in an obviously disingenuous tone. Turning to Alison, she added, "Thanks for inviting me, Ms. Kendall. So nice to see you." The words sounded as if they'd come straight out of a book on etiquette.

Isabel felt vaguely guilty for witnessing Sandy's discomfort with such pleasure, but after Friday night, she simply couldn't help it. Isabel waited until the door closed before producing a copy of the *Slenderella* e-mail and handing it to Alison. "I'd like your input before acting on this, as a room parent, that is. I don't think it's appropriate to use the parents' e-mail list to solicit business." Isabel watched Alison scan the page, then added, "I'm unaware of any school policy so I thought I'd check with you."

A smile crept onto Alison's face. "*Slenderella*. How amusing." She looked up at Isabel. "But I get your point. Thanks for raising it. I'll have Mrs. Watson send out a notice clarifying usage of the e-mail list. Anything else?"

Isabel had thought this exchange might help her gain some intimacy with Alison; at a minimum she had hoped the e-mail would be an entrée to a deeper discussion about Phoebe, maybe even broach what had transpired the previous year, but she could tell when a conversation was over. So, despite her disappointment, she smiled and thanked Alison. "If Amanda or I hear anything more from any of the parents we'll let you know. We hope to keep an open dialogue."

At the door, Alison gazed into Isabel's eyes and said in a faintly reproachful tone, "Don't worry about Phoebe. She appears to be a good student, someone who cares about others. She has character, and that counts for a lot in life."

Unlike her usual measured responses, Isabel was quick to react. "But I do worry about her. I'm her mother. If I don't worry, who will?" The startled look on Alison's face made Isabel regret her tone and she tried to make up for the lapse. "I'm sorry, I didn't mean to sound harsh. Perhaps another time we can have a more in-depth conversation about Phoebe. There are some things you may not be aware of." Somewhat wearily, she added, "I know you're too busy now and I have to get back to my office. So perhaps another time?"

"I'm sorry if I overstepped my bounds," Alison said. "I didn't mean to. Yes, certainly. I'd love to get to know Phoebe better, and you as well. It's just that in our meeting she was so disappointed about not being able to attend the dance."

Isabel's eyes widened; she felt pierced. She wanted to say something to explain herself, but could think of nothing. "Like I said, there are things I doubt you are aware of, but thanks for telling me. I appreciate it, I really do."

On her way back to the office in the back of a cab, an unsettled Isabel wondered exactly what Phoebe had revealed to Alison. As the cabbie angled through traffic inside the canyon of buildings on K Street, the comment that really nagged at Isabel was Alison's subtle suggestion that she allow Phoebe to attend the dance.

· ● · ● · ● ·

That evening when Isabel came home, she called for Phoebe. "Honey, come down here a minute, I want to talk to you." She thought she heard her daughter's music two floors up. Using the intercom system, she added, "It's important, Feebs."

She considered what she was about to do. The issue she faced was about consistency. All the books said that children needed consistency and clear boundaries. But wasn't there also a role for compromise? Compromise in legal situations often presented themselves unexpectedly. And it was up to a clever lawyer to take advantage of such moments. So maybe this was one such moment. Just then a sullen, sulky-faced Phoebe entered the kitchen.

"Come here, honey," Isabel said, outstretching her hands. Phoebe stood her ground. Isabel moved toward her and placed her hands on her daughter's arms. Gazing into her beautiful honey-colored eyes, she said softly, "I've come to the conclusion that I was wrong, that I reacted precipitously. You *can* go to the dance, darling."

Phoebe looked at her with disbelief. "I can? Really?"

"Yes, really."

Phoebe screamed and hurled herself at her mother, clutching her about the neck and hugging her. "Oh, Mommy, thank you."

Chapter Fifteen

Thursday, October 9, 2008

In the hopes of avoiding Jessie without being obvious about it, Phoebe ducked into the girls' bathroom and waited in one of the stalls for the morning buzzer to sound. She felt terrible about it, but once Jessie knew she could go to the dance she'd be badgering her to come spend the night afterward. And that was the one thing she couldn't do. Well, her mother had left it up to her, but she'd decided to reward her mother's kindness by steering clear of Jessie, at least until after the dance.

She sought out Noah right after English class and, smiling sweetly, told him the news. Instead of grinning back at her, happy at this turn of events, he cocked his head to one side and looked at her strangely. Oh, God, now he doesn't want to go with me? A bad feeling swarmed through her insides.

"I'm sorry, Phoebe, but I can't go. With you, I mean."

Each word felt like a karate kick to her gut. She wanted to wilt to the floor and disappear. She found it difficult to meet his uncomfortable gaze, and though she didn't want to sound wimpy or whiny, her voice sounded weak when she asked, "Did I do something?"

"No, it's just that I got another date," he said, quick to add, "because you couldn't go. It got set up last night."

"Really?" Phoebe's eyes fixed on the waxed wooden floor at her feet. "Who? Who are you going with?" She looked up at him, eyes wide.

It seemed as though he didn't want to tell her.

"Oh, man, this is awkward. It seemed like a good idea last night," he said. "And I figured you knew." He stood there staring at her.

"Noah, just tell me. Who is it?"

"Jessie."

"*Jessie*?"

"She said you wouldn't mind since you guys are best friends and you couldn't go. You know?"

"No, I don't." Phoebe was flabbergasted. But this time, hot, steamy anger, not tears, threatened to contort her face. She wished he'd say he would break the date, but he didn't. Why hadn't Jessie said anything to her? She could at least have texted, asking if it was okay. Why hadn't she? About something so important.

She didn't remember how she got there, but she found herself sitting fully clothed on one of the toilets studying her feet, her small Swiss Army knife in one hand. The sadness and pain that had raged through her were beginning to subside, though she felt a killer headache coming on. Her left sleeve was rolled up and wads of bloody toilet paper were stuck to her arm.

· ● · ● · ● ·

Today Phoebe was grateful that Jessie had a different lunch schedule, something that had happened when Jessie's classes had shifted a few days ago. There was no way she wanted to see her. Bad enough they had biology together. Each time she even thought about what Jessie had done, fury galloped through her. How could she?

Between morning classes, Phoebe searched for Emma, but her friend seemed absent from school. Finally, in the lunchroom she sat beside Skyla and blurted out the entire sordid story, hardly caring who heard, though only Skyla's entourage – Molly, Cara, Daisy and a few others – sat within hearing range and listened with rapt attention.

"So Noah is going with Jessie? I thought she was your friend?" Skyla said, underscoring the word *friend*.

"I guess she thought it would be okay since I couldn't go." Phoebe could see the crazy logic in Jessie's move, but still.

Skyla arched her brows in her usual dramatic way. "Yeah, right."

Already Phoebe regretted having told her. "I don't want to think about it."

"Do you still want to go?" Skyla asked in a silky voice.

"I don't know. Maybe a little," she conceded.

"Well, who would be your second choice?"

Phoebe thought for a moment. She almost said, Dylan, but she wouldn't do what Jessie had done. She shrugged. "I dunno."

"I know. Let me ask Kevin or Max if they have a friend for you. How about that? You don't mind that he might be a sophomore?" Her tone was teasing and sly.

The idea appealed to Phoebe more than she could have imagined and her spirits lifted. Still, she couldn't believe she wouldn't be going with Noah. Without realizing it she touched her arm where she'd wounded herself earlier. If she did go there'd be no sleeveless dress for her. She glanced at the clock on the wall. "I should get going," she said. She wanted to avoid running into Jessie at all cost.

· ● · ● · ● ·

Before her last class, Phoebe stared emptily down the double row of lockers on the second floor, hoping to find Emma there. How would she get through biology? She'd thought of a dozen things to say to Jessie and a dozen ways to act, but on entering the classroom, she struggled to maintain her composure, her emotions as readily apparent as if stamped on her face.

"What's *your* problem?" Jessie asked, her eyebrows dipping into a V.

"My problem? What's yours? You asked Noah to the dance. What were you thinking?"

She seemed confused by the question and hesitated before responding. "What d'you mean? Now you don't have to worry that he'll ask somebody else. I thought you'd be happy." Jessie stood with one arm on her hip, looking aggrieved and slightly disgusted.

"Happy? I'm totally NOT happy! Why didn't you text me first? Then you would have known my mom said I could go."

"Yeah, and if you'd texted me last night none of this would have happened either. It's your stupid mother's fault, not mine."

Phoebe turned away. For several minutes she and Jessie refused to look at each other. Then Jessie said, "Anyway, I'll tell Noah he can go with you."

"It's ruined, Jess." She shook her head.

"Yeah? Well, here's a crazy idea; why don't you stop talking about me to Skyla!"

When biology ended she ran into the bathroom again and cried. It took her several minutes not to look like a clown with red-rimmed eyes.

· ● · ● · ● ·

Isabel was in the kitchen fixing dinner.

"What are *you* doing home?" Phoebe snarled.

"That's a nice greeting," Isabel said, giving her daughter a sidelong glance from her place by the stove, where she was stirring Phoebe's favorite dumpling soup. "I thought it would be nice to have supper waiting for all of you."

Isabel was about to offer her daughter a snack, but before the words escaped her lips Phoebe shouted, "Oh, so you can feel like you're being the good mom? But who cares about food when you don't have friends? When your whole life is messed up?"

"What on earth is going on?" Isabel couldn't believe what she was hearing, not after last night's embrace, after the best evening they'd spent together in a while. What had happened?

Phoebe's words tumbled out willy nilly, tears streaming down her face, as Isabel tried to make sense of them. As best she could tell Noah was going to the dance with *someone* else, Phoebe refused to say with whom, and the reason for that of course was all her fault, though Phoebe now was also angry with Noah. And for some indiscernible reason Phoebe was now relegated to attending the dance with "some loser" that Kevin or Max would find for her.

Isabel wanted to ask who Kevin and Max were, but knew better than to interrupt her distraught girl. Clearly, an avalanche of pent-up resentment had broken loose. Isabel rounded the counter to put an arm around her, but Phoebe recoiled. "Don't freaking touch me!"

Isabel took a step back. Trying to keep her tone neutral, she said evenly but sternly, "Do not use language like that on me, young lady."

Phoebe scrunched her face in anger and mocked her mother. "Young lady? Well, thanks to you this *young lady's* life sucks!"

Isabel felt like yelling back, reminding Phoebe that she'd caused her own mess, but restrained herself by counting. Ten, nine, eight...seven...Who am I angry with? she thought. In that moment she truly didn't know. Six, five, four...What do I really want now? She knew it was to get Phoebe to calm down. Once that happened she'd pour herself a little wine. Hopefully a teenage Jackson wouldn't prove as difficult.

At once Phoebe burst into tears. She slumped onto a barstool at the kitchen counter and released deep gulping sobs. Isabel watched her a moment before saying, "Oh, Phoebe darling, come here, honey. You've had a bad day, but it'll be okay. You'll see. I promise." She opened her arms to her daughter, and though at first Phoebe resisted, with a bit more coaxing, she collapsed into them.

· • · • · • ·

That evening, as arranged by Skyla and her date Max, a sophomore named Michael called Phoebe on her cell phone and invited her to the dance. Without even thinking about it, she accepted. Shortly after the call, she looked him up on Facebook, and there he was. Not bad looking. Kind of cute even.

A while later, Jessie texted her. *I'm sorry. It's not too late. You can still go with him.*

Phoebe texted back. *Too late. Going with Michael Singer.*

The next day Michael approached her at her locker, seemed nice enough, and the drama that had heaved and pitched inside of her settled down. Of course, she would still prefer to be going with Noah, but if that wasn't to be, oh, well.

At home that night, Phoebe asked her mom to help her pick out a dress for the dance the following weekend, to which her mother responded, "Of course, honey, I'd love to."

Phoebe could tell that her mother's huge smile was genuine. They hadn't gone shopping together in quite a while, and she was looking forward to it as well. Only then did she remember all the gashes and wounds on her arm and thighs. Her stomach felt sick. How would she hide them in the dressing room? What would her mother do if she saw? Guilt and shame slid through her in equal measure. Maybe she would go alone, though the thought of it made her want to weep.

Chapter Sixteen

Friday, October 10, 2008

Sandy often found comfort cruising Westfield Mall, her second favorite place in the world, after her own home. Over the course of her fifteen years with Bill, she'd spent countless hours dipping in and out of stores, and so on Friday, still trying to erase the memory of the email from Mrs. Watson and that awful meeting with Isabel and Ms. Kendall, she decided to do the thing that most soothed her soul and took her mind off her troubles: she would go shopping.

Golf alone just wasn't any fun. Today, the mere thought of golf brought on the long ago memory of her final date with her stepfather, Les. But now was not the time, and so she chased this tangent from her mind.

After a quick coffee with a neighbor she'd recently befriended,

Sandy spent several hours of concentrated effort poking through sale racks, searching for items on Jessie's wish list and making nearly a dozen purchases.

Around one o'clock, her arms weighed down by shopping bags, she decided to hunt for a place to have coffee, and maybe, just maybe, she'd treat herself to dessert. Sandy knew she ought to have a salad or a cup of soup, but just then the urge to satisfy her sweet tooth was winning out.

The habit had developed in her teens, when she'd slipped over to Mrs. Eddinger's Nantucket-style cottage across the street to escape yet another of her mother's dreadful silences, the occasional memory of which could still bring tears to her eyes. No matter the time of day, Mrs. E had welcomed Sandy, had had gentle words for her and something sweet to eat. Entering her home, Sandy would relax into the elderly woman's soothing voice, and the rich, sumptuous world of cakes, pastries, cookies, and pies.

Now, it was a habit she fought. If she didn't, she knew she'd end up like Margaret – what she called her mother on those rare occasions they talked, only twice since Jessie's birth – who'd eventually lost her pretty figure. She brushed away that memory too as she came upon the café outside Nordstrom's, where several people stood in line.

Sandy plopped her bags on the floor as her eyes took in the assortment of pastries: thickly frosted carrot cake, lemon meringue pie (fluffy meringue piled high), chocolate decadence cake (one of her favorites), vanilla-frosted cupcakes, a variety of scones, and a pear tart. Though the slice of chocolate decadence beckoned her, she chose the lemon meringue pie. Fewer calories, and she wouldn't eat the crust, or at least not all of it.

"I'll have a tall coffee," she said to the teenager behind the counter, "and leave room for cream." Pointing the long fuchsia nail of her index finger at the pie, she added, "And that. Yummy. It's fresh, right?"

The girl gave a disinterested nod as she went through the motions of preparing a cup of coffee. "For here or to go?"

Sandy smiled brightly. "For here. I can hardly stand up with all these bags. Need a quick pick-me-up, you know."

"Yep."

Sandy's enthusiasm refused to be diminished by the girl's tepid response. She chose the nearest empty table and seated herself so she had a view of the mall. She sighed audibly after taking a sip of the creamy coffee and tasting her first bite of pie. "That is sooo good," she muttered softly. "Mmmm."

Sandy had developed into a woman of indulgence only after she'd left home and after Bill began pampering her and making it his mission to make mounds of money for her to spend. He was the most generous man she knew. And, luckily, he harbored little jealousy. After a night of flirtation with other men at a party, she always made sure to be extra sexy for him. Made sure he knew she'd always be there for him. Made sure he knew that *he* was her number one.

She gazed at the shopping bags, several of which contained items for Jessie, who'd been out of sorts the previous night. After considerable wheedling, she'd gotten Jess to reveal how hurt and angry Phoebe had been because she'd invited Noah to the dance. To ease Jessie's confused feelings, she'd bought not just one but two dresses for the fall dance at Nordstrom's, jeans from J. Crew, a white t-shirt from Banana Republic, and a strapless black bra from Victoria's Secret.

She never tired of seeing the expression of happiness on Jes-

sie's face when she bought her something, an item casually mentioned while she and Jessie chatted in the kitchen over a snack.
Something that had ground to a halt at a critical moment in her
own life.

She took a sip of coffee, dipped her fork into the lemon curd,
and began running her mind over old memories the way others ran
fingers over old scars. It wasn't often that she indulged or so sub-
jected herself, but recent events prompted this train of thought. The
way Isabel seemed to ignore and dislike her felt much like Margaret, who had, at times, spurned and envied her own daughter. For
the natural curves of her youthful figure, because of Les's wandering hands. But what could she have done? Her mother should have
protected her – thrown her stepfather out of the house, not her.

Adopting her mother's words, Sandy had told a few of her
very closest high school friends, "It's a story as old as the hills." She
imagined that one or two had passed her account along, despite
having sworn to secrecy.

Of course that wasn't the real story. And not the whole story
that she'd kept to herself all these years. Even though Sandy hadn't
been the smartest girl in her class, she was clever enough to understand human nature. And she knew that women tended to gossip,
especially about something as juicy and salacious as this. Salacious
wouldn't have been Sandy's word, but that's what it was.

Now, as she took another bite of the lemon custard, she thought
about events that had transpired more than half a lifetime ago.

When Les—that was his name—had entered her life, she'd
just turned fifteen. The first time she saw him, she couldn't believe
that such a handsome man was interested in her mother. Of course
she'd failed to recall her mother's once-upon-a-time beauty, by
then a bit faded, but she remained elegant and attractive nonethe-

less. Besides, her mother had fallen into a small inheritance upon the death of her parents. Something that never hurt a woman, especially one with children, when it came to attracting a man.

Not only was Les handsome, but he also had that rare thing called charm. And it drew Sandy because she'd spent so much time in the company of a mother who'd lost interest in her. The divorce had been difficult for her mother, but afterward the fact that Sandy had been her father's favorite seemed to taint her. Never again would she have the same closeness with her mother as her sister Ashley, with whom Margaret often cuddled up to read bedtime stories. Perhaps for that reason, Sandy found herself hungering for attention, like a flower hungers for sun. Early to develop into a shapely and luscious girl, Sandy fell readily into boys' kisses. So many boys. And for a time, this had stemmed the tide of her needs.

One night, not long after Les married Margaret, which also wasn't long after Sandy's sixteenth birthday in May of 1993, her mother announced over the dinner table that she was going out with a group of women friends and that Les shouldn't wait up for her. Sandy glanced at Les to see what he would say. For the briefest moment their eyes met, latching onto each other like sky and sea, and his mouth turned upward into a glimmer of a smile.

Her mother left shortly thereafter, and the two of them went about cleaning up the dishes. Light banter, a bit of joking turned more serious when Les suddenly said, "So, tell me about your boyfriends."

The comment took Sandy aback because she didn't know what he was after. "What do you mean?" she said.

He rubbed a dishtowel across a shiny metal lid and lifted it up to see if it was properly dried. Sandy imagined he was examining his own striking, dark haired, blue-eyed image. "Well, do you like what they do to you?" he asked.

"Do to me?"

"Sure," he said with a half smile, "the way they – " he paused then as if evaluating his choice of words, "the way they, uh, kiss you?"

She laughed at him. "Why, do *you* want to kiss me?" The words slid out smoothly, playfully. Daringly. She wasn't sure whether her question had been an innocent flirtation or an invitation, but regardless it led to the next thing, which was him leaning in to kiss her. And she kissing him back. A long, slow, delicious kiss.

The experience didn't resemble the inexpert kissing of most boys she knew. Nor did the sensations he aroused in her approximate anything she'd felt with any teenage guy. What happened that night ignited something. A sensuality that radiated throughout her body, a desire that beckoned from between her legs.

From that night on they met often, simplified by the fact that as a freelance writer and video producer, Les mostly worked from home. His sensitive touch drove her wild. And it hadn't taken long before they'd gone all the way. Despite everything else that happened, even now she relished the memory.

Still, it was the worst kind of wrong to know you wanted something you shouldn't have, and she thought he felt that way too. They never spoke of their taboo activity, and perhaps by not giving voice to it they were able to hang on to a fictional version of events.

Being a fast learner, Sandy taught many a boy to better love and satisfy her, but few came close to those times with Les. During the summer, he also began teaching her the finer points of golf, a sport she became increasingly fond of and good at. On the way to and from they'd stop in assorted places. A remote bathroom in the country club, the lavish basement of one of Les's friends, the backseat of his Range Rover.

She felt daring and each encounter thrilled her until she began to feel dissonance in the air. Between herself and her mother. Her mother and Les. What she couldn't know was that the sexual tension between herself and Les was palpable. It electrified the rooms they occupied. Her mother didn't need evidence to know of its existence. She sensed it with every cell of her being. And resented it. Began resenting Sandy even more than before.

This brought Sandy to the part of the story she didn't like to remember. And with practiced precision, she turned off the memory like a spigot stops the flow of water.

The idea that someone might uncover pieces of her past sometimes petrified her. Bill, especially, couldn't know the way she'd deceived him. Surely he'd leave her. Their recent move to Bethesda had helped. When asked about her roots, she remained vague. "Baltimore area. So boring I had to come live near the President. And yes, I have been to the White House," she'd say, beaming. She didn't exactly lie, because she, along with hundreds of tourists, *had* visited the White House, but she certainly had no qualms about twisting the truth. The distinctions between the two had become malleable. "What's the difference as long as it doesn't hurt anyone?" she'd think. Though whether hurting someone truly bothered Sandy, well, that was questionable.

Sandy had gotten lucky when Bill entered her life; his timing had been perfect – she'd just turned 18 and things were rotten; in fact her whole life had fallen apart several weeks before. So now, she did her utmost to keep Bill happy, and really that was pretty easy. Give him a good meal, a few laughs, clean laundry, some steamy sex and he was good to go. Besides, in a sense, she'd given him Jessie and he loved the girl deeply.

That was the thing about Sandy, she never forgot the people she owed, nor did she forget the ones who'd slighted her. Like her mother. And that damn Isabel, she'd really gotten under her skin. She still couldn't believe the note from the headmistress about some stupid policy for the "appropriate use" of Georgetown parents' e-mails. If that didn't have Isabel Winthrop written all over it, she didn't know what did. Sandy took a giant bite of lemon meringue pie. Did Isabel really think she could get away with that?

The truth was, though, Isabel's consistent year-long rejection had wounded her, more deeply than she cared to admit. So when she thought of Isabel now, she didn't cry, no, she launched into an angry internal monologue, something Sandy was prone to, just like overindulging on sweets. And once she got going little could stop her. *That evil woman does not know who she's messing with,* she thought. *I'm going to make her suffer.*

She would make sure of that. But how?

Sandy sucked a thick mound of meringue off her fork. Oh, God, that's good. Another bite followed a long sip of coffee. She wound her tongue around another spoonful of lemon custard, drew it into her mouth, and sat there thinking. How to get to that woman? Really get to her.

Then, part of the answer materialized, as it always did. It had been sitting right there in her brain since her earlier memory of Les; in fact, she'd already made a start without fully being aware of it. Ron!

The delightful hum of shoppers buzzed around Sandy as she sat there, smug and cat-like, polishing off the last of her dessert.

· ● · ● · ● ·

At home in her kitchen, Sandy pulled out the Academy phonebook and turned to "M" for Murrow. A glib smile rose to her lips.

She'd never forget the tortured look on Isabel's face a mere Friday ago. Now, insert needle and twist. True Ron hadn't responded to her first email, but she hadn't really expected him to, and long ago she'd learned the value of persistence. Besides that email had only laid the groundwork for another more specific one.

So, what would she say? That she wondered if they could talk about the girls. Not a get-together, she'd save that for later. She figured it would be awkward for him to turn her down, and he certainly wouldn't be telling Isabel about it. So on her kitchen computer she typed up a short note:

Could we have a quick chat about our girls. Things are a little tense!

I'm sure you understand. ☺ *Sandy.*

While waiting for a reply, Sandy clicked on the Internet icon. She went to Facebook, typed in Isabel's name, but no, she still didn't have an account. So she went to Liz VanDorn's page to see what Academy moms were gabbing about. Nothing interested her. Why should she care about which college so-and-so had gotten into, or somebody's "fabulous" new job, or some silly morning news item? The photos she examined more closely and commented on a few.

Next, she opened up Jessie's page and scanned recent postings, checking on who, what and how many posts – the more the better in her opinion. She relished the notion that Jessie could be popular. But wait, what was that?

An exchange with Phoebe in Jessie's private message chat box. A day ago.

Jessie: *Are you still mad at me?*

Phoebe: *Not mad...*

Jessie: *Then what?*

Phoebe: *Confused, maybe.*

Jessie: *But I said I was sorry. Noah likes you, not me, you know.*
Phoebe: *Let's drop it, okay?*
Jessie: *Ok, best buds for life?*
Phoebe: *Sure.*

Sure? Sandy thought. Does it get any less convincing than that? She wondered what Phoebe might be saying about Jessie. Her eyes narrowed in thought. She hoped that her ill-timed suggestion to invite Noah wouldn't backfire on her. She didn't want Jessie hurt, or, God forbid, to become an outcast.

After the meeting at Ms. Kendall's office she'd stewed all afternoon. *Doesn't want Phoebe to hang out with my kid? Fine.* But she simply couldn't let Isabel get away with dissing Jessie. That's when the idea of Jessie inviting Noah had popped into her head. *See how Phoebe likes that.* No girl wants her crush to go on a date with someone else. Especially not her best friend. And yet she'd twisted the idea into a reasonable suggestion. And Jessie had bought it hook, line and sinker.

She checked her emails. Still nothing from Ron. He'll come around, she told herself.

Late afternoon, as she unconsciously popped a peanut into her mouth and sipped a can of Bud Light, she sat at the kitchen counter studying Phoebe Murrow's pudgy eighth-grade face in Jessie's Woodmont yearbook. She decided the girl's innocent looks probably belied her true nature. Lurking in there was someone just as mean as her stupid mother, though even Sandy knew Isabel wasn't stupid, which made the situation all the more vexing. What are you saying about my daughter, Phoebe?

Wiping her greasy fingers on her new pink sweats, she left the kitchen and sprinted up two flights of stairs, though by the time she reached her messy office, she was huffing and puffing. Time to cut back on dessert, beer and peanuts. And get back on a *Slenderella* diet.

She sighed and checked her computer for that elusive email from Ron. The email that would get things rolling. The very thought of it made her smile. Just you wait, Isabel, you have no idea who you're messing with.

Part Two
Revenge

Chapter One

Saturday, October 11, 2008

Phoebe slipped into a long-sleeved shirt, but there was simply no way that she could go shopping with her mother. Her arms were a mess. She kept staring at them as if some magical words might make the wounds disappear. To put her mind elsewhere she opened her computer, and logged onto Facebook. A new "friend" request. Hmm. Someone named Shane Barnett.

She re-read the name, but it meant nothing to her. Since the beginning of school, Phoebe had been friended by dozens of new kids, and her texting and tweeting had exploded. She thought Shane might be a friend of Max's, but on closer inspection that didn't seem to be the case. Shane's profile said he went to Walter Johnson High School, which she knew was over in Bethesda near Westfield Mall. His message indicated he was new and that he wanted to get to know some of the kids in the area. He'd already friended Jessie and Emma, and a few other girls, though not Skyla. As she took in his Facebook photo she couldn't get over how adorable he was. He had a familiar look.

She accepted his friend request and sent him a quick note. *Welcome*, she wrote, noticing he was instant messaging. *Where are you from?*

A shout from her mother interrupted her.

"You all set, Phoebe?"

"I don't think I feel well," Phoebe shouted down from her room.

· ● · ● · ● ·

"Oh?" Isabel said to herself. As she made her way upstairs, a feeling of disappointment invaded her. She'd been so looking forward to their shopping trip; at least a month had passed since their last intimate mother-daughter outing. Had Phoebe come down with something? She'd seemed all right a little while ago at breakfast and even the night before.

The carpeted stairs muted Isabel's footsteps, perhaps the reason that Phoebe looked so startled when Isabel walked through the open doorway into her room. She noticed Phoebe hurriedly pushing down her left sleeve, or maybe she was just imagining it. The thought that Phoebe had cut herself again lodged itself in her mind. Although she hoped, as Ron often suggested, that she was just concocting things.

"What's wrong, sweetheart?" she asked, concern etched on her brow. "Should I take your temperature?"

Without looking up at her, Phoebe shook her head. "I just

don't think I'm up for a big shopping trip."

Isabel sat down on the end of the bed a couple of feet from Phoebe and put on a cheerful face. "So let's make it a short, very focused one. Because if we don't find a dress for the dance today, honey, I don't know when we'll get the chance. It's next weekend, you know."

Phoebe responded with a slightly aggrieved "I know."

"So what's wrong?"

She shrugged. "I dunno."

Isabel wondered if she'd returned to moping about what had happened with Noah, maybe once more wanting to make her feel guilty. And Isabel couldn't blame her, she felt awful about it. She wondered, too, who Noah was taking to the dance, and if perhaps that didn't play a role in Phoebe's state of mind. But instead of probing, she did her best to enliven Phoebe's mood.

She suggested they go to Georgetown instead of a mall, preview a few stores by doing a little window shopping along Wisconsin and M Streets before checking out Claire's Boutique, a cute shop with unique teen dresses, pricey and high-end, but stylish. The kind of clothes she thought Phoebe might actually like.

She scooted closer to Phoebe, who then rested her head against Isabel's arm.

"I've got it, Feebs!" Isabel had suddenly hit on an idea that might pique her daughter's interest. "Let's go to one of your favorite second-hand shops and see if you can find something there?"

Phoebe twisted her head and looked up at her mother. A sweet smile blossomed on her face. "Really, Mom? Okay, let's go."

· ● · ● · ● ·

They began their search at Secondhand Rose, though Phoebe didn't find anything there and then suggested going mainstream, which both surprised and pleased Isabel.

As they cruised the countless boutiques up and down Wisconsin Avenue, Isabel felt sunny and upbeat; she chatted about this and that and pointed out various items of clothing, ("wouldn't that look terrific on you;" "check out this color, Feebs, it goes perfectly with your eyes"). Together they ducked in and out of one store after another, until Isabel felt certain that Phoebe had forgotten whatever had thrown her off-kilter earlier. Now she was clearly into the spirit of shopping. And Isabel willingly pulled out her credit card more than once.

Finally, they arrived at Claire's Boutique, Phoebe appearing more enthused and happy than in quite some time, which generated an equally uplifting effect on Isabel. They each collected an armful of dresses, and followed an ambitious young sales clerk to a large dressing room. "Here you go," she said. "Let me know if you need any help."

Phoebe entered with Isabel close on her heels. But at the curtain, Phoebe blocked her path. "You wait out here, okay, Mom, and I'll model them for you."

"Okay," Isabel said agreeably, though she would have preferred going in to watch Phoebe try on each dress, helping her zip and adjust them, and chatting with her as she did. But knowing how fragile these interactions with Phoebe could be, Isabel was careful not to mar their adventure together. So she sat down a few feet outside the dressing room and rested on an upholstered chair.

It was then, in that relaxed moment that an unbidden thought screeched into Isabel's brain. Phoebe doesn't want me in the dressing room because she has something to hide! She had trouble breathing when her mind gave voice to what her daughter was hiding: scars and wounds from cutting herself. As the ugly thought gained purchase Isabel had to restrain herself from jumping up and barging into the fitting room.

After a couple of minutes, Phoebe emerged. "What do you think?" she said, tilting her head to the side. She stood there and modeled the short black dress, with its gauzy long sleeves, taking mincing steps to turn around.

"It's okay, what do you think?" Isabel said, trying to focus on the dress, not the sleeves of the dress. All the dresses Phoebe was trying on had sleeves, she now realized.

"It's not the one," Phoebe said.

"Just what I was thinking," Isabel concurred.

Once Phoebe stepped back into the dressing room, Isabel returned to the racks, browsed for a second, pulled a dress from one of them, hardly bothering to check for size, and practically ran back to the dressing room. Without hesitating, she yanked the curtain aside, just in time to catch Phoebe peeling off the dress she'd just tried on.

"So I saw this, honey—" Isabel said, but halted in mid-sentence as her eyes fixed on Phoebe's mutilated arm in the mirror.

Phoebe wore a look of horror as she stared back at her mother's reflection. Her hand flew to cover the mosaic of cuts and scabs that disfigured the area just above and below her elbow. "Mom, why'd you come in?" She groaned as the dress fell to the floor, revealing more wounds on her thighs.

"Oh my God, Feebs," Isabel said as she took a step closer to her daughter. *What have you done, my darling girl?* she thought.

Phoebe's face puckered with shame.

Isabel's eyes glistened. "Oh, baby." It was all she could say, as tears streamed down her face. "I'm so sorry."

· • · • · • ·

While Isabel and Phoebe were out dress shopping, Ron took Jackson to his soccer game. He stood on the sidelines watching, then stepped away from the other parents to type an email to Sandy. She'd written the previous day and he hadn't figured out what to say or whether to confide in Isabel. *Of course, I'd be happy to talk with you,* he wrote. *Why don't you call me at the office next week? Maybe Monday? Ron*

Though distracted by Sandy's curvy figure in his mind, he turned his attentions back to the field just as Jackson scored. All around him shouts kicked into the air: "Goal!" "Way to go, Jackson!" "Yes!"

· • · • · • ·

On Sunday Phoebe stuck close to her mother, who'd set up a series of appointments for her with Dr. Sharma, beginning the following week. She felt catapulted back in time, as if she were 10 or 11, not almost 14. For once she didn't mind being fussed over. Her mother insisted on tending to her wounds, dressing the scars, scabs, and wounds with a Vitamin E ointment. Her father prepared a fun breakfast ("All right, Princess Blueberry Muffin, what'll you have?"), and with her mother, she took a leisurely walk in Rock Creek Park early afternoon.

They came to a halt at an overlook to watch the stream glitter in the sunlight, winding between the forested hills awash with fall. Phoebe began crying, as if the water had roused deep-seated emotions. "Mom, Noah is taking Jessie to the dance!" The despondent words tumbled out as though the two of them had been in the middle of a conversation.

Her mother's brow furrowed. "Really? How did that happen?"

And that was all Phoebe needed to unleash the thoughts and emotions she'd suppressed for the past few days. She explained the tortured logic Jessie had used to justify her actions. It was Jessie, after all, who had approached Noah.

This time it was Phoebe's turn to feel surprised by her mother's behavior. She said very little, though the expression on her face revealed the depth of her dismay. And if Jessie had been persona non grata with her mother before, this secret didn't help, but Phoebe didn't care. No, her best friend had betrayed her, and now she sought solace, which only her mother could give.

Late afternoon, Phoebe went to her room to do some homework. She listened to the Jonas Brothers, Miley Cyrus, Adele and other popular singers on her iPod. Now and then, she checked her Facebook page then turned to Noah's, and for a few minutes scrolled through his photos, of which there weren't many. And happily nothing about going to the dance with Jessie.

She'd forgotten all about Shane, until she saw that he'd answered yesterday's question. *Dad got transferred down here from Baltimore.* She began messaging with him and found out that he was on the Varsity football team. Still preoccupied with Noah, she ran out of clever things to say.

Then, almost as if sensing her discomfort, he wrote: *gotta go to football practice. Later.*

Phoebe was surprised he had football practice at this late hour on a Sunday, but didn't give it more than a passing thought.

A while later, Skyla called. She wanted to know all the details of the dress she'd gotten. And she spoke of the coming dance. But nothing about Shane. Skyla always wanted to talk about the latest guy with whom she or Phoebe had become Facebook friends. This neglect surprised Phoebe a little, *and*, she realized, it disappointed her. While chatting, she saw that Shane had left her a private message. *Your eyes are so cool. I wish I could see them in person.*

A thrill coursed through Phoebe, and she actually felt herself blushing. Eager to end the call, she kept her answers brief without being rude. "What's with you?" Skyla asked at once. "Nothing," Phoebe said, "let's talk tomorrow," and then hung up.

Since Shane didn't attend her school, she felt less inhibited in her response, so she wrote exactly what she thought: *Thanks, maybe you can?* ☺ *BTW: You remind me of the guy in* Twilight.

You remind me of Emma Stone. ;-)

Phoebe laughed aloud, feeling a sense of unrestrained glee. If he thought she looked like Emma Stone, then they truly were meant to be friends. She was about to ask how he knew she adored the actress's looks, but before she could, he'd written to her again.

Do you have a boyfriend? No, don't tell me, of course you do. To which she wrote: *No, not really. How about you? Do you have a girlfriend?* To which he responded: *Of course not, otherwise I wouldn't be flirting with you!*

She touched the word "flirting" on the screen and rubbed her finger across it, as if by doing so she could somehow reach through the netherworld of computers and connect with him. After they signed off, Phoebe printed out his Facebook photo and pinned it to her bulletin board. And studied it repeatedly. In bed that night, Phoebe tried to imagine what it would be like to meet him.

Chapter Two

Monday, October 13, 2008

"Ron, is that you?" Sandy said. "Is this a good time?"

"Sure, sure," he said, sitting at his desk, toying with a miniature basketball, "what's on your mind?"

"Well," she said, "it's just that Jessie feels awful about having invited Noah. She told me Phoebe was upset, but she was just trying to help. You know? So I hope you can let her know that. And I hope the two girls can get back to the good old days." A long purring sigh reached through the phone and grabbed him.

"Of course, not to worry," he said in a rush. "These things always sort themselves out." Though in this case he wondered if that was true.

"Do they?" she said, as if reading his mind. "I don't know. I'd like to think so." She paused. "You know what I'd really like?"

"What's that?"

"To make you happy."

Ron wasn't sure he'd heard correctly. Before he could ask there was a click on the line.

· ● · ● · ● ·

As Sandy hung up she watched her reflection in the round mirror she'd placed on her desk beside the computer screen. But it wasn't what it seemed, not some narcissistic addiction to her image, but rather a reminder not to eat. If she did, she'd have to watch herself do it. A very effective method, if she had to say so herself. It was one of the simple diet tips she sent out periodically to her list of customers.

Which, oddly, reminded her of Les, who'd taught her a few tricks. She recalled how, on occasion, she'd stood in front of a mirror with him off to the side behind her or he'd sat on her bed directing her. "Now take off your blouse. No, no, not so fast. Slowly, darling." And so on. Of course it always ended with them pawing at each other, but she'd loved his stories, his impromptu explorations of her body. There was something languid and tropical about him. Or maybe it was French. He occasionally threw out a French word or two. "Je t'aime" were the only ones she recognized.

His voice though was a bit like Ron's, they had similar velvety baritones, she now thought. They even vaguely resembled one another. She sighed, recollecting how her mother's growing suspicions had precipitated a change in Les's voice. She could hear the anxiety. "We need to stop this," he said one day during her senior year.

She'd looked at him quizzically. "Stop what?" She'd been so

sure he was planning on running off with her the minute she grad-
uated that when she told him so, he'd laughed. Not exactly in a
mean way, but dismissively as if she were a child. "I can't believe
you had any such idea." And yet she had. She could have sworn
he'd said as much.

"You've lost your mind, my sweet," he added.

Sandy had fantasized a life with him, a life away from her
mother, a woman so lacking in affection, so distant, so uninterest-
ed in her older daughter.

It all dated back to the divorce, when their father came to pick
them up every other Sunday. Sandy began to dread those meetings
as it cast her further and further from her mother; she became an
island her mother rarely visited. And though Sandy wanted her father's love and understanding, how could a single day with him
replace the thirteen in between when she felt adrift. Alone. As if
understanding her quandary, he began to come less and less until she hardly saw him at all. Until she felt neither the love of her
mother nor her father.

We don't fully understand such things as children, her one
and only therapist had said, and maybe never, because all too often
such experiences become one of those shadow feelings that follow
us through life without our ever coming to terms with it. We run
from it, hide from it, only now and then catching a glimpse of that
shadow, seeing that it's still there, sewn to us by a thin but strong
thread. And so we build castles around ourselves, armor ourselves
against the pain of loss, never fully realizing what we've lost and never knowing what might have been had circumstances been different.

So it was with Sandy. She'd invited Les into her castle and
wanted to keep him there. When she continued to pursue him, often taking unreasonable risks and threatening to expose their af-

fair to the mother who'd neglected her, he took her for a drive one late afternoon two months before Sandy's graduation. He suggested the exercise club where she liked to go.

Darkness had already settled in for the evening as they pulled into the club's parking lot. But he stopped her from exiting the car. Instead, he kissed her with the fierceness of Genghis Khan, a little joke between them. Which was followed by stormy screwing. When the two of them climaxed, Sandy's orgasm came in explosive waves, unlike anything she'd ever felt. Then, softly, she heard him say, "I love you," and he kissed her again.

Now, for sure, she thought, Les would start the car and they'd drive away together. As she waited, however, the deadening words arrived: "But we have to stop. It's over, darling. Don't you understand?"

She cried out and told him she didn't understand, not one bit, not ever. Without further discussion he started the car and aimed it home.

That's when Sandy decided to get back at Les in the only way she knew. She would find a very cute guy to begin hanging around the house with. To openly kiss whenever Les was around. See how he liked that.

Her thoughts returned to Ron, and she wondered how Isabel would like the kisses she'd give her husband. Staring in the mirror beside her laptop, she didn't see herself, but imagined those tousled looks of Ron's. Just like the Kennedys, and their very Irish charm. She'd send him another email soon, but she'd wait. It worked best that way.

· ● · ● · ● ·

"Jane, you have no idea what her arms looked like," Isabel said, using the speakerphone in her office, and subconsciously staring at her own arms. "It was like a killing field. Stab wounds, cuts, scabs, raw tender flesh. Oh, my God, it was devastating. How could she have done that? And how could I have not known? I feel like the world's worst mother!"

"Oh, Iz, don't beat yourself up over it. You're an incredibly dedicated mom. You two will find a way through this." Jane paused. "I'm so sorry for Phoebe. And for you, you poor thing. What are you going to do?"

Just hearing her friend's voice soothed Isabel's frayed state of mind. She described her plan of action. That Phoebe would see Dr. Sharma once or twice a week, depending on what she thought after the first session; that she planned to do more research on cutting; and that she really did think keeping Phoebe away from Jessie was the right thing to do. "Can you believe how that girl justified having Noah take her to the dance? It's sinful! Really. How does she come up with that crap?"

"Well, in a twisted way, I guess you could convince yourself that you're keeping your friend's boyfriend from other girls. But, I agree, who thinks like that? And without even asking Phoebe! You've got your hands full," Jane said, then added, "but you know what they say?"

"What?"

"This too shall pass."

"I suppose."

"Anyway, Phoebe's a kind, smart girl, and she'll be all right."

Her reassurance sounded like Alison Kendall's, but coming from Jane she felt better. "You promise?"

"I guarantee it!"

Generally, on Mondays Isabel tried to schedule as few meetings as possible. Which meant that now she had a few minutes to kill before her first of the day, a pro bono case. But her mind wasn't yet on that appointment.

After what she'd seen on Saturday in the dressing room, and despite Jane's no-nonsense pep talk, she was still angry with herself for having allowed Phoebe to stop seeing Dr. Sharma. Clearly, she'd been in denial. She logged onto the Internet and Googled "cutting." It seemed far more information existed now than when she'd researched it before. The second site she landed on featured an article that grabbed her attention. "Cutting to Escape from Emotional Pain?" by Edward A. Selby, Ph.D. She printed out the piece and began to read. Automatically, she reached for her highlighter and began marking a few passages. As she went along, more and more lines of type shouted out at her.

The author was asking the question Isabel sometimes still asked herself: "Why on Earth would someone purposely want to cut his or her self?" The fact that something like 4% of the U.S. population self-injured, millions in other words, with the number of adolescents rising to "as high as 14%" was frightening. How had this happened? It only seemed like yesterday that so many girls suffered from anorexia and bulimia. Was this the new method of coping?

The unsightly highlights felt like an affront. She could hardly bear to read more. But she told herself to toughen up. She scanned the rest and made notes on one of the legal pads, things she'd discuss with Ron and also Dr. Sharma:

- the number one reason for self-mutilating is to reduce negative emotions (author claims this seems like "such a bizarre reason!")
- like Phoebe, many people say they do it to "stop bad feelings"
- they are trying "to cope with stressful situations or upsetting

problems" the way some "people use alcohol or drugs"

• many become dependent on dealing with their problems this way.

These things fit Phoebe's situation, she thought, but what didn't was the notion that people who self-mutilated often had problems in school or at work. Phoebe did great in school, or at least she had last year when this whole thing began. She wondered if she should ask Phoebe how her grades were. Of course not, she thought to herself.

The next thing she read stopped her. She flipped the cap off her highlighter and pressed the tip hard on the copy of the article she'd printed out, sliding it across several passages. "The worst thing of all about NSSI is that it is strongly connected to later suicide attempts and death by suicide."

She jotted "strongly connected to suicide attempts" on her hand-written list. The only hope the article gave her were the soon-to-be-released "new and exciting findings on this topic." Terrific! Isabel thought. Oh joy, she imagined Phoebe saying. And the only advice was to see a therapist. At least that she'd accomplished. Now she recollected what Dr. Sharma had explained to her last May – that cutting had similarities to eating disorders, both used the body as a means of self-expression. A kind of canvas, as with body piercings. She thought of Emma and wondered what, if anything, lay behind that girl's unhappiness, assuming of course that she was unhappy.

Isabel gazed outside. From her fifth story window she had a view of numerous other 19th-century renovated brick buildings in DC's Penn Quarter and the tops of dozens of trees, a fall spectacle at this time of year. Though she knew the dome of the Capitol hovered somewhere in the distance, from her office neither the famous building nor the machinations of Congress were visible.

As much as she'd wanted more information on cutting, now that she'd read this, she found herself sinking into despair. How could her dear sweet girl do such a thing to herself? Was it all because she'd grounded her? Despite her own father's strictness, she'd never resorted to such extreme measures. Of course Phoebe wasn't a carbon copy of herself. But why this? Because of Noah and Jessie? The whole thing made her sick to her stomach.

On Saturday, after their shopping spree, her call to Dr. Sharma had been panicked. At least she'd had the presence of mind to schedule an appointment with her, not only for Phoebe but also one for herself and Ron, "to develop a strategy to help Phoebe cope." Their meeting would follow the first three with Phoebe, which would take place over the next ten days. Dr. Sharma had suggested that she get the lay of the land with Phoebe before meeting with her and Ron. Isabel checked her calendar to make sure that she'd added the appointment.

Staring at the date, Isabel reassured herself there was no danger of suicide, not between now and then. Absolutely none. Especially if she saw Dr. Sharma. Why on earth had they ever agreed to let Phoebe end her sessions? Such a juggling act to be a parent, a loving parent, *and* to take one's child's thoughts, wishes, and opinions into account. But things had gotten in the way too: there had been several interruptions in her therapy during summer vacation, then they'd ended therapy with the start of the school year (a *new* school, for heaven's sake), and, of course, she couldn't leave out the world of wishful thinking. Phoebe had seemed happy, everything had seemed okay.

Isabel's office buzzer sounded. She punched the intercom button. "Your one o'clock's here, Ms. Winthrop."

Isabel picked up her yellow legal pad, tore off the top sheet and shoved it into her drawer along with the article, grabbed a pen and headed for the door. She wondered about the parents of the boy she was about to meet. Her pro bono task would be to help him get into the right school. He suffered from numerous learning disabilities and they'd had absolutely no luck getting support from the DC public school system. With everything she had going on, she felt some reluctance to take this on, but she'd promised one of the partners. Anyway, she'd get the new associate, Jason, to do most of the legwork.

At the door she took a quick look in the mirror. She noticed the cruel little lines etching themselves into her brow, but it wasn't surprising, not with everything she had going on. Maybe less work, she thought. With that, she plastered a smile on her face and exited her office.

· • · • · • ·

Over the next couple of days, as the dance drew nearer, Phoebe received more private messages from Shane, all friendly and complimentary, with one about her friends. *Who's your best friend,* he'd written. After some thought, she wrote back: *Emma Blau, Skyla VanDorn, and 'til recently, Jessie Littleton.* He'd stopped corresponding then, and she worried a little, though later he sent more flirty messages. When she reviewed these, she saw that on Sunday she'd suggested getting together, but he hadn't responded.

Maybe he was shy, she thought, and considered writing him and offering again, but when, and how? That's when she realized that she wished *he* was taking her to the dance, not Michael, who, when she checked him out again on Facebook, didn't even come close in the looks department. And, after their initial exchange, he'd only spoken with her a couple of times. By Wednesday she couldn't resist floating the idea.

After school that day, she saw that Shane was on Facebook, so she posed the question privately this way: *If I asked you to a dance, would you go?* This gave her an out in case he couldn't or had no interest.

Phoebe's eyes stayed glued to the computer screen, waiting for an answer. Surely he saw that she'd written him. After a minute or so, which felt like forever, her cheeks grew hot with embarrassment. Oh, gosh, what have I done, she thought. At least another minute went by without a response. Then, finally, the answer appeared.

Defintely...depends on when ☺.

Phoebe noticed the misspelling, but who cared. *It's on Friday night.*

Would love to, but I've got a game.

Some other time, maybe? ☺.

Yep.

She felt giddy with relief and joy, and simultaneously grateful that he couldn't make it. It would have been mean to cancel on Michael, and no way did she want to incur Skyla's wrath. After all, she'd been a good friend this year, and it was bad enough that she and Jessie were on shaky terms. But now it seemed inevitable that sometime soon she'd get to meet Shane.

Chapter Three

Saturday, October 18, 2008

The reflection that stared back at Phoebe grimaced at the sight of the three quarter-length sleeves. Sleeveless, even strapless, was the in-thing. And there was no way for her to pull that off. Not tonight. Not at this dance. She just hoped she wouldn't be the only one wearing a dress with sleeves. Still frowning, she berated herself for what she'd done, though Dr. Sharma had eased her feelings of guilt at their session this past week.

"You've done nothing wrong. You're trying to cope with overwhelming feelings, Phoebe, and that's completely understandable. You're not alone." The doctor had helped order her thoughts a bit, had even explained how emotionally perceptive she was, perhaps a bit over-sensitive, but that was far better than being insensitive and unsympathetic. She'd suggested ways of avoiding triggers, though they both knew that was easier said than done.

Dr. Sharma had also explained that her mother's near collapse in the dressing room had been an act of love. Though what didn't help was that her mother now seemed to be watching her like some Über-Mom – Jessie's word for moms like that.

Jessie. Now, when she thought of her friend – former best friend? – she often grew sad, and couldn't help entertaining thoughts of cutting herself. She didn't feel like that now, but when she did Dr. Sharma had suggested she tuck those thoughts neatly into a box in the back of her mind and deal with them later, preferably in Dr. Sharma's office.

"Phoebe, you ready?" her mother called up the stairs.

Only a few more minutes before her parents were taking her to Skyla's, where everyone was gathering for the "photo shoot." Though not Noah and Jessie, and not Emma; they hadn't been invited to Skyla's. As she applied some lip gloss and a tiny bit of mascara, she thought about running into them later in the evening, a notion that unleashed a wave of panic.

All week, things had been awkward between her and Noah; how could they not have been? He'd seen her with Michael, in the hall and at her locker, and she remembered blushing and looking away, unable to meet his gaze. Michael was okay, but she'd much rather be with Noah and wished she had the nerve to tell him. A smile came to her lips though when she imagined what she'd say. *Hey, Noah, you're so cool! Kiss me!*

And that reminded her of Shane. He'd written her private Facebook messages every day, though he seemed to want to know stuff guys weren't usually that interested in: who she was going to the dance with, why she wasn't going to Jessie's after-party, and even what her dress looked like. She downplayed Michael, saying she didn't really know him, though he seemed nice. *Why aren't you going to Jessie's?* he'd demanded to know, which had also struck her as odd. Why would he care, especially since she'd told him Skyla was one of her best friends, but she dutifully told him that since Michael was friends with Skyla's date, she'd have to go there. But did guys really want to know about these things? Maybe Shane was different – most guys didn't seem to understand girls – and somehow that made him even more appealing.

Phoebe hadn't confided in Skyla about her growing interest in Shane; after all, she hadn't even met him. Besides there was Michael. She also hadn't told her about cutting or her visits to the shrink, and she prayed Jessie wouldn't sink so low as to unveil her secret now that they were, well, not best friends. Then she picked out a pair of glittery earrings and put them on.

· ● · ● · ● ·

They all gathered, some thirteen couples, on the back patio of Skyla's house for the "photo shoot" before the dinner. The parents took group shots, and then a few of each couple with everyone standing around watching. It was all a bit much for Phoebe, who tried to put on a happy face. It did not help that her mother kept mouthing the word "smile" and opening her eyes wide in that irritating way she had when trying to emphasize something. And Michael seemed to have a death-grip around her waist.

At last they all piled into a limo bus destined for the restaurant, the parents waving vigorously as if they were leaving for a distant country. Though everyone sat beside their dates, a lot of the girls chattered with one another like voluble monkeys while the guys looked vaguely uncomfortable in their ties and silly sports jackets.

Once the lights on the bus dimmed, Michael's arm crept around Phoebe's shoulder and he whispered something. She couldn't hear what, so she inched closer, asking him to repeat, which she then realized must have been a ploy he used to kiss her, as his other hand slid beneath her dress and up her thigh.

Noah's image swam into her mind. She almost started crying and tugged his hand away from her leg. "D—d—do you have to do that?"

Without skipping a beat or appearing the least bit shamefaced, Michael reached inside his jacket and withdrew a small silver flask. A smile materialized on his lips. "Have some of this," he said. "It'll make you feel better."

Yeah, right, she thought. Nevertheless, she tilted the flask up to her mouth and took a swallow. She coughed a little – the stuff tasted vile and burned her throat, but she was desperate not to embarrass herself. Though of course, she *was* like a fledgling bird, ready to spread its wings yet unsure how to fly. A novice, not only at drinking but kissing and dating.

A cheer rose up from the back of the bus and Phoebe pivoted to see what was going on. Two of the guys were chugging beers, apparently having a race. More cans of beer sprouted, like bouquets of flowers from a magician's sleeve, and a bunch of guys joined in the drinking, which initiated a chant that grew in volume: "Chug, chug, chug *it*!!" The first guy to finish crumpled the beer can in his fist, then tossed it over his shoulder. The others followed suit.

The bus came to a sudden jerking halt. A light went on inside and the bus driver stood up, facing them. "All right, any more of that and I'm taking you all back to the VanDorns'." His dark eyes swooped through the bus, stopping every so often to make contact with one of the boys and staring them down. "Understood?"

No one said anything. The boys nodded obediently.

"Understood?" he said more loudly.

"Yes, sir," a few of the guys ventured.

Though no one believed he'd follow through, since their parents had hired him, they obeyed and the remainder of the ride to Sequoia, a glamorous Georgetown restaurant overlooking the Potomac, passed uneventfully.

They dined in one of the restaurant's semi-private rooms, where alcohol again grew pervasive, with flasks and "water" bottles containing gin or vodka appearing beneath the table, in the bathrooms, and so on. Wherever Phoebe turned, she was being offered a drink. And she dutifully imbibed, only tiny sips, but still she could feel its effects.

Just before the bus arrived at the dance, mints in various shapes and forms made their way from front to rear, and back again. The "water bottles" remained on the bus.

· ● · ● · ● ·

Fall had invaded the school gymnasium. To enter, couples passed beneath an archway of yellow, orange, and scarlet balloons and once inside they found matching balloon bouquets floating throughout the huge room. Brightly colored autumn leaves, attached to construction paper, approximated foliage. Hundreds of twisted rolls of crepe paper of similar hues were draped across the ceiling and met in the center, where a huge rotating, mirrored ball reflected the blaze of color across the room.

No sooner had Phoebe and Michael stepped beneath the balloon arch into the decorated gymnasium knotted with teens – a transporting, even slightly magical event that gave Phoebe her first real smile of the night – than she spotted Noah and Jessie, Emma and Nick. Though earlier she'd feared running into them, now she gazed longingly at the covey of kids she still considered her real friends.

In contrast to her own outfit, she noticed that Jessie's strapless dress was little more than a tube of black figure-hugging material ending maybe five inches below her crotch. Big dangly gold hoops swung from her ears, and at least a dozen gold bangles encircled each arm. She swayed slightly on black stiletto heels that seemed a little too big. Glancing at her own feet – encased in a new pair of Tory Burch flats – Phoebe wondered what it would be like to have a mother who'd let her dress like that. Gratefully, she noted that Emma wore a long-sleeved dress.

For an instant she contemplated joining them, but what would she say? Determined to make the best of things, she turned back to her group, hovering near Skyla, who seemed wildly happy.

When Skyla bounded onto the dance floor, dragging Max along, Phoebe abandoned Michael and followed her into the swarm of bouncing kids, many of them girls without their dates. There, hidden inside the throng, Phoebe swayed her hips and tossed her arms with slightly drunken abandon. At last she was having fun.

During several slow dances, she pretended that Michael was Noah and then Shane, though when he shoved his boner into her thigh, she pulled away and gave him a look. Now and then he snuck drinks from his flask, which he never omitted to offer her. If caught, she knew she'd be in big trouble, but the alcohol seemed to be helping her get through the night, so she took the occasional surreptitious sip. The next time he closed in on her leg, Phoebe felt far less timid and laughingly said, "What is wrong with you? Cut it out, okay?"

After another hour of dancing, Phoebe suddenly felt the floor tilt and saw the lights swirl. She mumbled an excuse to Michael and lurched off to the bathroom. She collapsed into an empty stall, where she knelt at the base of a toilet and heaved up her dinner. Disgusting. She hated the putrid taste in her mouth. Teary-eyed, she searched through her purse for a mint. Girls' laughter resounded against the tiled walls and she imagined they might be laughing at the sound of someone throwing up, but she was too sick to care.

At one point, she thought the door to her stall pushed open and someone's hand brushed her hair. When she turned all she saw was a blur of flesh and black fabric. "Jessie?" she said. But whoever it was had gone.

She finally peeled herself off the floor and peeked out of the stall into the bathroom. A few girls stood around talking; a couple of them were at the sinks examining their faces in the mirrors and putting on make-up. She avoided their gaze as she exited the stall and headed straight to the row of gleaming white basins where she washed her face, then repeatedly gargled water and spit it out. Still, her mouth tasted awful and she had a whopping headache.

As best she could she wiped the smeared mascara from beneath her eyes. She finally found a mint in her beaded purse, popped it into her mouth and sucked vigorously. After applying some lip gloss, she exited the bathroom.

"There you are," Skyla cried, waving with her corsaged wrist. "Come on, time to go. Everybody's been waiting."

Michael seemed understanding and wrapped his arm around her, guiding her out to the bus. On the ride to Skyla's, Phoebe tried to sit still to quell the nausea and to keep the pounding in her head from getting worse. She really couldn't believe how horrible drinking made her feel. She also couldn't believe that Michael had started groping her again.

She brushed his hand away and whispered, "I feel like crap, okay?"

He held his hands up in mock surrender. "Okay, okay."

At Skyla's house, the kids tumbled out raucously and filed inside, but all Phoebe wanted was to go home, lie down, and surrender to the oblivion of sleep. She began hatching an exit plan. She'd go in for a little, have a snack to settle her stomach, get her act together, then sneak out and walk the short two blocks home.

· ● · ● ·

She glanced at the time. It was just past eleven. She'd managed to lose Michael and thought she might sneak out, even though her mother hadn't set curfew until midnight. "Oh, go ahead, honey," she'd said. "I want you to have happy memories of the dance." Phoebe knew her relaxed attitude had to do with her guilt about Noah and the sight of her cuts. They'd truly affected her mother. Destabilized her, if such a thing were possible.

If her mother knew how much drinking was going on, she'd probably go ballistic, Phoebe thought. Just then, someone came around and poured something clear into all the girls' glasses. Phoebe took a tentative sip. Another alcohol-laced drink, but she set it down.

"Hey, d'you see that crotch hugger Jessie was wearing? Jeez, talk about flaunting it." Molly, one of Skyla's lieutenants, searched the group for agreement.

"Yeah, what's up with that?" Sophia said.

Though Phoebe feigned disinterest, she was on the verge of defending Jessie. She might be mad at her, but who were these girls to talk about Jessie that way?

Just then Molly turned to Phoebe. "And what's the deal with asking Noah? I thought she was supposed to be your friend?"

Phoebe responded with a tired shrug. Her anger over the whole Noah "thing" had waned. Just as she was about to wander off, something Molly said stopped her. "How about that cute Shane guy?" she said with a wide-eyed grin. "I want a chance to hook up with him!"

"No, no, me first," Sophia added with a mischievous grin, "like in a dark theater!"

"Oh, keep dreaming," Skyla broke in. "Not a chance!"

"He hasn't even friended you, has he?" taunted Molly, who everyone knew tried very hard to imitate Skyla, in style if not substance. Long blonde hair, lots of pastel clothing, your basic Lily Pulitzer prep.

Skyla gave her the evil eye, then said, "As if I care," a comment that fractured the room with more teasing and laughter. Phoebe watched with dismay, and thought that maybe she should encourage Shane to friend Skyla. It struck her as odd that he hadn't, after all Skyla was the prettiest girl in ninth grade.

Amid the hectoring chatter, Phoebe snuck away to the food table and grabbed a pumpkin cookie frosted with a macabre face. She imagined Mrs. VanDorn and Skyla spending the past few nights baking and decorating them, and thought of asking her for the recipe so she could bake some with her own mother. As she nibbled on the cookie, Phoebe's fragmented thoughts returned to Shane. His image shimmered in her mind, glistening in the distance, like the grand city of Oz. She thought of their Facebook exchanges. He wanted to meet her. Did he want to meet the other girls too? Did he private message them? She hoped not. *Don't have too much fun,* his last entry had teased. No need to worry about that, she thought. And then imagined what she'd tell him about the dance. With that came a desire to see him, to be with him.

She snuck up the stairs, hoping to avoid Michael, who she'd last seen playing pool in another room. She figured he wouldn't miss her as she tiptoed down the hall away from the sound of laughter, bypassing the bathroom, and sneaking out a side door. She hadn't expected anyone to be on the porch, though. Maybe they won't notice me, she thought. Just then a board creaked beneath her feet.

"Leaving?" someone asked.

Squinting into the dark, Phoebe saw that it was Daisy, swinging with Alex on a suspended bench. Hoping they wouldn't make a fuss, Phoebe replied, "I just live a couple of blocks away."

"What about Michael?" Daisy said.

"What about him?" Phoebe said, her tart reply pleasantly surprising her.

The crisp air helped to refresh her and strengthened her resolve to date Shane, before the other girls had a chance to, which made her look forward to something rather than back at the stupid Adams Morgan incident. She had a goal and she looked forward to making it happen.

She'd barely entered the night shadows, when footsteps echoed on the sidewalk behind her. She began to walk faster.

"Hey, Phoebe!" It was Michael. When he caught up to her, he grabbed her by the arm. "What the hell? Why'd you leave without sayin' good-bye?"

"Sorry," she murmured, hoping Daisy and Alex couldn't hear. "I was tired and didn't want to bother you. Seemed like you were having fun." She tried to pull away, but his grip grew tighter. With her free arm, she pointed in the direction of her house. "I don't live far."

His offended eyes searched hers. "Don't I at least get a good-night kiss?" Before she could say no, his mouth pressed against her lips.

"Stop it!" she said in a loud whisper as she pushed her hands against his chest, trying to shake him loose.

"Come on, baby, just a kiss."

His breath reeked of beer, and she could once again feel his stupid cock hard against her thigh. "No!" she said. "Let go!" Only somewhat irritated a moment ago, she now felt an urgent need to get away.

"Max said you put out," he said, his words slurring a bit. "Guess he was wrong?"

"Max said that? I don't even know him!" She angled her body away from his chest, again trying to pull free, but his fingers dug into her arm.

His voice softened. "Come on," he said, again trying to kiss her.

"No, Michael, stop it."

Just then, a scene from a TV show punched into her brain. Instead of continuing to resist, she pretended to give in to his kiss. Once his grip relaxed, she kicked him in the shin as hard as she could and took off.

He let out a cry and stumbled back. "You little bitch!" he shouted after her.

Phoebe made it to the corner, where she briefly glanced over her shoulder. He was squatting on the ground rubbing his leg. As she rushed toward her house she looked back once more, but no one was there.

Chapter Four

Sunday, October 19, 2008

The doorbell rang and Isabel went to answer it. She was expecting to see Phoebe and Michael, not this mess of a girl who ran inside, angry and shouting.

"Phoebe, what on earth—" she said as she closed the gap between them. "What happened, sweetheart?"

All Isabel could hear was that Michael was a total creep, that she never wanted to see him again, that she hated him, and that he was *so* stupid. Then she revealed a little of what he'd done a few minutes earlier. She admitted to having taken sips of alcohol, hating it, and begging for forgiveness. "Please don't punish me. I'm sorry," she said. And Isabel knew this wasn't the time to even reprimand her, including for walking home alone, but she couldn't help wondering why awful things kept happening to her daughter. Was this normal?

· ● · ● · ● ·

"What are *you* doing here?" Phoebe snapped at Isabel the following morning.

Isabel hadn't intended to fall asleep, but her daughter's nasty tone put her in no mood to apologize. "I was taking care of you. Remember, last night?" she answered tersely.

"How could I forget?" Phoebe shot back. "If you'd let me go with Noah none of this would have happened."

God, why was everything her fault? She almost lashed out; only the memory of their intimacy the night before prevented her.

Phoebe rubbed her eyes and forehead. "Oh, my head," she yammered.

Isabel got up and returned a minute later with a glass of water and two Advil. She held them out to her daughter.

"Mom, I'm fine," Phoebe said, though she accepted the pills and took them along with several swallows of water. "Remember you promised not to tell Dad. About Michael. He'll go crazy." Then she stared at the doorway as if to say, now get out of here. A moment later she dropped back onto her pillow.

This adolescent phase couldn't end soon enough, Isabel thought. She was halfway out the door, when something pulled her back. "Phoebe?"

"What?" she said without opening her eyes.

"First of all, I didn't promise *not* to tell Dad, and secondly, I think we should talk with Michael's parents."

The shriek that erupted from Phoebe's throat sounded like a

caterwauling monkey. "Are you insane, Mom?" she shouted. "You are not—" and now she popped up in bed like a trick Halloween cadaver, "—you are absolutely not going to do that! And neither is Dad! No way!"

Isabel stared at her daughter. Hormones didn't begin to explain her mood swings. At moments like this she felt there was something seriously wrong with her. Speechless, she made a hasty retreat down the steps in the hope that Ron might prop up her depleted spirit. She also wondered if he would agree with Phoebe's request.

· ● · ● · ● ·

The unmistakable and alluring smell of bacon wafted into her room. Phoebe pulled an old hoodie over her flannel PJ bottoms and went down to the kitchen, her stomach growling with hunger. On Sundays her dad traditionally cooked a big breakfast. Pancakes, with or without chocolate chips, eggs any style, including *huevos rancheros*, one of her favorites, French toast, the works. Whatever they wanted. Plus bacon. There was always bacon. And she loved sitting on a bar stool at the counter watching him and talking or arguing, though if the latter, it happened mostly in a good-natured way.

This morning when she stepped into the kitchen, Jackson was already perched on his stool, scooping up milk and Cheerios with a large spoon. As often as not, her brother still preferred cereal, despite the fact that the only brand Isabel allowed was plain Cheerios. The rest of that "junk" contained too much sugar. And Jackson refused granola and other healthy alternatives.

Phoebe squeezed his arm as she sat down beside him. "Hey, Jackson, was'up?"

"Nuttin', s'up with you?" he said, continuing to slurp down his cereal. "D'you have fun at the dance?"

She peered at him, a little surprised he'd ask, then looked suspiciously at her father.

"Daddy?" she said, examining his face.

"What do you want for breakfast, my little Miss Muffin?" Ron said innocently.

Phoebe rolled her eyes. "I'll have French toast, Daddy. And three slices of bacon, and some milk. Lots of syrup. The Vermont kind, okay?"

"Coming right up," he said. "So how was the dance?"

"Yeah, Feebs, how *was* the dance?" Jackson said, making a goofy face at her.

She groaned. "You haven't heard, Daddy?" She tucked one of her legs under her bottom and leaned toward him on the counter. "Mom hasn't told you?"

"No," he said.

She studied him as he worked. "That's hard to believe."

"Well, let's just hear how it went, Pumpkin Noodle."

"Daddy, you're so silly. Anyway, it was just fine...that is, until my date...well, until he turned into an asshole."

He glanced over his shoulder as if to ensure Isabel wasn't there and then gave her a half-smile. "Easy does it. What happened?"

Jackson leaned in as if to listen more closely.

"Well, he was a jerk. Boys can be really stupid, Dad." She glanced at Jackson. "Don't be a jerk when you grow up, okay?" she said before turning back to her father. "But the other parts were fun. We danced and there was lots of food, and, you know, it was good."

"That's great honey," he said with his back to her.

What Ron really felt like doing was wringing that asshole Michael's neck. But with everything else that had happened thus far in Phoebe's freshman year, he couldn't risk adding one more disaster to her young life. No, he needed time to think about this boy. As he considered how to teach Michael a lesson, maybe not now, but at some point down the road, he flipped the slices of bacon, one at a time, with a fork he'd like to shove in the kid's face.

"I need your help with something," Phoebe said.

"What's that?" he said, sensing what was coming.

She looked over at Jackson but he'd turned on his Gameboy and was concentrating on the small screen of the handheld device. "Mom said she wanted to call Michael's parents."

"Really?" He slid a plate of pancakes before her. "You think that's a bad idea?" He wanted to add, *Would you want him treating other girls like that?*

"Yeah. That's nuts, Dad. I'd be, like, so ridiculed. You know what I mean? You can't let her." She tilted her head at him curiously. "And not you either. Anyway, he's out of my life. He is so not happening. So what would be the point?"

"Hmm...here's the syrup."

"It's not important. I just want it to be over. Okay?" She glanced up at him as she reached for the glass container. "Today's a bright new one, right, Dad?"

He fixed her with a loving stare. "Yup, it's a bright new one." For her sake, he certainly hoped so.

After drenching the French toast in maple syrup, then soaking a morsel in the thick golden liquid, Phoebe said, "I think there's a different boy I like."

Ron almost said "Noah?" but as a reporter he'd learned to let his sources do the talking. The same was true with kids.

"Who would that be?" he finally said.

"His name is Shane. He goes to another school."

"Oh? How'd you meet him?"

She seemed to consider his question before answering. "Well, I haven't exactly met him, he friended me. On Facebook."

Ron took in a breath. How safe was it to meet people on Facebook, or any other Internet venue? He knew how Isabel felt, and mostly on this subject he agreed with her. But then again, that was how kids communicated these days. He busied himself preparing Jackson's plate of food as he searched for a reasonable follow-up question. "What school does he go to?"

"Walter Johnson. Plays football. He made Varsity."

"That's pretty good for a freshman."

"No, he's a sophomore." She grinned.

"You've gotta watch out for those sophomores." He flashed a smile back at her.

"Yeah. But he seems really nice, Daddy. And he's new to the area."

This set off another alarm, the word *predator* insinuating itself into his thoughts. "Well, maybe he can come over sometime?" he said, quickly adding, "But you know, Princess French Toast, it'll have to wait a couple of weeks."

"I know," she said grudgingly.

"Have you told Mom about him?"

"No."

"Well, maybe you should?"

"Maybe."

"She loves you, you know."

She looked doubtful. "I guess."

"Phoebe," he said in a faux disappointed tone.

"Okay, okay. I know she does."

· ● · ● · ● ·

Back in her room Phoebe checked Shane's Facebook page, but he wasn't online. Then she examined her various friends' Facebook pages to see what they'd posted about the dance. Skyla, predictably, had written little more than *So cool*, and included at least ten images of herself and Max. Jessie had added a few of Emma's photos and gushed about the evening, which clouded her mind briefly with unhappy thoughts. At least Noah had posted nothing; maybe he hadn't had fun, and maybe he'd missed her. But she knew she couldn't let her mind spin out in that direction. Anyway, she didn't care about Noah anymore; she was waiting for Shane to contact her. To ask her out.

Instead of doing her homework, Phoebe was drawn to the pile of used clothes in the corner and picked up an old lacy blouse, a pair of jeans, an old man's jacket. She held the articles up, studying each one, believing that if given the chance at another life the items knew just what they wanted to be. Other pieces followed. Some she discarded, others she set aside.

At her sewing machine she began ripping apart the lacy blouse, separating the lace from the cotton, then she cut open the seams of a pair of jeans. This was the first task: taking clothing apart. Then she could better assess the materials she might use to forge something new. Immersed in her work, she forgot all about Facebook, Shane, Michael, Noah, Jessie, her mother – everything was lost to her except the world of her imagination.

Phoebe wholeheartedly believed that Nana Helen inspired her creations. She'd died when Phoebe was 11, an event that had etched itself into her memory as one of the saddest in her short life. Not only had Nana taught her how to sew, but Phoebe had also inherited her grandmother's strawberry blond wavy hair and fair skin, so unlike her mother's dark tresses, olive complexion and aquiline nose. Her own pug nose, which freckled in the summer, looked just like Nana's in a photo taken not long after her arrival in the US from Hungary. When Phoebe examined her hands she saw Nana's, except that Nana hadn't chewed her fingernails or cuticles.

Sometimes when she sewed, a kind of magic happened. In the midst of manipulating the fabric – bunching it, straightening it, or guiding it into the path of the needle – she suddenly felt the material develop a rhythm all its own, and it began to fly beneath her fingers as if it knew the exact shape of the piece she intended to create. When she told her mother this, she'd laughed, not meanly, but the way adults sometimes laugh at childish statements. Phoebe had given her a slightly wounded look and thereafter had stopped confiding in her about her deepest, secret, intimate dreams.

· ● · ● · ● ·

Sandy was a little surprised by Jessie's post-dance report. She'd expected nothing short of: *Oh, my God, Mom, I had such a fabulous time.* But complaints were what she got: *I didn't wanna go with Noah; that was a really dumb idea, Mom. Why didn't Dylan ask me?* And, according to Jessie, it was Phoebe who'd had all the fun. Dancing and laughing with her new set of friends.

This pained Sandy. So much of her life revolved around making Jessie happy. She took to heart her daughter's grievances, and spent much of the afternoon trying to figure out how "to make it better." From the time Jessie could talk, Sandy had sworn an oath to her little girl. *Mommy will make it better, no matter what.* Not like her own mother.

Mostly, what Margaret had done was shockingly neglectful, and certainly Sandy hadn't forgiven her. There was perhaps the small but not negligible fact that Sandy's relations with Les had played a role in her mother's reaction, though Sandy failed to see it this way.

After vowing to get back at Les, Sandy had kept her promise. She began to bring boys home, mostly when her mother was at work. She'd lie around making out with them on the family room couch, almost always with her stepfather nearby, working in his study on various writing assignments, or so he said. She sensed how much this bothered Les, who occasionally came out and asked her to keep it down. Things changed though when Sandy brought home a guy she actually liked, the first one she took to her room, to fuck, no holds barred.

A few days later, Les stood at her bedroom door, watching her. "So who's your new fellow?" he asked. She could tell her wild episode had rattled him and that now Les wanted her, while her own feelings for him had slowed to a simmer. Still, she couldn't help taunting him.

With a sly smile, and pointing at her bed, she said, "That's where we did it, Les."

In the next moment he stepped inside her room, grabbed and kissed her. A rough, needy kiss. She willingly gave in to him, allowing him to tumble her onto the bed. When they'd finished Sandy said a bit breathlessly, "I thought our *last* time was at the gym?"

He gave her a sheepish look but said nothing.

"Well, guess what? I don't care any more, Les." She gave him a self-satisfied, vengeful grin, enjoying her tiny victory.

She never knew if her mother had sensed this breach or Les had been indiscreet, but in any case Margaret stomped into Sandy's room that night and told her to get out. Screamed at her. "You think you can just do whatever you want. Well, you can't! I want you out."

"Are you kidding me, Mom? I'm your daughter."

"Not anymore you're not." She stood with her arms crossed. "Get your stuff and go."

Sandy had gone to her girlfriend's to spend the night, assuming her mother would calm down and invite her back. But she never did.

And that was how Shane the popular, handsome football star had entered her life and exited a couple of months thereafter. Bastard that he turned out to be. She should have been his date to the prom, she'd dreamed of walking in on the arm of the Prom King, but she wasn't. No, pregnant with Jessie and uncertain of the girl's paternity. Bill believed she was his. Good old Bill, she now thought gratefully.

While mulling over how to improve Jessie's frame of mind, she decided to bake some chocolate chip cookies, and make an extra dozen or two for her neighbor, Mrs. Wilkins, whose son was arriving home after a year in Iraq. Sandy liked to pretend the gracious older woman was her mother, a little like Mrs. E; they'd have imaginary conversations, her favorite being ones where Mrs. Wilkins couldn't wait to introduce her to the daughters of her friends.

Later, she sat at her computer composing Shane's next round of Facebook posts and private messages, determined to rectify the wrongs of the world. To make Jessie happy.

· ● · ● · ● ·

Because life beyond fabric had ceased to exist, Phoebe did not hear her mother's shout. Then her cry rang out a second time. "Phoebeee, DINNER!" Could it be that late already? The clock said six-thirty. A bright, shiny moon hung outside her window. She stared at it as if it were trying to tell her something. Then she remembered her mother's cautionary words last year when all her problems seemed to revolve around Skyla. *The moon is a reminder,* she'd said, *that sometimes things are not as they seem. The moon appears to cast its own light, but it's merely a reflection of the sun.*

She gazed at its brilliant surface a moment longer. Then returned her attentions to her sewing. She just needed to finish this one seam before heading downstairs. Once done, she quickly scanned her Facebook page.

A note from Shane! Her heart sped up as she read: *How was the dance? Wish I could have gone with you.*

"Phoebe! Come on!"

"Coming!"

Her youthful lips curled into a smile as she hurriedly typed back: *Me too! I've been working all afternoon on a new jean jacket (I sew) and just saw your note.☺ ☺ Will write more after dinner. How was the football game? Did you win?* With that, she raced down the stairs.

"Oh, my gosh, Phoebe, you look like the proverbial cat that swallowed a canary! What happened?" her mother quipped as she walked into the kitchen.

Gleaming, a broad smile on her face, she said, "Yes, I ate the canary, mom, and it tasted really good." She licked her lips.

Her mother rolled her eyes. "Teenagers!"

After dinner, as soon as she'd helped with the dishes, she bounded back upstairs and found another private message from Shane: *Yeah, we won. Wish you'd been here.* Excitedly, she wrote back, telling him that the jean jacket could be his if he wanted it. Of course she'd have to get rid of the lace, but that was easily remedied.

She had other personal messages too. One from Emma: *We missed you last night. Did you have fun? How was Michael? He's kind of cute.*

To which Phoebe responded: *Don't let looks fool you. Missed you too.*

Then Shane wrote again: *Jean jacket? Nice! What happened at the dance?*

Phoebe: *The guy I went with was a creep.*

Shane: *What happened?*

Phoebe: *He was drunk and sort of attacked me, but please don't tell anybody.*

Shane: *For real? He attacked you?*

Phoebe: *I don't really want to talk about it. He's history.*

Shane: *Just tell me, you can trust me.*

Phoebe: *I will when we meet. I promise.*

Shane: *What about Jessie and Emma? Did you see them?*

She wondered why he was asking her, since she'd already told him she was going with a different group. *Things are a little tense with Jessie.*

Shane: *Tense, huh? Why?*

Phoebe knew she couldn't tell Shane about Noah, so what should she say? She wrote: *Oh, just stupid girl stuff. Drama. You know?*

Shane: *Not really, but then I'm not a girl. What happened?*

Phoebe: *It's boring, you don't want to know.*

Shane: *Sure I do. I won't tell anyone. We're not even at the same school, remember?*

Phoebe wondered why he wanted to know these things, and even considered telling him, but it was far too complicated. To get onto another subject, she wrote: *I'll tell you another time about all that stuff. What do you like to do besides football?*

Shane: *I like golfing...and movies. Wanna go sometime?*

She couldn't believe he'd just asked her, though in the next instant she grew irritated because she couldn't go. *I'm grounded for another week or so, but after that I'd love to.*

Shane: *Grounded, huh?*

Phoebe: *Another long story, but basically I sort of lied to my mom.*

Shane: *Sort of?* ☺

Phoebe: *I didn't tell her where I'd been. Mainly because I was in Adams Morgan where I wasn't supposed to be. So it was more like she assumed something and I let her. You know what I mean?* She wanted to be honest, but was afraid the truth might make him think poorly of her.

Shane: *She grounded you for a month? Except she let you go to the dance?*

Phoebe: *Yeah. She's a little crazy. It's a long story...let's save it for when I meet you!*

Shane: *Your mom does sound crazy...maybe more like she is a...rhymes with witch?*

Phoebe stared at what he'd just written, then wrote: *Totally. Tell me about the game.* She went back and erased the word "totally" and replaced it with "I guess," just in case her mom checked her Facebook private chats, though she hadn't done this in a while, at least not that she knew of. And the agreement was that she'd do it in front of her. Only then did she notice she'd said her mom was crazy. Oh well, hopefully she wouldn't check.

Shane: *It was great. Too bad we don't play you guys! Send me a picture. Love your Facebook pics. Gotta do some homework.*

Phoebe: *Yeah, me too. I will. Send me one of you? In your*

football uniform?

Shane: *Sure. Bye.*

Phoebe dropped back onto her pillows and stared up at the clouds painted on the blue ceiling. She was in love. Her first thought was to text Jessie, then she remembered they were barely talking. Although if Jessie wrote to her, she'd respond. She would. She returned to daydreaming about Shane. That's when it struck her. Why hadn't she thought of this before? She Googled Walter J High School and looked for the football team. Shane wasn't in the team photo. She wondered why. A while later, she printed out another of his Facebook photos and pinned it alongside the one already on her bulletin board. She loved the idea of him observing everything she did.

Glancing back at the computer, she saw a note from Dylan: *Hey Feebs, can you come over after school tomorrow? Help us figure out cool outfits for our band.*

She hesitated, wondering what Jessie would think, then decided to say yes, though she'd have to clear it with her mother. But she felt fairly certain she'd let her go since she "adored" Mrs. Thomas, who lived in Georgetown not in evil Adams Morgan.

Chapter Five

Monday, October 20, 2008

"Sure, honey," Phoebe's mother said in response to her question about going to Dylan's. Though she added, "If only you could be as enthusiastic about other things as you are about sewing. My God, there'd be no stopping you." When her mother made comments like this, Phoebe wasn't sure whether to feel flattered or offended.

"By the way, I've been thinking about you doing some volunteering next weekend."

"Volunteering? Where?" She frowned at her mother.

"Well, we do live in a political town, and there is an amazing presidential race underway – as you know, we might elect the first African American president! – and I do have lots of contacts on the Hill." She gave Phoebe a searching look.

"But, Mawm, I hate politics."

"Well, you owe me some time and it's never too soon to do something good for the world," she paused, "*and* something that'll look good on your resumé."

"My resumé?"

"For college."

"I'm a freshman!"

"It's never too early to start."

Phoebe was about to argue the point when she remembered it would probably lead to a lecture. "Oh, joy! See you tonight," she said as she walked out the door to catch the bus.

"I almost forgot," her mother called after her. "Mrs. VanDorn and Skyla are coming over this week to talk about the birthday party."

· ● · ● · ● ·

Ron opened his email and almost instantly his eyes were drawn to two messages. Or rather the senders of those two messages. One was from Gil at the *Washington Post* and the other from Sandy.

The latter would contain a pleasant surprise, he hoped. As for the *Post* email, it would bring either good news or bad. Gil's previous email hadn't sounded particularly promising. Which one to open first.

Finally he double-clicked on the *Post* message.

Dear Ron,

We'd like to talk to you. Give us a call and let us know when it's convenient. My assistant, Sarah, can be reached at the number below. Hope you can make it today or tomorrow.

Best, Gil

He read it twice before thinking, shit, they're gonna offer me a job. His next thought was to call Isabel.

He dialed her cell. It rang but she didn't answer. He left her a hurried message, then returned to Gil's email and read it again. He glanced at his watch. It was a little past nine. Best not to be too eager. He decided to call Gil's assistant after he'd gone through the rest of the day's emails. Though Sandy's roused a certain curiosity in him, he also felt a little dread. He hated it when people left the subject line empty, which she'd done. Maybe he should just delete it.

Good God, man, he said to himself, just open the damn thing. He clicked on it.

Hi Ron,

Just thinking about the girls and, you know, what I mentioned the other day. Just wonder if I could take a little of your time over lunch to talk about it? This week I'm free just about any day except Thursday...so let me know.

xox, S

Those three letters before her signature – xox – caught his attention, and his imagination. Either they meant nothing, or everything. With Sandy he figured there was no telling. Isabel would most certainly say she hadn't signed her note that way by accident. Of course, she'd never know about this. Just as she'd never known about the two one-night stands he'd had while on the road as a young reporter. Yes, she'd found out about a third one, but that's because he'd been cocky and careless. Not that he was about to have a one-night stand with Sandy.

He was struggling with his answer, when he decided to put Sandy off by saying that this week was insane, and the only day he could even think about having lunch was Thursday, the day she couldn't. Just as he finished writing, the phone rang. It was Isabel calling him back.

·　●　·　●　·　●　·

A savage look crossed Skyla's face. "Well, how do you expect me to do anything if you won't tell me what happened?" The other girls at the lunch table – Molly, Cara, Sophia and Daisy – hunched in eagerly awaiting Phoebe's answer.

"I don't *want* you to do anything," Phoebe whispered. "Michael was drunk and really, well, really—" she hesitated, trying to find the right word to placate Skyla without blurting out the whole sordid ordeal, "—he got really pushy. All right? That's it, it's over."

Skyla gave Phoebe an intense stare. "Fine with me," she said, though Phoebe could tell it wasn't. "It's all Jessie's fault, you know. If she hadn't asked Noah, then none of this would have happened! Right?"

Phoebe hadn't thought of it that way and was now eager to change the topic. She glanced around the table and asked if the girls knew that Dylan was forming a band, one that lacked a name and a backup singer.

Skyla's eyes widened with interest. "I'm a pretty good singer, you know."

"Really? I didn't know that," Cara laughed. "Let's hear it."

"Yeah, come on," several others joined in.

It surprised Phoebe that Skyla was letting her minions get away with that sort of talk, though she'd noticed the same thing at her house after the dance. Not always, but often she seemed like a new Skyla.

"Well, not here," Skyla said with an offended pout, "but I *am* in the *a capella* group." Then quietly she asked Phoebe to put in a good word for her. "Ask Dylan if I can try out; I'm really good. Do you think they'll have tryouts?"

"Sure," Phoebe said, noting the change in Skyla's tone and demeanor, and intrigued by her mercurial shifts. She didn't tell Skyla that Dylan was not a big fan of hers – "the pink girl," he'd called her on more than one occasion.

"We can talk about it at your house. You know my mom and I are coming over on Wednesday, right?" Skyla said. "We should probably figure out who we're inviting, what kind of food to have, a band or a DJ, all that stuff, you know?"

"Yeah, sure," was all that Phoebe said, then sat there listening to Skyla reel off ideas and eyeing her overly ornate cursive as she made lists of food and people in her notebook.

In Phoebe's last class of the day, once more facing a question about her date with Michael, this time from Jessie during lab, Phoebe said, "You don't wanna know."

"That bad, huh?"

Phoebe nodded, happy that Jess seemed to care, but refused to elaborate, nor did she ask about Jessie's evening. She wondered if Jessie had been the one to help her in the bathroom, but felt too embarrassed to ask. Since Jessie didn't mention going to Dylan's, Phoebe didn't either. If Jessie found out Dylan had invited Phoebe and not her it would probably erase any progress they'd made. By day's end, she felt a thaw between her and Jessie. It would have been a stretch though to say they'd resumed their best buds' status.

· ● · ● · ● ·

When Ron spoke to Sarah, Gil's assistant, he made an appointment for the following day, Tuesday. That would give him time to discuss his strategy with Isabel. And it gave him an ounce of control, the sense that he wasn't groveling. That he wasn't just going to drop everything and run over to the *Post*'s offices on 15th Street.

He sat at his desk tapping out a story on the computer, trying to concentrate, but his mind wandered.

While he wanted to continue to cover the White House for the *Post* – after all, he was good at it, and as far as he knew that's what they were looking for – what he really hoped was to get on board the media bus, now, and follow the Democratic presidential candidate in the final weeks of the race. What Barack Obama had put in place was the most exciting campaign since John F. Kennedy's, one he'd read volumes about.

While many of his colleagues had been traveling around the country tailing McCain, Palin, Obama or Biden, he'd spent most of the campaign in White House briefings on the economy with Bush – a lame duck President if he ever saw one – and his staff. He was dying to get in on the action. Even if it was only at the end. What he needed were some new angles on the campaign, stories no one had yet done. He'd come up with something, and tomorrow, as part of his discussion with the *Post*, he'd offer to write a feature or two for the paper, even as he wrapped things up at AP. He vibrated with excitement. He could see an entirely new future. The timing couldn't have been more perfect.

Just then another email arrived from Sandy. He opened it, surprised yet again to see what she'd written.

Hi Ron, well, I changed my appt on Thursday to see you.

So where should we meet and what time? xox, Sandy

Oh, Christ, he thought. He stared at her message – what should he do? – then he struck the delete button. He'd deal with her later.

· ● · ● · ● ·

At Dylan's, Phoebe helped collect chips, Gatorade and sodas to take to the studio apartment above the Thomas's three-car garage. Beneath a bright blue sky, they walked across the courtyard behind the main house and climbed the stairs to the studio. Here, where the guys would practice, drums had already been set up, along with speakers, an electric keyboard and two guitars – a bass and a lead. Dylan told her that Eric Clapton used the same type of guitar he'd gotten on his birthday. He plucked its strings in a way that produced a pleasing melody.

"Come here," Dylan said. "Let me show you something."

She went over to him. "Hold the guitar as if you were about to play it," he said, handing her the instrument. He was close to her. She could feel his breath on her face as he pulled the guitar strap over her head. "Go ahead, play a few notes."

She felt awkward, but did as she was told. Despite the randomness of the notes the melodic sound that erupted from the speakers amazed her. Though she'd tried playing the piano, she hadn't been very good and didn't consider herself the least bit musical. "Wow, that's sick," she said, pleased and smiling.

"You like it?"

"Yeah." She played a few more notes before he relieved her of the guitar. In one smooth motion he drew the strap over her head and leaned in to kiss her. Shane's image, and then Jessie's, popped into her head, the ghosts of her conscience. Before she could push him away though, his lips brushed hers. In the next instant the sound of the door below opening then slamming shut rescued her. Phoebe dropped to the floor in a squat and busied herself poking through her backpack. Footsteps bounded up the stairs.

A moment later, Sam and Nick burst into the room. They fist-bumped Dylan and gave Phoebe a hug, then sprawled long-legged on beanbags, grabbing chips and chugging sodas. As Phoebe took a few sips of a Pepsi Dylan's kiss lingered in her mind. Though she wouldn't let things go any further because of Jessie, she could imagine falling for him. He was adorable with that bleached surfer-boy hair.

Once more the hollow echo of footsteps sounded on the stairwell. Then girls' voices. Jessie and Emma popped their heads inside. "Hey, guys. Sorry we're late." Jessie's eyes briefly rested on Phoebe, a questioning look skittering across her face.

If only Dylan had mentioned that not only Sam and Nick were coming, but also Jessie and Emma. Now Phoebe felt a little weird, wondering what Jessie might be thinking, especially since neither she nor Jessie had discussed it earlier. With the exception of Noah, who couldn't make it, this was the first time they'd all been together since that awful Friday in Adams Morgan. The irony of the gathering wasn't lost on her. The gang her mother didn't want her hanging out with was assembled here. If only she could send a photo to her mom's phone.

Determined to hang on to the good feeling she'd had much of the day, she joined in the banter as they kicked around names. The Argyles—"Oh yeah, one for preppy socks," someone shouted, "NO f'n way!" Iron Majesty – a take off on Iron Butterfly – got a drum roll, and Simply George actually got a few claps, but Phoebe was surprised when the one she offered – Guys in Black Suits – got everybody's vote. Including Jessie's, if a bit grudgingly.

Already she imagined the band dressed in dark suits with narrow lapels, thin black ties, and white t-shirts. Maybe a couple could wear fedoras. She announced that she'd go on a quest for old suits and accessories – "ties, hats, that sort of thing" – maybe over the weekend.

When Dylan offered to go with her, Jessie jumped in with an edgy, "I thought you were grounded," words aimed at Phoebe. A taut silence followed.

Phoebe was about to answer when Sam stepped in. "Chill out, Jess." Everyone except maybe Dylan understood that she was jealous.

Jessie shot back, "So who asked you?"

The intensity of her narrowed gaze seemed to startle Sam. For once he was at a loss for words. Jessie burst out laughing. "Gotcha'!" The others joined in, nervous titters breaking the awkwardness of the moment.

Nick had risen to pick up one of the guitars and began strumming it. Sam swung his leg around the drummer's stool, and with his foot on the pedal tapped a steady beat on the bass drum, while he struck the cymbals lightly with the sticks. Noah was supposed to be the group's drummer, causing Phoebe to wonder what would happen now that he wasn't supposed to hang out with Nick and Sam.

Phoebe exchanged a glance with Emma, who mouthed the words "Dylan" and "later." Making sure Jessie's gaze was fixed elsewhere, Phoebe mouthed back, "I know." For the remainder of the time they spent together, Phoebe kept an eye on Jessie, hoping to resurrect their friendship, and hoping to disabuse her of any concern regarding Dylan. Now that the fall dance was behind them she also wanted to tell Jessie about Shane, and to say she'd moved on. Noah was a thing of the past. "I'm sooo over him," she imagined saying, though she would still like him as a friend.

Talk turned to tryouts for a female singer. And once again, when Phoebe spoke, mentioning Skyla's claim to excellent vocal chords, Jessie appeared disgruntled. Phoebe was about to apologize with something like: "I didn't mean she should be the one,

I was just..." but such defensive gestures were lame. Moreover, Phoebe knew the problem wasn't in what she was saying—friends didn't take to heart every little remark; no, it was everything else that had passed between them. And Dylan's ambivalence toward Jessie didn't help.

Phoebe left then, not wanting to be the source of Jessie's annoyance, and not wanting to subject herself to her reactions. That was something her mother had tried to instill in her last year, when she'd had so many problems with Skyla. "Why hang around where you're not wanted?" her mother would say. "You can make other friends." And she had. She'd found Jessie.

On the way home, she kicked the leaves on the sidewalk, watching them scatter. She noticed too that where it had been sunny earlier, now a wall of grey-bellied clouds hung overhead. Her mood had changed accordingly.

She vowed to tell Dylan that she really liked Shane. Well, maybe, but she would definitely tell him that she was Jessie's friend and he shouldn't try to kiss her again.

By the time she arrived at her house, darkness had set in despite the early hour – it was only a little past six o'clock. She hated that about fall. She also hated coming home to a dark, empty home. It was creepy. She ran inside and began flipping on all the lights. Why was nobody home? She suddenly felt like collapsing in a heap and crying.

Chapter Six

As Isabel stepped foot in the kitchen, she heard Phoebe bark, "Why do you have to work all the time?" Her daughter's opening gambit was followed by: "Why can't you just be a stay-at-home mom like all the other moms?"

Though startled, Isabel mustered an even-toned response. "Honey, we've been over this. First of all, you and Jackson have what you have because Daddy and I both work hard. And, second, you know, as well as I do, that plenty of moms work."

Often enough Isabel wished for more time off and shorter hours, but the truth was she loved her work. She couldn't understand how women who stayed at home felt satisfied. Endless volunteering? Baking cookies? Going out to lunch with friends? Tennis, golf? How could any of that compare to winning a tough legal case in court? Did she want more time with her children? Of course, but no way would she trade places with all those women who'd forsaken their careers.

Phoebe glared at her. "Like I care about all that stuff. I'd rather you stayed home." Then her voice softened. "Why won't you?"

"You'll understand when you have a career of your own." Isabel began pulling leftovers out of the fridge.

"No, I won't, because I won't have a *career*." She spat the word. "I'll be designing clothes and working from home like Jessie's mom! She's always there after school. And she actually cares what happens to Jessie!"

Phoebe's comment stabbed her. Little else that her daughter could say would have a more damning effect. But Isabel tried to remember that this was a young girl talking, a girl who knew little about the world but her own selfish needs and desires. Desires which, by the way, were volatile and all over the map.

She wanted to say something, but what? "Honey, tell me what happened at Dylan's? Are you still designing the band's outfits?"

"Yes, but what do you care?"

"I care a lot. Maybe you and I can do something this weekend?" She poured the contents of a stew that Milly had made into a pot and placed it on the stove.

Then, as though a magician had snapped his fingers, Phoebe transformed into a well-adjusted teen who began telling her mother with great zeal about the band's name and how she planned to scour used clothing stores for dark suits and how she would make some sketches of guys wearing thin ties and vintage-style fedoras, just like ones she'd recently seen on a few celebrities. "And maybe you'd like to go with me?" she concluded.

Isabel stopped stirring the stew and looked up. "There's nothing I'd love more than that, Phoebe."

It took Phoebe a moment to register her comment. "Oh, Mom, I know that's not true!"

And they both began laughing.

· ● · ● · ● ·

Sandy observed her daughter slouching into the kitchen, a downcast expression on her face. "What's up, honey?"

"Nothin'," Jessie said, her backpack landing on the floor beside the table. She pulled out a chair, the legs scraping the pale wood, and dropped into it.

"Doesn't look like *nothin'* to me. Want a celery stick?"

"No, I don't want a celery stick!" She gave her mother a look of disgust. "Chips and a soda."

"Okay, but I thought—"

"Well, you thought wrong. Do you want to know what happened or not?"

"Of course, I do. One soda coming up." Sandy crossed the room to the fridge, pulled out a diet Coke and deposited it on the counter. "Here you go, sweets."

Jessie briefly glowered at it before popping the tab and taking a sip. "Unbelievable. Phoebe at Dylan's alone," she looked at her mother to make sure she was listening, "alone with him! They pick the band's name, the one *she* suggests, and when she talks about going to used clothing stores, Dylan's all over it. She knows I like Dylan," she said plaintively, her eyes widening, "I told her so, and now she's trying to steal him—" She glanced at her mom. "I think she's still mad at me for asking Noah to the dance."

Sandy looked at her daughter protectively. With each image of Phoebe – cunningly smart, curvaceously sexy, and deceptively devious – her insides heated up, and she barely heard what Jessie said about Noah or Dylan. Her mind had jumped ahead to how she would quiz Phoebe, how she'd get her to tell *Shane* the truth. But would she tell Shane about Dylan?

Then she noticed Jessie looking at her, anticipating a response. What had she been saying? Snapping back to the present, she forced calm on her rampant mind. "What was that, honey? Something about Noah?"

"I think she's still mad at me for asking him to the dance." Jessie's brow arched in an accusatory fashion. "Remember? That brilliant idea of yours, the one that would make Phoebe so happy?"

Sandy hadn't anticipated this glitch. Actually, she hadn't thought much about it at all. So, things *had* backfired. Well, hell, Rome wasn't built in a day. Now what advice to offer?

Before she'd had time to fully formulate the thought, the words tumbled out, "We'll have a party, and you'll invite Dylan. Tell him we'll hire his band. Of course he'll have to come over and check out the space and discuss money. I can pick you guys up at school—"

She hadn't finished speaking before Jessie shouted, "Oh, Mom, you're brilliant! Did I ever tell you that?" She skipped out of the room, her mother feeling relief and redemption. A solution to every problem – that was her motto. You just had to think about it.

One thing seemed to elude her though, no matter how hard she thought. And that was making Jessie popular. Getting lots of boys to like her. Girls too. She didn't know why, it just seemed important. Like something that spelled success in life. Besides, it couldn't hurt. Having parties couldn't hurt either.

After finishing a Chinese carry-out meal with Jessie and Bill, she left them sitting in the family room watching TV. Up in her office she scrolled through her e-mails to see if she'd heard from Ron – not yet. Then she looked for new *Slenderella* orders. Nope, none. Damn that Isabel. Sandy routinely cursed her for all sorts of reasons, but even more so since the e-mail that banned use of the school directory "to solicit business." More than once she'd fretted over the nasty chit-chat that must have ensued among the snitty moms.

Memories of real and imagined slights, along with Phoebe's most recent betrayal, tumbled through her mind in a chaotic stew. She studied Shane's Facebook page.

Hope you like my picture. I didn't get yours? Looked up Walter J, but you weren't in the team photo.

Sandy blanched. She'd hoped Phoebe would forget her request. A moment's thought and her devious brain found a solution. *I arrived after they'd taken the shots.* But it also brought to mind the need for greater caution; she ought to check the website for wins and losses, which she hadn't done. She began to wonder if *Shane* was worth all the trouble.

A few seconds later, Phoebe wrote: *Do you want to get together?*

A smirk played on Sandy's lips. The message from Phoebe, God bless her, was perfect. She felt absolutely giddy. Now to stir the pot *and* gather some intel. *Love your pic. How about this weekend?* she wrote back, fairly certain Phoebe was still grounded. But perhaps she'd shed some light on her upcoming shopping date with Dylan.

Phoebe: *I'm still grounded on weekends, but maybe I could meet you one day after school?*

Little liar, thought Sandy. Now, how to flush her out about Dylan. But first, in response to Phoebe's question, Sandy's fingers skipped lightly over the keys: *Can't, football practice.* The answer had come easily. How many times had she watched Shane Barnett on the football field? Of course that had been in the fall before she knew she loved him. All the girls had watched Shane; he'd been Mr. Popularity. And then in April she'd imagined marrying him, to spite Les, but mostly because she'd truly fallen for him. Countless afternoons in the spring she'd sat in the bleachers watching him on the baseball team, waiting to steal a kiss, to make out with him until her chin was raw. To let him feel her up. To let him fuck her. Which he had, in more ways than one. How was it that memories of Shane always created such emotional turmoil?

She shook him from her head and read Phoebe's response: *Right. Oh, well, guess we'll have to wait until I'm un-grounded.*

Shane: *Hey, your friend Jessie's having a party. Maybe we can meet then?*

Phoebe: *She invited you?*

Sandy again panicked. Was Jessie so mad that she hadn't invited Phoebe? She'd been so sure Jessie would post a blanket invitation on her Facebook page that she hadn't even checked. Something she quickly remedied. And sure enough her predictable daughter had announced it online. Invited the whole damn grade! *Party at my house. Save the date.*

Good girl, Jessie.

Shane: *She posted it on Facebook.*

Phoebe: *I don't know. I have to ask my mom.*

Shane: *Oh, come on, your mom can't be that big of a...you know what!*

Phoebe: *Maybe she'll let me go.*

Shane: *Promise to ask her?* Hope you can't come, Sandy thought.

Phoebe: *Okay.*

Shane: *Can I tell you a secret?*

Phoebe: *Sure...what?*

Shane: *Of all the girls at your school, you're the only one I want to go out with.*

Phoebe: *Well, I really want to go out with you too.*

With a come-on like that Sandy figured she could pry just about any info out of Phoebe, including what she was doing with Dylan. *Who are your favorite guy friends,* though, failed to elicit the answer she was looking for. Of course, the girl wasn't stupid. No, she was cunningly smart. When Sandy asked what was on tap for the weekend, Phoebe claimed to be going shopping with her mother. Fucking liar! You're going with Dylan, admit it!

· ● · ● · ● ·

Ron loved Isabel's white silk pajamas. The way they outlined her breasts and accentuated her legs always put him in the mood for sex. He figured she wore them because the thought of him working at the *Post* turned her on. Fact was, though, he didn't actually have the job yet. Gil hadn't mentioned an offer, just that they wanted to see him. Yet why else would they want a meeting?

"You've got the jitters, I can tell," Isabel said.

"Is it that obvious?"

"Mmm...hmm. Come to bed, honey, it'll be fine. You'll see."

He'd drummed up a couple of story ideas. Like tailing Sarah Palin. Getting a real inside look. She seemed like such a ball-busting ice maiden. He wanted to see if he could make her defrost. A charming come-on. He mentioned the idea to Isabel, who laughed. "You are incorrigible."

They spent a few minutes devising a strategy for his meeting, nothing spectacular – she predicted the *Post* would make him an offer, he'd push for a little more money or stock in the company, maybe a higher-level title, then he'd take it – after all, writing for the prestigious paper was what he wanted, so what would be the point of playing hard to get?

He gazed admiringly at his wife. In situations like this, Isabel was so logical, so reassuring. She's definitely the brain in the family, he thought.

He eased back against the pillow and reached for Isabel's hand. "Craziest thing," he said. "I got an email from Sandy today. She wants to go to lunch to talk about the girls. Of course I'm not going, but I was thinking maybe you could reach out to her?" When he turned and saw the look on Isabel's face, he realized the ill timing of his remark.

"Really? That's what you think?" she said.

He watched as she rolled over, her silky back now facing him. "Come on, Iz." He touched her shoulder but she shrugged him off. She'd been all ready for sex. Why in the hell had Sandy popped into his head? He felt like getting up and going into the other room to masturbate, but suddenly he was too tired, and his cock, which had sprung to life a moment ago, now simply withered in his hand. Goddamn it.

Chapter Seven

Tuesday, October 21, 2008

As Ron left the *Washington Post* building, he had to wipe the shit-eating grin off his face. He wondered if passersby noticed that his feet weren't even touching the ground. He'd done it! A new job, start as soon as you like, sure a story on Palin would be great, a little more money why not, though he'd have to oversee a few interns hell-bent on doing political stories. To follow in the footsteps of Woodward and Bernstein, the famous Watergate reporters. No problem, he thought, already savoring his new status.

He stopped off at Starbucks to grab some coffee before going back to the AP office, where he now had the unpleasant task of giving management notice. Of course, he'd offer to stay the requisite amount of time, but would request early departure. He knew they could survive without him. They might even be happy, given that they could replace him with someone younger, someone for far less pay.

In line ahead of him, he saw the back of a woman. Her ass-hugging jeans, her curvy figure, and the way she stood with a hand on one hip all reminded him of Sandy. He stared at her streaked hair, almost thinking it might be her. He willed her to turn, though when she did she looked nothing like Sandy, nor was she dressed in a cleavage-revealing top. He tugged his phone out of his pocket and called up her name in an email, then began to type. *Thursday looks good,* he wrote. *I don't have long, but meet me at the Quill in the Jefferson Hotel on 16th St at noon.* Satisfied, he tapped the word "send."

Already he imagined how impressed she would be when she heard his news.

· ● · ● · ● ·

Today, when Phoebe opened her locker, hanging inside she found two images taped onto one piece of paper smiling at each other. One half was of Noah at the fall dance and the other of herself. The torn edges met in the middle. She knew it was Emma's work. The two routinely rendezvoused at their neighboring lockers, and each time they did, it boosted Phoebe's spirits. She realized how much she truly appreciated her willowy friend.

The images made her smile. Instead of showing her and Noah as they more often appeared – with shy grins or reticent smiles – they were laughing and dancing, not with each other, of course, though Emma had made it appear that way.

Underneath she'd written the caption: *What shoulda coulda woulda been! Maybe next time?!!*

Phoebe thought about this, then decided she'd eventually reply by using images of herself and Shane. She neatly placed Emma's note between a stack of books, wrote a quick message back, and shoved it through a crack in Emma's locker.

· ● · ● · ● ·

It surprised Ron that he felt slightly nervous as the day for his lunch with Sandy approached. Now that he'd made a reservation at the Jefferson, he wished he'd invited her for a drink later in the day. Though he swallowed the crazy thought that surfaced briefly — making a hotel reservation and ordering room service — he understood his urges and knew he'd have to tame them. Nevertheless, as he sat at his desk, he couldn't help the wave of images that arose: first, Sandy slowly and teasingly stripping, revealing her large beautiful breasts, then kissing him with her slick tongue, sitting down on his lap and finally letting his thick cock slide in. In his imagination she was a perfect piece of ass, talented in the art of sex, waiting to devour him.

Chapter Eight

Saturday, October 25, 2008

Isabel navigated the narrow, sun-drenched streets of Cleveland Park as she and Phoebe headed out to do some shopping. They'd decided to go to Westfield Mall on Democracy Boulevard, then head off to Georgetown, first to a thrift store and then to Dylan's. In an effort to conserve driving time, Isabel had set up an afternoon appointment with Amanda to review room parent tasks, while Dylan and Phoebe browsed more secondhand clothing stores.

While shopping with Phoebe, Isabel hoped to ask how things were going with Dr. Sharma. She had to wait for the right moment, but when it came she'd ease into the conversation. *How are you feeling about things, honey? What did Dr. Sharma say?* And so on.

She'd ask her, too, how she felt things had gone with Skyla and

Liz a couple of days ago. Maybe that was the better place to start.

"Are you looking forward to your birthday party with Skyla?" she asked once they entered the mall, which literally vibrated with activity.

"Yeah, sure."

Her answer seemed awfully lukewarm, Isabel thought. Hmm...how to probe without prying? "That doesn't sound entirely convincing. Are you sure you want to go through with it?"

"Yeah, it's fine."

Clearly something else was on her mind.

"Anything you want to share with your mom?" Isabel poked her playfully.

"Well, as a matter of fact, there is," she said quite seriously. "There's this guy I've met and I'd like to invite him."

"Well, that shouldn't be a problem, should it?" Isabel asked. "Is Skyla objecting?" She'd noticed how much Skyla controlled the planning while chatting with her and Liz. Not to mention how clearly Liz was using the party as another means of currying favor with her and Ron. Another attempt at gaining entry to the Chevy Chase Club was underway.

"No, though I haven't mentioned it to her. He goes to another school," Phoebe said.

"Oh? How do you know him?"

"He friended me on Facebook."

"Oh," Isabel said again, feeling some anxiety about this. "So you don't actually *know* him?"

"Well, not yet."

Their conversation was cut short when Phoebe ran over to the cosmetic counter to test a new shade of lip gloss. Next they bought a pair of leggings for her at J. Crew. Twice she entered a dressing room and allowed her mother to join her. Neither time seemed quite right to dive into the sacred realm of cutting. Somehow, the intimacy of the situation – Phoebe was letting her see her scarred arms and legs – precluded any of the conversations Isabel had imagined. It relieved her that Phoebe hadn't further inflicted injury on herself. And, really, wasn't that enough?

Isabel purchased a pair of slacks at Nordstrom's and a sale shirt for Ron. They looked for a new video game for Jackson, discovered the store was awaiting a shipment, then left for a thrift shop Phoebe had discovered on the Internet.

Unwittingly, the route Isabel had chosen took them past Walter Johnson High School. Right past the chain link fence that surrounds the football field, where a raucous football game was underway, the bleachers crammed with students and parents. Cheers, shrill whistles and all the sounds that accompany a high school football game rose above the traffic noise.

"Go, Wildcats, go!!"

"Oh, my gosh, Mom, could we stop?" Phoebe said, craning her neck as she looked outside.

"What on earth for?" Isabel said.

"This is where Shane goes. He plays for Walter Johnson," Phoebe said, as if Isabel should know.

"I take it Shane's the guy you mentioned earlier?" Phoebe nodded. Isabel added, "But, we have things to do, honey."

"Fine!" Phoebe crossed her arms and stared out the window. "We can never *do* anything! You're always on a schedule. God, Mom, you are sooo *not* fun!"

Isabel stared at her daughter. How had they gone from having a perfectly lovely day to this? As much as she loved Phoebe, she couldn't wait until they could look back on these moments and laugh. One thing she was sure of: it couldn't happen soon enough.

She sighed. "I don't think I deserved that, Phoebe. But if you really want to stop here, then fine. We can always go to the secondhand store another time."

A wide grin replaced the scowl. "Really, Mom? Thank you. Thank you. You're the best."

Isabel had to stop herself from rolling her eyes, shaking her head and heaving another sigh as she maneuvered the car into the jammed parking lot. "Now, can you tell me a little more about all this? Who is this boy?"

Phoebe's face transformed yet again – a bashful smile replacing her enthusiasm. "Well, a few weeks ago Shane friended me. He's new to the area and," she glanced at Isabel sheepishly, "and he, well, he really wants to meet me."

Though having Phoebe "meet" some stranger through the Internet conjured all the worst images, she was now glad she might actually lay eyes on him. It was this that allowed her to keep the alarm out of her voice. "Oh. Who else has he friended?" This was a call for caution and a return to Facebook ground rules. Isabel would discuss it with Ron; they'd set up new guidelines for the use of Facebook, and computer use in general (for both kids); they had set up controls, but she now realized their standards had relaxed at the very time when they ought to have become more vigilant.

"Pretty much all my friends," Phoebe said.

"Skyla? Jessie? Emma?"

"Jessie, Emma, yes." Then she added, "All of Skyla's friends. They all think he's adorable, Mom. He is sooo cute. Wait till you meet him."

"Okay, but what about Skyla?"

"No...and I'm not sure why. I'll ask him."

"Which is why you're worried that Skyla might not want to

invite him?"

"A little." But then excitedly she added, "He asked to see *me*."

"You, and no one else?" She hoped Phoebe couldn't hear the distress in her tone.

"Well, I don't know for sure. He asked if I could meet up with him this weekend." She sounded so full of eagerness, full of innocent desire, until she added, "But I told him I was grounded." She released a disgruntled snort, which Isabel ignored.

Isabel found a narrow parking spot and pulled in. "I guess we're okay here for a few minutes. Be careful getting out."

Phoebe nodded. "We don't have to stay long. I just want to be able to tell him later that I watched some of the game." She turned to Isabel, her eyes alit like amber jewels. "Maybe I'll even see him!" Isabel nodded.

Inside the stadium, they stood at the end of the bleachers gazing off at the jerseys and helmets crashing into one another on the field. The other players huddled in tight packs along the sidelines behind their coaches, and two sets of cheerleaders thrust their pom poms high into the crisp air. A huge cheer rose from the fans. "Who's the best? Wildcats! Yes!"

"Do you know his number, honey?" It would ease her mind to put a face to a name. If she could see his face behind the mask. If he shed his helmet. But at least to have seen this mystery boy, even from a distance, would help.

Before Phoebe could answer, another shout erupted. "Push 'em back, push 'em back, way back!"

Phoebe grabbed her mother's arm. "Wait here a sec', okay?"

"Where are you going?"

"To ask someone Shane's number."

"Okay, but you have your phone with you?" Isabel couldn't

help asking.

"Really, Mom?" Her eyes widened. "I mean really?"

"I'll wait right here." She stared after her daughter. Phoebe wore the leggings they'd just purchased and a long-sleeved lacy t-shirt with her navy blue Georgetown Academy sweatshirt draped over her shoulders. She had to admit that since Phoebe had slimmed down, she cut quite a figure, maybe accentuated by the tight clothes. No wonder this boy was after her. She'd have to talk to her about that. She knew how carnal boys were at this age, which reminded her of that wretched Michael. Not contacting his parents had galled her, but the implications for Phoebe had been too formidable. She did confide in Jane, and they'd agreed to spread word through the grapevine about his behavior without mentioning Phoebe.

Isabel checked her watch. It was nearly 1:30. As she gazed emptily at the game, she wondered about this latest development. It seemed only minutes ago that Phoebe had been mad for Noah. Now she seemed gaga over someone named Shane. Internet aside, she wasn't crazy about the fact that he attended a school way out here, but she tried not to be judgmental. After all, he might be a very smart, nice boy. More importantly, she would make a point of being present when Phoebe met this young man, whoever he was.

Less than ten minutes elapsed before Phoebe returned, her brow furrowed.

"What happened?" She wondered if Phoebe had inadvertently discovered this Shane character was a *player*.

"Well, I asked a couple of people and they didn't know him. No big deal," she said, clearly trying to brush aside her disappointment. "I'll ask him." Then a smile returned to her face. "At least I can tell him I saw part of his game."

"It's a little odd though, isn't it?" Isabel's interest was piqued. No one knew him. That could be coincidence, after all, he was supposedly new, but as a member of the football team, you'd think...

"No, Mom. I mean I only asked three or four people. You can hardly expect everybody that goes to a game to know him," Phoebe retorted.

She supposed Phoebe was right, but made a mental note to keep tabs on this situation. In fact, she'd encourage Phoebe to invite him to her birthday party, no matter what Skyla wanted. After staring at the guys on the field for a few more minutes, Phoebe seemed ready to leave.

"Should we grab a bite in Georgetown?" Isabel asked once back at the car.

"Sure, if we have time." Phoebe gazed outside, as if her mind had already bounced elsewhere. "There's something I want to ask you, Mom. And it's kind of big. And important." Phoebe turned and looked at her mother, apparently waiting before continuing.

"Okay, I'm all ears." Now what, she thought as she carefully backed out and pointed the BMW toward the main road.

"There's a party in a couple of weeks and I'd really like to go. I think I've been acting responsibly and doing everything you asked me to. Right?"

Isabel suspected there was a catch to Phoebe's request, so she proceeded cautiously. "Yes, you've been fairly good." She almost brought up the fall dance, and the fact that drinking had obviously taken place, but decided now was not the time. "And we really appreciate it. So who's having a party?"

"Jessie."

Isabel's hands gripped the steering wheel more tightly. Why couldn't she get Phoebe away from her? Then she recognized Sandy's strategy. Be Party Central, have the house where kids congregate. Make your kid popular. If she didn't think Jessie was eager for popularity too, she'd actually feel sorry for the girl, burdened with a mother like that. She took in a deep breath. "You really want to go? Despite all the stuff that's been going on between the two of you?"

"What stuff?" Phoebe asked innocently.

"Come on, Phoebe, you know what I'm talking about."

"You don't want me to go, I can tell. It's because *you* don't like Jess. Tell the truth."

"I haven't said anything yet. Can we talk about it before you decide?"

"But I think Shane is going to be there." Phoebe's voice had turned into a whine.

"I see," Isabel said cautiously. "What about Noah? Don't you like him anymore?"

"Sure I do, but only as a friend."

"But you haven't even met this guy. How do you know you'll even like him?"

"I just do."

Isabel found this sad. The mercurial life of teens. "All right, but let's ask Dad about the party and...and this situation with Shane."

"Situation?"

"You know what I mean."

"Anyway, he already knows about him, Mom."

What!? She felt like shouting, but all she said was, "He does?" She'd deal with him later.

"Yeah, I told him last Sunday, after … you know, the whole stupid Michael thing. So, is that a strong maybe?"

Strong maybe? Had she said that? She didn't think so. "All right, we'll discuss it," Isabel said, although in her mind it was a *weak* maybe, if anything.

Chapter Nine

Around 1:30 in the afternoon, Sandy dropped Jessie and Emma off at the mall in search of party decorations and returned home to pay some bills that had piled up. She hadn't seen Jessie quite so psyched about anything in a while. It was a huge relief and a personal victory. Thank God Dylan had responded so enthusiastically to the request that the band play. But then why wouldn't he? She'd offered to pay them $200!

Though she agreed with Bill, who called the money "no small potatoes," he'd said it in a way that was unlike him. As if he resented it, and that seemed strange, because to him $200 barely counted as pocket money, an attitude she'd adopted over the years. *Chump change,* he might say.

In fact, earlier in the day he'd said a few other things that had put her in a sour mood. Like, "Ya know, I'm not sure you should try to *buy* Dylan for our daughter. You really think that's a good idea?"

She'd tried staring him down, then said, "I don't know what you're talking about," while fiddling with her hair, twirling a lock round and round her finger.

He smiled, a maddening smile, really, and said, "Oh, I think you do." But he hadn't left the conversation there. He'd been more insistent than usual. "Don't you think she should have the opportunity to work that sort of thing out herself?"

"Well, what I'm thinking is that you should just stop asking questions," she said, trying to gain the upper hand.

He frowned. "Don't go overboard trying to make Jessie happy, okay?" he said before walking out the door and leaving her sitting there to stew. The nerve!

Now, as she sat before the computer, about to fulfill a few *Slenderella* orders, she was tempted to call Ron. No, she told herself, not yet. She'd intentionally waited to call or write him after their "brief" lunch, which had turned into an hour-and-a-half event. Men hated overly eager, clingy women and she didn't want him to think she was one of those. But they'd had fun. More than fun. He'd lusted after her.

It began when he'd reached for her hand across the table in a quiet booth at the Quill. She quickly figured out he'd chosen this spot so his flirtation would go unnoticed, and she'd gone to great lengths to present both her most earnest and most vulnerable sides. She laughed demurely, all the while observing him, clear-eyed, like a panther stalking her prey, and knew that he underestimated her.

But she'd also underestimated his effect on her. They'd each had a glass of wine, which she sipped and he drank rather quickly. He ordered another. When their food came, she picked at it, he'd noticed, and she brushed off his suggestion that she didn't like the salad, saying she was so impressed with his "new job and all" that she forgot to eat. A flirty smile, a bit of light laughter, when all the while she felt like ravaging him. God, he was cute.

As she recollected the memory, Bill briefly entered her thoughts and she apologized to him despite his earlier behavior. *You have your fantasies, too,* she claimed.

"Does that mean you'll be on the road a lot?" she'd asked Ron slyly.

"It does," he said, staring into her eyes, then letting his gaze drop, running over her throat and down to her breasts, where they remained, rather brazenly, as he asked, "Do you like to travel?" before lifting them again to see her lips part then turn into a becoming smile.

"Sometimes, but I'm kind of a homebody," she said, which was only half true.

She'd toyed with him this way. Had let him stroke her hand with his finger, at one point she'd kissed two of her own fingers and placed them on his mouth. "I really need to get going," she said, though she'd had to tear herself away. Even now she grew hot at the memory.

"Do you?" he asked, his tone braided with regret.

She thought he might just run to the front desk and do whatever was needed to get her up to a room. A man ripe for the picking, but she'd felt so turned on that if he'd pursued it, she would have agreed in a hot second.

"Maybe we can do this again," she said, "when *you* have more time."

He looked slightly off balance, as if surprised she was leaving, but nodded. When they got up from their chairs she went over and gave him a little taste of what might be in store for him. "You are one handsome, successful man, Ron Murrow," she whispered in his ear, then touched his jaw with her fingertips, drew his face toward her and kissed him lightly on the lips. "Thank you for a wonderful lunch." She didn't wait for him to answer, but instead hurried off, knowing he was watching her as she sashayed away.

Now, she clicked on "new email" and dashed off a thank you note. It would only be a matter of time before he'd contact her and want to "see" her again. Interestingly, they'd never touched on the subject of Jessie and Phoebe, the presumed reason for lunch, though she had told him about Jessie's party and said she hoped Phoebe could make it. Which wasn't true. It was Ron she could hardly wait to see again. Each time she thought of him, she tingled with excitement. This was something she hadn't expected, but she couldn't help recalling his slightly cocky attitude, so irresistible in a guy. All because he had a new job.

· ● · ● · ● ·

Though Amanda didn't work, Isabel thought she might as well have since she served on several boards, corporate and non-profit, and raised money for everything from the Choral Arts Society to the Capitol Hill homeless shelter. Thus far Amanda and Isabel's views on all the room parent issues blended beautifully, and while Amanda had a more easygoing nature when it came to child-rearing, one Isabel attributed to the fact that she had sons and not daughters, she certainly agreed with Isabel about getting a handle on "this drug thing" when she brought it up.

"The pitfalls of parenthood," Amanda said lightly, "are legion. No wonder our teens resent us. All we do is say 'no,' 'be careful,' and 'don't.' 'No drinking, no drugs, no sex!' 'Be careful driving, don't stay out too late, make sure you call me,' blah, blah, blah!" She laughed.

"It's so true, but what are we to do? Abdicate our responsibil-ities? Like some parents we know?" She looked at Amanda mean-ingfully then leaned in. "Can I be candid with you?"

"Of course."

"I take it you've heard about the party coming up at the Littletons'?"

Amanda snorted softly. "Have I ever! Sandy had Dylan over on Thursday, presumably to check out the space where the band will play. Of course I offered to drive him over, but she wouldn't hear of it. No, she picked him and Jessie up after school and then drove him all the way back here two hours later, but not without first calling and begging to feed him dinner, after I'd specifically said he needed to be home. He procrastinates like crazy when it comes to doing his homework. So of course I said no, but it was a bit awkward."

Isabel nodded her head. "I understand completely."

"Confidentially, I think Jessie might have her young heart set on Dylan. Poor thing! She has no idea what she's getting herself into," Amanda said with an arch look.

Isabel smiled. "He's adorable and you know it."

"Someday. Hopefully. We'll see," she mused.

"Well, I, for one, am beginning to see the merits of arranged marriages!" Isabel said with a grin.

"There's an idea. Can you imagine?" Then her expression grew serious. "So, let me guess, you're worried Sandy and company will let the kids drink?"

Isabel frowned. She'd heard that at a party the previous year, when they were away at Christmas, Sandy had done everything but place beer in the hands of the kids. And another in the summer. "That's right," she said. "I wonder if she and Bill have any intention of providing oversight. I mean the real kind. Not just pretending."

"How about if we send something out reminding parents of their responsibilities as hosts and chaperones of a party?"

"Maybe we could offer to chaperone?" Isabel said with a laugh, though it brought to mind Ron's suggestion of reaching out to Sandy. This memory briefly clouded her thoughts, until she heard Amanda say, "That would be quite an experience. Of course, Dylan would kill me, or maybe the other way around."

They both chuckled and Isabel forgot all about Ron, thinking how much fun it was to be working with a woman the caliber of Amanda Thomas, someone who shared her sensibilities.

They spoke a while about the issues of drugs, drinking and sex and finally decided to send out an e-mail underscoring the "no alcohol" rule at parties. They would list all the ways kids tried to sneak it in – water bottles, flasks, etcetera – and places they might store it outside. If parents failed to uphold this most basic rule – *NO alcohol at parties* – then the ones to be blamed for drinking problems were the parents.

And Isabel, as an attorney, would add language about how parents were not only responsible, but could also be prosecuted, especially if something horrible happened after a party where alcohol "had been served or allowed." It wasn't unusual for upper classmen to crash such parties, which raised the issue of drunk driving. Perhaps she would cite recent incidents in which teens had either died or suffered serious injuries.

They'd end the missive by encouraging parents to keep an eye on their children and watch for any possible alcohol or drug use. And, of course, there really was no replacement for staying in close contact with one's sons and daughters.

Armed with this, Isabel left for home, though without Phoebe. She and Dylan hadn't returned yet, and Amanda insisted she'd bring her home in a while. They both laughed simultaneously, thinking of Sandy. "Please don't go out of your way. Really, I don't mind if she takes the bus," Isabel said.

"All right, I'll leave it up to her. But if I don't take her, I'll let you know."

Isabel prayed that by hanging out with Dylan, Phoebe would get her mind off this Shane person, whoever he was. She'd thought about raising the topic with Amanda, but then decided to keep it to herself. She'd discuss it with Ron later, including why he hadn't told her about him.

On the drive home, her thoughts turned to Ron. To events of the past week. If she didn't know him better, she'd think the *Washington Post* offer had completely gone to his head. Of course, he had every right to be thrilled. It was his dream job, but the way he'd behaved, so annoyingly self-assured, like some teenager. At first, she'd thought it was her imagination, until Thursday night, when he suddenly seemed not only cocky, but also somewhat distant. Men could be such children, she thought.

At home, Isabel found herself alone climbing the stairs to Phoebe's room; Ron was still at Jackson's soccer game. She'd decided to go through Phoebe's things, something she'd avoided for weeks; there hadn't been much point since Phoebe was grounded, and the truth of it was she hated the sneaky dishonesty of it. On the other hand, she'd long ago convinced herself that in order to keep her daughter safe, she needed to know what was going on. Especially after the discovery of her secret romance.

The bulletin board drew her attention and there, dead center, a photo of a boy she assumed was Shane, her daughter's romantic obsession. She had to admit he was ruggedly handsome. So easy to lose yourself in starry-eyed dreams about someone you don't know.

Her eyes cast about the room, briefly landing on Phoebe's very colorful childhood painting – "I See the Moon," she'd called it. It reminded her of the talk she'd had with Phoebe about the illusory appearance of things, and even people. Then she'd used the moon as a metaphor for Skyla, now she added Shane to the long list of things to discuss with Phoebe.

She roused herself back to her task. Where to start?

Well, drawers were always the first place she looked. She glanced in the usual places, beneath panties and t-shirts and bulky sweaters. Nothing. She opened her jewelry box, a multi-drawer affair, but again found nothing unusual. She noted that Phoebe still kept a couple of baby teeth in a tiny see-through jewelry bag, a lock of her strawberry blonde baby hair tied with a piece of pink yarn, and a narrow blue ribbon that had once graced the knitted cap of her favorite bear. She'd always intended to stitch it back on, but there it lay.

She fondled the hair. How quickly time passed. In the blink of an eye her daughter had gone from innocent babe to budding adolescent. She touched the baby hair to her cheek, sniffed it, and then gently placed it back in the jewelry drawer, tears welling up. She wiped them away and moved to the dollhouse. Her fingers grazed the roof as she recalled the hours she'd spent playing here with Phoebe. The tiny furniture, the toy people. Their funny pretend conversations. Peering inside, she noticed the miniature couch. It was out of place. She was about to move it when the phone rang and she left the room.

· ● · ● · ● · ●

Instead of completing *Slenderella* orders, Sandy turned her attention to Shane's Facebook page, where she noticed several new friend requests. Including one from Skyla, who she'd excluded. Because Skyla was nearly as much to blame as Isabel for her daughter's recent distress. Her lips curved into a faint smile, considering the request, then sent Phoebe a note asking if she'd mentioned Jessie's party to her parents. *Dying to meet you.* Not! What she really wanted to say was: how were things with Dylan? Did he kiss you? Instead she wrote, *Heard you're designing the band's outfits. What do they look like?* More importantly, would she finally admit having spent time with Dylan? Doubtful.

She stared at Shane's photo, suddenly hating herself for having used it, for not having anticipated that the mere sight of him would force her to relive a past she'd relegated to a remote part of her mind. In fact, she'd made a point of not keeping up with her old friends. So God only knew where Shane was. Now, she routinely wished the pox on him. Especially when she recalled the unceremonious way he'd dumped her, without any consideration for the fact that he'd gotten her pregnant. Something neither Bill nor Jessie could ever know.

With an obsession born of habit, she went to the bookshelf reserved for the paraphernalia of her teen years and found her senior yearbook. Class of 1993. When she pulled the book down, it fell open to of the Senior Prom. And there was Julie Donovan smiling her toothy smile beside Prom King Shane Barnett, captain of the football team. Sandy almost threw the book down. How could such a long ago event still get her all twisted in a knot? She was going to be his date, until she'd gotten pregnant. And then Shane had decided he'd rather go with Julie. Julie, whose parents weren't divorced. Julie, who hadn't fucked her stepfather. Cute fucking Julie!

Sandy flipped the pages to her class's senior photos, skimming the face of each boy she'd screwed around with – there were maybe a dozen – allowing old memories to sift through her, until she landed on Shane's. Even now his mischievous smile goaded her. The bile of old hurt and anger rose up inside her as if he'd betrayed her yesterday. He'd crushed her.

Occasionally, he still tormented her. In one dream he'd spied doodles in the margins of her notebook—a series of linked "S's," his initial and hers, swinging down the page like monkey arms. His hyena laughter haunted her. She slammed the book shut.

Oh, well, now he'll break another heart and this time she wouldn't be the one to suffer.

Sandy distracted herself from this odious memory by fulfilling orders and coming up with new *Slenderella* "ads" and new lists of people to contact. She'd recently joined Linked-In and had developed a Facebook page for the product.

At once, an email arrived from Amanda Thomas and Isabel Winthrop. She scanned it. In an instant she knew its message targeted her. Just like the one from Alison Kendall. And this time it focused on "chaperoning," in other words, Jessie's party. Her emotions ricocheted from hurt to pissed-off to embarrassment. It sent her mind into a tailspin, as she imagined what the women would say about her. She tapped her fingernails on the desk, listening to the hollow sound. "Fuck them," she said, trying to sound tougher than she felt.

Before heading out for her pedicure, she checked the *Slenderella* Facebook page, then again Shane's to see if Phoebe had responded (she hadn't). Of course not, she's still with Dylan, she thought. Next she checked Jessie's. For the sake of appearances, she made sure "Shane" wrote on Jessie's and a few of the other girls' pages with some regularity, and now saw that Jessie had written to "him": *Come to my party. Bring some friends! Can't wait to meet ya!*

Right. Hate to disappoint you girls, but Shane will not be coming to your party.

Then she heard a voice mocking her. *Shane? Ha, ha, ha. You'd better watch out or he'll fuck you again. How long do you think you can keep up this charade?*

Sometimes Sandy wished she could turn to someone for guidance, but Mrs. E had died some years ago, and when it came to her mother she was greeted by a stunning, deafening silence. On occasion she heard Margaret's nasty recriminating voice in her mind. Lately, a new unpleasant voice had entered her head and Sandy wished it would go away.

"Damn it, I know!" she said loudly, sensing that sooner or later this Shane, like the real one, might fuck her. So the sooner he did his disappearing act, the better. This was something she occasionally fretted about, especially when she mind-tripped in the middle of the night. But he hadn't finished the job she'd created him to do.

· ● · ● · ● ·

Later that night, Sandy checked to see if Ron had sent a reply. When he hadn't, more disappointment flowed through her, but she chided herself (*he will, you know he will*), then on Shane's Facebook page she saw the private message Phoebe had left: *Yes, designing outfits, cool, huh? But even cooler I got to see a few minutes of your football game today!!*

Sandy actually shook her head to make sure she'd read correctly. Such a thought had never occurred to her. She read on: *My mom and I were passing by after a trip to the mall. Tried to find out your jersey number, but couldn't find anybody who knew you. What is your number?*

The words sent Sandy's heart racing and sweat bloomed in her armpits. Again, she heard the mocking voice: "One of these days Little Miss Muffit will get caught in her own spider's web." Now that sounded like her mother, which irked her. But it irked her even more when her mother was right, like now.

Should she just pretend she hadn't seen the message? Christ, what was she going to say? What had those kids said to her? She could imagine Phoebe asking, and someone saying, "Who?" But as she followed this line of thinking, she began to calm down. Phoebe was just a kid, one who – from what she could tell – was infatuated, a lovesick little puppy. Shane was as real to her as her stupid mother. She wouldn't even stop to wonder if there was a Shane. No, kids were gullible. Her secret was safe.

But she had to respond. And that was annoying, because she'd actually have to do some work. She checked her watch. Better get it done now. She Googled "Walter Johnson High School football team." After a few clicks she saw a photo with a list of the team members' names beneath it. The boys were seated on a set of indoor bleachers. Of course, she'd already told Phoebe Shane had arrived at Walter J after the photo had been taken. But she'd have to make sure she didn't assign him someone else's number.

She studied the photo again, noting that some of the boy's heads obscured the numbers of the kids behind them. She obsessed on this a few minutes, chewing her pinky nail to the nub. She even threw a pencil across the room. She wanted to scratch Shane's eyes out. "Damn you! You're such a pain in the ass," she muttered, then realized the obscured jerseys worked to her advantage.

The number she decided on was 10; it looked like none of the kids had that number. If Phoebe checked the website, she wouldn't find anything to contradict this, would she?

Trying to keep herself from completely losing it, she wrote a cagey note back to Phoebe:

Won the game! With the help of Number 10. Which could mean that was Shane's number or not. *I bet you're a 10 too! I want you to be my number 10. Are you coming to Jessie's party? I'll show you what a 10 is all about! Did you ask your mom?* Sandy's hands shook. She exited from Facebook and went to the kitchen where she pulled a Bud Light from the fridge. She guzzled half the beer, then slammed the can on the counter.

"Take it easy, babe."

Startled, Sandy twirled about. "Oh, it's you."

"Who'd you think it was?" Bill said.

"Nobody," she said with a sigh.

He put his arm around her shoulder, pulled her close and asked what was wrong. She kissed him lightly. "Nothing, hon," she said. Together they had another beer. Their afternoon spat forgotten, she thought about what a find Bill had been. A very basic sort of guy, but the best sort of basic, the answer to all her anguished prayers half a lifetime ago.

Finally, her besieged mind settled down. Much later, in the middle of the night, after she'd made love to, then fucked Bill – the second time more of a release for her than for him – she realized what had escaped her before. All she had to do, if worse came to worse, was to disappear Shane. Like all those milk carton kids. And no one would be the wiser.

Chapter Ten

Monday, November 3, 2008

It was the day before an historic presidential election, but this was of little consequence to Phoebe, Emma, Jessie, and all the band members, including Noah, who'd reconvened at Dylan's for a last practice session before Jessie's party on Saturday. At least initially, Phoebe thought things were going well. Especially between her and Jessie.

"Okay, guys, let her rip!" Nick shouted. The group began to jam loud and hard, with Jessie taking a couple of eager turns at the mike.

Phoebe looked on, tapping her foot to the beat of the drums. The second time she felt Dylan's gaze on her she turned away to stare out the window, noticing the flurry of leaves floating to earth. It seemed that Dylan had a thing for her, and if it weren't for Jessie, she wouldn't mind. It was nice having a boy like her, two boys even, because she'd noticed Noah watching her too, but all she could think about was Shane. Only a few more days before she'd see him at Jessie's party, though her mother hadn't given final approval. But she had to go, she just had to.

She'd already begun embroidering a 10 in Walter J's colors – kelly green and white – on the pocket of the jean jacket. A pocket located directly over his heart. She'd even imagined both of them getting tattoos, absolutely *verboten* by her mother, hers a 10 inside a heart, and his would be the same but with her birthday inside, the number 18, something straight out of a modern-day *Romeo and Juliet*. Or something like that.

The group took a short break to try on their band outfits. For a few minutes the room turned into a blizzard of clothing and half-robed bodies. Phoebe caught both Emma and Jessie staring at the guys' naked torsos. She too was impressed by Noah's muscular biceps, but busied herself yanking clothing out of several shopping bags – secondhand dark blazers, white t-shirts and skinny black ties – and tossing them to the guys, while Jess and Emma kept up a steady flow of comments. Laughter tumbled through the room as freely as opinions. "Too neat," "loosen the tie," "untuck the t-shirt," "yeah, awesome." "Super cool!"

Phoebe declared that Dylan and Nick, the two guitarists and lead singers, should wear slightly beat up felt fedoras pulled low over their brows. She went over to fit them properly on their heads.

After they were all dressed, the guys picked up their instruments, took their spots on the "stage" and struck a series of cocky and comic poses, the entire session recorded in video and static images by Emma, who promised to post them on Facebook and YouTube, and even send out tweets, announcing the formation of the group.

"Yeah, and their first paid gig is at my house," Jessie piped in.

Dylan stroked the strings of his guitar a few times, then rotated his arm 360 degrees and screeched out a few notes Jimi Hendrix style. The others chimed in with their own instruments, and Jessie was again given a chance to sing.

Still, it didn't mean she was *in* the band. That was to be decided at some later time.

After a second break, and seemingly out of the blue, Emma, looking quite serious and wide-eyed, posed the question, "Do you think we're going to grow up to be like, well, pretty much like our parents?"

A wild series of shouts ensued, denying that any such thing could or would ever happen. But once the chaos subsided, Noah, sitting on the drummer's stool, announced with great seriousness, "No doubt. You know, genes and all!"

"Oh, God, that sucks," several of them exclaimed.

"But probably accurate," Emma said. Her very black bangs, cut bluntly across her forehead, revealed her equally dark brows and earnest eyes.

Phoebe thought it was a little odd that Emma, the least conforming of any girl she knew, would ask such a question and wondered if the question was as innocent as Emma now appeared. She couldn't imagine Emma ever becoming like her mother. Or anyone's parents. Especially if she kept adding more piercings. Recently, she told Phoebe she wanted one in her tongue, to which Phoebe had said, "Wouldn't that get annoying?"

Emma had shrugged. "Maybe, but then life's annoying."

In a recent exchange Phoebe had learned that Emma's father, a year after her birth, had left his wife and child for another man and moved to LA to work for some Hollywood studio. He rarely called or wrote. Now and then he sent money. Emma harbored another secret she'd shared with Phoebe. Someday she'd go out to California, find "that bastard," and guilt him into supporting her through college.

Phoebe spoke up. "It may be in the genes, Noah, but we have reason and free will," she said, recalling a recent discussion in English class. Turning to the group, she added, "Are your parents replicas of their parents? There might be a resemblance, but they're not copies. We *are* individuals. We *are* different." And recalling what Emma had told her, she said, "I'm certainly not going to be like *my* mother." Then, realizing how that sounded, she stopped to examine her friends' faces. All but Emma stared at her. A little embarrassed, she added, "You guys?"

They all chimed in with: "Yeah, no way!" Except Jessie. Hand on jutting hip, she announced, "Well, I'd be happy to be like my mom *or* my dad. They're great!"

"Good for you, Jess!" Nick shouted, and they all laughed. Jessie's face flushed despite the make-up she'd used to cover up a mini-bout of acne. Phoebe wanted to come to her rescue, but what could she say?

Later, when Phoebe left, she was pretty sure Noah timed his departure to coincide with her own. Out on the sidewalk, he synchronized his footsteps with hers. The whole thing felt a bit awkward, and she wondered if she ought to tell him about Shane.

"You're coming, aren't you?" Noah asked quietly. "I mean to Jess's party."

"Yeah," she said. Then, "Yes, definitely." She'd die if her mother prevented her.

"Oh, great. Me, too."

"I hope so. You're in the band!" She laughed a little.

He kicked at the leaves, appearing ill at ease. "I think it'll be a blast," he said, though his tone didn't sound convincing.

"Yeah, I hope so."

As they neared her bus stop, Phoebe saw the 32 approaching. Although there was plenty of time, she shouted, "That's mine, gotta run. Sorry." She gave him an apologetic look, but actually felt relieved. Seated at a window, Phoebe noticed that Noah, his expression a bit bewildered, still stood where she'd left him, as if hoping to catch a glimpse of her.

She turned her gaze back inside the bus and pulled *To Kill a Mockingbird* out of her backpack. She had no trouble imagining Scout as a friend and wondered if she ever felt about Atticus the way she felt about her mom – that he spent far too much time at his job.

· ● · ● · ● ·

Forks, knives and spoons clattered noisily onto the glass kitchen table as Jessie dropped them beside each plate.

"Christ, Jess," Sandy said, "you wanna break the frickin' table? Go easy."

Jessie grunted, "Whatever."

When Bill strolled in, Sandy gave him a warning look, aiming her eyes at Jessie. "Beware, teenage beast on the prowl," her look suggested. They sat down and began to eat.

It wasn't long, though, before Jessie spilled her discontent, complaining about Dylan and Phoebe, her words twisting this way and that until she'd again accused Phoebe of making a play for Dylan. She described the afternoon's events a second time, all the while inhaling forkfuls of mashed potatoes. "I'll never get Dylan."

Sandy responded lightly, "Well, for starters you might try

slowing the carb intake, hon'. Have you looked in the mirror late-ly?" Sandy gave Jessie huge latitude, but one thing she couldn't abide was people feeling sorry for themselves, wallowing in their misery. She was all about picking yourself up and figuring out how to get what you wanted. "If you're fat and your face is full of zits, well, then you get what you deserve, don't ya?" she added mat-ter-of-factly, though with a dimpled, disarming smile.

Tough love wasn't one of Sandy's tactics, but she could see some-thing radical was needed to jolt her daughter out of the valley of self-pity and get her back on track. What with the party five days away.

Jessie slammed down her fork, rose from the table, picked up her half-full plate and practically tossed it in the sink. "Thanks a lot! Maybe you should take your own advice, Mom!"

Mission accomplished, Sandy thought as Jessie flounced out of the room. She'd apologize later and have the mom-daughter talk that always followed such mini-dramas, but for now she'd at least stopped her daughter from eating all that food. In a while Jessie would calm down and then she'd join her upstairs and together they'd hatch a plan. How to get beautiful for the party and take back Dylan: diet and exercise (with the help of *Slenderella*), a five-day facial program, just the right cleavage- and thigh-revealing clothes, get her hair done, etcetera, etcetera. The steps to success broken down into bite-sized pieces.

Bill brought plates to the sink as Sandy stacked them in the dishwasher. In a low voice, without sounding accusative, he said, "A little rough on her, weren't you?"

"Not to worry, babe, I've got it covered." She turned and light-ly rubbed her hand over his crotch. "Got you covered too," she whispered in his ear.

His voice turned husky in her ear. "You always do," he said

and gave her ass a squeeze. That meant sex was a sure thing later on, and she loved Bill for the way he turned her on. Though she knew that sometimes her sexual appetite outpaced his. He was probably one of the few men in the world who on occasion didn't act on his wife's come-ons.

The truth was Sandy loved sex. Whether Les's careful lessons had enflamed her sexual desire then taken it to stratospheric heights, or she was just built that way, she didn't know. By being married, though, she sometimes missed the fun of getting guys to do exactly what she wanted. A little coaxing and moaning, a little sucking on their dicks, and they'd do just about anything. Anyone who didn't, she had tremendous respect for.

Until that lunch, she'd thought Ron might fall into that latter category, but now she was pretty sure he'd be a willing victim. She considered him a topnotch catch for all sorts of reasons. He was cute, for sure, but on their recent date he'd even promised to get her into the White House, which made her think of *doing it* in the Oval Office! Since their lunch she sometimes lost sight of her original goal – rubbing her achievement in Isabel Winthrop's face – but she reminded herself of that now. If he didn't email again soon, she'd think of another reason to contact him.

She finished the dishes, and instead of watching her favorite show, *Desperate Housewives*, she caught a few minutes of the pre-election day newscast. Things had reached a feverish pitch, something she wanted to be able to discuss with Ron. She'd tell him she cast her vote for Obama, because that's what he planned to do, though she couldn't understand why when DC residents' votes didn't count in national elections. In contrast, though her ballot counted, living in Maryland and all, she doubted she'd go. Lines would be unbearably long, and she figured Obama would win without her.

On her way upstairs to talk with Jessie, she thought about passing on a few of her "how to get your man" tricks. She *was* a freshman in high school after all. Maybe she ought to introduce her to birth control pills. She grabbed a pack from her bathroom then went and knocked on Jessie's door, though she entered without waiting to be invited in.

"Hi, toots, what's up?" she said to Jessie, who was propped against several pillows on her bed, her knees slightly bent, her laptop resting against her thighs.

Jessie looked up, an Eeyore expression on her face.

"Don't be glum, puss." Sandy went and sat down beside her. "Okay, here's what we're gonna do," she said and laid out the plan for the next few days until the party. "See? It's that easy. And by the way, Mick Jagger had it all wrong. He said, you *can't* always get what you want, but I say you can!" She chuckled at her own cleverness.

Before she left, she laid the package of birth control pills on Jessie's bed. "Now, hon, I'm not condoning sex with boys, but I am trying to be realistic. You do *not* want to get pregnant. You just wanna have fun." She smiled at her daughter. "Remember, more than anything boys want to have sex. But you're in charge. You put out when you want and when you're ready. Don't give it away for free or too often, because that's just plain cheap. You understand?"

Jessie stared at her mother. She chewed on her lower lip. "I think so."

"And don't forget, I got your back. Any questions, you come ask your ole' ma! Okay?"

"Okay, Ma," Jessie said, elongating the word "Ma" and rolling her eyes.

"Do as I say and I have a feeling Dylan won't even give that Phoebe girl another glance," she said as if Phoebe were some stranger. "I can't believe he'd care about her when he can have you." She was at the door, about to exit, when she stopped and swiveled to face her daughter. "Anyway, didn't you tell me that Phoebe was all sweet on that guy Shane?"

Jessie nodded.

"I'll bet Dylan doesn't know that?" She tossed her daughter a meaningful look.

"Nope," Jessie said, grinning.

Adopting a look of concern, Sandy added, "She isn't still doing that awful cutting thing, is she?" She paused, observing her daughter nod yes. "Sure hope she outgrows it. Sleep tight, Jess. Mama loves ya."

With that, she closed the door and swayed her hips down the hall to her bedroom. On the way, she made a detour to her office to see if Ron had written back yet. She rubbed her hands in glee when she saw his simple, elegant one-liner:

"Great seeing you, too. Maybe we'll meet up after things die down post-election?"

On her way to bed, the mere notion of seeing Ron was making her feel super turned on. I know, she thought, I'll invite him to help chaperone the party next Saturday. That seemed as good an excuse as any to initiate contact and brought a huge smile to her lips. She prayed Bill was still up. If not, she'd have to wake him, gently. Slowly. The way he liked it. And fuck his brains out.

Chapter Eleven

Wednesday, November 5, 2008

The morning after Barack Obama's momentous win, Isabel felt justified heading into work late. She could almost feel the elation sweeping over Washington – with its largely Democratic constituency – and imagined the celebratory mood in her office. She had offered to buy a few items for a party they were hosting later on. First, she needed to do something else.

Ron and Jackson had left a few minutes earlier and she'd watched Phoebe run down the sidewalk to catch the bus. *If* Phoebe was going to Jessie's party, she needed to get a handle on Shane. And in Isabel's mind a great big "if" still existed despite Ron's proclamation: "Of course she can go." She'd raised other factors besides Shane. The hostess, for example. Ron had reacted as if she were an incorrigible child. "What is it with you and Sandy Littleton? It'll be fine, Iz."

She logged onto Phoebe's Facebook page, then connected to Shane's to see what he was up to. He seemed older than 15, but maybe not. Hard to tell. But Phoebe was right, he was good-looking. That stray lock of hair, those intense eyes. A slight air of mystery. That caught her short. No, mystery was not good, not for her daughter, not with a stranger and not when she could police Phoebe's Facebook site, at least officially, only until she turned 14. Only one week and six days away. According to Facebook rules she'd then have to become one of Phoebe's "friends," which gave her no access to private messages.

She recalled the moment Phoebe had turned 13, the legal age for Facebook, when her pubescent daughter had asked that she be allowed to have her own page, and of course Ron had supported her wish. Ever since, it seemed as if life for Phoebe had been on a downhill slide. Not that Facebook had caused it, but somehow her mind linked the two.

She reviewed the comments Shane had posted on her wall. Nothing out of line there. Then she checked the private messages between the two. A few seemed unusual for a boy. Why would he want to know about her outfits, for example? And other guys? There seemed an unusual number of references to Jessie as well. But she continued on.

Aha, so his jersey number was 10. But the next few sentences nearly made her gasp. *I bet you're a 10 too! I want you to be my number 10. Are you coming to Jessie's party? I'll show you what a 10 is all about!*

You will do no such thing, not if I can help it, Isabel thought. She would tell Ron. This should change his mind. Innocent, right!

There was no way she would let her daughter go to that party and meet up with this vulture. Another one ready to steal her daughter's innocence. Oh, God, male hormones. Surely, Ron would agree with her.

As she began moving back in the history of Phoebe and Shane's messages, she ran across: *Oh, come on, your mom can't be that big of a...you know what! Rhymes with w-i-t-c-h!* And Phoebe had called her "crazy." Well, as she scanned the rest of their frequent interactions, she felt that she had plenty of ammunition to keep her from attending the party. Of one thing she felt certain, it was time to have a mother-daughter talk – not just about this guy, and guys in general, but once again about being careful of what she said to others on Facebook. She could easily imagine things getting out of hand. Because there it was in writing. But first she'd talk to Ron. Hopefully, for once, he'd see things her way.

When she reached him, he said a little breathlessly, "It'll have to wait til tonight, Iz; I'm hot on the trail of an Obama story." She hung up, feeling proud of her husband and his renewed enthusiasm for work and career. Of course it could wait.

· ● · ● · ● ·

Phoebe and Skyla hopped off the bus and walked to school together, as they did quite often. Along the way, Phoebe mentioned that things between her and Jessie had gotten pretty tense again, and that she thought it might be about Dylan. "I feel like I don't even know her anymore. It's weird, you know?"

"Jessie, well, she's not really the kind of girl I like to hang with," Skyla said in her know-it-all manner. "No offense, Feebs." Then she put her hand on Phoebe's arm and fixed her with a confidential stare. "Did you know her mom got pregnant with Jessie in high school."

Phoebe had never heard this and wondered if Skyla was making it up. "Are you sure?"

"Just do the math." She smiled at her own cleverness.

"I always sort of liked her mom."

"Seriously? You haven't noticed how her mom dresses? Like totally—" she searched for a word, but couldn't come up with one. "One time I saw her thong sticking out when she bent over! It was so gross. It's like she wants guys to notice her, you know?"

"Really?" This all came as news to Phoebe and she tried to imagine how Skyla knew. Probably something her mother had said. She gazed off, staring at the campus entryway in the distance. Red brick pillars connected by the famous Georgetown Academy wrought-iron arch, with the curlicue letters "GA" in Victorian script. The need to defend her old friend rose up in her. "Even if it's true, Jessie can't help what her mom does, or did."

Skyla smiled knowingly. "No, but you know what they say."

"No, what do *they* say?"

"The apple doesn't fall far from the tree. Jessie dresses kind of slutty too, in case you haven't noticed. I guess it's in the genes, Feebs."

Phoebe stared at her a moment. Had Skyla found out about Monday's conversation at Dylan's? "So you think being mean or jealous or whatever is inherited?"

Skyla screwed up her face, looking slightly confused. "My advice: steer clear of her. But that's just me." Then her eyes transformed into glittering emeralds. "Let's talk about our party, okay?" And for the next couple of minutes Skyla veered off in this new direction.

Though Phoebe nodded and added a word here and there, all she could really think about was Shane. Finally seeing him, actually meeting him, and maybe – well, probably – kissing him.

· • · • · • ·

As Sandy got ready she kept worrying that Ron would cancel on her. She'd gotten a text from him mid-morning: *Are you up for adventure? Meet me at the Jefferson at 1. Text me from the lobby.* Did this mean he was getting a room for them? The thrill that coursed through her was palpable. And the word "adventure" kept echoing in her mind. She was in a kind of feverish state, almost like a teenager on her first date with a really hot guy, and she was also talking to herself, trying to keep her emotions in check.

She tried on an assortment of outfits, casting aside one after the other, until she finally found a slinky, pale pink cashmere dress with a black suede belt to cinch about her waist. Black suede high-heeled boots to match. The ensemble would show off all her best features. But first she chose her lacy under-garments, all in creamy whites, and dabbed herself with perfume in all the important places.

As she got dressed, a hodgepodge of thoughts spun through her mind. Anxious thoughts. Would some last minute work assignment trump their date? Was this a "one-time" fling for him? How could she make sure Isabel eventually found out? Did she want Isabel to find out? What did she want? Only then did she think of Bill and Jessie. Certainly they couldn't find out.

After slipping into her dress, she gave herself one last long look in the mirror. Her reflection was pretty close to perfect. She gave herself a dimpled Marilyn smile, imagined what Ron would feel when he saw her and ran out the door.

The room she left behind looked like the proverbial tornado had just struck. But with her thoughts so far away, she hadn't noticed. She hadn't had an affair in a long time.

· ● · ● · ● ·

That evening over dinner Sandy noticed an unusually reserved Bill. It made her uneasy, but she said nothing. She didn't
want to provoke him, not with Jessie there. Finally, in their bedroom, he launched a small grenade: "Can you tell me where the hell
you went this afternoon?" Anger creased his brow.

Shaken, Sandy said, "What do you mean?" Though now she
understood his earlier mood. Bill had only one rule: *No fucking
around.* He'd made that clear when he proposed to her. And there
had only been a couple of times that he'd questioned her this way.

"I came home this afternoon and your shit was all over the
place," he said.

How could he possibly know she'd gone to The Jefferson? It
was rare for him to come home mid-day, which tempted her to ask
why he had, but she thought better of it. She'd returned home after
a frustrating few hours and hurried to make dinner, failing to take
note of the mess when she'd briefly gone upstairs to change. "Went
out with some of the Academy moms and wanted to look my best,"
she finally said. She grabbed a fistful of clothes and tossed them into
her roomy closet. "I'll get to it later, hon'," she said over her shoulder.

She took a moment to freshen up in the bathroom then
hopped onto their king-size bed. "Now come here and tell me about
your day," she said breezily.

He eyed her then acquiesced. As he talked, she relaxed. Slowly, she began unbuttoning her sweater, one by one, keeping her
eyes on him, just as Les had taught her. She continued undressing
until there was nothing left between her bare skin and the air but

a lacy thong and bra. She beckoned him. "Come here, baby?" She leaned back against the pillows and began to fondle her breasts.

A moment later, Bill had stripped down, and she felt the rough suck of his mouth on her nipple, his roughness being something she liked. She breathed a sigh of relief as he touched the wetness between her legs.

Though less than nothing had happened with Ron, she'd have to be more careful in the future.

· ● · ● · ● ·

It hadn't begun as an argument. Ron had showered, then after a little chitchat about the overwhelmingly positive international reaction to the first black president of the United States, Isabel switched gears and gave him a rundown of the private messages between Phoebe and Shane. He shrugged.

"So you think all that talk about making her his number 10 means nothing? She's your daughter, don't you feel a need to protect her?" Isabel said, hoping Ron would have a last minute change of heart about letting Phoebe go to the party.

"For heaven's sakes, Iz, stop worrying about it," he said dismissively, adding, "I trust Phoebe to do the right thing."

"I trust her too, but he's older and you know how boys are." She looked at him for some sign that he agreed, but his eyes were trained on the newspaper, which he'd brought to bed. She was changing into her silky pj's. "Between her meeting some phantom kid we've never met, a cute guy who will no doubt break your daughter's heart, and being at that woman's house where I just know they'll look the other way on the whole drinking business, how can you not worry?"

Ron seemed about to snap at Isabel when instead he finally looked up and took note of the pajamas he'd given her. "Well, there is a solution." His voice contained a teasing tone.

She stopped and peered curiously at him. "What's that? You'll go there as a reporter and cover it for the society page of the *Post*?" She laughed.

Suddenly in an indulgent and obvious good mood, he smiled. "Something like that." He patted the bed next to him and Isabel extended her leg beneath the sheet, then slid in. They scooted close to one another under the covers. "I was invited to be one of the chaperones at the Littletons' party," he finished.

"You've got to be kidding?" She turned and stared at him in disbelief.

"Nope. I was asked today."

"Bill?" she said hopefully. He shook his head, and she said, "Sandy?"

"Uh-huh."

"The nerve of her, Ron! How could she ask my husband? No one does that. No respectable woman anyway."

He shrugged, recalling the sultry tone of Sandy's voice. *Ron,* she'd said on the phone, *I have a favor to ask.* Despite his last-minute cancellation, due to a pang of guilt and the need to be on top of election results, Ron was surprised at what a perfectly good sport she'd been. She'd said a few other things too, but he wouldn't be mentioning those either. His thoughts switched back to the matter at hand. Of course he understood Isabel's indignation. Women asked other women. Not their husbands.

"I have half a mind to call her."

Ron, looking slightly alarmed, stayed her arm as if she were about to reach for the phone that sat on the bedside table. "Iz, you know I'm not going, don't you?"

Her face crumpled a little, and her head lolled onto Ron's shoulder. "That woman is the bane of my existence," she said.

"Don't let her be," he replied softly and kissed the top of her head.

She pushed the newspaper out of his hands. "You've read everything there is to read about the Obama win," she said, "so let's concentrate on something...something more important." She bussed his cheek and slowly moved her hand below his navel.

He breathed in the familiar scent of Isabel's hair, drew her to him and kissed her neck and face, then ran his hand down the length of her spine, cupping her buttocks and letting her feel his hardness. They made love the way they always did, not too vigorously, but lovingly. It was comforting, but for some reason, afterward, Isabel wept a little.

Chapter Twelve

Saturday, November 8, 2008

"Mom, can't you hurry up a little? At this speed we'll never get there!"

"I'm going the speed limit," Isabel replied.

Phoebe released a loud sigh.

Isabel still regretted letting Phoebe go to the party. Her consent, though, had come with two conditions. One: any alcohol and she was supposed to call home immediately; and two: curfew was at 11 o'clock. Isabel would arrive promptly, waiting outside to pick her up.

Despite what Phoebe had said a week earlier – that she didn't care about staying past ten-thirty, the time when Shane had to leave – she'd put up a vociferous fight to make it later, worthy of any defense attorney's final rebuttal in a trial. Turning a brilliant smile on her mother and hugging her, she'd begged, "Come on, Mom, make it eleven. Please."

And Isabel had acquiesced, thinking about what Dr. Sharma had said. "I think you can trust Phoebe to do the right thing. And if you *let her know* you trust her, I don't think you'll be disappointed."

Now Phoebe grew chatty, happy even, talking to the three girls in the back seat – Skyla, Molly and Daisy. It was good to see her this way, and yet Isabel couldn't entirely shake worrying about her, vulnerable as she was.

"Do you think I look okay?" Phoebe said, then added to the girls in back, "Can you believe I'm finally going to meet Shane?" A couple of days earlier, she'd marshaled the courage to tell Skyla and her troop of friends about his desire to go out with her, and to her relief discovered he hadn't asked anyone else.

Don't remind me, Isabel thought, and felt the need to interject. "That should be interesting, but you don't know him, so be careful, honey."

"Oh, Mawm, what can happen?" Phoebe asked impatiently. "Right, Skyla?"

"I'll watch out for her, Ms. Winthrop. I promise," Skyla said in her take-charge voice.

"Hmm," Isabel said, glancing at Phoebe. *How eager she is.* She couldn't help feeling as if she were sending her lamb to slaughter. All those hormonal boys, all those temptations, all that poor decision-making, and then there was the bigger issue: all at Jessie Littleton's party. Isabel imagined boys and girls pairing off and drifting into dark rooms, drinking alcohol that had been smuggled in, kids guzzling beer and perhaps smoking pot, with no one to stop them, and all the while Phoebe saying, "What can happen?"

She wanted to lecture her. All four of the girls. To itemize all the things that *could* and often *did* happen, but she'd already done that and it would only alienate Phoebe, who was hopefully smart enough to avoid the myriad temptations, especially the kind that got you into trouble.

"Mom, you've got that look on your face!" Phoebe said, cutting into Isabel's thoughts. Then her voice softened. "It's gonna be all right. I promise." Phoebe smiled at her, and Isabel smiled back, reveling in the sweetness of the moment like every other imperfect parent who loves her imperfect child.

"All right. Have a good time. I'll text when I'm out front, okay? But don't keep me waiting." Glancing over her shoulder at the girls in back, she added, "You three have another ride, right?"

In response, Skyla articulated each word as if Isabel were hard of hearing. "Yes, Ms. Winthrop, my mom is going to pick us up."

"Okay, there it is." Phoebe pointed at a house that was big, really big, boastful and showy, but attractive too. She realized then that in the twelve months of Phoebe and Jessie's friendship she'd never once been here. What did that say about her? That Bethesda, a nearby Maryland suburb, was an inconvenient drive from Cleveland Park? She suddenly felt terrible that Sandy had always driven them, and Isabel had let her. I suppose I should have been more grateful for that, she thought.

She drew up to the curb and the girls got out. She watched them giggle as they made their way to the front door. Waiting for someone to let them in, she drank in every inch of the well-lit place, which was just shy of a mansion. In fact, the mini-manse took up two lots and had the feel of a ski chalet, one you might find in Aspen or Vail. It was constructed of stone and wood shingles, an elaborate peaked archway over the front door, and a dark metal-roofed porch that ran the length of the house. A wide driveway led to a three-car garage located on one side of the house, and a perfectly manicured garden wrapped around the other. It looked twice the size of her own home.

The beep of a text. From Phoebe. *You can go now. Bye!*

She glanced up just in time to see one of the double doors open and swallow the girls. Despite craning her neck, she hadn't been able to tell if it was an adult who'd let them in. She shifted the BMW into gear and rolled away from the curb. She hadn't traveled fifty feet when in her rearview mirror she noticed the headlights of a car drawing to a halt in the spot she'd just vacated. She slowed the BMW enough to see who was getting out.

Several teens erupted noisily from the vehicle and slammed the doors. Halfway up the sidewalk to the Littletons, they stopped. And so did Isabel. She rolled down the window and observed the scene through her side and rearview mirrors. There was whispering, a bit of head bobbing, laughter and then movement – a multi-legged, shape-shifting creature closing in on the front steps. Once more, the door opened and inhaled the group.

The temptation to circle the block and continue observing the house for a bit stirred inside her. She even wished she could go inside to assure herself there was no alcohol. A brief battle raged, but then she headed home. She wouldn't be so worried, she told herself, if this party were anywhere but at Sandy's.

· • · • · • ·

Moths danced in Phoebe's gut as she glanced about the room in search of Shane. She was downstairs, on the party level, in one of several large rooms filled with her classmates, most of them people she'd come to know over the past couple of months. When she spied a shock of hair that matched Shane's photo her heart thumped loudly in her head. The boy turned. It was someone else. She needed to get a grip.

Just then Mrs. Littleton wound through the room, waving and welcoming everyone as if she were a celebrity. She wore a very huggy, green sweater with a plunging neckline and super-tight pants. Even though she didn't mean for it to, the word *slutty* popped into Phoebe's head. "There's lots of food and drink. So don't be shy, help yourselves." She stopped briefly to speak with Dylan, then called out, "If anybody needs us, Bill and I will be upstairs, okay?" She brandished a smile then disappeared.

A few seconds later, Emma presented her with a beer. "You look like you could use this."

Phoebe gave her a questioning look. "Really? You sure this is okay?"

"You kidding? We're at the Littletons', remember?"

Then without any more thinking, she grabbed the can and poured liquid down her throat. "Careful," Emma said, "not too fast. Remember what happened at the dance?" Which is the first time Phoebe thought that perhaps it had been Emma who'd stroked her hair when she'd gotten sick that night.

In the corner the band was setting up its equipment. The two girls moved closer and watched. Noah looked up and waved Phoebe over. "You wanna come?" Phoebe asked Emma, but her friend urged her to go ahead. "I'll go see what Nick's up to." She waggled her eyebrows like Groucho Marx and tapped a pretend cigar.

Still smiling from Emma's antics, Phoebe offered Noah a sip of her beer. He took a slug and wiped his mouth with the back of his hand, approximating the gestures of a pro, when Phoebe knew he was an amateur drinker at best. She also wasn't sure what to say. Between her wandering thoughts and questions – what would she say to Shane when he arrived, what would his voice sound like, would he like her once he actually met her? – she finally managed, "You look good, Noah. Good luck."

"Yeah, thanks." He sat down on the stool, pushed the sleeves of his jacket up to liberate his forearms, and took a few preliminary taps, grazing the top of each drum, then banged the bass with the foot pedal. Boom. Boom. Boom.

"Don't worry, nobody'll even be listening," she said, followed immediately by an embarrassed smile. "Sorry, you know what I mean."

He nodded. "I'll look for you when we take a break."

"Okay," Phoebe said, though she hoped he wouldn't. How awkward if he found her with Shane. She took another sip of the beer then set it down and wandered off in search of Emma or Skyla or maybe even Jess. In the background, she could hear the band warming up.

A dozen kids, five of them girls, were scattered around a ping-pong table, which had been prepped for a game of beer pong. Skyla was among them. Phoebe watched as the blonde tilted a plastic pong cup an inch above her mouth and allowed the beer to cascade into her mouth.

For a nanosecond, her mother's admonition flashed through Phoebe's mind – *if there's any alcohol, you call me, is that clear?* – then she joined the others and took her chances, tossing the feather-light ping pong ball at one of the many cups lined up on the other side of the table and keeping a lookout for the adorable, inimitable Shane.

· • · • ·

At home Isabel managed to distract herself by pouring a glass of her favorite white wine, then sat down with Jackson on the sofa in the family room, half an eye on the TV, where Spider-Man bounded from building to building, bringing some thug to justice without much ado. If only real life were so easy, she thought.

She'd spent half the day meeting with her new client, listening to all his lame excuses for misusing campaign funds. After a recitation of all the things he'd done for DC, he explained why he and his friends had flown first class to the Bahamas, why his wife had needed a new fur coat, and they'd both needed Rolex watches, never mind the thousands they'd spent on Michael Jackson memorabilia.

She'd listened patiently and then helped him to understand the likely consequences of his actions and how difficult it would be to keep him out of jail. "The best we can probably do will be to mitigate your sentence," she had said. When he stared at her dully, she added, "For example, two years in jail, not four or five." Perhaps this had been her subconscious way of hoping he'd leave and search for another attorney, she now thought.

It was already 8 o'clock and Ron still wasn't home. She looked forward to telling him about the Littleton's huge house, though perhaps she wouldn't. It still bothered her that he'd again mentioned Sandy at the very moment they were snuggling and ready to have sex the other night. She lamented the Freudian implications then chided herself for thinking that way.

She reached for her wine and with her other arm cradled Jackson a little more tightly. It was something he still occasionally allowed, especially with no one else around. They both stared at the TV and watched Tobey Maguire in his admirable rendition of Peter Parker.

When Ron finally came home, she asked what story had

kept him so late. "Or were you out celebrating your job at the *Post* again?" Several nights he'd called saying he was having drinks with some of his new colleagues. She hated the fact that she was beginning to wonder.

Ron studied her a moment, began to say one thing then seemed to change his mind. "You really interested, or you just want to know whether the story has a chance of winning your illustrious husband the next Pulitzer?" he said with his new air of confidence.

She shook her head at him. "Don't be so cynical, of course I'm interested."

He went to the fridge, pulled out a Stella, and said, "Believe it or not, I'm looking into how Obama's campaign used social networking so effectively and how that'll change all future political fundraising. Also, its need for regulation. You know, how people using social media might cross certain boundaries. How it might violate people's privacy." He flipped the cap off the bottle and tossed it toward his son. "Think fast, sport."

Jackson's hands shot out and captured the prize. "Got it, Dad."

"Hmmm...sounds like it might have potential," Isabel said, "to win the Pulitzer, I mean." They both laughed. "Come, sit down." Reassured by the exchange, she patted the cushion beside her, then took another sip of wine.

He trotted over, plopped down, and turned his attention to the TV. "What's this? Your mother's letting you watch *Spider-Man*?"

"Yup."

"What'd you do right?" Ron said to Jackson as he placed his arm possessively around Isabel, and in turn she squeezed his thigh. Jackson snuggled against her other side, the three of them nestled comfortably on the couch, the very image of a Norman Rockwell painting.

· ● · ● · ● ·

After Phoebe had drained several more small cups of beer, which made her feel slightly woozy, she glanced past the ping-pong table around the room. Somebody was making out in the corner. Several somebodies. And still no sign of Shane, despite the fact that it was already 8:30.

The band, in full swing, could be heard throughout the lower level, an area so extensive that one could truly get lost. Phoebe heard Jessie's voice singing backup on a couple of songs. For someone with trouble staying on key, she sounded pretty good and Phoebe felt glad for her.

Just then Skyla came toward her. Phoebe grabbed her arm and whispered into her ear, "If you see Shane, tell me, okay?"

"You'll be the first to know," she said, tossing back another miniature cup of cheap light beer. About to return back to the game, Skyla stopped. "Hey, have some fun. Don't worry about that guy. After all, who the hell is he? I mean no one's even met him." Perhaps she noticed Phoebe's distraught look, because she added, "He'll show, Feebs! Anyway, if he doesn't come he's the one missing out. Haven't you noticed all the guys checking you out?"

It was such a Skyla thing to say, though for a moment Phoebe wondered if it could be true. She was about to respond when Nick's voice came through the loudspeaker announcing that anyone who wanted to sing could come and take a turn at the mike. Without another word, Skyla darted toward the makeshift stage in the other room. Phoebe was left considering whether guys, besides Noah and Dylan, really were looking at her?

After a few minutes, she squeezed her way into the room with the band and watched as Skyla readied herself to sing, tapping the microphone and adjusting it to her height. She leaned in close to Dylan and they exchanged a few words, probably about what to sing, and then in a flirty gesture she grabbed his fedora and placed it on her own head at a jaunty angle. Dylan gave her an appreciative nod, counted, "One, two, three," and the music began. Phoebe was mesmerized by Skyla's near perfect imitation of Taylor Swift's deep country voice as she belted out the words to "Our Song," with Dylan and Nick singing back-up.

With the ease and grace of a rock star, Skyla shimmied across the floor, then trained her eyes on Dylan and sang to him as if they were performing a duet. Phoebe glanced around hoping Jessie wasn't around to see. The band sounded good. Really good, Phoebe thought. And there was an on-stage connection between Skyla and Dylan that made it fun to watch. Skyla even looked a little like Taylor Swift.

Out of her peripheral vision, Phoebe noticed Jessie maneuvering into the room, slipping between people and drawing closer to the stage, a scowl etched on her face. A chill ran through her when she saw Jessie's eyes squinting and leering at Skyla. It was obvious she wished her away from Dylan and out of her house. Probably wished she'd never invited her.

As she continued to watch her angry stare, Phoebe felt as if Jessie was the new someone to watch out for. How could that have happened, she thought, as she began to make her exit. She'd loved Jessie, just as she'd loved Skyla before she'd turned on her. Why were girls so fickle? In some ways, it seemed easier being a guy; maybe she should stick to having mostly guy friends. Music cascaded around Phoebe, the noise dimming as she retreated from the room. She most definitely didn't want to be there if words were exchanged between Skyla and Jessie.

She wandered upstairs to see if Shane had gotten stuck up there. Maybe he'd arrived late and had been waylaid by Mr. or Mrs. Littleton. Which brought her back to marveling at how casually they treated alcohol. It shocked her. Plus she knew her mother would have a total fit if she found out. Well, she wouldn't. Besides, Phoebe had brought some mints to mask the smell, and would be sure to use them before getting into her mother's car. God, she would freak. But then Phoebe couldn't blame her. After all, it was her mother's job to make sure she didn't drink or do other stupid stuff kids her age did. Standing alone in the hallway, a momentary feeling of warmth toward her mother washed over Phoebe.

She continued her search for Shane. She poked her head into the kitchen, where half a dozen kids were pulling beers and sodas out of the fridge to take downstairs, then entered and exited other rooms, eventually stumbling upon a few kids making out. She gazed at them longingly, but Shane was nowhere to be found. A pang of disappointment stabbed through her. He isn't coming! She thought of checking her iPhone to see if he'd sent her a message on Facebook, but before she could a female voice sang out, "Looking for someone?"

As Phoebe pivoted she came face to face with Mrs. Littleton. A huge smile dimpled one of Mrs. Littleton's cheeks. Her platinum blonde hair was piled loosely atop her head, with alluring loose strands framing her face. She was so different from her mother that Phoebe sometimes didn't know what to make of her. She seemed fun, but something told Phoebe she might be someone to watch out for too. The way she was looking at her, so intently, her head tilted to the side, like a curious bird.

"I'm looking for a guy named Shane," Phoebe said in her still small not quite 14-year-old voice. "He's not from the Academy. He goes to public school," she felt compelled to add.

"Oh. What does he look like?" Mrs. Littleton asked, with a strange little smile.

As best she could, Phoebe described him. With the odd way Mrs. Littleton continued to observe her, she felt increasingly uncomfortable.

"You like him, don't you?" Mrs. Littleton said, a faint smile returning to her lips.

Phoebe's cheeks flushed red and her ears grew hot. "Uh...I don't really know him yet, but," she was about to say she'd like to know him, instead she added, "he said he'd be here." She began edging backward toward the stairs that led down to the party.

Sandy made a tsk-tsk sound. "Guys can be so unreliable." Then under her breath, seemingly to herself, she added, "I should know." Phoebe wondered if what Skyla had told her the other day was true. That Mrs. Littleton was or had been slutty. Sandy lifted a Bud Light out of a cooler on the floor and extended it to Phoebe, who stared at it in confusion. Just then an arm slipped around Phoebe's waist. *Shane!*

But no, it was Emma. Her friend accepted the icy can from Sandy, muttered thanks, and the two fled the kitchen.

"She can be a little much sometimes," Emma offered, as if reading Phoebe's thoughts.

"Yeah, but she doesn't usually act like *that*." *So weird,* Phoebe thought.

About half an hour later, feeling a bit queasy, Phoebe stood with her back against the wall half-watching another round of beer pong, her friends getting even more plastered, though Jessie wasn't among them. She seemed intent on singing with the band, probably to keep Skyla away from Dylan. Thinking about this and feeling increasingly sad that Shane hadn't shown up, she startled when a guy's hand suddenly shot past her eyes and landed on the wall behind her, his face so close she could smell his breath. Certain it was Shane, she gasped.

"You're so pretty, Phoebe, you know that?"

She felt herself blushing. Before she could think what to say, he was kissing her neck. Then her mouth, and she was kissing him back even though halfway through the kiss she knew it was Noah, not Shane.

Chapter Thirteen

Anxiety wormed its way back into Isabel's thoughts. Jackson had been sent to bed, and the effects of the wine had worn off. First came a moment of panic that began with a sensation like a stone thrust into her gut, followed by fear radiating in waves through her chest. Something was wrong. Or she was having a heart attack. She ran in search of her cell phone, located it on the kitchen counter, and checked for any missed calls or text messages. Nothing.

A few minutes later, around 10:15, she grabbed her purse and on her way out the door shouted to Ron, "I'm going to pick up Phoebe."

"But I thought you didn't need to get her until eleven?"

"I'm stopping for some gas," she lied. "Anyway, it won't hurt if I'm there a little early."

"You sure you don't want me to go?"

She pretended not to hear and shut the door behind her.

Slowing to a cruise as she approached the Littletons' – Party Central! – she found a parking spot with a perfect view of their house. The car sat in the shadow of an ancient oak. She wondered briefly at the fact that the developer, that is Bill, had had the sense not to cut it down. Maybe he'd left it because of its proximity to his own house, for both aesthetic reasons and the added value. Yet how many others had he felled for the sake of profit?

The sound of tittering disrupted her thoughts.

She peered into the darkness, but saw nothing. Then, continuing to train her eyes in the direction of the sound, she made out two people entwined in a passionate embrace alongside the Littletons'. She couldn't help watching and wondering if it was anyone she knew. Anyone but Phoebe, she hoped. Phoebe with anyone but Shane?

Then two more teens emerged from behind bushes at the side of the house; they were laughing, one passing a bottle to the other. A bottle of beer? Vodka? Gin? Could it be water? Of course it's not water. No sooner had the thought entered her mind than a bottle sailed through the air and crashed into the street, the breaking sound of glass rupturing the silence. It was followed by a gasp, a loud exclamation – "Jeez-us! Come on!" – and more laughter.

Four kids scampered to the front of the house, turned to the right and headed north before jumping into a parked car, gunning the engine, and tearing off into the darkness. Half a block later, the headlights of the car finally switched on.

Fury shot through Isabel. Of course, what had she expected? That Sandy would respect the e-mail she and Amanda had sent out? Damn her!

The Bethesda cops had a bead on most parties in the area and routinely broke them up, dragging every kid they could lay their hands on to the police station. And, of course, the flagrant permissive host parents, too. She wasn't about to let Phoebe get arrested. She needed to get her out of there.

Her watch said 10:45. Phoebe would be ticked off if she called now, but what choice did she have? A few seconds later, Phoebe's phone began to ring. She'd explain to her what was going on. A text would simply take too long. She drummed the fingers of her free hand on the steering wheel. Come on, Phoebe, answer.

The couple engaged in making out continued. Isabel eyed them. Phoebe's voicemail engaged. "Hey, this is Phoebe. You know what to do...so do it, okay?"

Isabel hastily explained that she was early, that she saw some kids drinking, and added, "You know our rule about that, Feebs. So come on out, I'm here waiting for you across the street." The last thing she wanted was to embarrass Phoebe by going to the door. Nor did she relish the thought of encountering Sandy.

She'd give her five minutes. In the meantime, she decided to investigate, to gather evidence of drinking. She got out of the car, grateful Ron had requested an extra feature that allowed the doors to close with barely a click. It didn't take much before she found the bottom half of the broken bottle. Gingerly, she picked it up from the gutter, careful not to slice her fingers, and lifting it to her nose, confirmed it had indeed contained alcohol. In this case it smelled like that awful spiced rum.

A few more kids sprouted from the back of the house and entered the side yard. They headed to roughly the same spot where the previous rowdy group had been. She hoped they hadn't seen her. From the noise and laughter, it became apparent they were too absorbed in their own activities to notice her. Obviously, someone had stashed alcohol there, the kids all knew and were helping themselves. An old trick. Something her own classmates had done.

But as seniors, not freshmen. And in this case she suspected Sandy and Bill had made it far too easy for the kids to slip outside. Their ineffectual version of chaperoning.

In the car she found a reusable grocery sack in the back seat and deposited the broken bottle inside. *Let me introduce item number 1 as evidence, your Honor.* Her impulse was to call Ron. Her finger hovered over the home number as her thoughts returned to the kids who'd driven away a few minutes earlier. Certainly they'd been drinking, and a breathalyzer test would confirm just how much they'd consumed. Her mind jumped to the various hazards they faced: DUI arrests, car accident, a crash in which they were killed, occupants of another car dead, or worse: all of them DOA. Teen drunk driving horror stories abounded. It was a nightmare. How did parents survive such devastating events? Where did they find the strength?

She glanced at the time: 10:54. She called home. Ron's groggy voice answered. "What's going on?"

Isabel quickly relayed what she'd witnessed.

"It's a party, Iz," he said sleepily.

"Are you kidding me? This is what you expected? Why on earth didn't you say so?"

There was silence on the other end. "So what do you want me to do?"

"Call the police," Isabel said.

"I'm not calling the police. Have you forgotten you have a daughter in there?"

"*We* have a daughter in there, Ron."

"So go get her and bring her home." She could hear Ron breathing, thinking. He added, "Don't you remember what it was like when you were young, hon'?"

Somewhere in the back of her mind the word *"hon'"* registered. It wasn't a word he normally used. "Not that young! They're
only thirteen!"

"Fourteen."

"Christ, Ron, thirteen or fourteen, what does it matter? Anyway, we didn't have people like Sandy Littleton shoveling alcohol
down our throats."

"That's a little extreme, don't you think?" he said. "Just go get
her, and we'll talk about it when you get home." He hung up.

Rattled by his summary dismissal, she felt anger boiling up inside of her. How could he side with the Littletons? Correction, with
Sandy. She tapped another text into the phone to Phoebe: *I'm outside. You have 2 minutes to get out here. Otherwise, I'm coming
in. There's drinking and you know...* She erased the last sentence,
wrote *I already left a voice message,* and hit send. She watched the
little dialogue bubble turn blue and then a few seconds later came
the popping sound that indicated the message had been delivered.

She bit her lip and took in a deep breath. The blackened tree
branches grew eerily into something out of a horror film. She felt
unnerved, unhinged, as if something really bad was about to happen. Every few seconds she glanced at her phone, willing Phoebe
to contact her. Two more minutes passed. What if the police were
less than a block away?

Unable to wait longer, she tore open the car door and ran up
the walkway. She didn't care if the kids saw her or not. She strained
to see if Phoebe was part of the couple still in the throes of passion,
but couldn't really make out more than shadows.

At the door, she composed herself. Who would answer? What
would she say? She dreaded embarrassing Phoebe, but finally she
rang the doorbell. Laughter filtered outside. After another minute

of standing there, she tested the doorknob and found it unlocked. Before she could let herself in, the door opened and several teens, none of them familiar, tumbled past her with furtive glances, a bit of giggling, and mumbled hellos.

She stepped inside and stood in the large foyer, momentarily at a loss. Should she call out to Sandy or Bill? As she paused there, deciding, she couldn't help taking a quick look around. The living room was off to the left and done in creamy shades of white, beige and pink. Though the lights were low, she could see dried flower arrangements and pillows of the same hue throughout the room. It surprised her that reproductions of Monet's "Water Lilies" and several other Impressionist paintings hung on the walls. Surely they could afford better than that?

At once, in the corner furthest from her, two of the pillows moved. Then they lifted off the sofa. She tore her gaze elsewhere, realizing she'd been watching two teenagers making out, then peeled off in the direction of noise and light.

The enormous kitchen was a mass of food and ice chests over-flowing with sodas. On second glance she saw that some of these were cans of beer. Bud Light! Kids meandered about, grazing on an assortment of teen party food – open boxes of Domino's pizzas, several metal baking trays of mini-hot dogs, platters of cookies and bowls of chips and dips. All this, along with empty beer and soda cans, lay scattered on a long granite kitchen counter, a large oak table, and the counters of an island that housed a sink.

She was staring at the beer in the ice chests when she felt someone's eyes on her. It was Jessie. Isabel called out to her, ig-noring the alcohol and pretending politeness. "Hey, Jessica, do you know where Phoebe is?"

Jessie flicked her eyes away from what had captured Isabel's attention and now looked at her curiously, perhaps wondering if Phoebe would be in trouble. "No, Mrs. Murrow, I don't."

Automatically Isabel said, "Winthrop, not Murrow." Catching herself, she added, "Oh, for heaven's sakes, where are your parents?"

"They're upstairs."

"Upstairs? Well, could you please help me locate Phoebe?"

"Uh, okay."

Isabel wasn't sure if she should follow the girl downstairs, or strike out in another direction, finally deciding on the latter. She peered into a few more rooms on the first floor, where she found more kids making out and drinking, then turned to the stairs, climbing them as if a string were drawing her toward some unavoidable destiny. "Sandy? Bill?" she called out. Despite two stories of separation, the loud thump of drums and guitars reached her.

At once Sandy's head popped around the edge of a doorway and into the hall. "Isabel? What are you doing here?"

"I'd like to ask you the same thing."

"Well, I live here," Sandy said, looking annoyingly composed and amused.

"Do you have any idea what's going on downstairs?"

With the same stupid grin, she answered, "Last time I checked the kids were having fun. You remember what that's like, don't you?" She hesitated, then added loud enough for Isabel to hear, "Or maybe not."

Isabel shook her head. "I can't believe you. There's beer in the coolers!"

"Now how did those get in there," Sandy said, phony consternation knitting her brow.

"What on earth are you thinking? Kids are drinking and then leaving your house."

"Well, stop worrying, for gosh sakes. This isn't your party."

"You don't care if someone gets killed?" Isabel tried to keep her emotions in check.

Sandy cocked her head. "In case you forgot, they're not old enough to drive."

"Well, some of them must be because I saw a few kids driving away – in cars. And you're giving them alcohol. Last time I checked that was illegal!"

"Oh, chill out."

Isabel felt her anger about to rage out of control. "Christ, you are a piece of work."

"If it's so awful, just take your precious Phoebe home, and everything'll be all right. I promise." Then, with a coy smile, she added, "Oh, and tell Ron hi."

Isabel squinted at her a long moment, then turned on her heel and swept down the hallway. Now, as for Phoebe. Where the hell was she?

About to descend to the first floor, she saw her daughter at the base of the stairs looking up, her face twisted in confusion and anger. "Mom, why are *you* here?" she hissed.

Taking the steps quickly, Isabel responded in a loud whisper, "I'm taking you home is why. Let's go."

Phoebe dashed ahead of her out the front door. As Isabel watched her go she used the remote to open the car doors. Then, following her daughter outside, she hesitated before joining her in the car. With her back to Phoebe, she pulled out her phone and without thinking touched three numbers.

There was an immediate response. "Emergency 911, dispatcher 5021, ambulance, fire or police? How can I help you?"

"Police," Isabel said.

In a matter of seconds she was transferred. Hastily, she said to the woman who'd answered, "I want to report there's alcohol and underage drinking going on without adult supervision." Staring at the house address, she gave the woman the number and street name.

"And your name?" the policewoman asked.

Isabel hadn't thought of this. Of course, they'd want to know. Instinct prompted her to quickly tap the red "end" button. Right after she did, she realized the police could discover her name by simply checking the caller ID. So the cat was out of the bag on that one. Too, they might think it was a crank call, in which case they probably wouldn't forward the information to the police on patrol. Well, if that's what happened, then fine.

Isabel hurried along the curvy pathway and got into the car. She sniffed the air and caught the scent of alcohol. She wanted to ask Phoebe to allow her to smell her breath, but stopped herself. What would be gained by that now? Maybe she'd have Ron do it. Why hadn't she thought to buy a home breathalyzer? Because until recently there'd been no need to.

Silent and sullen, Phoebe refused to even acknowledge her. In a way, Isabel was grateful, at least she wouldn't have to tell her she'd just called the police on Jessie's parents. Who might or might not get arrested.

Using the hands-free mechanism in her car, Isabel quickly phoned half a dozen parents, including Amanda Thomas, to let them know what was going on at the Littleton's party. Phoebe gave her a blistering look the entire time, until she suddenly shouted at her mother to stop. Isabel was about to yell back until she realized it wasn't what she thought. No, her daughter was about to throw up. She barely had time to pull over before Phoebe yanked open the door, and leaning half her body over the threshold of the car, retched into the street.

When they got home, Isabel was going to give Ron a piece of her mind.

Chapter Fourteen

Sunday, November 9, 2008

Around ten o'clock the following morning, a bedraggled Sandy and Bill had barely stepped inside their home when Sandy called out, "Jess, hon'? You home?"

Bill's sister, Cynthia, shouted, "In here. In the kitchen." She'd picked Jessie up from the police station in the middle of the night.

Sandy tossed her coat and purse on the tufted ivory leather bench in the hallway and made for the kitchen. Bill followed her, grumbling about needing a strong "cup of jo'." The hours they'd spent at the police station wrangling with the cops until their lawyer had shown up had put them both in a foul mood.

Though still a mess, thanks to Cynthia, the kitchen was a little neater than when they'd left at midnight, handcuffed and marched outside by the police, neighbors gawking at them.

Jessie jumped up from the counter, where she'd been eating a bowl of cereal beside her cousin Carson, and ran to greet them. "Mom, Dad, you guys okay?" She peered at them through blood-shot eyes, as her aunt and Carson looked on.

"We're okay, honey," Bill said. "How about you?" To his sister, he mouthed the words, "Thank you" and "maybe you'd better go."

Before Jessie could answer, her mother released a stream of curses about Phoebe and Isabel, ending with, "That little witch, wouldn't you know it...just like her mother," her features contorted in frustrated anger.

Bill fixed his wife with a stare that said, *Cool it*, and nodded his head in the direction of Carson, who, with some prodding from his mother, was getting off the barstool to leave.

"I will not!" Sandy shrieked. "I've had it. I've tried everything. Being nice to Isabel, inviting her over, driving her daughter all over town, trying to be her friend." Of course, she was conveniently for-getting her own recent behavior, but then Isabel didn't know about that. "And all for what? No, I'm done with them! Phoebe getting sauced right along with her friends, then tattles to her goddamn mother, that holier than thou, stuck-up bitch."

"Mom, I don't think...well, Phoebe wouldn't do that," Jessie said, though her tone suggested uncertainty.

"Phoebe told her mother; why else did that freaking Isabel show up?"

"How do you even know Isabel called?" Bill said, trying to be the voice of reason. "It could've been somebody else...or the police just got wind of it."

Her lip curled in a look of disgust. "Like I said, Phoebe told, then Isabel called the cops. Right, Jess?"

Jessie stared at the Froot Loops in her bowl as if they might give her the answer. "Come on, Mom, there's lots of ways. All she had to do was come in the house, which she did. She was even in the kitchen. I told you not to—"

"Not to what?"

"Be so obvious," she mumbled, adding, "never mind." Jessie stared at a handful of Froot Loops on the table and arranged them into two eyes and a frown. Then she ate them one by one as her mother continued to vent. The sound of her fury rose and fell. Such outbursts were actually rare, but when they happened Jessie wanted to hide, much the way she used to curl up under her bed out of the reach of thunderstorms.

"The nerve of her, to call the police on the parents of her daughter's best friend." She gave Jessie a hard stare. "Oh, don't you go all soft on me. I know what you're thinking. 'Used to be best friends,' right?" She practically spat the words as Jessie studied the terra cotta-tiled floor. "I wouldn't do that to people I hate," Sandy shouted. She hadn't been this angry since Shane's betrayal.

Jessie eyed her mother with a flash of disbelief, though she had to admit that calling the police was pretty bad. What if Phoebe *had* told her mom? But no, Feebs had been having fun. She'd played beer pong, had a few drinks, or at least she'd been carrying a beer around. And she'd been talking to Noah, had even made out with him.

Without saying anything, Jessie quietly left the table and went upstairs to her room. There she pulled out her cell phone and typed a message to Phoebe. *You there?*

She waited for a reply. Her head was hurting; the whole night had gotten to her, so she lay down on her bed and grabbed the fuzzy bunny Phoebe had given her during the summer. She rubbed a finger over the bunny's heart, which Phoebe had embroidered in rainbow colors, Jessie's favorite.

At once her phone buzzed. She grabbed it. A text message from Phoebe: *Don't call me,* it said. *I don't want to talk.*

Tears sprang to Jessie's eyes. What? How could she?

She threw the rabbit aside and bolted out of bed and down the stairs, two at a time. "I think you're right, Mom. About Phoebe."

Sandy was thrusting beer cans into the trash with wild energy. She didn't stop until she'd finished. "What makes you say that?" She peered at Jessie intently.

Jessie didn't want to tell her that she'd tried to contact Phoebe, not after what her mother had said earlier, but she told her anyway. "Then she texted me a message, saying not to call her." Despite her efforts not to, she burst out crying. "I was her friend, Mom."

Sandy came to her daughter and wrapped her arms around her. It felt good to hold her. "It's okay, sweetie puss. What comes around goes around."

A frightening glint lit up Sandy's eyes.

Jessie pulled away. "What are you going to do?"

"Me? *I'm* not going to do anything," she said, her mouth twisted into a wry smile.

Chapter Fifteen

Monday, November 10, 2008

At school on Monday morning, Phoebe got a series of looks and a few sniggers. It didn't take long before she caught a whiff of the buzz circulating the hallways: that either the cops had heard about the party or someone had called the police on the Littletons. The consensus, still unknown to Phoebe, was that most likely *someone* (and many fingers were pointing at Phoebe's mom) had called.

Until Emma filled her in, between second and third period, about everything but Phoebe's mom, Phoebe also hadn't known that the cops had dragged the Littletons down to the Montgomery County police station in Bethesda and that at least twenty kids, including Jessie and Emma, had been cited for underage drinking and assigned court dates. Phoebe stared at Emma and gave her friend a forlorn look. "I'm sorry," she said. And she was, though she didn't know that worse was yet to come.

Skyla had been spared, along with Dylan, Noah and several others, all of them picked up by Skyla's mother. When Emma mentioned Noah's name, the memory of their kiss returned to Phoebe, but she brushed it from her mind. If Shane had been there that kiss would not have happened. What should have been the most wonderful party had morphed into a nightmare.

Phoebe'd been isolated after arriving home that night. No phone, no computer, no TV. No electronic devices of any kind. Though her parents had spared her the humiliation of cancelling her birthday party, Isabel had heaped other demands on her. Community service hours (just as the kids who'd been caught would have to serve), a short research paper on teen drinking, additional chores, and other things TBD – to be determined. She'd wept pitiful tears and apologized for drinking – "I used poor judgment, I'm sorry," she'd said – but her mother had little sympathy for her. "One day without electronics, Phoebe, surely you'll survive."

On the way up to her room, Phoebe had muttered loud enough for her parents to hear: "Solitary confinement without privileges. My life ruined. AGAIN. I should just kill myself." In reality, she knew things could have been worse. She hadn't gotten grounded again, except for Sunday. And that was behind her now. And that meant she would see Shane in five days. She clung to his long ago promise that he'd come to her party, despite his no-show at Jessie's. She was sure he had a good excuse. Probably football related. She'd checked his football schedule for her birthday weekend and there were no games on Saturday to keep him away.

Over the course of the morning, she'd gotten a few nasty stares from those who'd received citations. Jessie passed by once and refused to speak to her. Phoebe, dreading any sort of confrontation, was actually grateful. Shortly before lunch, however, Jessie stopped her and, with a look that could drill holes into the wall, accused her mother of having called the police.

"My mom? No." She squared her shoulders and met Jessie's glowering stare. "Why would you even think that?"

"Because she hates my mom."

"What are you talking about?" Phoebe asked, though this time her ignorance was feigned.

"Oh, as if you don't know. I bet your mom called the cops. Why don't you ask her and see what she says." Jessie glared at her. "And what's with that text you sent me on Sunday? *Don't call me, I don't wanna talk?!*"

Then, pivoting on one foot, she turned and left Phoebe gaping after her. What?! She hadn't texted that message! Which meant what? That her mother had? Worse yet, *had* she called the police on the Littletons? No, she couldn't have. She'd been with her the entire time after they'd left the party. Nevertheless, the thought burrowed its way into her mind. Please, don't let it be true, she said to herself.

The rest of the day she made herself very small and avoided contact with just about everyone; even Skyla had shown little interest in sitting with her at lunch. When Phoebe told her about the exchange with Jessie, Skyla peered intently at her and asked, "Do you think your mom really did it?"

"No! I don't," Phoebe said in a defiant whisper.

Barely taking note of Phoebe's distress, she said, "I sure hope this doesn't affect our party. You don't think it will, do you?"

"Of course not, why would it?" Phoebe snapped, though she too worried something bad might happen. Like Shane not coming.

Like kids hating her again. She couldn't handle that.

In the pit of her stomach she got the same roller coaster feeling she'd had on and off all fall. How could things be so good one day and so awful the next? Why was life so unpredictable? She almost ran into the bathroom, the urge to cut was overwhelming.

On the five o'clock bus home from school, she gazed emptily out the window, buildings and traffic passing by in a blur. She clung to the idea that she would talk to Shane after school. No one would be home to stop her from using Facebook, except maybe Milly, and she would never interfere. At last she'd find out what had happened on Saturday, why Shane hadn't come to Jessie's, and he'd reassure her that he *would* show up at her party. He just had to. Then everything would be okay.

Chapter Sixteen

Late afternoon, at home in her well-appointed kitchen, Sandy paced. Thirty feet one direction, thirty feet back. Her rage from the previous day hadn't subsided; no, it had increased in intensity, like one of those tropical storms that gathers force off the Florida coast.

Muttering, she continued past white-painted French doors, past cabinets Bill had custom-built for her, past a crowded granite-topped island, past the handsome, carved wooden table, where she now stopped to take a bite of chocolate cake. She slid the morsel into her mouth, chewed thoughtfully, took a sip of coffee, then angled her fork and sliced off another piece.

As she stared outside into the darkness, all she could think of was the grief and humiliation that Isabel had heaped on her. Calling the cops on her and Bill was the last straw.

In the backyard, the tall branches of the leafless trees thrashed and bent beneath the fury of an invisible wind. Sandy stopped eating. She watched the wild towering oaks. Something raw and savage was taking place out there and it appealed to Sandy, though she couldn't say exactly why. She simply liked it. Just as she liked this cup of coffee and the last sliver of Chocolate Decadence awaiting her fork. She speared the cake, sank her teeth into it, then drained the coffee, fully savoring the taste of both.

A faint smile appeared on her perfectly heart-shaped lips. Another bite. Yum, so delicious. As she swallowed, an unbidden memory of Mrs. Eddinger arose.

A furrowed brow replaced Sandy's brief smile; her mouth, when not chewing, grew pursed, and her eyes narrowed. She wanted to tell her, "Mrs. E, I've been wronged, Bill has been wronged, Jessie's been wronged. It's not fair! Something has to be done."

If Mrs. E had been there, she might have said, "Now, Sandy, don't you think you're over-reacting, a little?" Tilting her head she often added, "Be careful. Remember, some things you can never take back. Right, honey?"

Occasionally, when Mrs. E said such things, Sandy had reconsidered and exercised self-restraint. She had often followed Mrs. E's suggestions, especially her time-honored edict: *Do unto others as you would have them do unto you.* Today, however, she only heard that strange, mocking voice turn the phrase on its head: *Do unto others as they do unto you!* and recalled that long ago unforgiving look on her mother's face when she'd ordered her out of the house. And the police, those awful police, as they'd barged into her home.

The wind blew. Sandy almost thought she could hear the trees scratching the dark heavens and the faint whisper of Mrs. E. Sandy reviewed the many good deeds she'd done over the past year, with which she'd hoped to gain entry into the tightly knit group of mothers.

So how was it that despite all her efforts she'd been rebuffed? Painfully so. Especially by Isabel.

She ticked off the slights one by one: Isabel had rejected her attempts at friendship, embarrassed her before the entire school, forbidden Phoebe to see Jessie. And now a call to the police. The entire mom population would be texting and gossiping about her. Isabel's insults mounted until she felt kicked around like someone's unwanted mutt.

The whispering ended, and, strangely, so did the roaring wind. A kind of quiet crowded around her large, extravagant house as if waiting to see what she might do. Tonight her resolve to spread goodwill failed to gain purchase. The time had come to "disappear" Shane. And on his way out, thought Sandy, he'll wreak a little havoc, a mess that Isabel will have to mop up.

So, what to write to Phoebe to end *Shane's* online courtship?

As she poured herself more coffee she noticed the time. A little after five o'clock. Phoebe would be home soon, if she wasn't already. Over the past month, Sandy had become intimately acquainted with the girl's habits.

She climbed two stories to her home office. By the time she reached the messy room, a little short of breath, she knew she had to lay off the cake and get back on her diet. *Slenderella* for breakfast, lunch and dinner. Otherwise she wouldn't fit into her holiday outfits, and she'd worked so hard all summer to get into a size six. Which these days, even she knew, meant a size eight. She couldn't bear to think she might need a size ten.

What she wouldn't give for a cigarette, it made dieting so much easier, but no, she'd kicked the habit with Bill, and for Jessie, formerly Phoebe's best friend. *Formerly.* That word unfolded another series of painful memories, hardening Sandy's resolve to punish Isabel.

Sitting at her computer, she tapped her acrylic turquoise nails against the keys: *I don't want to see you.* She stared at the words for several seconds, added *Ever,* and reread the private message to Phoebe. She stuck a finger in her mouth and chewed on the cuticle, trying to imagine the look on Phoebe's face when she saw that Shane had dumped her.

"Poor Phoebe!" she said aloud, and for an instant she actually meant it. Then she pressed "enter" and sent the seven-word message through cyberspace, unleashing her venom into the world.

She turned the radio on low and settled into her chair to wait, keeping half an ear on the front door for Jessie's arrival from school. Jess couldn't know what she was doing. She sat before Shane's Facebook page, eyeing the little symbol beside Phoebe's name, waiting patiently for it to light up, not unlike a cat waiting to pounce on an unsuspecting creature. She turned up the radio and tapped her fingers in rhythm to a Bob Marley song.

· ● · ● · ● ·

Then, finally, the first message from Phoebe appeared: *You're joking, right?*

Sandy's lips curled into a tight smile as her fingers skipped across the keys. *Not joking.*

Phoebe: *Shane, what are you talking about?*

Now Sandy's mind raced, rat-a-tat like a machine gun. "What am I talking about?" Sandy said aloud. "*This* is what I'm talking about." She wrote, *Your mother called the police on Jessie's parents...you tattled about the booze at the party! And then the Littletons were arrested!* And that's only the half of it, she thought.

Phoebe: *How do you know that stuff when you weren't even there?*

Sandy froze. What could she say? The cursor hovered over the little red button. Ready to close Facebook. She sat up straighter and took a breath. *Don't you worry how; I just do,* she wrote.

A few seconds later, Phoebe wrote: *Why didn't you come to Jessie's? You promised.*

Hmm...Sandy thought Why? And then it came to her: *Because I heard you've been messing around with Dylan.*

Phoebe: *Who told you that?* Sandy stared at the words before realizing the obvious. The time had come to write on Phoebe's Facebook wall, where everyone could see what *Shane* was saying and join in the fun. *I don't tell on my friends,* Sandy wrote with smug satisfaction.

Phoebe, still private messaging, wrote back: *It has to be Jessie, but if it is, she's lying.*

Sandy couldn't believe how easy Phoebe was making this. Again she posted her response on Phoebe's wall: *You're calling Jessie a liar?*

Sandy saw that in a pathetic attempt to defend herself, Phoebe had finally switched to making her responses public: *No, I meant if she said that about me, she's not telling the truth. Why don't you believe me?*

Let me count the ways, Sandy thought. How about this: *I don't trust you. I heard you said Jessie was fat and no boy wants her, especially Dylan. That's bitchy. Nobody likes bitchy girls.*

This provoked a slew of jeering posts from Phoebe's *friends* just as Sandy had anticipated. She pumped her fist into the air with glee.

That's not true, Phoebe wrote and then begged for a chance to talk on the phone.

Sandy could almost hear the pleading in her voice. "Not happening, girl. Never happen! You got that?" She could imagine the tears and the wailing, while outside the trees tossed about.

· ● · ● · ● · ● ·

Again waiting for Phoebe to respond, Sandy imagined, as she had many times before, being invited by Gail, or Jane, or Liz, or even Amanda to one of their girl dinners or lunches. Perhaps being married to Ron, not Bill, would increase her chances of such an invitation. She had no intention of leaving Bill – she loved him, she did – but she enjoyed the fantasy nevertheless.

Maybe I'll give old Ron a call, she thought. She hadn't spoken to Isabel's husband in a few days, and she loved titillating him, which also genuinely turned her on. She touched Ron's number and waited to hear his slightly Bostonian accent.

The women she envied swam through her mind. Maybe she'd organize a luncheon. But she knew they wouldn't come, not after what Isabel had done, tarnishing her reputation yet again. Sandy felt like a pariah, a bit of flotsam floating downstream, never quite reaching the riverbank, never gaining access to all the action. It seemed as if history were repeating itself.

Shane, shocked by her admission that she'd failed to use contraceptives, and looking at her as if she were crazy, had said, "You think the prom king should go to the prom with a pregnant girl?" He smirked. "I don't think so."

She'd made the additional mistake early on of having confided in him about Les – not that she'd had sex with him, but that he lusted after her – because Shane's final comment to her had been: "How do I even know it's mine? Could be his." She wanted to slap

him. The comment had frightened her, though, because she realized it could be true.

A voice startled her. It was coming through the cell phone.
Someone had answered her call. For a fleeting moment she saw
Shane's image. It took her a second to gather her wits. Then she
said, "Hi, Ron," in her most alluring tone. "How ya been?"

Chapter Seventeen

Isabel couldn't believe Phoebe's stressed out call, the way she'd just hung up, and then her refusal to answer when she phoned her back. She kept glancing in her rearview mirror to see if the cop who'd stopped her a few minutes earlier was behind her, but she didn't see him. How could she have left the scene? Now she stepped on the gas though she kept an eye on the odometer. And that gibbous moon, staring down on her, a mocking grin on its misshapen face.

Oh, God, she could kick herself for having called the police on Saturday night. She always said you shouldn't do things in the heat of anger. Now she'd have to explain everything to Phoebe. She tapped their home number and waited for someone to answer. Despite two more calls to Phoebe, plus one to Ron, she got no answer. *Damn it!*

· ● · ● · ● ·

Ron pulled away from the curb where he'd parked for about five minutes while he and Sandy spoke. She'd made him rock hard, and now he was pounding his hand on the steering wheel to a Stones' tune. "Who says you can't always get what you want?" he shouted. With a smooth sweeping motion, he turned the steering wheel hand over hand, and headed north on 16th Street away from the *Washington Post's* offices.

"I am on a roll," he said, punctuating each word, and then shouting, "On-a-fucking-roll!"

At the top of his game, that's how he felt. He'd just gotten approval from the White House for an interview with President Obama! Christ! I've got a great job, great kids, perfect everything, he thought. Well, maybe not everything. He was having a little trouble balancing a wife with the notion of a fuck buddy. He'd just set up "lunch" with Sandy for Friday.

A wife and a mistress didn't really go together, but he knew guys who did it. And he couldn't stop thinking that she was a vixen. He'd always love Isabel, but he wanted to fuck this babe. The honk of a car reminded him that his driving had slowed to a crawl. He sped up and turned his thoughts to dinner, wondering what Milly had made.

· ● · ● · ● ·

Phoebe fought back her tears. Jessie and Shane had been right. Her mother *had* called the cops. And now everyone would HATE her for what her mother had done. Worst of all, Shane was no longer interested in meeting her and he WASN'T coming to her party! She'd NEVER get to know him. She'd never be his "number 10!"

Phoebe marched over to the dollhouse and retrieved the box cutter, then marched back and saw what Skyla had written: *This better not wreck our party. What the heck did you do? And your mom!!? Whoa!? So uncool.*

Oh, please, not again, Phoebe thought as she stared at Skyla's note. Not another year like the last one. And now this one seemed infinitely worse.

How low! You are such a piece of trash! someone else wrote.

Phoebe gaped at the words when suddenly a post appeared from Vanessa, a former Woodmont friend of hers and Jessie's, who she hadn't seen since the summer: *You're a cutter! I saw the scars. How weird! What's wrong with you?*

"No! Please," she whimpered. Vanessa and Emma were the only girls besides Jessie who knew about her cutting. And now her secret was exposed! How could she?

Oooh, ick. How sick.

Shane: *God, you're such a loser!*

Vanessa: *Your mom called the police! If I were you I'd leave home or slash my wrists. Get it?*

The words on the screen grew into a grating noise. She closed her eyes and covered her ears. This can't be happening. Please make it stop. When she opened them, she saw another note from Shane: *The world would be better off without you. Don't you know that?*

Phoebe slammed the computer shut. Somewhere in the distance the phone rang. She vaulted off her bed and ripped Shane's photos off the bulletin board, the thumbtacks flying across the room. She tore his image into shreds, allowing the pieces to flutter onto the thickly carpeted floor.

· ● · ● · ● ·

Engrossed in sending Phoebe one last message, Sandy jumped at the sound of Jessie's voice. "What the heck are you doing, Mom?"

Sandy hadn't heard her arrive. Now she felt Jess right behind her. "What are you talking about?" she said without turning around. Her fingers fumbled with the cursor and finally managed to close Facebook.

"Mommm!"

"Oh, stop your yammering," Sandy said, keeping her back to Jessie.

"How'd you do that? How could you write a message from Shane?" Jessie asked, a rare urgency in her tone. "Turn around! Answer me!" shouted Jessie.

Sandy should have known that it would only take an instant for the neurons and synapses in Jessie's brain to put two and two together: Shane hadn't come to her party because there was no Shane. Because she, her mother, was Shane! Which is why she was writing messages that appeared to come from Shane.

In those same few moments, Sandy collected herself and rotated the swivel chair to face her daughter, all traces of guilt and anxiety erased from her countenance. She, Sandy, had rectified an injustice. Jessie, on the other hand, looked like she might puke.

"Sit down, honey, we need to talk," Sandy said.

· ● · ● · ● ·

In a trance, almost as if sleepwalking, Phoebe entered the bathroom without closing the door and without switching on the light. She laid the box cutter on the edge of the tub and began peeling off her clothes. One by one, each article fell to the floor as water splashed and filled the tub. Light from the hallway spilled inside, illuminating a vertical slice of the darkened room. The water shimmered as she entered. Shadows hovered and climbed the walls like so many wraiths.

The words *you're such a loser* and *I don't want to see you ever* cycled through Phoebe's mind. *The world would be better off without you.* A shiver ran through her body as she sank into the tub. Steam rose into the air, obscuring the dim light in the room. She lay there for a few minutes, tears seeping from her eyes, dripping down her cheeks, and running along her slender throat. Everyone hated her. Everyone.

She lifted the box cutter and twisted the dull metal tool in the air before dragging the blade across her left wrist. The gash separated the skin. She stared at the open wound with cold detachment and waited for the blood to appear. At first there was no sensation, then, as always, the pain of the cut overtook the thoughts in her head, and all her confusion began to recede, like a wave rushing back out to sea. But this time relief lasted only a few precious moments. Then the cacophony of voices assaulted her anew. *Ooh ick, you're sick. I never want to see you. You're a liar. A slut. We don't trust you. We hate you. Why don't you just end it? The world would be better off without you.*

Phoebe balled her left hand into a fist and made several more slices across her thin bluish veins. The skin curled open and more blood pulsed to the surface. She tilted her wrist and watched dark pearls of liquid splash into the water – drip, drip, drip – then spread like ink. She'd actually never seen ink in water, except once on a show about squids and the way they squirt the toxic substance at their enemies, giving them time to disappear behind an ever expanding bluish-black cloud.

· • · • · • ·

Isabel maneuvered the car along the curves of Rock Creek Parkway. She pressed harder on the gas pedal, watching the speedometer climb to fifty, half an eye on her rearview mirror, the other on her iPhone. "Damn it," she said aloud, fumbling with the icons, touching the wrong one, banging "end," striking another, wishing she'd learned to use voice commands. Finally, she tapped Ron's name and listened to the phone ring. "Damn it," she said viciously, "answer the fucking phone!"

· • · • · • ·

Driving north on Wisconsin, Ron glanced at his cell reluctant to answer Isabel's call. But, finally, he turned down the volume on the radio. "What's up?"

"Are you home yet?" Isabel's tone was urgent, borderline hysterical.

"No, what's wrong?" Since Saturday's fiasco, things had been touchy between them. He'd made it clear he thought calling the police had been unnecessary, and in an added imperious tone told her it could have negative ramifications for Phoebe, a comment that had been met with stony silence.

"Well, how far are you?" she insisted.

"A couple of blocks," he said, his voice gaining an edge. And it wasn't entirely true. "What's going on?"

Isabel filled him in on the panic-stricken conversation she'd had with Phoebe, and her subsequent refusal to answer the phone.

"Okay, calm down," he said, even though he felt like lashing out. Why *had* she called the fucking police? Even now he was tempted to say, I told you so. Goddamn it! On the other hand, he thought she was over-reacting.

"I'm heading home," he heard Isabel say, "but I want you to know that I got, uh, stopped for running a red light." Her voice sounded breathy, not like herself. "I left the scene before the policeman returned with my license."

"You're kidding?"

"No, I'm dead serious."

"Christ, Izzy."

"I know. I'll deal with it later. But if he catches up to me before I get home, well, you'll know where I am." She managed a little laugh.

"Christ, Izzy."

"You already said that. Just hurry up."

An epithet was on the tip of his tongue, but she'd already ended the call. The needle on the speedometer of his SUV edged up. If anything happened to Phoebe, he'd never forgive Isabel.

· ● · ● · ● ·

A few minutes later, Isabel wondered if Ron had arrived home yet. She'd forgotten to ask his exact location. He'd said a couple of blocks. But was he really that close?

Isabel made good progress on the parkway. A little surprising since it was rush hour. She even passed several cars, completely ignoring the solid double yellow lines, and turned off at Porter Street. Only a few more blocks. At the intersection of Porter and Connecticut she again lucked out. A place where congestion was a near certainty this time of day, she only had to wait through two changes of the traffic light, where normally she had to wait twice that long.

Less than a block from home though, she could see the flash of red lights glowing on the tall oaks surrounding her house. Of course, she should have realized the police would be waiting for her. The cop had her license, which contained her address. For an instant, as adrenalin rushed through her veins, instinct told her to flee, but in the next her rational lawyerly mind breached the wall of fear, and she knew what to do.

Still, anxiety gripped her. Her hands clutched the steering wheel. She told herself to buck up, that it was now or later, and coming home would at least illustrate that she'd been honest earlier when she told the cop she was rushing to get to her daughter.

However, when she pulled up, not only were two DC police cars – flashing lights and all – blocking the driveway in front of her house, but an ambulance also stood out front and numerous neighbors were gawking nearby. Just then the door of the house opened, an EMT backing out, carrying one end of a stretcher with a white sheet draped over a human form.

Isabel leapt out of the car. A guttural cry rose up her throat. "Noooo! Noooo!" she screamed. "Please, God, noooo!"

Part Three
Justice

Chapter One

Wednesday, November 12, 2008

Light fell in patches on the floor beside Isabel. Soon fall would officially give way to winter. Though in some ways she dreaded it, there were other aspects she had always liked: the cool weather, snow floating past the solarium windows, everything frozen, in hibernation, as if you could suspend time. As if you could stop time altogether and reverse the order of things. If only she could. She would give away all their money and all her possessions; she would give up her job and stay at home; she would give her life, gladly, if only she could get Phoebe back.

As if in keeping with some inner rhythm, tears pooled in her eyes and a sob rose from the depths of her soul. She allowed herself to cry for several minutes before mindlessly drawing a tissue from the box on the small wicker table. The image that kept swimming to the forefront of her mind was of Phoebe, lying in the Intensive Care Unit, tubes extending from her mouth and arms, sheets shrouding her body, already as if only half-alive and being readied for the next world.

Then, in an almost ritualized fashion, Isabel wiped her eyes and blew her nose, and repeated a quick prayer, her mantra: *Please, God, save her. Please.*

The computer sat in Isabel's lap, waiting patiently. She was afraid to open her email account. She couldn't believe how many people had sent notes over the past two days saying how sorry they were and asking if they could help, a heartfelt one from Liz Van-Dorn and even Sandy Littleton, who'd signed hers with: "Love to you and Ron, from Sandy, Jessie and Bill."

As much as Isabel resented her, she was both surprised and appreciative that the woman had had the graciousness to write. Though she hadn't heard from Jessie, she did receive messages, calls, and cards from Emma, Skyla, and a dozen other girls, including a couple who had been involved in the piling on of insults and taunts. She couldn't bring herself to respond to the latter, not until she'd carefully considered what to say.

Although each person had been alone at their computer during the hazing, mob mentality had ruled and drawn out the vicious, dark side of each participant. It was something she thought about constantly. Yet what could she possibly say or do?

In the two days since the nightmare event, the number of email messages had mounted to the point that she'd stopped reading most of them, much less answering them. In that time she'd discovered it was far easier to use Phoebe's Facebook as a means of communicating to the world of well wishers, nosy neighbors, annoying problem-solving control freaks, the outright unabashed voyeurs, and to some extent even her friends and Phoebe's.

She stared at Phoebe's Facebook photo. The curve of her full lips, wavy hair tucked behind tiny ears, the bashful smile. Such innocence, such vulnerability, such naiveté. That in contrast to the cruelty of the girls and boys who'd bullied and shamed her, and the horrible twisted Shane, who'd led the charge, whoever he was.

Yesterday, she'd called Walter Johnson High, only to discover that no one with his name was registered at the school. When she spoke with the principal and told him what had happened, he immediately promised to do what he could. Not long after sending him a copy of "Shane's" photo, he confirmed there was definitely no such student at "Walter J."

As words began to form in her mind, Isabel typed a note on Phoebe's Facebook wall: *This is Phoebe's mother, Isabel Winthrop, writing this. Ron and I want to thank all of you for your concern, your notes, and prayers. We remain in a state of shock and disbelief at what happened, as you can imagine, and we do appreciate your desire to help. What would be most helpful is to contact us if you know anything about Shane, the boy who initiated the bullying against our daughter. If you do, please call us at our home number and leave us a message if we don't answer. We check regularly.*

An update on our Phoebe: she's still in a coma in Georgetown University Hospital. She hesitated, trying to determine what else to say.

Without fail, at moments like this, she was catapulted back into the hospital waiting room. Reliving each horrible moment. Sitting and waiting, pacing and waiting. She and Ron in a state of limbo. In purgatory. When Dr. Bailey had finally entered the room, surrounded by a coterie of interns and residents, consternation had been etched across her brow and Isabel's stomach sank. She was sure Dr. Bailey was about to pronounce the time of Phoebe's death.

"Phoebe's condition is very, very serious," she said. "Blood loss, as you can imagine, was extensive. We've transfused her with several units of blood, stitched up and bandaged her wounds, and put her on an IV, but so far she's unresponsive. In other words, she remains unconscious. She's in a coma. As far as how much damage was done, either to organs, like her kidneys, liver and so on, or to her brain due to lack of oxygen, that's hard to tell right now."

Isabel and Ron stood there mutely. For once, neither of them had control over events. It didn't matter how smart or rich they were. "What might be reasonable to expect, Dr. Bailey, I mean in the way of recovery?" Ron had managed.

"It's hard to know, everyone responds differently." The doctor gazed at each of them. "Young women her age and in her state of health, with comparable blood loss are revived a majority of the time." Then she lowered her voice, and Isabel noticed that people had turned to stare at them. "The question we can't answer is how long her brain was deprived of oxygen... about how long she was in an unconscious state before the emergency medical team arrived. That would have a bearing on recovery."

Isabel tried to do a mental calculation of how much time might have elapsed between her last call to Phoebe and when she'd entered the tub. She assumed some minutes had passed after the call and Phoebe's last Facebook entry, but she'd have to check Phoebe's computer for that. Then several more minutes before the idea even occurred to her, more time to fill the tub, and then how long until she entered the tub and cut herself...she could hardly bear to think of it.

"It couldn't have been very long," Isabel said tearfully, "but I can get a more accurate measure after we go home and check her computer." Not only that, but she'd compute how long it took to fill the tub and find out the exact time when Ron called 911. One statistic she knew: she'd arrived home almost 20 minutes after last talking with Phoebe. For some reason, she'd checked her watch.

The following day, among other things, she'd determined that Phoebe could have been unconscious anywhere from a couple of minutes to seven or eight, which really wasn't very helpful, since each minute counted in the most horrific fashion. She knew that the longer the time without oxygen to the brain the worse the prognosis.

Now she thought, *Oh, dear God, please let it have been a very short time.* Then, after staring outside at the barren trees and sodden sky, she continued writing the Facebook message, but first adjusted the part she'd already written about Shane:

We welcome any assistance you can give us to find "Shane," who we discovered does not attend Walter Johnson High School, as he claimed. Please pass along any ideas or leads you might have. All will remain confidential. Finally, I want everyone to know that we will not rest until we have found Shane and he has been exposed for his cruel and vile behavior, and that he is brought to justice. Thank you, Isabel Winthrop and Ron Murrow.

She studied what she'd written before making it final. The birthday party had been cancelled; she didn't need to mention that, did she? After a few minor edits, she struck the "enter" key, releasing the message into cyberspace. The good and evil of social networking.

The previous day she had contacted Facebook and reported that a "cyberbullying episode" had occurred on their site, the main points of which she outlined then detailed. She went on to explain that she was an attorney and Phoebe's mother, attempting to find the culprit, the leader of the pack, someone with the Facebook name of Shane, whose real identity she hoped to uncover, and that she would appreciate their assistance in this regard. Though the day would come when she'd demand they remove or ban "Shane" from Facebook – it shocked her that he hadn't yet disappeared from the site – for the time being she explained it was a convenient way to send "him" messages and hopefully track down the real person behind his page. They agreed to help in any way that "did not violate privacy laws."

When she read this response, her eyebrows shot up. Screw your privacy laws, what about my child? After they acknowledged reading the awful things that had been said to Phoebe, "the verbal exchange" as they called it, she'd made a copy and erased the hateful posts that had led her daughter to attempt suicide.

Having digested every word on "Facebook Safety," she now knew that she could remove any of Phoebe's "friends" from her Facebook page if she wanted to, but for the time being she left them. She was sure the minute a post went up from Phoebe (or in this case, from herself), everyone would be reading it and then talking about it, though most likely through private messaging. No one could keep people from gossiping, and she thought that perhaps this now worked to her advantage.

Before ending her session, she placed two fingers to her lips, kissed them, then touched them to Phoebe's image on the computer screen. Her poor baby's life hung in the balance. Tears began to form in her eyes again, and she had to take several deep breaths to keep from breaking down for the hundredth time that day. In a few minutes she'd go to the hospital and relieve Ron so he could pick up Jackson at Woodmont. She had come home earlier to change clothes and gather a few books and magazines to take with her, though she suspected they'd go unread.

Her life now consisted of maintaining a 24-hour vigil at Phoe-be's bedside and saying silent prayers around the clock. Though she attended church rarely, Isabel believed in God, in a higher force. That and one other thing fueled Isabel's ability to keep go-ing: Justice, with a capital J. She would make whoever did this pay.

· ● · ● · ● ·

Sandy panicked when she read the post from Isabel. Her body literally quaked with fear. She stared at Shane's face. "You fucker," she said aloud. "You fucked me again. Goddamn it, I hate you!" She wanted to throw something at his stupid face. Her hand landed on a paperweight perched atop an unwieldy stack of papers and fold-ers, but she knew destroying her computer solved nothing and that she needed to keep her wits. Her mother's haranguing voice rattled about in her brain. *Hope you're happy with what you've done, you little harlot.* Sandy ran her fingers through her hair, grabbed a fist-ful, and tugged it back. Hard. She released a feral groan.

How was she going to remove Shane from Facebook? It ter-rified her that somehow someone would be able to trace his page back to her through the separate e-mail she'd set up. She needed to erase that trail. But she was no more capable of that than fixing a gourmet meal. What could she do? Jessie would refuse to help and she couldn't hire someone, for who could she possibly trust? Her thoughts gyrated like images in a kaleidoscope, each one scattering in a dozen directions. She sat transfixed, unable to make a deci-sion. Could someone really discover she was behind Shane?

The need to destroy all evidence was paramount, to the point that she barely gave Phoebe a thought. Nothing beyond: how could that stupid girl have done such a thing? Provoking suicide certainly hadn't been her intention. That counted for something, didn't it?

Sandy wanted to call Bill, but knew that was a non-starter. If he found out about what she'd done, he'd be furious. He'd kill her. Well, not literally. But he might divorce her and she really couldn't handle that. Which reminded her. She was supposed to have a date with Ron on Friday, the one they'd made while she was saying all those mean things to Phoebe. She couldn't imagine he'd remember, though maybe she should write to him. But what would she say? She toyed with a few variations of the same email until she heard the front door.

As she expected, when Jessie came home, she again resisted helping her. The painful session was not without recrimination. "Mom, you're totally unbelievable. You know that, right? You're the worst, you really are," she said, a disgusted baleful expression on her face. Sandy kept a deaf ear to her reproach.

"What if people find out?" Jessie said in a whiny tone.

At which point, Sandy swore her to secrecy. Well, not exactly, but she pointed out the downside to people knowing it was *Jessie's* mom who had perpetrated this. Emphasis on Jessie.

Chapter Two

Thursday, November 13, 2008

The following late afternoon, at Georgetown Hospital, in the hallway outside the ICU, Isabel saw a young man sitting in one of the plastic chairs, bent over, cradling his head in his hands. She wondered what ill fate had befallen him or his family, when, as she brushed past him, he glanced up. "Oh, hi," he said, his red-rimmed eyes scrutinizing her. "You're Phoebe's mom, right?"

"Yes, I am. And you are?"

"Noah. I'm a friend of Phoebe's at Georgetown." He looked as if he might cry.

"I see." So this was the boy she'd kept her daughter from going to the dance with. Oh, God, why had she done that? She almost broke down at the thought.

"How is she?" he asked softly.

"Not very good, Noah. It's nice of you to come." She wasn't sure what else to say.

He grew thoughtful. "I want to help. Is there anything I can do, Mrs. Murrow?"

Coming from this boy, the name that usually caused her to wince now didn't bother her in the slightest. In fact, she welcomed it. Mrs. Murrow. Somehow it underscored and strengthened her kinship to Phoebe and Ron, despite his recent coolness toward her. Why *had* the name bothered her so much in the past?

"All right, Noah, I'll let you know." She was about to turn away when she stopped. "Actually, there may be something. I'm trying to find out who that Shane person is. Was. Apparently he's not a student at Walter Johnson." She thought a moment. "I can't understand why someone would prey on my daughter that way, or do such a thing to anyone, for that matter. You wouldn't have any idea who he is?"

He shook his head no, but then something seemed to occur to him and his eyes lit up. "I might be able to find out though. I'm pretty good with computers, and if I can't I know some guys who are—" he hesitated, "—well, who are even better. Would you mind?"

She looked at him gratefully. "Not in the least. You have our number and I imagine you're in the school directory?" She glanced at the ICU door. Something was tugging at her to get inside.

He nodded, then gazed up at her bashfully. "Uh, is there any chance I could see Phoebe? Just for a minute? There's something I want to tell her." He stopped, again appearing as though he were on the verge of tears.

She felt like embracing him, but deemed such physicality in-appropriate, after all, she hardly knew him, so she merely placed her hand on his arm. "They have pretty strict rules around here, but let me check," she said softly. "Maybe we can get you in. Wait here a moment."

· ● · ● · ● ·

Though Mrs. Murrow's departure and return took only a couple of minutes, to Noah, it seemed forever, and he worried that access to Phoebe wouldn't be allowed. Then he heard her say, "It's okay. You can come."

Along the way, she whispered to him. "I hope you realize this is not the Phoebe you know." He nodded, stepping carefully around an amalgam of machinery, medical equipment and IV poles that hovered like metal angels at each ICU bed. Together they threaded their way between visitors, nurses, and patients, the latter mostly appearing to be asleep or comatose.

Still, he wasn't prepared for what he saw when they arrived at her bedside. He swallowed and said a quiet hello to her father, then stood there awkwardly. Phoebe's chest rose ever so slightly with each breath the ventilator pumped into her lungs, a ghastly hollow sound. He could hardly bring himself to look at her face, especially with the breathing tube contraption taped firmly into place around her mouth. He listened to the blip and whirr of the electronic equipment that monitored Phoebe's vital signs and kept her alive. Her mother was right, this wasn't the Phoebe he knew; he just hoped the real Phoebe still lived in there, somewhere.

He'd seen a show once where someone snuck into a hospital room at night and flipped each machine off in succession, then watched the person die. That someone had loved the patient, a girl, but knew being a vegetable wasn't what she would have wanted.

Noah glanced first at Isabel then Ron, as if for approval, before speaking to the girl he'd kissed less than a week ago. "I'm here, Phoebe. It's me, Noah, your friend. Everybody says 'hi,' and they hope you'll get better soon." His voice faltered, and he paused to regain control. "If you want, I'll come visit you, and read to you. I'll get the books you like. *To Kill a Mockingbird* is one of them, right? Anyway, if it's okay with your parents I'll start tomorrow."

He forced himself to look at her face with its disconcerting deathly pallor. "Maybe if you can hear me, squeeze my hand. If you can't, like maybe you're too weak, that's okay, don't worry about it." He waited, but there was no response. Not that he'd really expected one, although he'd read that people in comas could hear – it was the last of the senses to go. Still, he had his doubts.

"Skyla said she really wants to come too, so maybe she'll bring *People* Magazine and read to you about all the latest *important* news." A faint smile appeared on his lips because he knew that if Phoebe could hear him, she'd laugh. As he continued to hold her limp right hand, he noticed the bandages around her left wrist. He couldn't help staring at them. Then, sensing Phoebe's parents' eyes on him, he quickly averted his gaze.

"Thank you for coming, Noah. It really means a lot to us," Mr. Murrow said. And Isabel added, "Please let Phoebe's friends know how grateful we are for thinking of her. We truly appreciate it."

With determination etched into his youthful brow, Noah said, "We'll find who did this, Mr. and Mrs. Murrow. I promise."

· ● · ● · ● ·

After he left, Isabel sat down beside Phoebe and wept. Noah's visit had reached into the softest part of her and reignited all the guilt she'd experienced the past two days. Had it been all her fault that Phoebe had done this? Had she been too hard on Phoebe? Should she not have grounded her, or at least let her go to the dance with Noah? Should she have refrained from calling the police on the Littletons? This bothered her most as it seemed to have unleashed Shane's hatefulness. Why? It didn't make sense. But then, when had bullying ever made sense?

Isabel second-guessed herself on a dozen fronts and struggled with these thoughts as she began massaging her daughter's right arm and fingers. Though logically she knew Phoebe's suicide attempt hadn't been *all* her fault, the answer to the other questions seemed to be yes. And that placed the blame firmly at her feet.

She rubbed Phoebe gently and vigorously, in part because the nurses had informed her and Ron that it was important to keep stimulating Phoebe's circulation, and also to move her limbs to inhibit muscle atrophy. Then again, she'd overheard a resident whisper that it gave parents something to do. Real muscle atrophy took months before it became serious. Still, it made her feel useful and allowed her to touch her daughter.

Ron looked haggard and spent, his eyes red from lack of sleep and his own bouts of crying. He remained beside Phoebe opposite Isabel. Though he hadn't said anything, Isabel sensed his anger and resentment toward her. She wished he'd just speak plainly, but mostly he was silent. "Christ," he said, "this sucks."

Isabel nodded. "Poor baby," she said, as she continued to massage Phoebe's left leg.

"I'll be all right."

"I didn't mean you," she said, an edge in her voice.

"Right. Guess not."

"I'm sorry," she said, though she wasn't. How could he possibly think she was referring to him? And yet she knew his behavior wasn't entirely out of character. Plenty of times Ron had acted childish and self-centered, though perhaps not unlike many men, she decided.

To stanch the flow of such negative thoughts, Isabel turned her mind to the only thing she cared about now besides her baby getting better, and that was to develop a strategy for her latest case: finding her daughter's predator. "Look, we need to find out what laws exist that can be used to prosecute people for doing what he did. Have you run across anything for that piece you mentioned you were working on?"

Ron scowled at her. "What piece?"

"The one on social networking," she said, glad to have something to occupy her mind, even if only momentarily.

"Are you kidding? How would I have had time for that?"

"Well, I would have thought—"

"Thought what? That I'd be hard at work investigating the pitfalls of social networking while our daughter is...is lying here...like this? Jesus, Iz."

Her finger shot to her lips, indicating he should keep his voice down. "Let's not argue. I just think we owe it to her to find out who this Shane person is and bring him to justice. I, for one, will not rest until we do."

"A lot of good that does." His lip curled in disgust.

"What are you saying?"

"I just think we need to stay focused on her. We can deal with that later. Anyway, it won't change what's happened. Why are you so intent on that? What does it accomplish? Where does revenge ever get anyone?"

"I can't believe you're saying that. Anyway it's justice, not revenge. Doesn't Phoebe deserve that? Maybe you'd better go pick up Jackson," she said brusquely.

Ignoring Ron's heavy sigh as he lifted himself out of his chair, she turned her attentions back to Phoebe, listening to the steady blip, ping and whirr of the machines that were keeping her daughter alive. The mechanical sound of her breathing.

After he left, she grew teary-eyed because they'd snapped at one another exactly when they needed to be supportive, and then she experienced a growing inner steeliness, a quality she'd always possessed, but now it felt like a hardening shell that would protect her from the feelings that threatened to drown her in self-pity and guilt, that threatened to immobilize her. She couldn't afford that, not when so much was at stake. She would find Shane and bring him to justice. And she'd do it with or without Ron, with or without the justice system.

Chapter Three

Monday, November 17, 2008

Ron drove slowly, following the road that wound through Rock Creek Park, noticing the thinning canopy and the increased light that always came with November. He knew homeless people roamed and even lived in the park and wondered if the lack of foliage gave them fewer places to hide. He had an insane desire to hide too, but in his case it was from people's glances and stares. He'd barely started at the *Post* and already he was the source of water cooler gossip. The kind of notoriety no one wanted. It was human nature for people to talk, but he couldn't help wondering what they were saying. All the wrong things, he was sure.

On Friday he'd stopped in for a few hours, grabbed a cup of coffee and in the hallway overheard someone saying, "Hey, d'you hear that awful thing about Murrow's daughter?" He fled to his office, a little stunned and off-kilter, and turned to his voice mails, hoping to regain his bearings.

The first message caught him off guard: "Hi Ron, this is Sandy Littleton. I'm sorry we won't have a chance to talk today." That's when he remembered they'd planned to meet. "I just want you to know how sorry I am about Phoebe." She spoke in a soft baby doll voice. "How is she? Anything I can do just let me know. Can't imagine what you're going through, so if you need a break, a shoulder to cry on, call me."

The moment he'd finished listening to her message, all he could think about was meeting up with her and literally crying on her shoulder. Since the *event* – he didn't know what else to call it – he'd felt like a fish without oxygen, trapped in a house that provided only dark, somber reminders of what had happened on the third floor. And seeing Isabel only seemed to make matters worse. Then, being in the hospital, a stark depressing place filled with sick and dying people, he could hardly stand it. He needed a break, he deserved one, he told himself, and now after a long weekend he was counting on Sandy for a breath of fresh air.

Finding a place to park on this slightly remote stretch of road alongside the Potomac, especially at this time of year, offered little challenge. Many spaces were available. At the last moment before exiting the car he grabbed his shades and slipped them on. Of course the sun shone, but it was a protective maneuver, in case someone passing by knew him.

Jack's Boathouse was empty, as he'd imagined. Being early, he sat down on one of several benches to wait. Lanterns of various colors were strung along the small wooden structure, a thriving, fun establishment during the season when it was open. Both a place where you could rent a paddleboat or a canoe and also have a drink. Ron had brought the kids here to go canoeing. And he and Isabel had ridden bikes on the nearby Crescent Trail, which began just a few yards further down the road.

He wished he hadn't thought of Isabel just then. She was the last thing he wanted to think about. What had happened to Phoebe, more or less, could be traced back to her. Several times, he'd come close to saying so, but it would be cruel and at the last second he'd stopped himself.

Sunlight danced on the river, a sight that today did not stir him. Instead it reminded him of the stained water in the bathtub, Phoebe's body floating there; he'd been sure she was dead. His little girl. Dead. A sob erupted from deep within.

He startled when a hand gently caressed his shoulder. Instead of swallowing his tears, Ron turned and buried his head in Sandy's midriff. All the pain he'd choked back erupted into an endless stream with Sandy stroking his head and muttering, "There, there, it's all right. I'm here. I'm here. Let it out."

· ● · ● · ● · ·

Georgetown Academy's modern, high-tech performing arts center had been constructed a few years earlier with the generous $200 million donation of two dozen donors, all of them alumni. On days when there were guest speakers or special meetings it alternated as an assembly hall. While normally going to and from such events served as an excuse for incessant chatter among the girls and rowdiness among the boys, today's assembly featured a subdued group of students. Almost funereal. They trudged into the large, expensively-furnished auditorium and took their seats without being chided.

There was Skyla and her troupe of friends looking appropriately downcast; Dylan and Noah and Emma, though she was without her usual sidekick, Jessie, who had not been seen or heard from in several days; and the rest of the ninth grade, minus a few absentees. In other words, all the kids who knew Phoebe, and all of them aware of what had transpired.

Noah was lost in thought about Phoebe when he noticed Jessie plop down into the chair on his right. He frowned. In his mind, her hair-brained logic around the dance had caused Phoebe to lose faith in him. But even more than that, on hearing of the exchange that led to the attack on Phoebe, which revolved around some supposed thing Phoebe had said about Jessie, and then blaming her for the police thing, well, he really wanted nothing more to do with her. The whole thing was so lame. She was bad news and he turned his head away. He almost got up to switch seats, but just then Ms. Kendall cleared her throat and tapped the microphone on the stage, imploring a few last stragglers to "grab a seat, any seat, and listen up."

Alison Kendall, neatly dressed in a navy blue pantsuit and white silk collarless blouse, stood behind the lectern, adjusted the microphone, and began. "We are here to discuss an awful event that occurred a week ago. Actually that's an understatement. It was a horrific event." She scanned her audience to secure everyone's attention. A few students shifted in their seats.

"First, let me give you a brief update on Phoebe Murrow's condition because I know that you are all concerned, as are all of the teachers and staff at Georgetown Academy. At the present time, she remains in a coma, and the doctors have no way of knowing whether or not she will survive, and if she does, whether or not there will be brain damage.

"I imagine this is difficult for you to hear, but I tell you this bluntly because it's important that you recognize people's behavior has consequences. Extreme and disastrous consequences even." She stopped and allowed her eyes to sweep from one side of the large room to the other.

She continued. "Nothing can change what has happened to Phoebe, but we *can* take steps to prevent something like this from happening again. So...let it be known that online bullying, or any bullying for that matter, is absolutely unacceptable at this school and we have zero tolerance for such behavior. There are and will be repercussions."

A chill air sucked all noise out of the room, a place normally so friendly and full of life that it almost seemed as though the entire group was collectively holding its breath. No squirming, no whispering, nothing, not even the rustle of paper, a nervous cough, titter or giggle as they waited for Ms. Kendall to resume.

"I know that news travels fast, and so you may already be aware that several of your fellow students have been suspended for what happened last Monday. We are taking time to examine each person's involvement on a case-by-case basis before taking further action." She allowed the words to sink in, and as she did, she thought of the pushback she'd gotten from two of the students' parents. Not only had they cursed her, but they'd threatened to withdraw considerable financial support pledged at the beginning of the year. More importantly, they asked her why the school was involved at all since no laws existed to prevent cyberbullying.

Alison couldn't believe they'd taken such a stance, but then both of those parents were attorneys. Sadly, they were right. No laws existed, so no law had been broken. Which meant there was no way to bring law enforcement to bear on the situation, as she'd learned in her brief conversation with Isabel Winthrop.

Furthermore, she knew this incident had the potential to make or break her career here, but she was willing to take that risk. She refused to be indecisive in a situation as dire as this. Not only was every parent and student watching her, not only was the board discussing this and advising her, but the community at large and even the media had her actions in their crosshairs. Word had spread quickly about what happened to Phoebe Murrow, and her phone had been ringing nonstop. She needed to be stern and unwavering, and above all else she needed to do the right thing. Furthermore, a private school, one as elite as Georgetown Academy, had much greater latitude in its involvement in the activities of its students, on or off campus.

If the decision had been hers alone she would already have expelled the students known to have participated in the online intimidation, an incident that might, in fact, turn out to be the cause of Phoebe's death. But the Board had insisted the students get a fair hearing before taking such final action. Yet it wasn't about fairness. If the child came without the vestige of wealth, he or she would probably get the boot.

From everything Alison knew, Jessie Littleton was not involved, and she hoped it remained that way because she was another student whose expulsion would be complicated by the fact that her father had committed over a million dollars to the capital campaign, a sum to be doled out over the next four years. Clever, she now thought. But she also liked Jessie, who she'd noticed had entered the assembly late.

Actually, Alison Kendall relished a good fight. Especially for a worthy cause. It's what she was trained to do. She looked out over the attentive student body.

"I will end with this final note," she said. "Though all of you are probably aware that someone by the name of Shane initiated the Facebook attack on Phoebe, it has come to my attention that this person, if I may call him that, is not a student at Walter Johnson High as he claimed to be. If any of you here know anything that might be helpful in discovering who he is, and where he can be found, please report it to me.

"It will be much appreciated, not only by us here at the school, but also by Phoebe and her family," Alison Kendall continued. "Furthermore, I will look favorably on anyone who is truthful and comes forward to take responsibility for his or her actions. As you know, that's a basic tenet of our school, and we take it seriously. Being ethical, honest, and responsible." She cleared her throat.

A few students shifted in their seats. Noah felt Jessie's eyes on him, but refused to glance her way.

"There is a reward being offered by Phoebe's family for anyone providing information that might lead to the person behind this. Regardless, I encourage you to reveal anything you know that might shed light on this...well, this entire awful situation. And please, students, don't think of it as tattling, because it isn't. Know that you're being a responsible citizen who refuses to give in to peer pressure. That's all I have for now. Any questions?"

She was about to dismiss them when an arm cloaked in a black sleeve went up. It was Emma. Alison admired her for being such a little rebel, in style and substance. "Yes?" she said.

"I want to announce that a group of us are getting together today to form a support group for Phoebe and her parents. I thought we could start by making her a card and getting everyone to sign it?"

"Excellent idea, Emma. I'll let you organize that...if you need my help, just let me know. Maybe the art teachers would like to help? Anyone else?"

A little self-consciously, Noah raised his hand. He suggested the idea of coordinating students to visit Phoebe and read to her. "I've already checked with her parents." He mentioned the constraints of ICU visits – two visitors at a time – and also received Ms. Kendall's blessing.

She glanced around for any further hands, and seeing none, dismissed them.

·•·•·•·

Sandy continued to murmur soothing things in Ron's ear. "It'll be all right. You'll see. Ph...ph...Phoebe," she said, stumbling over the name, "she'll come out of the coma and she'll be good as new." She sat beside him, one arm wrapped around his shoulders and the other caressing his leg, his hand, his cheek. "It'll be all right," she whispered, telling herself the same.

"Have you gotten any leads on this awful character...what's his name...Shane?"

He shook his head, his eyes like a downcast dog's. "No, but Isabel's doing everything she can to find out."

"Of course she is, I just can't believe someone would, well, do, that," she said, then stared out at the middle of the river where several groups of college students rowed past them in sleek boats that skimmed the water. "Come on, let's take a little walk," she said. "I promised to get your mind off things and that's what I'm gonna do."

She took him by the hand and led him down a few steps toward the water, then turned to the right behind Jack's Boathouse. From the road no one could see them here; only a few bike riders had even passed by the entire time they'd sat on the bench, at least half an hour.

Scarlet was not a color Sandy often wore, but that's what she'd chosen today. A pale gray tank top under a scarlet sweater with pearl gray buttons. It was tight and she could only button the sweater to just beneath her breasts, the better to show them off, she'd thought as she was getting dressed and assessing her reflection in the mirror. Her black pants were tight too, like a second skin, but she had practice unzipping them. No underwear either. Not even a thong.

Ron said nothing, just followed her like a puppy until they came to a halt. He leaned against the structure's gray planks of wood, which the sun had warmed, and Sandy stood in front of him, placing her back against his chest, gazing out at the water as she pulled his arms around her. She held them tight. And he let her. She felt him relax. They stood that way, like a couple in love, watching the flowing river, the silence ruptured by a few squawking gulls and a helicopter passing overhead.

Ron's hands, pressed against her belly, felt warm. Slowly, she moved them up to cup her breasts. At the same time she tightened her buttocks and pressed against him, feeling for hardness, which came soon enough. His hands broke free of hers and slid beneath her tank top, beneath her bra and onto her nipples, which he rolled between his fingers.

Moments later, she was kissing him, slipping her tongue between his lips. He responded with a fierce, needy desire that roused her.

Together they found a more secluded spot nearby. In a matter of seconds Sandy had stripped off her pants and shed her sweater, and Ron had pulled out his cock. The rest was easy.

Afterward, the chill air gave Sandy reason to zip and button hurriedly. As he watched her, his eyes taking in every inch, he said in a hushed tone, "You'll keep this quiet, right?"

Though she'd expected something like this, it disappointed her. She lifted her eyes to meet his and peered at him, like an abandoned fawn, but said nothing. She put on her coat. "Take care, Ron," she finally said and left.

· ● · ● · ● ·

After Ms. Kendall's departure noise filled the void: The shuffle of feet, the low murmur of voices, a few kids calling out to each other, nervous laughter. Noah again felt Jessie staring at him. "Why do you keep looking at me?" he said in a hushed voice then turned to follow Dylan, already halfway down the row.

Noah had barely taken a step when he felt Jessie's hand on his arm. "Noah," she said.

He shrugged her off and continued moving away from her. But she followed him. "Please," she whispered to his back, "I need to talk to you. It's really important."

When he finally turned to look at her he saw tears glistening in her eyes. "What do you want?" he said harshly.

"Not here." Her eyes looked puffy and she seemed exhausted, a far cry from the bubbly, exuberant Jessie he was familiar with.

Reluctantly he agreed and told her to follow him. He moved slowly so that most people had passed them before he veered off into one of the small rooms in the building where students took private lessons from assorted music tutors. He really didn't want to be seen with her.

He closed the door. "So what's up?"

"You hate me, don't you?"

Unsure how to respond, he said, "If you're here to tell me that you had nothing to do with it, you can just stop, okay? It's obvious you put one of your friends up to saying that stuff to Phoebe. Or... are you here to confess, is that it?"

When he saw how miserable she looked, he stopped. "Okay, sorry, but what do you want?"

"I know who Shane is." Her words came out in a whisper, but they punctured Noah's self-righteousness. He took a step back.

"You know?" he said. "Then why aren't you telling Ms. Kendall?"

She stared at the floor, silent.

"How do you know? Who is he?"

She licked her dried, chapped lips. "Not *he*."

He peered at her quizzically.

"She." She gave him a beseeching look. As if she wanted him to guess. But then added, "My mother. My mother did it."

Confused, Noah continued to stare at Jessie. "Your mother?"

She nodded, then told him how she'd found her mother and had stopped her, but also that her mother had used her gift of *persuasion* to get her to dismantle Shane's Facebook page. She wasn't sure whether that had been a good or a bad thing.

"But why? Why would your mother do that?"

"Because she's crazy," she said, lines creasing her brow.

"Yeah, obviously," he said, trying to control the swirl of thoughts and emotions that engulfed him. "But why are you telling *me*?" He was still uncertain whether to believe her. He'd known Jessie to lie. Or at least exaggerate. But this was pretty serious.

"Because, like Ms. Kendall said, we have an obligation to tell the truth, and I had to tell someone. I trust you, Noah. You need to tell Ms. Kendall or Phoebe's parents, or something. But nobody can know I told you." She was about to break down.

"You want *me* to tell?"

She nodded. "You know *I* can't."

"No matter who I tell," he said cautiously, "you know it's gonna spread like...like freakin' wildfire... the whole school will know. You know that, right?"

Staring off into the mid-distance she nodded. "I'll probably have to leave, school I mean, but—" she left the thought dangling, as though she hadn't gotten that far in her thinking.

A thousand questions ran through Noah's mind. He especially wondered about the image of Shane. "Whose photo was that?" he asked.

She again lowered her gaze to her feet and shrugged.

He didn't believe she didn't know. "So you had nothing to do with it?"

She shook her head. "Nothing, I swear, other than getting him off Facebook. You have to believe me. I would never do such a thing. I promise. I'm as sorry about what happened to Phoebe as you are."

He stared at her skeptically. "So exactly what am I supposed to say about how I found out?"

"I was hoping you'd think of something. You're smart." Her eyes latched onto his; they seemed filled with fear and desperation. He'd only seen such looks on people in movies, ones about to get caught. Or killed. "I wish I could see Phoebe?" She seemed to be asking if he thought it was a possibility.

"I don't think so. Not once her parents hear this. I can't imagine they would want that. Can you?"

Chapter Four

Around five o'clock that day, Isabel's toughest at the hospital yet, she came home, having put her work on hold indefinitely. She'd hoped to avoid this, thinking that by keeping her thoughts positive, somehow Phoebe would emerge from her coma, brain intact, and she'd be back at work in no time. Cerrtainly by today, one week later, but that hadn't happened.

It pained her to reassign all her clients – she'd thought a little work might ease her through the day – but her mind simply spun off every few minutes; her concentration, on which she prided herself, was shot.

She spent some time with Jackson, but after fifteen minutes of chatting idly, as he sat at the kitchen counter eating cookies and drinking milk while she stood across from him with a cup of coffee, it became clear to both of them that her attempt at acting normal was anything but, and so, with wisdom that far exceeded his ten years, he excused her from her motherly duty.

"Mom," he said, "I get it. You're worried about Phoebe. I am too. Just do what you need to and don't worry about me."

She looked at him with tremendous affection and went to his side to hug him. "Oh, darling, I'm so sorry we're neglecting you. This is a tough time for all of us. Thank you for being such a grown-up about it. You're wonderful, you truly are. You know that don't you?"

With a grin, he said, "Yup, I know, Mom."

Which is how she found herself upstairs in Phoebe's room, lying on her bed beside Hagrid, staring at the ceiling, the same ceiling that her daughter had stared at countless times. "Oh, Phoebe, Phoebe. I'm so sorry." She stroked the cat mindlessly as her eyes traversed the beams, from one end to the other, to the mobile of glow-in-the-dark stars and planets that floated overhead and had since Phoebe moved into this room at the age of seven.

Isabel recalled that move, how Phoebe had said she wasn't afraid to be all the way up here by herself, but Isabel knew that the small nightlight she installed and the bright glow that the mobile cast over the room had helped her sleep. It showed that underneath it all, her daughter was a brave girl, or at least tried to be.

She raised her hands and studied her nails. They were a mess, yet she couldn't care less, all she wanted was to lie here with Phoebe beside her. How often the two had lain on this bed, Isabel reading to her before going to sleep – all the classic fairy tales, *Harry Potter*, the Lemony Snickett series, countless others.

That's it, she thought. Like Noah, I'll read to her. It will help pass the time and perhaps the familiar words will reach my sweet girl, wherever she is. In a moment she would get up, but now she just wanted to lie here a bit longer, the cat's fur warming her. She drank in Phoebe's spirit, suffused as it was in all the things around her. In the furniture, in the lime green and purple bedspread and curtains, the dozens of stuffed animals, the little girl saddle and riding gear, the doll house, the clothes and shoes in her closet, the school pennants and knickknacks, and even in that pile of used clothes in the corner.

Her eyes settled there. And guilt engulfed her. She closed her eyes and recalled the stupid arguments they'd had over Phoebe's secondhand clothing fetish, over her friendship with Jessie and Emma, and over her own desire to protect Phoebe and, perhaps, direct too much of her life. But, I love her, she thought. I only wanted the best for her. Breathing deeply, she steepled her hands in prayer, her fingertips touching her lips.

Please, God, forgive me for all the things I did wrong as a mother. But, you know that I love her. With all my heart. You must know that. She squeezed her eyes together more tightly. *Just please let her be okay. Take me if you have to take a life, but let her live. She's just a young girl. Please, I'll do anything.* She thought a moment about what else to add. *And thank you for hearing my prayer.* She hadn't prayed this much since she'd wanted her own pony. Though Lucky had materialized on her tenth birthday, she wasn't at all sure that God meddled in human affairs, but if by any chance *He* or *She* or *It* did, then she was submitting the most earnest, most genuine plea of her life.

She glanced at her watch. It was nearly six o'clock. In a few minutes she'd head downstairs and defrost one of the many meals that friends and neighbors had left for them. Perusing Phoebe's bookshelves, her fingers hesitated on one of the *Twilight* paperbacks, but she wasn't wild about them and decided to take her daughter's favorite *Harry Potter* book instead. She'd choose one other volume after dinner.

Maybe she'd ask Jackson for his choice, or perhaps Ron would want to contribute an idea, which reminded her that he'd said he was going to stop by the hospital mid-afternoon, but he hadn't. Maybe he was angry with her; she knew that over the past few days they'd taken their frustration and fears out on each other. She'd do better. They were a team. This was a time to stick together. What would she do without him?

As she headed downstairs she wondered where he was; perhaps he'd gotten stuck with a last minute deadline. These things happened routinely. Maybe traffic had been bad.

· ● · ● · ● ·

Ron had found himself feeling particularly unsettled after his riverside tryst with Sandy. He really hadn't expected things to go that far. To distract himself, he'd returned to the *Post* and fiddled around at the computer for a while, then for the purposes of the social networking article and to assuage his guilt, he'd looked up Shane's Facebook page, only to find that it was no longer there. He frowned at the screen, certain the guy had folded up shop, hoping to disappear.

He felt his reporter instincts kick in and began doing some research, going to a few sites on cyber-bullying. That's when he ran across the Megan Meier case, the poor little thirteen-year-old who'd hung herself after Lori Drew – a mother! – had pretended to be a fifteen-year-old boy on MySpace, gotten her to like him, then turned against her! What a horrible thing. So horrible, he couldn't bear to read more than one article.

Over the next couple of hours, he kept thinking he'd go over to the hospital, but repeatedly he delayed facing Isabel, hoping to regain a semblance of calm and composure.

As night painted his windows black, he knew he'd have to go home sooner or later. But the thing that kept him glued to his chair was the look Sandy had given him before she'd left. At five o'clock, he was still trying to interpret that last moment with her. Why had he asked that stupid question? *You'll keep this quiet, right?* For reassurance, he told himself, though she hadn't given him any, had she? With that doe-eyed look was she saying, of course I will, why are you even asking? Or would she get angry with him and out of revenge tell someone? There were women like that, though on this front he'd been lucky in the past.

On the drive home, he wasn't exactly filled with remorse, but something like it. Regret? In any case, he wouldn't do it again. And that gave him some courage, plus a moment in which to relish the memory. She was a good fuck, he had to admit. And tomorrow he'd call her. Flirt with her a little. Just enough to keep her quiet.

· ● · ● · ● ·

"Where have you been?" Isabel asked when Ron walked into the kitchen.

"Where do you think I've been?" he shot back, a little surprised by the vehemence of his response. He slipped off his coat and dropped his briefcase onto a chair.

About to give Ron's testiness a nasty retort, Isabel caught herself. Don't argue, she told herself. "I just thought you were coming to the hospital? I was surprised not to hear from you."

"I'm trying to make a living, Iz. I just got hired and now I have to at least show up."

"Okay, sure. But didn't you say they told you to take off as much time as you needed?" She stopped and studied him. He was uptight, no denying that. "Never mind. I know you're doing what you have to do." She could hear him suck in a deep breath.

"Look," she went on, "I've heated up some dinner, so why don't you stay home tonight and relax with Jackson while I go back to the hospital?"

"I thought I should go," he said, though without much enthusiasm.

"You look beat. Go tomorrow? Anyway, I was almost out the door. I—" she hesitated, "—I'm going to read *Harry Potter* to Feebs." She peered at him sadly.

"How is she?"

Isabel swallowed. "The same." A mournful sound bubbled up. "Oh, Ron."

In two long strides he bridged the gap between them and held her. "She'll be all right. You'll see."

Her eyes brimming with tears, she said, "She will?"

She could see that his eyes were uncertain, but nevertheless he nodded, and she was grateful for that. It was then that he mentioned the disappearance of Shane's Facebook page.

· ● · ● · ● ·

At the hospital she encountered Emma and Noah sitting outside the ICU having what appeared to be an intense conversation. Their countenances lightened at the sight of her. Both jumped to their feet, and Emma shook her hand. "I'm really sorry, Ms. Winthrop, I truly am. I can't imagine how you must feel. This is so, so awful."

In an instant, Isabel could tell the sincerity and maturity of this girl with all the piercings. How much she cared about Phoebe.

Why hadn't she realized this before? "Thank you, Emma, thank you for being Phoebe's friend." When she'd read the stream of horrible things people had written on Facebook, Isabel had noted names, and Emma's had been absent. For that matter so had Jessie's.

"Phoebe's easy to love," Emma went on. "I don't know why all those kids said that stuff. It's really depressing. But there are lots more who are really worried about her. We made her a card." She held out a huge piece of cardboard with a collage of her classmates' images crisscrossed with their words of concern and love. The card was titled: *In the Moon of the Falling Leaves,* which Emma explained was a Native American reference to fall. "Would it be okay if I went in to see her?"

As Emma awaited her answer, Isabel thought she noticed Noah cast a meaningful glance in Emma's direction.

"Yes, I'm sure Phoebe would love to hear your voice." She explained the theory of how hearing was the last to go and first to come back. "Let's go in."

As she began to walk toward the ICU doors, Noah called out, "Do you think I could talk to you a minute while Emma's with Phoebe?"

She looked at him curiously, then said, "Sure, let me just escort Emma inside." Isabel's heart rate sped up. Had he discovered something about Shane? Did she really want to know? Of course, I do, she thought.

· ● · ● · ● · ●

Noah's palms felt sweaty, even the area where he'd someday have a mustache had grown moist. He'd rehearsed his lines, but at the sight of Phoebe's mom returning from the ICU, he grew even more nervous than before.

She sat down on the adjacent chair and looked at him expectantly.

"Well, earlier today I, I ... someone...uh," he stammered.

"Yes?" she said.

He took a breath and continued, "I got some information today about this Shane guy, but I think I'd better check it out first. You know, make sure it's true."

"What have you found out, Noah?"

"Well, that's what I'm trying to say, I don't know that I should tell you until someone can confirm it. Like my friend, the one who's really good with computers. You know?" He could see that she wanted to know what he'd discovered, but he was afraid to tell her. What if it wasn't true? That would be huge.

"If you weren't going to tell me, why—" she said, leaving the rest unsaid.

"I'm sorry, but I thought it would be helpful to know that I might be close to finding out."

"I think I can handle it, even if the information turns out to be inaccurate. Why don't you just tell me?"

Sitting beside her, he realized just how rash he'd been to come here. In his eagerness to reassure her, he was actually making her more anxious. She was staring at him, waiting. "Where did you get this information, maybe we could start there?"

She wasn't going to let go of this, he could tell. Shit, shit, shit. Her eyes were piercing. Emma had encouraged him to tell.

"It came from Jessie," he finally blurted out.

"Jessie Littleton?" she said.

He nodded.

"I see," she said.

He swallowed hard, his Adam's apple bobbing up and down. "Yeah, that's why I thought I should double-check. 'Cuz it could get really messy if she's wrong. Do you know what I mean, Mrs. Murrow?"

She took a moment to think, then she said, "I do. Thanks for telling me." Pause. "And let me know as soon as you find out anything more. Okay?" She smiled and gave him an understanding look, which he didn't understand at all.

Chapter Five

Tuesday, November 18, 2008

Sandy was afraid to open her eyes. Each time she did, there in the mirror, staring at her, was Phoebe. She closed her eyes again, and then she heard Phoebe speak. "Why'd you do it? I'm telling. I'm telling everyone what you did." Then she disappeared and Sandy woke up, shaking, gasping for breath.

A few hours later, she sat at the kitchen table clutching her cup of coffee studying the dark brew. Yesterday, after her "date" with Ron, she thought she'd put an end to this nightmare, but the image of Phoebe in the mirror hovered in her mind like an apparition. She started at every noise. Several times, goose bumps rose on her arms. Get a grip, she told herself. She thought of calling Bill, but what could he say that would be helpful?

It wasn't until her third cup of coffee that an idea finally occurred to her.

She picked up her cell phone and tapped in Ron's new work
number. He didn't pick up, and after briefly hesitating, she said,
"Hi, Ron. This is Sandy. Just wanted to check on you." She paused.
"I'd like to bring your family dinner, would that be okay? Loved
seeing you, call me." She left her number and hung up.

Clutching the mug in both hands, she took another long sip of
coffee. It made her feel better to have done that, to be doing something, anything to shake the image of Phoebe out of her head. That
little idiot! Why'd she go and try to kill herself? For the life of her,
Sandy couldn't fathom such a thing. *"Sticks and stones may break
your bones, but words can never hurt you,"* she muttered under
her breath.

She was feeling pretty rotten about what had happened, but
her mind trotted out any number of excuses: She'd been cutting
herself long before last Monday. The reason for that must have
something to do with Isabel. Living with her! For that she actually
felt sorry for Phoebe. Poor thing. And for Ron.

In that regard, she wished circumstances were different.
Ron was good in the sack, but she knew their times together were
numbered. It actually made her sad, except for that dumb question he'd asked. That hurt. Well, today was his lucky day; she'd
cut him a break and reassure him when he called. *Of course, I
promise not to tell.* And maybe, just maybe she'd turn him on
again for good measure.

· ● · ● · ● ·

On Ron's way into the office – he'd just dropped off Jackson –

traffic slowed to a crawl. A woman in the car next to his reminded him of Isabel. The way she held herself so upright when driving, the way she wore her long dark hair, and even her profile was stunningly similar. One big difference, however. This woman wore a smile. Of course, neither he nor Isabel had much to smile about, but it shouldn't be forbidden, should it?

Just before taking off this morning, Isabel told him what Noah had revealed the previous night. "I'm going to call Jessie and find out what she knows," she concluded.

"Shouldn't you wait, like he said? What if it's nothing?" He wondered if this could be his excuse to call Sandy. And ask her what she knew.

Isabel began to respond, but then Jackson had walked in. To disengage from the conversation, Ron cracked a joke, and Isabel shot him a look. Poor kid, Ron thought. He was trying to keep things halfway normal. What was the point of such a morbid atmosphere? After all Phoebe was alive. With any luck, she would regain consciousness. She'd be okay.

Observing the woman's smile made Ron want to jump into her car and trade a few war stories. He felt weary of Isabel's attitude, and her need for "justice." Why couldn't she spend more time bolstering his feelings of hopelessness instead of constantly attacking him? And this notion that Jessie knew something, well, maybe *he* should contact Noah.

He lifted his cell phone half-heartedly to check for voice mails at work. He clicked through the calls, saving or deleting them, when he heard the sound of Sandy's kittenish voice. Her offer to bring dinner. Relief flooded through him. All that worrying. For nothing. He couldn't help shaking his head and smiling to himself. She was something else. Then another call, a number he should write down.

He rifled through his jacket pocket for a slip of paper. He felt one and fished it out. The words "call me" were scrawled on it. Squinting at it, he could tell it wasn't his own handwriting. When he flipped it over he saw that it was Sandy's business card, the word *Slenderella* typed in an attractive cursive font. How the hell had that gotten there, he wondered.

Scrolling through his mind, he finally recalled last wearing this jacket on the night of the parents' party, and then he remembered Sandy curled up at his side flirting with him, and Isabel's angry, jealous reproach. Now she was offering to bring dinner. Pretty nice of her, he thought, considering how much Isabel detested her. Gutsy too, though, in light of yesterday. He had half a mind to accept the offer, only thing was Isabel couldn't know.

He jotted down the number he needed, still shaking his head at the strange coincidence of finding Sandy's card. A few moments later, believing that the universe was conspiring in his favor, he punched Sandy's number into his iPhone. His finger remained poised above the green "call" button and hovered there for several seconds before descending.

· ● · ● · ● ·

"Yes, there is brain activity, but not much has changed since we spoke on Saturday," Dr. Bailey explained to Ron and Isabel in her straightforward manner. "That doesn't mean things won't change. You never know. Hopefully her brain is just taking a rest and repairing itself. But we can't be certain." She took a breath and galloped on as several hyper-attentive interns listened nearby. "What we do know is her blood pressure and oxygenation are currently stable. Her kidneys appear to be working, she's producing urine, and her electrolytes are within normal limits; in other words, her fluid is essentially in balance."

The doctor had been half an hour late and now it was two o'clock. Her words weren't as reassuring as they'd hoped, and Ron felt Izzy tensing up beside him.

"If I didn't know better, Dr. Bailey, I'd think you were trying to confuse us with all that medical talk." Isabel managed a wry smile. The doctor responded with a slight apologetic shrug. "Can you give us some idea...I mean, how much longer do you think—" Isabel stopped, unable to finish her question.

"It's hard to tell when she'll come out of the coma. Everyone responds differently."

"What I think Iz was trying to say," Ron intervened, "is what happens if there's no improvement? How long should we keep her on life support?" He glanced searchingly at Isabel, who averted her gaze. Still, he knew that's what she'd meant. It was on his mind too.

Dr. Bailey's deep brown eyes probed Ron's, then Isabel's. "It's really premature to think about that. She is oxygenating, she is no longer bleeding, her fluid and pH are in balance. She still has a chance."

Ron felt Isabel's hand squeeze his own. "A chance?" she said and turned away momentarily to hide her tears.

"Yes, absolutely." Then Dr. Bailey added, "Perhaps it would help you to consult our chaplain or one of our social workers?"

These words shook Isabel. In the fashion of a litigator who intends to uncover the truth, no matter the cost, she turned back to the doctor and asked, "What happens when you remove someone from—from all this?" Isabel aimed at the tubes that slithered down Phoebe's neck, over her chest and along her arms.

The doctor explained in a low voice: "First, we would extubate her; that is, the breathing apparatus will go. Then, if she continues to breathe on her own, we have the option of inserting a feeding tube or waiting to see if she comes out of the coma."

"So you're saying if she doesn't come out of the coma and we don't insert a feeding tube, she'll starve to death?" Isabel blurted out.

"Yes, but if she has no brain function, then—" Dr. Bailey stopped. Isabel could tell the doctor believed there was no point in being overly graphic; people could fill in the blanks. They weren't stupid. But Isabel pushed her, "*Then* what, doctor?"

"Then there's no sensation," she said, speaking softly, "hence, no awareness of the pain."

· ● · ● · ● ·

Ron wasn't at all sure it was a good idea to meet Sandy at the Georgetown Mall, but after the session with Dr. Bailey he needed a drink. And besides, he felt it was safer to see her in a public place than a remote one, where he could get into trouble again. But now, here at the base of the mall's vast three-story atrium, he knew he'd have to come up with a plausible alibi if he encountered someone familiar. The thought of wearing his sunglasses passed through his mind, but that was ridiculous. The Georgetown Mall wasn't that well lit to begin with.

While waiting, he sat at the bar of the Japanese restaurant on the lower level and ordered a pot of sake, nice and hot. He'd almost asked for two at once. The first shot went down easy, and he decided that if anyone saw him here with Sandy, he'd just say he'd come from the hospital to pick up some carry-out and by coincidence ran into her. It was pretty lame, but no one could prove it wasn't true. Especially since he was sitting here alone now.

He ordered a second sake, appreciating the way it slid down

his throat and warmed him, the way it was beginning to anesthe-tize him to the news from today's meeting. As usual, the doctor had been maddeningly non-committal about Phoebe's prognosis. He could read between the lines though. It wasn't just *when* she might emerge from the coma, but *if.*

He poured himself another tumbler and stared at the clear liq-uid inside the miniature porcelain cup. He couldn't help returning to the scene that had indelibly etched itself into his mind, the one he most wanted to erase: the dreadful moment he'd found Phoebe.

If only he'd arrived a few minutes earlier, or if he'd raced up-stairs the moment he came home. But no, he'd shouted up to her, assuming Isabel's frantic call had been an over-reaction. When there'd been no answer, he'd slowly climbed the stairs to her attic suite, thinking he'd find her on her computer, probably on Face-book. He checked her room and saw her stuff lying about. Only then had he knocked on the partially open bathroom door. "Phoe-be?" he'd called, sensitive to her need for privacy.

He could tell someone was taking a bath from the mist curl-ing inside the room, but it was dark, and that seemed strange. He waited another couple of seconds, seconds he now knew held an urgency he'd failed to recognize, then called Phoebe's name again. No answer.

He'd pushed the door open and stepped inside. On seeing her body floating in the tub, he'd cried out, "Oh, my God, baby!" He switched on the light and almost fainted at the sight of the red-tinged water.

"Oh, my God, Phoebe! What—why?" Frantic, he'd grabbed a towel and lifted her out of the tub. She felt so light, a girl who'd worried about being overweight, and here she was a young woman, beautiful and blossoming, her blood everywhere. He gently laid her lifeless body on the bathroom rug and stabbed the numbers 9-1-1 into his cell phone. He was half-crazed by the time he got someone to understand what was happening, and they claimed an ambulance was on its way.

They kept him on the line, telling him to wrap bandages or towels around her wrist, anything to stop the bleeding. "Check her pulse," they said, but he was afraid to, and when he did he couldn't feel anything. They told him to give her breaths, and this he did by pinching her nose and breathing into her mouth. Then he placed his hands on her chest and pushed as he'd seen doctors, nurses, and emergency rescue crews do on television.

If only he could forget that image. Forget that he'd wasted precious minutes on the side of the road, talking on the phone. Had he done that? He'd almost forgotten. He took the tiny cup of hot sake, threw it into the back of his mouth and felt the soothing alcohol glide down his throat and into his gullet. Now he truly understood the meaning of drowning your sorrows in drink. Nevertheless, the image clung to him and refused to let go. Mingling with it was a vision of Phoebe in the hospital, plastic tubes stretching around and away from her body, her sallow skin, her hair lying in greasy strands, her spirit all but stripped from her physical being. How much longer before they'd have to make a decision about what to do next?

The bartender, a Japanese man in his mid-thirties, looked at him with concern. "More?"

Ron nodded. Might as well, he thought. Then he remembered why he was there and checked his watch. Sandy was late. He should just leave, he thought. He didn't want to see her. For heaven's sake what was he thinking when he'd agreed to meet her again? Then he clearly remembered that it had been Sandy flirting with him on the phone that day! That day when Isabel had urged him to hurry home. Oh, God. Motioning to the bartender, he told him to cancel the drink and bring the check.

"Hi, Ron," Sandy said softly.

He felt as if she'd caught him in mid-flight. Blushing, he turned to face her. She took a seat on the barstool beside him, and shaking her head said, "Sorry I'm late. Traffic." She looked genuinely apologetic. He watched her place a bloated plastic bag at her feet. Carry-out food. Now there was nothing to do but stay a minute. He was strangely at a loss for words.

"Would you like a drink?" he asked.

"Sure, what are you having?" She sounded young and uncertain, which surprised him.

"Sake. You want some?"

"I've never tried it, but why not? It's a mess out there. Heard there's some bad weather coming in."

He cancelled his check and placed two more orders of sake. They both sat quietly.

After taking several swallows, she said, "How's it going? Anything new with Phoebe, I mean."

Somehow those few words caused him to well up and his throat to constrict so that he couldn't speak. He shook his head. "Not good," he finally managed.

She again placed her hand on his arm. Her mouth close to his ear, she whispered, "Let it out, Ron. Don't hold it in. What's the point in that?" Her voice sounded full of tenderness and concern, though if he'd listened more carefully, he might have heard that it was also laced with something else. Fear. The fear that Phoebe would die and she'd be found out.

Sandy rubbed his back with one hand and with the other lifted the tiny cup and drained its contents. "Tell me what's going on. What are the docs saying? How's Isabel? Jackson? Tell me everything. I'm here to listen. Or we can just sit here and drink. Whatever you want, Ron. You can count on me. Nothing tougher than what you're going through."

Downing his fourth tiny cup of sake, Ron told her everything the doctor had said. He didn't even care if anyone saw them. Let them. What the hell! She was kind enough to listen to him blab.

And then he told her how he'd found Phoebe, how the EMTs had come and thought it was too late until one of them found a weak pulse, how they'd managed to get her down three flights of stairs on the gurney, how she looked so vulnerable and helpless, how he prayed every hour of the day even though he wasn't religious, how stressed out and impossible Isabel was, how this was the worst event of his life, and how no parent should have to suffer such a thing. He described everything but the fact that he'd wasted precious minutes on the side of the road talking to her and setting up a *lunch* date.

Several times he considered mentioning Jessie, that maybe she knew the culprit, but he felt awkward and refrained. After finishing his story he cried and felt a little better. He was so grateful that she'd listened without interruption, only brief murmurings that soothed him.

· ● · ● · ● ·

Sandy took over without him noticing and paid the bill, then began steering him toward the elevators to the underground garage, and finally to his black SUV. He used the remote to open the car and slid in behind the wheel as she scooted into the passenger seat.

"I put the heating directions on top," she said, pointing at the large shopping bag at her feet. "So all you have to do is follow instructions. You can do that, can't you, Ron Murray?" She laughed a little at her joke and so did he.

She reached for his hands. "Now don't hesitate to call me, okay? I'm here for ya. And don't worry about yesterday. Our secret," she said coyly and winked. She grasped his chin firmly, tugging it toward her so his mouth could meet hers. Then she gave him another nice, long, hard kiss, and allowed him to suck her tongue into his mouth like a greedy teenage boy. Like all those boys who'd wanted her. Like Les and Shane and all the rest.

Once again, she caressed his crotch, now bulging with a hardened cock, unzipped his khakis and stroked and fondled him, then unzipped her own pants and placed his fingers inside her wetness to let him feel how turned on she was.

"Easy does it," she said, lowering her head and putting his fat cock into her mouth. She heard a satisfied grunt. Then, as her tongue titillated and teased him, she thought she heard him say, "Damn it, Sandy, no," then "Oh, God, Sandy, fuck me," and then, "You fucking beautiful bitch, you fucking bitch." In less than two minutes she'd finished sucking him off.

He let out a strangled cry that sounded throughout the cavernous garage. The scattered few who heard him weren't sure if it was a cry of alarm, joy, or relief. Maybe all three.

· ● · ● · ● ·

Twenty minutes later, Ron pulled into the circular driveway. He'd half-expected – no, he'd hoped – Isabel would still be at the hospital. But her BMW sat there, like some shady character lurking in front of the house. He'd hoped to take a shower, but now realized that might seem peculiar. It wasn't as if he'd gone to the gym and worked out or played squash.

He glanced at himself in the rearview mirror, making sure there wasn't any stray lipstick on his face, and with both hands raked his fingers through his thick wavy hair, hair that for an instant conjured Phoebe and shamed him. Next, he examined his features – what did a guilty expression look like anyway? – then he took a deep breath and exhaled. For some reason he was feeling a lot less steady today than yesterday. Maybe because yesterday more time had elapsed between seeing Sandy, no, between fucking her and seeing Isabel.

He switched off the radio, though he hadn't heard a word of NPR's evening news. From the time he left the garage until a moment ago, all his thoughts had revolved around Sandy. He'd had no intention of fucking around again. How was it that she'd gotten him into his car, taken his dick into her mouth and made him come? It was all the anxiety, stress, and pressure, he told himself. For a moment, though, he couldn't help recalling how great his orgasm had felt.

He rubbed his hand across his lips with the memory, then noticed Sandy's tangy odor. Shit! His heart started hammering. He stuck his fingers in his mouth and licked them vigorously, then wiped them on the floor mat. He had to get himself together and walk into the house as though nothing had happened. He took several more breaths to calm himself.

Finally, he turned the engine off. At the front door he adjusted his expression once more, serious but not too serious, sniffed his fingers again – he'd wash them immediately – and inhaled yet one more deep breath, then released it. Thus fortified, he inserted the key into the lock, and, shopping bag in hand, stepped inside.

He listened for sounds coming from the kitchen, hoping there wouldn't be any, but of course there were. The banging of a cupboard, the refrigerator opening and closing, water splashing in the sink. He wanted to go hole up with Jackson, but on days that Isabel was home he always went in to see her first. Today of all days, he couldn't change his entry routine, and so he dropped his briefcase on the hallway bench and made his way into the kitchen with the sack of food Sandy had given him.

Isabel's eyes locked onto his the moment he entered. "What's wrong?" she said, as if sensing something amiss.

Heading for the sink, he answered, "Nothing, I'm, you know, as okay as somebody can be," he looked at her helplessly and added, "under the circumstances." Then he said, "I should have called. Got some carry-out." *From Sandy*, he thought. He was careful not to lie. Of course he was splitting hairs, withholding information was as good as lying, wasn't it? He thought of Phoebe and how upset Isabel had been all those weeks ago.

"Oh, good," she said. "I was just trying to pull something together, but my heart's not in it. What'd you get?"

Then he remembered that Sandy hadn't told him, only that she'd left heating instructions inside. Oh, Christ. He stared at her blankly as he dried his hands. "Hey, I have an idea," he said. "You probably need a drink as much as I do. Why don't you go make us two gin and tonics and I'll heat the stuff up, get dinner on the table? I'll surprise you. How's that?"

She came over to him and wrapped her arms around his neck and kissed him. Full on the lips. At first rigid, he finally managed to give in to the kiss, but all the while he couldn't help worrying about any lingering scent of Sandy. When Isabel pulled away and looked at him, his heart thumped a little harder.

"Oh, Ron, our baby," she said, her lip quivering.

Relieved, he embraced her again and pulled her tightly to his chest. "She'll be okay. We have to believe that, honey baby." He couldn't remember the last time he'd called her that. Holding her at arms' length and fixing her with a commiserating grin, he said, "Okay, get me that drink, and I'll whip up dinner." He felt himself acting far too happy. Dial it down, he told himself.

But Izzy didn't seem to notice. She gave him a wan smile. "Okay."

The minute she left, he pulled the containers out of the Dean & DeLuca bag and searched for the instructions. There they were. He perused them quickly, noting the childish loopiness of Sandy's script, then wadded up the sheet of paper and threw it in the trash. Heating dinner wasn't exactly rocket science. In any case, the note was mostly about how much she hoped they'd enjoy the food and how sorry she was about Phoebe.

He was glad he hadn't mentioned anything about Jessie. Surely, if Jessie knew something, Sandy would have told him.

He was busily microwaving each dish and setting the table, when Isabel returned with two drinks. She looked at all the food. "Looks like you got enough for the whole neighborhood." He realized that Sandy had bought far more than they'd eat in three, or even four, days' time. He reached for his drink. "Oh well, we can always eat leftovers, or we can freeze some of this stuff."

Silently, Ron patted himself on the back with the way he was handling each little twist and turn in their conversation. It didn't hurt that Isabel seemed in much better spirits, but still things were working without a hitch. He promised himself that although no one was hurt by his fooling around, tonight really had been the last time. For the first time in a week, he actually felt like he still loved

Isabel. It hadn't been all her fault. No, he bore part of the blame. He almost felt like clinking glasses, but the image of his baby girl in the hospital stopped him.

To his surprise though, Isabel raised her glass, eyes glistening. "Do you know what day it is?" she asked.

Before he could respond, the phone rang and Isabel walked over to answer it. Ron put down his drink, took one of the dishes out of the microwave and added another, wondering what Isabel had been referring to.

"Oh, hello. Thank you," he heard her say. "She's, uh, still the same." Pause. "Of course I know Jessie."

Jessie? Ron wondered, then saw Isabel's body stiffen.

"What's that?" she asked.

Slightly alarmed he moved to her side to listen in, but she moved away from him. He watched her face grow ashen and several lines crease her forehead. "What else did Jessie say?"

On hearing those words, Ron was sure his cover had just been blown. But how could Jessie know? And who the hell was on the phone? Rifling through his brain for an out, he heard Isabel say, "Yes, of course. But he's sure that's what she said?" Then, "Well, thank you. Goodbye." She ended the call, staring vacantly into space.

"What was all that about?" Ron asked, stricken with fear to hear the answer.

Isabel listed slightly, her shoulder touching the wall. "That was Noah's mother," she said, her tone devoid of emotion. "Yesterday at school Jessie told Noah that Sandy...that Sandy was Shane, and she wanted us to know. Noah did some additional checking and found that Shane's Facebook page had been linked to an IP address of Sandy's, or something like that." Isabel looked bewildered, staring off at a point just beyond Ron.

The effects of all that sake combined with the gin was cloud-ing Ron's ability to think. "You're not making sense. What do you mean Sandy *was* Shane?" What the hell was she saying?

"*Sandy* was behind creating him. He wasn't a real person, and he wasn't even some teenage boy. *He* was Sandy." The color had further drained from her face. "It was Sandy. Sandy led our daugh-ter on; she was the one who taunted and bullied her. She—" her voice trailed off.

The room tilted around Ron.

"I'm going to kill her," Isabel said.

Chapter Six

Ron needed time to think. Had he really screwed around with a woman who'd done this to his daughter? His daughter who might be permanently brain damaged – who might die. Oh, God.

Minutes earlier, despite Isabel's repeated urging, Ron had refused to accompany her, saying they couldn't just leave Jackson. "Look we need to get actual proof that Sandy was involved. You can't just go over there half-cocked," he said.

Isabel had grown violent then. "What's wrong with you?" she'd shouted. "How much more confirmation do you need?"

"What if you're wrong?" he'd heard himself say, though it was more a defensive measure than a real question.

"Did you not hear a thing I just said? Noah confirmed it." She spoke loudly, punctuating each word, as if he were an idiot. "They traced Shane's Facebook page back to Sandy's computer!"

"Well, what if it was Jessie using Sandy's computer?" He'd suddenly latched onto this explanation to dodge the hideous reality Isabel described. But this sounded far-fetched even to his own ears. Why would Jessie tell on herself?

"So you're just going to stay here? How can you be so passive?"

"And you, what are you going to do? Just walk in there and accuse Sandy? What will that do to Jessie? Have you thought about that?"

That slowed her, but only for a moment. She said she needed to look Sandy in the eye; then she'd know the truth. With that she grabbed her keys. Isabel's ferocity had reminded him of an enraged tigress protecting her young. She'd slammed the door, but her image stayed with him.

He wanted to call Sandy and yell at her himself. But what would he say? *You fucking bitch, did you do it, did you fucking do it?* How could she have? Was it possible? Or maybe he should warn her: *Look out, my wife's on a fucking rampage!* But he couldn't do that either.

Isabel's parents had agreed to sit with Phoebe for the next few hours no questions asked, which allowed him to stay at home with Jackson. And for a little while longer pretend none of this was true.

Sitting there on the couch with his son, nursing his gin and tonic while watching some inane sitcom, Ron began to feel sick to his stomach. He fretted about what Isabel would say or do, and God only knew how Sandy would respond. He still hadn't digested that Sandy had sent these daily posts. It seemed impossible. Was that why she'd come on to him? As one thought tripped over another, Ron glanced at his watch.

How long before everything would come crashing down on him, them, everything that hadn't already? Even through his muddled brain he recognized what an ass he'd been to fuck around with

Sandy, of all people. And if there was one thing he'd learned over time, it was that life has a way of paying you back for your stupid, dumb-ass moves.

He lurched off the couch and stumbled to the bathroom.

· ● · ● · ● ·

Isabel rehearsed and revised what she planned to say. In the end, she knew she'd be on automatic and whatever came out of her mouth, well, those were the words she'd deliver. This was not like a case she'd litigated, where she practiced and rehearsed her opening and closing statements until she had them just right. No, this was unlike anything she'd ever encountered.

In the November darkness, standing at Sandy's front door, she hesitated. Maybe Ron was right. They should be absolutely certain. Of what though? No, if there had been any doubt, Noah's mother, a math professor at Georgetown University, wouldn't have called. Still, she wished she knew more about computer technology. Then, before she lost her nerve, she lifted the knocker and rapped on the door. The truth would be in Sandy's eyes.

She waited. It was only a little after seven so maybe they were having dinner. She sniffed, but didn't catch any smells of food. Her intense state and the brisk air sharpened her senses. She stared at the huge oak, thinking of all the strange family events it had witnessed. All the secrets it held. A few moments later, the door opened.

Bill looked quizzical on seeing her. Isabel didn't hesitate. "I'm sorry to be interrupting, but I have something important to discuss. With you and Sandy. May I come in?"

He hesitated, and Isabel saw conflicting emotions ripple across his face. She supposed a few hours in jail could do that, especially if you were pretty sure the person standing before you had prompted the arrest.

"Of course," he said, stepping aside and motioning for her to enter. "Sandy's in the kitchen."

She followed him. Midway down the hall, he turned to her. "I hope there isn't bad news—" he paused, as if catching himself, "—I mean, how is Phoebe?"

Isabel shrugged. "No change as of a couple of hours ago."

She wondered if he knew of Sandy's involvement, but doubted he did. He padded along in front of her in his jeans, white t-shirt, and thick socks. The uniform of construction work.

When they arrived in the kitchen, both Sandy and Jessie's heads jerked up in surprise. "Oh, gee, you didn't have to come all the way over here to thank me," Sandy blurted out.

"Thank you?" Isabel said, struggling to keep herself from launching across the room and striking the woman.

"For the food I gave Ron. Your dinner."

It took a moment for this to register in Isabel's brain, and when it did she fought to contain her feelings. Why hadn't Ron told her? When had they met? Where? As several more thoughts and questions fired through her brain, Isabel saw that Sandy perceived the deception, which added to her fury. Another second passed before she regained her equilibrium.

Jaw clenched, she fixed Sandy with a hostile stare. "No, I'm here about something else." She paused, searching for the right words. She had to do this right. She had to know. "It's come to my attention that Shane, Facebook Shane, is not a real person." She spoke in a formal tone, as if addressing someone in a legal case. "Not real," she said for emphasis.

She scrutinized Sandy, almost certain she detected unease

flicker through her eyes, then continued. "In fact, I've been informed that *you* were behind creating Shane." Her eyes held Sandy's as she let the words rest in the air before going on. "Which means that *you*, Sandy, are responsible for what's happened to our daughter." The image of Phoebe lying comatose floated before her. "Our—" For an instant Isabel's voice faltered, though her gaze did not. Then she added, "Our precious Phoebe."

"What are you talking about?" Sandy said. With an indignant look, she flipped her hair over her shoulder and threw a narrow-eyed glance at Jessie, who visibly shrank back.

So, at least that much was true. Jessie *had* told Noah.

Isabel refused to lift her eyes from this wretched woman, forcing her to meet her gaze. "So you're telling me you had nothing to do with it?"

This time Sandy shouted, "Are you nuts? Of course not!" Jessie looked terrified, and Bill appeared ready to say something but seemed to think better of it.

"We have proof," Isabel said. She pulled a piece of paper out of her purse and unfolded it. "This *young man's* Facebook page has been traced to your computer's IP address." She scrutinized Sandy's reaction to this bit of information and saw her eyes flit about the room, as if they could spirit her away. The paper contained Shane's Facebook photo. Straightening the creases, she laid it on the table. When Bill saw it, he recoiled. To Isabel's amazement evidence was adding up, just as in one of her cases. Now she felt 99 percent certain there was a connection.

She thrust the photo at Sandy. Continuing to approximate her courtroom manner, she said, "I'd like you to look at it, Sandy, and tell me who this is."

Sandy pushed the image away. "Get out of here, who cares

who it is! You've always hated me and now you're trying to ruin my life."

"No, Sandy, I'm trying to find the person who perpetrated such evil on my daughter, the person who has ruined *our* life. I'm sure you'd do the same." The timbre of Isabel's voice sounded strong and commanding. "So tell me you don't know who this is and that you had nothing to do with him or putting his image on Facebook. That you had nothing to do with falsely creating a person to prey on my daughter. Look me in the eye and tell me that."

For a moment, Sandy's glare weakened and she turned to Bill. "Honey, do something," she pleaded. He stared at her. Then, with renewed defiance, Sandy squared her shoulders and shouted at Isabel, "I had *nothing* to do with it! Satisfied? Now get out."

"So who did, Sandy? Who used your computer?"

When Isabel continued to stand there refusing to budge, Sandy screamed, "Out! Get out of MY house!"

· ● · ● · ● ·

No sooner had Isabel gone than Bill fled the room, and Jessie began crying.

Taking in several deep breaths, Sandy squinted at her. "You little weasel, you told on me didn't you?"

"You did this awful thing, Mom, and that's all you can say? What about Phoebe?" Jessie flung the words at her mother. "Poor Phoebe." She was on the verge of tears. "And me? What'll happen to me? I'll get kicked out of school, and you don't even care?"

"No one's going to kick you out," Sandy said evenly. They wouldn't dare, she thought, not after all the money Bill committed. Would they?

"Oh, yeah? Well, how can I stay there? Everyone will hate me!" Jessie shouted. She glanced around the kitchen, her eyes skimming the room, landing on a large unused cookbook that sat on the counter. With one arm, she swept it onto the floor, propelling it in the direction of her mother, but it merely dropped with a loud thump. She kicked it. "Ouch, damn it!" She leaned over and rubbed the toe of her foot.

"Well, why the heck d'you go and tell?" Sandy shook her head uselessly. "Nobody had to know. They wouldn't have if you hadn't told." Her voice sounded plaintive and filled with rare doubt.

"Didn't you hear? They traced the email address to your computer! You're so stupid to think there aren't other ways of finding out?" Jessie shouted and glanced around the room for her father, unaware he'd left. "How could you do that, put a fake person on Facebook? And why'd you stick your big fat nose in my business? Why, Mom? Why?" Her eyes grew wet with tears. "You've messed up everything!" She fled the room, a loud "I hate you" trailing behind her.

Sandy clutched the kitchen counter, tracking her daughter's departure. She tried to swallow, but it felt like a vulture's egg was stuck in her throat. She could hardly breathe. Oh, God, what have I done? Jessie was probably right; this time she *had* ruined their lives.

· ● · ● · ● ·

Isabel had no idea how she'd gotten into the car or how she was managing to drive. Or even where she was. Fury howled inside of her. She cursed Sandy and kept muttering to herself, "I'm going to kill her, I'm going to kill her." The only question was how. I could buy a gun, she thought, or maybe a blowtorch. She imagined aiming each one at Sandy's face and watching her crumple with fear.

A cold sweat enveloped Isabel. Her mind leapt between two irrevocable moments: from learning that Sandy had cooked up the phony Facebook Shane to the instant she'd known something had happened between Sandy and Ron and back again. If she could surgically remove these two moments, she would. How was it possible that this wretched woman had single-handedly destroyed all that was dear to her?

She dialed Ron's cell. When he answered, she shouted, "You fucked her, didn't you?" Then weeping, she added, "How could you? Today was Phoebe's birthday! And you forgot!" As if the two events were linked. She hung up and slammed the steering wheel, then yelped in pain.

One second she felt like ripping her own hair out, the next like clawing Sandy to a bloody pulp. Her breath came in rapid bursts. She had to calm down, she knew this, but never, not in her entire life had she been as angry and devastated as she was now. If she could have, she would have returned to Sandy's house and simply shot her. And that would have been that. But she didn't have a gun. At least not yet. And she'd never shot one, but how hard could it be?

As Isabel drove around town, yelling at Sandy and imagining her death, she noticed she was nearly out of gas. She found a service station and pulled in.

Chapter Seven

It was almost eight in the evening, when, across town, Alison Kendall called her board of directors, a group of twelve men and women, discussing the evidence that pointed to Sandy Littleton having triggered the cyber-bullying episode against Phoebe Murrow.

Earlier in the day, the instant they'd each received a call from Alison, the horror in her tone was something they'd never heard. It slapped them in the face and woke them up. She'd called to schedule an emergency conference call. From that moment, the board members knew they faced a public relations disaster of considerable magnitude, and some tough decisions.

She was now explaining the information that had been revealed to her by Noah after second period, and then confirmed over the telephone by Jessie. Alison assured them that Noah had provided an independent report from a computer expert with whom she'd spoken. She did not mention that he was a "hacker."

Yes, what had happened to Phoebe Murrow was terrible, beyond terrible, really the whole thing was unimaginable, but the board members quickly turned from their collective horror to their obligation as stewards of Georgetown Academy, their need to protect the school's image and reputation.

They launched into a series of discussions. Setting aside the personal implications for a moment, there were the obvious concerns if this became public knowledge: first, how would it affect future enrollment (would people worry about the quality of the parents who populated the school? Yes, yes, yes.); second, would the school be seen as having any culpability (hopefully not); third, should they hire a public relations firm for damage control (yes); and, finally, how would the media (assuming it got hold of the news, which it probably would) cast this story. The effect on future donations was spoken of sideways, mostly avoided.

But the tricky issue they saved for last: What should be done about poor Jessica Littleton? Though they would just as soon be rid of her, "in fairness to the girl, she'd done nothing wrong." Nothing was said about Bill's generous donation. And in truth, they couldn't exactly kick her out because of her mother's actions. So they decided to call her father the next day and have an informal discussion with him about what might be "best for Jessica."

Suggestions ranged from Bill moving her away from the area, but if not that, then at a minimum taking her out of Georgetown Academy, though they would leave the decision up to him. Yet, how could she possibly stay? On the other hand, what other nearby private school would welcome her? In some ways, Washington, DC could be a very small town.

Once the Board concluded the call, despite a vow of silence, several members called several other people about this development, and those people contacted yet others by cell and by e-mail, minute by minute furthering the chain of people who knew.

Earlier, Noah's techie friends, who had no allegiance to any of the parties involved, promptly spread the word throughout the hacker community. And pretty soon it was like an unstoppable freight train, in this case the cyberspace equivalent.

It didn't take long before news of Sandy's handiwork landed on Facebook, was being Tweeted and blogged about, and then picked up by various Internet news services. That Sandy had created Shane, that she *was* Shane, had just gone viral, and virtual justice was at hand, but neither Isabel nor Sandy was aware of this development.

· ● · ● · ● ·

The voice sounded distant, otherworldly. Sandy glanced down to discover that she was still leaning against the kitchen counter, and was equally surprised to find a glass in her hand, elevated a few inches above the dark granite. The bourbon was all but gone. How long had she been standing here? She glanced at the clock on the microwave. It was nearly nine. Another shout. Bill. But where the hell was he calling from and why wasn't he using the intercom?

"What?" she yelled back.

His voice rumbled down the stairs. "Get up here! Now."

A chill crawled up her spine when she realized he must be in her office. She'd been here for well over an hour, her mind traveling down all sorts of dead ends. She was afraid to go upstairs. She'd have to be Houdini to get out of this one. And now he was calling. She set the glass down, and on her way out of the kitchen she turned off the lights. Taking each step slowly, she heard her mother's voice taunting her, *So, what'd I tell you, you vile slut? And fucking Ron to boot? Thought you could get away with it? Hah. That'll show you!*

"Oh, shut up, Margaret!"

Bill sat at her messy desk, his arms folded across his chest, her high school yearbook open to the page containing Shane's senior photo. "Now suppose you just tell me what the hell you've been up to." His tone was hard-edged. "I don't want any lies. The truth, Goddammit!"

Sandy squeezed her eyes shut, hoping for a few tears, but none came. In a tiny voice she said, "I'm sorry. I screwed up." When she peered at him, she saw that he was staring at her without a hint of sympathy.

"Well, you got that right. What the *fuck* were you thinking? Jesus Christ, are you out of your mind? I can't even begin to imagine what got you going down that—"

"Let me explain, Bill," she said and began to move toward him.

He put up his hands. "I don't wanna hear it. You've done some crazy things, but I always thought you were worth it." He stopped and studied her. "How could you do that to a little girl? Even if you don't like her, or whatever the hell reason you—" His voice trailed off and he shook his head. "What if she dies?" he said softly.

In the next moment, though, his eyes seethed with contempt. "And why the fuck did you use Shane's picture? Goddamn you! You fucking bitch!" Then he again grew quiet.

"I should have known," he finally said. "She's his, isn't she?" He studied her reaction, but her eyes were cast down and she didn't move. "He's the one got you pregnant, not me. All these years I believed you, you conniving little cunt. Jess looks just like him." He stared down at the photo, tears brimming in his eyes.

For once, words failed Sandy, and she stood before him, powerless. He wasn't going to rescue her; no, he was turning against her. Just like her mother, just like Les, just like everyone before him.

In school not many topics had captured Sandy's attention, but the Spanish Inquisition had fascinated her. Often, she'd envisioned using medieval torture on her mother. Now the barbaric methods danced in her head. She imagined being hung from the rafters or burned at the stake, her skin peeling away, questions being hurled at her by Isabel and Bill, Alison Kendall and the Board of Directors, all the bitchy moms. *My sweet Jessie. God, Jess, I did it for you! Don't you know how much I love you!* All the while the strange voice scoffed at her.

"What are we going to do?" she eked out.

"*We?*" Bill said with disgust. "Get the hell out." He stood and hurled the yearbook across the room at her, but she remained there stock still. On his way out, he shoved her so hard that she flew against the wall, her head shuddering against the edge of the bookshelf. Pain shot through her as she sank to the floor with a whimper.

· ● · ● · ● ·

As Isabel stood at the gas pump, she felt impatient, watching the dollars mount while the gallons accumulated at a snail's pace. She was in no mood to wait until the tank was completely full, so she stopped the flow of gas. She went around to the trunk where she always kept sneakers and a set of black leggings and a dark gray t-shirt for her almost daily lunch workouts. As she withdrew them, she noticed a yellow two-gallon plastic can she kept in case her car ran out of gas. She stared at it. It seemed as if divine providence had placed the container there.

She returned to the pump and filled the gas can a little more than halfway. After screwing the lid on, she set it securely behind the driver's seat. Then she used the bathroom to change into her workout clothes and got back into her car.

It was a little before ten o'clock when Isabel parked a block away from the Littleton's. Though she hardly cared what happened to her, she still had enough sense to take precautions. Lugging the heavy plastic container, she trekked carefully through several backyards, none of them with fences, and peered into lit windows making sure no one saw her.

A few minutes later she arrived at the back of the Littleton's house. Almost all the lights were out, except a couple on the second floor and one on the third. As she set out to do what she'd imagined only a short while earlier, her breath came in big gulps. For several minutes she squatted in the shadows by the side of the house to stop her trembling. She tried to steady her hands as she unscrewed the cap. She inhaled the gaseous vapors, which braced her.

Do it now, she told herself. The image of Phoebe's lifeless face and limbs fortified her resolve. The bare branches of trees waved in the night sky. The only sounds were the faint soughing of the wind and the loud thump of her heart.

Staying in a low crouch she moved around to the front of the house, tiptoeing up the four wide steps to the veranda that ran the length of the house. She eyed the large picture windows that stared out at the front yard and the narrow panes of glass on either side of the mammoth custom-made doors that seemed to be watching her.

Unsteadily, she backed down each wooden rise as she poured the liquid onto the surface of the three lower steps. She avoided the one that connected to the veranda itself. That was as far as her plan went. If the fire climbed that last stair to the wooden deck, well, she'd leave that up to fate.

Several times she checked over her shoulder for passersby or late-night dog-walkers, and constantly she listened for cars, ready to sprint to the safety of the bushes and shadows alongside the house. She was imagining the damage – heavily charred steps – and figured it was minimal compared to what she really wanted, which was to burn the whole damn house down. She had to at least destroy some-thing. How else could she repay that horrible Sandy Littleton? But this was only the beginning. After the last of the gasoline dribbled onto the bottom stair, she pulled out a pack of matches.

Her hands shook violently. Finally, she managed to rip out a match and strike it against the coarse strip on the back. Nothing. She tore out another. It too refused to light.

She again steadied herself. The fumes of the gasoline reached into her nostrils. Calm down. Take a breath. Phoebe. Do it for Phoebe. Once more she tried. This time, the match flared to life. She threw it at the steps, but the tiny flame extinguished before arriving at its destination.

"Damn it," she whispered, separating another match from the pack. This one she struck carefully and again it caught. Shakily, she lowered the flame to a spot of fuel on the lowest step. At last a tiny fire danced and began to spread along that single stair. She imag-ined it engulfing the house, bit by bit, reaching inside the living room, then traveling upstairs into Sandy's bedroom. She imagined her shrieking in pain as the searing heat consumed her. But the fire on the step threatened to die.

Finally, Isabel took the entire matchbook, held it to the di-minishing flame, allowed it to ignite, then flung it onto the step with the most fluid. This time there was a pop and suddenly all three stairs were ablaze.

Isabel grabbed the gasoline can and ran behind the house. She took a moment to glance around and catch her breath, then crossed the backyard into the neighbor's property and crept away. This time, as she traversed the same gardens she'd traveled earlier, her right foot slipped into a dark puddle. She lost her balance and tumbled headlong into the sodden earth.

Instantly, frigid water seeped into her clothing. She gasped. Instead of jumping up, though, she simply sat there, her mind struggling to understand what was happening. Where she was. What she was doing. At once, though, her mind snapped into place and Isabel moved into action.

She got up on her hands and knees, grabbed the plastic container and desperately tried to force water into it. When that proved futile, she scrambled to locate her cell phone, found it, tapped it on. Its glowing surface lit up her frowning face. She took a deep breath and struck three numbers: 9-1-1.

About to punch the green call button, something stopped her. What was that? She looked up. A fat, wet drop of rain landed on her forehead. Then another and another. She stared up into the dark heavens in disbelief.

A moment later, her heart still sprinting, Isabel got behind the wheel. She prayed the fire hadn't gotten out of control. A fierce rain forced her to switch on the car's wipers. Her teeth chattering, she finally remembered to flick on the seat heaters. Two houses before the Littleton's she pulled up to the curb and peered at the dying fire.

Frightening thoughts tugged at her. What if the fire had torn through the house? What if something had happened to Jessie? Or Bill? The notion terrified her. While moments ago she might have cursed the change in weather, now she felt grateful.

Though she departed the Littletons' neighborhood with the image of the scarred stairs etched into her psyche, slowly, she began to feel as if she, not some vigilante, some alien being, were inhabiting her body again.

Now all she wanted was to be back at Phoebe's bedside in the embrace of her parents, who'd be waiting for her. A few blocks from the hospital she changed out of her wet clothes and discarded the leggings, t-shirt and gas can in a roadside trash container. She proceeded to the hospital, where she examined herself in the mirror of a bathroom near the ICU. She shook her head at the forlorn image, then thoroughly washed her hands before sniffing her hair and brushing the imagined smoke out of it.

Chapter Eight

Wednesday, November 19, 2008

It was shortly after midnight and Sandy was exhausted. After Bill had struck her, for the first time ever, she'd locked herself into her study and refused to come out. When smoke from the burned steps penetrated the house, she hadn't cared. Not just then anyway. Some tiny, diminishing part of her believed she deserved to die because of what she'd done, while a more substantial part believed she was the one who'd been wronged.

She wasn't even entirely sure there had been a fire, but if there was, intuition told her that Isabel had set it, or she'd sent someone, though she was equally certain that someone was *not* Ron Murrow. No, he wasn't the type. Whereas Isabel, acting all cool and lawyer-like, possessed a streak of meanness a mile long.

Sandy considered herself a keen observer of human types, but she also figured it would be hard to prove that Ms. High-and-Mighty had committed this crime. As her mind jumped from one thought to the next, she knew she could ill afford to make such an accusation as it would only further expose her and shove her deeper into a hole she was already struggling to get out of.

A year earlier, when Sandy had arrived in Bethesda, she'd imagined being invited to balls and galas and at some point making it into the Style section of the *Washington Post* or the society section of *The Washingtonian* magazine or even of *Bethesda Magazine*. But it had all proved elusive. And she certainly didn't want to be in the spotlight this way. She could already see the headlines: *Woman Uses Facebook: Causes Girl to Commit Suicide. Girl's Mother Retaliates, Starts Fire.* No, no, no.

She replayed Isabel's entrance into her kitchen several times. Though it had disarmed her, she'd relished the look on Isabel's face when she realized that her *dear husband* had lied to her. Sandy had been caught between wanting Isabel to know she'd had an affair with her husband and keeping that news hidden from Bill. At least now she knew Ron hadn't had the guts to tell his wife she'd given him a meal for the family, afraid what else she'd *given* him would be written all over his face. Men were so predictable.

Three delicious memories of Ron – their date at the Jefferson Hotel, Jack's Boathouse, and the Georgetown Mall garage – caused a smile to flicker across her lips. She'd especially enjoyed sucking him off. The way he'd groaned and shivered had truly delighted her. So satisfying the way she could make a man feel. It always amazed her how stingy women got with sex as they grew older. Like Isabel. Jesus fucking Christ, give a guy a break!

Outside, the heavy rain had turned into a wintery slush. She could hear its angry tapping against the window. Loud enough to creep her out. She wrapped her arms around herself.

If only she could find some wiggle room. But how, and where? She figured that nothing angered a man more than something that threatened his manliness. Suddenly Jessie, the kid Bill had loved, was the ugly reminder of a guy who'd come before him. No, of a guy who'd fucked his wife and gotten her pregnant in a way he couldn't and never would. She'd always taken the blame for not being able to get pregnant again, but now she imagined he saw through yet one more lie of hers. That he hadn't gotten hip to the truth sooner had surprised her: she hadn't wanted another fat belly ruining her figure. One baby was plenty. And how could she love another child as much as Jessie?

Maybe after he'd had time to think things through, Bill wouldn't leave her. The whole freaking mess would die down and he'd forgive her. But if he did want a divorce, well, she figured she'd get at least half of all their money and the property they'd accumulated. Her mind scrolled through their assets, something she kept track of. At least she wouldn't be broke. Maybe she'd move to another town and set up camp there. Maybe this time she'd go someplace warm, someplace less snotty, and find a nice old rich man to take care of her. Maybe she and Jessie would go to Florida. If Jessie would forgive her. But she couldn't think about that now.

With that in mind, Sandy got up, unlocked the door, and went downstairs to make herself a cup of coffee. In the morning she'd have a little talk with Jessie. She'd explain herself. Or try to. Would she understand that, bottom line, she'd done it for her? Okay, it was wrong to snoop. But really, after all the stuff she'd done for Jessie, didn't that count for anything?

As she wound down the steps to the first floor, the stink of smoke was more noticeable, and fanning her face with one hand, she called out. "Bill. Jessie." Several more times she hollered their names. She stopped halfway down the steps, finally realizing that nobody was home. They'd gone and left without a word. Frightened, she crept into her bedroom and locked the door.

· ● · ● · ● ·

Isabel cast a quick glance at Phoebe before greeting her parents and apologizing for being so late. Then she clung to her dark-haired mother like a desperate child. How had her life spun so completely out of control? Her mother fixed her with a kind stare and told her that although everything seemed bleak just now, it would turn out all right. That she ought to "give her problems up to God, to the powers that be" and give herself a rest. "You just have to let go and believe," her mother, a devout churchgoer, told her.

Like her father, Isabel had scoffed at this advice many times over the years, but now, she was willing to heed her mother's advice. So after a few minutes of quiet conversation, in which Isabel said nothing about Sandy Littleton's role in preying on Phoebe, and certainly nothing about the fire, she hugged her mother once more.

On his way out, her father stopped and clasped her hands. "Don't forget, I'm here for you too, Iz."

Isabel withdrew her hands. It was such a typical thing for him to say. All because she hadn't hugged him or given him any attention. A cavalcade of emotions assaulted her. She'd gone into law because she'd wanted to please him. Because like him, she liked the concreteness of rules and regulations. She knew of his aversion to the messiness of emotions. "Jesus, Dad, don't you know anything?" she found herself saying, "You're part of the reason she's in here.

Just like me."

He stiffened. "Why, whatever do you mean?"

In a sudden moment of clarity, Isabel pitied him. Too tired to get into it, she said quietly, "Just think about it. The demand to be perfect, successful, and all the rest runs in the family. And so does the need. Maybe some other time we can discuss it." Though she doubted that time would come. He stood there appearing puzzled.

She accompanied him to the door of the ICU, where her mother waited. She bade them both good-bye and went to the vending machine for some coffee. It would be a long night. About this she was certain.

Back in the ICU, reclining in the leather-cushioned chair beside Phoebe's hospital bed, Isabel quietly sipped her coffee and watched Phoebe's even intake and exhale of breath, which, despite the maddening sameness of it, went a long way toward steadying her nerves. Until her thoughts veered back to Ron and Sandy.

What *had* happened between them? Where had they met? For a moment she considered whether the encounter had been innocent, until the image of Sandy curled up beside Ron at the parents' party popped into her mind. And the night he'd used the word "hon." And other recent aberrant behavior. She sat upright. No, she couldn't allow her thoughts to venture further in this direction. She would read. From her oversize bag she withdrew that all-time great piece of children's literature, *Harry Potter and the Sorceror's Stone.*

On opening it, she saw the original publication date, 1997, three years after Phoebe was born. "I'll bet you didn't know that, Feebs," she whispered to her daughter. As if it were somehow significant. But painful thoughts followed. Her daughter had turned 14 while lying in a hospital bed. And Ron had forgotten her birthday. He'd been too busy meeting up with Sandy and then covering his tracks. The extent of his deception appalled her.

To keep from breaking down, she turned to the first page of the story and began to read about the Dursleys of Privet Drive, a couple who believed they were "perfectly normal."

Normal, Isabel thought. If only things could return to normal. But they were so far from normal it was insane, even when reviewing events from a detached distance. Her daughter lay inert after having tried to commit suicide, a woman – a treacherous woman – had used Facebook to prey on her daughter, her husband had lied to her about...about who knew what, and to top it all off, she'd just committed arson! Could things get any worse? Then she looked at Phoebe. At least she was alive. "Please wake up, baby. You hear me? Your mommy misses you."

Staring at the fanciful cover of *Harry Potter*, she thought, if someone wrote a novel about our situation, no one would believe it. Far too strange. And so was love...what people did in its name. She thought of the strange shapes of love. She sat, listening to the hum and bleep of the machines. *Let go and let God,* she heard her mother say. And as for her girl, she knew there was nothing more anyone could do for her. It truly seemed to be up to some higher force.

· ● · ● · ● ·

Perhaps an hour or so later, Isabel's calm shredded as the conversation with Dr. Bailey once more insinuated itself into her thoughts. She hadn't been very encouraging. If Phoebe didn't wake up soon, she and Ron would have to make a decision no parent should have to make. When to let their precious child go. The mere thought of it made Isabel's gut churn. She clutched Phoebe's hand, recalling Dr. Bailey's words.

"If she has no brain function, then—" Dr. Bailey had stopped. "Then there's no sensation," she'd said, speaking softly, "hence, no awareness of the pain."

To keep her despair at bay, she began massaging Phoebe's left hand, avoiding the bandages on her wrist. "Hello, sweet girl, how are you? I'm sorry it took me so long. Did you miss me? I missed you. I miss you every minute, every day." She closed her eyes and slowly but gently kneaded Phoebe's arm, then stood up and went to the foot of her bed. "Did you have a good visit with Grandmom and Grandpop?"

She lifted the covers off Phoebe's legs and began rubbing them, first one, then the other, humming the tune to "You Are My Sunshine." When she finished she placed the sheet and blanket back over Phoebe's legs, tucked them under her cold feet, and moved around to her left side to begin working on her other arm and hand, careful to avoid the IV tube taped to her wrist.

"Feebs, do you remember when you were little and we were at the beach? That thing I used to sing to you?"

She inhaled a deep breath and in a quiet voice, so as not to disturb the other patients and their families, began to say the words she used to sing, "I paint the trees green, the sky blue, I toss glitter on the sea… you know why?" She waited for the reply Phoebe had given countless times, *Why?* She watched Phoebe's lips with anticipation. Come on, baby, say it.

"Because I love you," she said, finishing the poem she'd made up for her baby daughter.

· ● · ● · ● · ·

Isabel startled at the sound of a voice. Her eyes blinked open. The *Harry Potter* book still lay open in her lap, a couple of feet away Phoebe was still unconscious, and Ron stood at the foot of the bed observing her, his face appearing to mask all emotion. In a split second though, the lurid events of the previous day came hurtling back into Isabel's mind.

What she wanted most in that moment was to yell at him, demand to know what had happened between him and Sandy, and call him a slew of names, but she resisted the urge. At a momentary loss for words, she glanced around the ICU. "We can't talk here," she said, a resigned look transforming her visage. "Say hi to Feebs," she ordered, "then we'll grab some coffee...in the cafeteria."

She could see that Ron had little desire to talk to her, about as much, she imagined, as he longed to meet up with her father to explain himself. No one got away with lies or half-truths with Mr. John Winthrop.

He nodded, then spoke briefly to Phoebe and bent over to kiss her cheek.

In the hospital cafeteria they encountered a hive of activity where graveyard nurses and docs bumped into the morning shift. They got in line for their coffees and some scrambled eggs for Isabel. After a wordless few minutes they sat down across from one another at a small out-of-the-way table.

Ron stared off, looking weary and uncomfortable. Isabel suddenly felt ravenous, having eaten little in the previous twenty-four hours, and inhaled a piece of wheat toast. After several bites of egg, she speared a piece of sausage and held it aloft as her gaze fixed on Ron. "I wonder what it must feel like to know you messed around with the woman responsible for your daughter being in a coma. I really can't imagine it." She watched him carefully.

The next sentence she had to coax out of her mouth because in reality she had little desire to learn the details of Ron's secret encounter. "Now, tell me exactly what happened."

Ron's breath caught. His eyes retreated from Isabel as he reached for his coffee. He took a sip, because he couldn't speak, not without stuttering and stumbling. It struck him odd, though, that Isabel's voice contained none of the rage he'd imagined. At least if she'd been furious, he could have refused to talk until she "calmed down."

Though he'd had all night to imagine what Sandy might have told Isabel, and how he should react, he was coming up empty. Sandy couldn't possibly have revealed their little sexual encounters, could she? Clinton's famous declaration – "I did not have sex with that woman" – jumped into his head. He'd actually been at that press conference and still felt a grudging admiration for the man who'd virtually been caught in the act and yet remained married *and* President. But then Monica Lewinsky hadn't tried to kill Chelsea.

Ron was still having trouble believing that Sandy had created Shane. That she was Shane. That the woman had purred in his ear and sucked him off after doing something so despicable. How had he let someone so corrupt, so rotten into his life? It simply didn't compute. His entire world had shifted on its axis. He only knew that he'd landed in some form of hell from which he was unlikely to extricate himself. Short of a miracle.

Unable to stave off the inevitable, he began one version of an excuse. "I knew you'd be mad if I told you she wanted to bring us a meal," he said haltingly, "but I thought it was a nice gesture, there was already enough water under the bridge." He was careful to incorporate as much of the truth as possible. "So I offered to meet her at the Georgetown Mall and get it from her. I had a drink at the sushi place, you know the one—" he looked to Isabel for confirmation, but she simply stared at him, so he continued, "— anyway, after she arrived we each had a sake, and that was it."

"A sake? With her? At a restaurant?" Isabel said. "At a time like this? On your daughter's birthday? Which you forgot!"

Ron's head fell into his hands. "Oh, God, I'm sorry." For a moment he closed his eyes.

Isabel refused to be softened. "Now, I want you to listen to me. Whatever else happened, and I suspect something did, I don't want to know. You know why?"

She paused, her eyes skewering him once more. "Because if that's the kind of man you are, you'll have to live with it."

He was about to defend himself, then thought better of it. What was the point of more lying?

"And the other reason I don't care is that last night I promised myself something. To stay positive and focused on Phoebe getting well. Everything else pales in comparison. Including you and Sandy." Though she spoke with determination and conviction, she felt tragic and sad and deeply wounded. "I can't let my mind and heart get all poisoned by crazy thoughts of that horrid woman with my husband. It just doesn't matter. It really doesn't."

Ron reached across the table to take her hand, but she pulled it away. Instead, she lifted a glass of water to her lips and slowly drank its contents. "And here's what else I want to tell you," she said. "Sandy denied having been behind Shane, but it was obvious that she did it. She screamed at me, told me to get out of her house. Which I did. But then I did something else." She took a few more bites of the eggs, this time half-heartedly. A sip of her coffee.

She dropped her voice to a half-whisper. "I tried to —"

She stopped. Why should she tell Ron about the Littleton's steps? It was far too complicated and she was too tired. In any case, she doubted the police would investigate. If they did, it was unlikely they'd suspect her. And should it come to that, it was best for Ron to remain ignorant.

She gave him one last look, said, "Never mind," and then abruptly rose from the table.

Chapter Nine

Thursday, November 20, 2008

When Isabel finally came home after another crushing day at the hospital, she could tell that Ron was making himself scarce, which suited her fine. Though she was enormously angry and hurt, she had in fact compartmentalized the entire tawdry episode she assumed he'd had with Sandy, because she was bound and determined to remain optimistic. She'd deal with her tattered marriage later. And really, it was the only way she could survive.

She headed for the kitchen, called out to Jackson, and said she was going to throw a pizza in the oven. "Is that okay?"

"Sure," he said, though his look suggested otherwise. Poor guy, she thought, and went to give him a hug. Though at first he resisted, finally he embraced her. "This has been tough on you, too, buddy, and I'm sorry."

Earlier, while ministering to Phoebe and walking the hospital corridors, Isabel's fight had come back. She renewed her vow to expose Sandy, but she'd do it openly and legally. She'd drag her through any court that would hear her case, and she wouldn't give up until Sandy paid for what she'd done. The scales of Justice, with a capital J, had to be righted.

One thing she regretted though was her attitude toward Jessie. She was, Isabel realized, an innocent in all this. Not only that, but she'd had the courage to unveil the truth about her mother's treachery. If she could do anything to save that child, she would, though at the moment she couldn't think what that might be. Get her away from her mother? Give her room to breathe.

She felt grateful too that the fire hadn't harmed the girl. Or Bill. *Thank God!*

The loud jangling of the kitchen phone startled her. She reached for it. "Hello?" she said. Ron must have picked it up simultaneously, wherever he was, because instead of hearing the caller's voice, she heard her husband say, "Ron Murrow here."

Then a nurse from the hospital announced herself. It was Nurse Laura, one of Phoebe's caretakers she'd grown fond of. She was efficient, courteous, upbeat, and attractive. Everything one could possibly want in a nurse, or really in most any human being.

"I think you should come to the hospital," Laura said. "It's urgent."

Isabel gasped. "Why? What is it?"

She only heard a few more sentences before she hung up the phone and was running through the hallway grabbing her purse and coat.

· ● · ● ·

Sandy wandered around the house aimlessly, trying to figure out what to take with her. She'd decided to leave, knowing no one was coming home or visiting her. Not in the near future anyway, maybe never. In fact, she hadn't seen Bill or Jessie since shortly after a certain someone had tried to incinerate their house. Even her handful of friends were avoiding her. Since Wednesday nothing but a great big fat silence.

It was doubtful, too, that she would hear from her mother or sister, interaction with "home" was rare, especially since Les had died, Les who would check on her from time to time, until he was killed in a car crash a couple of years ago. Still, she thought Margaret or Ashley might trip over some of the awful stuff floating around on the Internet and call to gloat, or for once actually show a little sympathy and defend her.

It scared her, not knowing what lay ahead. She'd had a couple of beers, chased down with a shot or two of whiskey, and now she felt wobbly. She had to get it together. She planned to leave under the cover of night. Escape was the word that rolled around in her head.

Without switching on the light, she searched Jessie's room. She wasn't entirely sure what she was looking for, some memento of her daughter, even though she knew that somewhere down the road, this single memory would make her sad. Very sad. She had little control over her crying and once again grew weepy; she pulled out a wadded up Kleenex from her pink sweatshirt pocket and blew her nose. Then she wiped her tears.

Moonlight streamed in, casting a milky glow over the room. On her daughter's dresser she spied a framed photo of the three of them. Jessie, with curly hair and a dimpled smile, had been four. Sandy picked it up and thought of their trip to Disney World, recalling how she'd been more excited than Jess.

As a child, Sandy had never been to Disney World. In fact, she'd hardly been anywhere, with circumstances as they'd been, her mother too preoccupied to travel, until Bill began taking her wherever she wanted because his business was making money hand over fist. And yet it was Disney World that had seemed nothing less than the fulfillment of her dreams. Back then. Until she'd become aware of how much more there was to see and do and—

A loud roar caused her head to jerk up. What the hell was that? It sounded like an airplane had just landed in her yard. She thought of the President's helicopter and ran to the window. Just then an explosion rattled the entire house. It seemed to have come from the living room. In the ensuing chaos, she dropped the framed photo, hardly realizing that she had. When she stepped to one side of the window for a better view, her foot landed on a shard of glass.

"Ouch," she screamed.

Though the pain registered somewhere in her brain, her mind was having trouble comprehending why a pick-up truck lurched back and forth in her front yard. Several times it drove a few feet across the lawn, then skidded to a halt, backed up and roared forward again, though in a new direction. At the same time, she saw several guys in dark clothes and hoodies run silently from the front of the house, avoid the truck, then speed across the street. They hopped into an idling SUV, which took off seconds after the last door slammed shut. The small truck jumped the curb and followed a moment later.

While all this went on, across the street she'd noticed a few neighbors' lights switch on and faces appear at several windows, probably trying to see what all the racket was about, but as soon as the SUV and pick-up were gone their faces disappeared and the lights went off.

Sandy was barely breathing. Afraid to go downstairs, yet knowing she'd have to sooner or later, she turned to leave Jessie's room. The moment she took her first step, she yelped at the pain that shot through her foot and up her leg. The piece of glass had embedded itself in her heel. She collapsed on the pale rug where she saw a pear-shaped stain of blood that had come from her wound. It made her woozy.

Oh, God, why is all this happening? And why the fuck isn't Bill here to protect me? What if those people come back? Should she call him? No, he probably wouldn't answer. In his one and only call the previous day, he'd said he and Jess had moved into a hotel, without revealing their location. He also said he'd told Jessie about the real Shane, that he was her biological father, after which he claimed she'd cried and asked if he still loved her because she loved him, and that he'd reassured her. Even if she wasn't his flesh and blood he truly cared for her.

Happy for your love fest, she now thought. But the fact that they'd so readily discarded her, well, it hurt more than she cared to admit.

Cradling her leg she searched her foot for the glass, which was hard to see in the dim room. But she didn't need the light to feel it. Once she got a hold of the offending fragment, she yanked it out, then got up and limped into Jess's bathroom. She cursed a few times while she sat on the edge of the tub rinsing her foot and applying Neosporin.

An image of Jessie as a young child in the bathtub lifted itself into her mind and though she wished it away, the memory refused to budge. The cute little toddler, then the gorgeous little girl, curly brown locks framing an inquisitive, happy-go-lucky face. Once again, tears welled up.

When she finally hobbled downstairs, her foot bandaged, she flipped on the lights as she went. In the kitchen she poured herself another big tumbler of Canadian Club to fortify herself before going into the living room to find out what those horrible people, whoever they were, had done. She got as far as the edge of the pale yellow Persian rug, where she stopped.

The huge picture window, with its view of the mammoth oak tree at the foot of their lawn, had been smashed, and an explosion of glass littered the room. She stepped back. Surveying the mess, she was again tempted to call Bill. But, knowing he didn't want to hear from her, in the next instant it pleased her to think that a few days from now he'd return home and discover the vandalism, the ruined yard and house. She tried to imagine the look on his face.

She rose back up the stairs, taking one step at a time, and began to pack. She had just returned to Jessie's room for a keepsake, a photo and one of her many stuffed bears, when the doorbell rang. Her first thought was reflexive, one she couldn't control: Bill's back, he's forgiven me. Thank heaven. Her second: Why's he ringing the bell?

· ● · ● · ● ·

Isabel drove through the dark streets along the all-too familiar path to the hospital, her hand fingering her hair, her emotions flip-flopping. One moment she was filled with excitement and hope and the next with fear and despair. The nurse's words were etched into her brain: "We can't say for certain, but it looks like Phoebe might be coming out of her coma."

"It could be a false alarm," Isabel said, turning the radio on, trying to find a channel that matched her vacillating moods. But even worse she couldn't quell her anxiety, the fear of what might greet her. What if Phoebe had lost her ability to speak or hear, or what if she'd gone blind?

She'd heard of brain-damaged people growing angry and violent, their personalities irrevocably altered. Who knew how long her brain had been oxygen-deprived from lack of blood? The longer the worse the outcome. Her stomach squirmed. *God, please let her be all right. Please.*

When Isabel arrived at the hospital, her legs felt leaden. Each step seemed like a huge effort, as if she were dragging her feet through sludge. She was afraid to enter the ICU and discover that the nurse had been mistaken. That it was nothing after all. What she saw from across the room when she stepped inside were Noah and Emma, each holding one of Phoebe's hands, and talking to her, though even from that distance, she could tell it was a one-way conversation.

Noah must have felt her eyes on him, because he dropped Phoebe's hand, then turned toward Isabel as she approached. But what drew her attention was a huge card on Phoebe's bedside table – with tiny images and the signatures of many of her classmates, and "Happy Birthday, Phoebe" in colorful letters. She felt so grateful that Emma and Noah had remembered, she hugged each of them in turn and thanked them for keeping Phoebe company.

"These past few days it's been rare that we could have dinner together at home," she explained, though of course that was only partly true. She hadn't actually had dinner with Ron, nor had she wanted to. Isabel had been telling herself she'd stop all pretenses; it was one of the bargains she'd made with God in exchange for Phoebe's recovery, but old habits die slowly. And the words had popped out of her mouth before she even realized what she was saying.

She gazed into Noah's dark eyes, such sweet pools of innocence, and almost explained her dissembling, but knew it would only confuse and burden him and Emma. It was enough that she'd caught herself. This flurry of thought occurred in a fraction of a second.

"How is she?" Isabel said, looking at Phoebe, who lay there quietly, as she had the previous ten days. Her stomach sank. "The nurse told us she moved?" she said.

Emma nodded. "She did. Twice. Once when we gave her a news flash."

"News flash?"

"Yes, we told her that Dylan and Skyla were an item now!" She smiled at Isabel, as if expecting her to understand.

Though Isabel returned the smile, she didn't pick up on the joke. "Maybe it was involuntary?" She glanced around. "Do you know where the nurse is, the one named Laura?"

Noah searched for her too. "She was over there a minute ago." He pointed to another patient's bed across the room.

"Excuse me, I'm going to see if I can find her," Isabel said, then threaded her way to the nurse's station in the center of the ICU.

"I got a call from Laura a short while ago," she said to a nurse whose eyes remained fixed on the computer screen in front of her, "about my daughter, Phoebe Murrow...that she was...that she might be coming out of her coma." Isabel's voice sounded tense and slightly high-pitched.

She wondered if the woman was even listening. "But she doesn't seem any different to me."

The nurse finally looked up. "Coming out of a coma isn't like waking up from sleep. And it's different for everybody, but I'll let her know," she said. "I'm sure she'll be right over."

Isabel thought about what she said. "Do you mean soon? Or when? What about Dr. Bailey? Is she around?"

It was only after Isabel returned to Phoebe's bedside that she realized the breathing tube had been removed. How could she have missed that?

"When did they take the tube out?" she asked Noah and Emma.

"About fifteen minutes ago," Emma replied.

"What if something happens?" *Like she stops breathing?* Isabel thought. "Shouldn't they be watching her?" She said this more to herself than to Emma or Noah, but he answered anyway.

"This thing on her finger," Noah said, pointing to Phoebe's right hand, "it's an oxygen saturation monitor. The nurse told me if it drops below a certain level some alarm will go off. But she also said to push this buzzer if I thought something was wrong." He lifted a thick white plastic tube with a button on the end.

"Oh, okay," she said. Noah's memory and obvious intelligence impressed her.

"Yeah, and one other thing. It sounded like Phoebe made a noise, sort of a groan, after they took the thing out."

"I heard it, too," Emma chimed in, a smile lighting up her porcelain features.

"Really?" Isabel said hopefully. "Oh, my gosh, do you think she might actually—" *come back to us?* She lifted Phoebe's hand. "I'm here, darling. Your good friends, Noah and Emma, are too. Isn't that lovely? And your father and brother are coming."

Until someone said something, she would ignore the "two-at-a-time" rule in the ICU.

Before she'd left home, Ron had taken her by the shoulders. "I think everything's going to be all right," he said, an uncharacteristic desperation in his eyes. She'd unlatched his hands, had trouble even meeting his gaze, though part of her had wanted to fall into his embrace. "Yes, maybe," she said. "Let's hope so."

Now Emma said she ought to get home, but would return on Saturday. After Isabel insisted that Emma take a taxi, "I don't want you wandering around out there in the dark," she pressed cab fare into the girl's hand and gave her another heartfelt hug.

Once she left, Isabel noticed a paperback copy of *To Kill a Mockingbird* lying open beside the card, the cover facing up. "Have you been reading to her?" she asked Noah. "It's one of Phoebe's favorites. But I guess you knew that?"

He nodded.

"Why don't you keep reading? I'd love to hear it too." She wanted to keep her mind occupied and could think of nothing more soothing than to hear this boy's voice.

And so he began to read, picking up apparently where he'd left off. But almost immediately Isabel's mind spun off. Until he said something about events leading to an accident.

Events that lead to an accident, Isabel thought. Will we ever be able to look back on this as an accident? She thought too about how every community, in a way, mirrored the small town of Monroeville, where prejudice existed and despicable things happened. After a few more sentences, in which Boo Radley and Dill were introduced, she found her interest flagging and only half-listened. Her foot tapped the floor with growing restlessness; she worried about where Ron and Jackson could be, and why the nurse or a doctor hadn't shown up.

Even as these thoughts marched through her mind, Ron came through the door of the ICU and Laura's dark head of wavy hair bobbed toward Phoebe's bed. Before she reached them, though, the nurse veered off to the left, saying something to Ron as she passed him. Now where was she off to?

At Ron's approach Isabel's brow knitted into a slight frown.

"Where's Jackson?"

Somewhat sheepishly Ron told her that their son had received a call from Matthew, one of his best friends and a neighbor. "Maybe it's for the best?" he said, as if sensing Isabel's disapproval.

Her smile was tight. Jackson hadn't visited, not once, because she and Ron hadn't wanted him to remember his sister this way. But tonight she wanted him here. Phoebe might respond to his voice, she thought.

Trying to keep her disappointment in check, she turned to Noah. "I imagine your parents might like to get you home? It's getting late."

He nodded. "But it's okay, Mrs. Murrow, they know I'm here." He pushed the novel into his backpack, which he hoisted onto his shoulder, and extended his hand toward Ron. They shook. He took one more look at Phoebe, told her he'd come the following day if it was all right – he eyed Isabel, who said, of course it was – and asked for a call if there were any further developments.

"Of course, we will," Isabel said. He took off just as the nurse arrived.

Chapter Ten

Sandy hobbled down the stairs to answer the door. Squinting through the peephole, she saw that it wasn't Bill; no, two cops stood there. She had half a mind not to answer. Were they going to arrest her? Had Phoebe died? Another hard knock. Heart pounding, she opened up.

The two men flashed their badges at her. She felt so close to fainting that she barely heard their names. They took their time examining her – up, down and sideways it seemed – which was really annoying because she looked like shit. They sniffed the air – could they tell she'd been drinking? Hell, that was no crime – then glanced at her foot and asked if she was okay.

Do I look okay? she wanted to ask, but instead forced a smile onto her face. "It's been a rough night," she said.

"We can see that. Can we come inside?"

"I'm kind of busy," she said. "What's this about?"

One of them pointed at the vandalized lawn. Then she realized that most likely they were here because one of her stupid neighbors had reported the "disturbance."

"How long will this take?"

"Just a few minutes."

As it was, they took their time and asked plenty, like did she have any idea why someone would do such things to her house. Her property. Though tempted to say something about Isabel, and even vaguely wondering if that had been Ron's SUV, she just shook her head. "Nope, no idea, Officer."

"We can report it as vandalism and further look into it, Ma'am," one of them said.

If only she could explain how much Isabel hated her and all the problems she'd caused. If only they would arrest *her*. "No, it's not necessary," she said reluctantly. "There's lots of loony bins in the world, Officer, and I guess they picked my house."

She flashed him a beleaguered smile, praying they would leave.

· • · • · • ·

Laura greeted Ron and Isabel in her courteous, efficient manner, pushed a few buttons on the bedside monitor and reviewed the log. Isabel was dying to ask for details about Phoebe, but waited. The nurse took a few moments to observe her patient, then finally turned to Isabel and Ron. "Everything looks good," she said brightly.

"But what can you tell us about her *status*?" Isabel cast a worried glance at Phoebe, wondering if she could hear her. She stroked the blanket covering Phoebe's torso as she used to do when she was young.

"Well, I'm pretty sure she moved, and random movement

could mean she's recovering. There's really no set pattern, but things like that, along with opening their eyes, responding to their surroundings in some way, an increasing awareness of themselves, these are the things we watch for."

"So you're not sure?" Isabel asked, already feeling the adrenaline from her earlier excitement recede.

"Like I said, I'm *pretty* sure," Laura replied, then turned her eyes to one of the monitors. "Your parents are here, Phoebe. Can you give us a wink?" She chuckled a bit. "Oh, I guess you only do that for Noah, is that right?"

Isabel watched Phoebe's face, and for a moment she could have sworn the girl began blushing.

As if her explanation hadn't been interrupted, Laura continued describing the stages of recovery. "Response to pain is the first sign of consciousness. When the doctor comes by she might do what we call a 'chest rub' along the sternum, which simulates pain. If the patient responds that's a good sign, though not entirely specific.

"Visual and auditory tracking usually come next. For example, if she turns when you arrive and tracks your movements, or appears to be listening to your voice, that's also a good sign." Laura's eyes moved from Phoebe to Isabel and Ron. "Many people respond to their name or a loved one's voice."

They'd been told this before and now Isabel wanted to call out Phoebe's name, but she would wait until the nurse had finished.

"Obviously if she can respond to our commands and talk to us, well, then we know she's really on the mend. Sometimes all this happens very quickly, other times it happens over a longer period. Everybody's different."

How often Isabel had heard that annoying phrase! What Laura had refrained from saying was that the extent of the damage also influences the level of recovery. And that was still the big unknown, a factor teasing, taunting, and mocking Isabel.

What if her poor girl was brain-damaged for life?

Isabel could wait no longer. "Phoebe, we're here, darling," she said. "Daddy and I. We love you."

A groan startled the three of them. In unison they stared at Phoebe, whose head turned from one side to the other, as if she were agitated. "Oh, Phoebe," Isabel muttered. Ron stood at the foot of the bed and squeezed her foot. "Feebs, how ya doin', kiddo? You waking up from a long nap?"

Isabel thought she might cry then. Phoebe's eyes seemed to flutter, and for an instant they opened halfway, only to close again. "Oh, Phoebe," Isabel said again. "My darling child. We love you so much. Can you hear me?" Tears brimmed in her eyes. She reached for her hand and squeezed it. "We're here for you, sweetie. Right here." What other things could she say to coax her daughter back to life?

She felt slight pressure from Phoebe's fingers on the palm of her hand, but it was so faint she thought she might have imagined it.

· ● · ● · ● ·

Isabel took in deep breaths of the frigid night air as she walked to her car in the hospital parking lot. Her mood had shifted dramatically over the last two hours. She almost felt ebullient, especially when compared to her emotional nadir of the previous couple of days. When she pulled onto the street, she found herself turning left, not right. She wasn't the least bit tired.

Instead of heading home to see Jackson, she aimed north, toward Bethesda. Ron would pick him up. What did it matter if she came home an hour earlier or later? And if for some reason Ron called wondering where she was, she'd tell him the truth, though she doubted he would.

She didn't know why, but she wanted to go to the Littletons'. Well, she did know. She wanted to see the damage she'd done to their steps – had it only been two days ago? – and she also had a few questions to ask Sandy. She wanted to know how her own actions might have contributed to Sandy's creation of Shane? She wasn't excusing Sandy's conduct, but on the other hand, she felt it was essential to recognize her own faults. She'd rejected Sandy on numerous occasions, and had reported her to the police. Was that enough to cause someone to do this to a young girl?

If she felt gutsy enough she'd even apologize for setting the steps on fire and make reparations. Her own form of restorative justice. She again wondered how she'd done something so completely out of character? And yet, in the course of her work, she'd often encountered quite normal people who "cracked" when under severe pressure. Somehow she'd always applied different standards to herself. I guess I'm more like everyone else than I thought. She sighed.

Taking the final turn onto the Littletons' street, Isabel saw two police cars, one in front of their house, the other in the driveway. The rooftop light on the latter was rotating, though without the usual sense of urgency. Curious, she continued driving toward the house. Then, as she drew closer, she saw that the police were nowhere to be seen. They must be inside, she decided, growing a little worried. Could something have happened to Sandy?

As soon as she reached the edge of the Littleton's property, she saw skid marks crisscrossing the front yard, huge gashes in a formerly perfect lawn, ones that obviously had been made by a large SUV or small truck. Then, she squinted to make sure, but it looked as though one of the large picture windows had been broken. And graffiti defiled the walls.

The words "Liar, Bully, Killer" were spray-painted in white, black and red. Just beyond the smashed window was the two-foot tall word "bit," which puzzled her, until she passed the house and saw the concluding letters, "ch," on the side wall.

Isabel was shocked by this display of hatred and animosity. It frightened her. And it reminded her of the Southern town depicted in Harper Lee's novel. She felt as though her own fury and outrage had been transmuted into other people's actions. This needed to stop. And yet this thought brought her up short.

Two days ago she'd wanted to kill Sandy. Still far from forgiving her, Isabel wondered if she'd be feeling as generous if Phoebe hadn't shown signs of lifting out of her coma. Then again the final outcome of Phoebe's condition remained uncertain, and might for some time. Nonetheless, she felt strongly opposed to vandalism and bullying. It was that sort of behavior that had sent her daughter to despair and to attempt suicide in the first place.

With the police there she wouldn't be knocking on the front door. So now what?

Chapter Eleven

Friday, November 21, 2008

By the time Sandy got packed and loaded the luggage into her car, it was one o'clock on Friday morning. It still ticked her off how long the cops had delayed her. Not to mention her injury, which had forced her to move far more slowly than she would have liked. Now, after reaching the Beltway, she took a sip of coffee from the thermos, and a bite of a chocolate chip cookie she'd grabbed along with a few candy bars, an apple, and a container of *Slenderella*.

Shortly before leaving, she'd received an email from *Slenderella* management terminating her contract. For "unspecified reasons." This had added to her eagerness to get out of town. Right behind wanting to escape the vandalism and the cops, who'd given her the creeps. They only left after she said, "I just don't want anything more to do with whoever did this," her mind conjuring up Isabel's image.

More or less, those had been Bill's final words too. "We don't want anything more to do with you." Which, in the end, made it easier for her to leave. Still, she prayed that Jessie would remember how much she'd loved her, how much she'd done for her, and come around.

Of course, she had gotten Bill to give her a monthly allowance until they were legally split. "Just give me what's mine and I won't bother you." He didn't say yes or no, but agreed to put money into an account for her, and added that he planned to close their joint account. For the moment, she still trusted him to treat her fairly. In case he didn't, she'd hire a divorce attorney.

But the thing that motivated her "to get out of Dodge" most was Isabel. After a few miles on the Beltway, she was relieved to be putting distance between herself and that wretched woman. It was clear now that no one knew what Isabel Winthrop was truly capable of. She'd tried to burn their house down! An incident that over the past few days had expanded in Sandy's mind. She imagined herself battling the growing blaze. She imagined Isabel wanting to burn her at the stake. Who knew what else she might do, not that she was afraid of her, but, after all, she *was* a lawyer.

Sandy pointed her car south on I-95, toward palm trees and warmth. It would be a long night, so she drank more coffee and listened to the radio, trying hard not to think about who else she was leaving behind besides Isabel Winthrop.

· ● · ● · ● ·

This morning, for the first time, as she was preparing to head back to the hospital, Isabel itched to do some work. Perhaps she'd have one of the paralegals bring her a few folders. At least then she could focus on something other than waiting for Phoebe to emerge from the coma's fog. To return to her former life. Though she knew that life would never be the same.

Oh, Phoebe, my darling girl. We love you so much. Maybe you'll surprise me and be in your own room today. The doctor had called a short while earlier to say that Phoebe had continued to make progress throughout the night and might be ready to leave the ICU very soon. *Please, God, let it be so.*

She smelled French toast and bacon as she wandered down the stairs and entered the kitchen. Ron didn't look up, but continued cooking. "What do you know? Sleeping beauty's up. What's your pleasure? Coffee? Juice? Eggs?" he said.

Isabel could tell he was working hard to sound cheerful and she felt uncertain about how to respond. "I could use some coffee," she said, aiming for a neutral tone. She knew he was elated about Phoebe and trying to get back into her good graces, but she couldn't simply ignore all his transgressions. She needed time to consider what he'd done and how to respond. She recalled the promise she'd made eight years ago, but for now she would do nothing that might upset Phoebe. So for the moment she shelved all thoughts of divorce. Whatever she decided, it would have to wait. I'll think about it tomorrow, she thought. And with that her mouth curved into a faint smile.

"Where's Jackson?" she asked.

"Probably on X-Box, winning a battle against the Evil Empire."

At the mention of the word "evil" she couldn't help Sandy's image appearing before her eyes. With a quick shake of her head, she chased it away.

"I'll get him," she said. "Maybe then we can eat together?"

"Your wish is my command."

• · ● · ● · ● ·

Dawn was breaking as Sandy drove south along the coast of North Carolina. She'd always wanted to see the Outer Banks. Despite the chilly temperatures, about an hour ago she'd put her car's top down and tied a see-through scarf around her hair, kind of like one she'd seen Marilyn wear. The icy wind braced her and kept her awake. She'd been driving a full five hours. A while ago she'd run out of coffee.

Now, on hearing the screeching gulls, she decided to pull over. Anyway, she could use a break. Just ahead, across the street from the ocean, a ramshackle little diner appeared. Once she'd parked and gotten out of her car she took a moment to stretch and yawn and breathe in the moist salt air. She was careful to put only slight pressure on her left foot as she crossed the small lot.

Inside the quaint empty diner, she plopped down on a stool and ordered a coffee from the woman behind the counter, "Black with two sugars and lots of cream," she said. Her eyes wandered over to the pastry shelf to see if they had any good pies or freshly baked muffins.

"Is that a sweet potato pie?" she asked, and when the answer was yes, she requested a slice, her eyes widening with delight, and her stomach suddenly ravenous. She could hardly remember the last time she'd eaten any real food, not that pie constituted a meal. She wolfed it down and considered having a second piece. Or maybe some eggs.

The smells and sounds of cooking filtered out of the kitchen.

Like a child, she took a couple of turns on the bar stool, then stopped to gaze outside. For a time, she watched the surf. A black pick-up swung into the parking lot. A muscular guy, wearing little more than jeans and a white t-shirt, got out and came inside. She turned a bright innocent smile on him. "Aren't ya cold, like that?" she said. "Brrr," and pretended to shiver.

"Nah," he laughed, then strode over to the counter and straddled a barstool near her. He cocked his head to the side and studied her. "Haven't I seen you somewhere?" he asked.

She wondered if he'd seen any of the awful stuff on the Internet. "Maybe," she said with a coy smile. "I used to model for ads now and then." Of course this wasn't true.

He seemed impressed. "What brings you to these parts?"

With that opening, Sandy launched into a story that unspooled like a skein of silk, the threads changing color with each new lie that emerged from her mouth. She loved his boyish laughter, his rugged good looks, his straightforward eagerness, and couldn't help the way her libido suddenly sprang to life. He seemed fair game. Maybe I'll stop here a while, she thought. Start out fresh. Be somebody new and different. Why not?

· ● · ● · ● ·

Over breakfast Ron told Isabel that he'd begun looking into cyber-bullying laws and some of the cases that surrounded the issue. The laws differed between Maryland and DC, but at least they existed; the strength of those laws, he believed, was another matter.

"You remember that Megan Meier case? The 13-year-old who killed herself?" he asked.

She flinched slightly. "The case where that sick woman, Lori

Drew, did what Sandy did to Phoebe? That one?" she said.

"Yeah, that's the one." His voice sounded far too enthusiastic to Isabel, but he didn't seem to notice. "Well, basically she's gotten away with murder. The government brought some pretty unique charges against her, but the judge didn't uphold the jury's guilty verdict. Granted that was before a number of the bullying laws came into existence, but I think it might be hard to convict Sandy since—" he hesitated.

Isabel saw the sweat on Ron's brow. It was obvious that Sandy Littleton now dredged up horrific and shameful memories for him. She felt him studying her.

Frowning, she finished the sentence for him. "You mean since Phoebe didn't die? I know, Ron," she said softly. "Anyway, I'm not going to do anything right away, but I will look into it. And once Phoebe's...well, once she's better, I'll check with her about what she wants me to do. I'm not going to push her. About this I'm going to take my cues from her. She's been through enough. Whatever she wants I'll do."

Ron reached across the table and grasped her hand. "I'm glad to hear that," he said, "really, I am." Though she withdrew her hand, they sat awhile, staring out the large kitchen window, where a bright red cardinal flew to the bird feeder that hung on the empty branches of a dogwood. His plumage was stark against the drab bark of the tree.

Though it was too early in the year, the sodden gray sky made Isabel think it might snow, something she and Phoebe had always loved watching out this very window, an event that, on weekends at least, often led to baking cookies and drinking hot chocolate. Isabel felt herself growing maudlin, in part because it seemed like such a long time ago that they'd done this together.

She suddenly straightened in her chair. "Of course I'll tell Phoebe why taking some sort of legal action might be the right thing to do." She heard herself and almost felt like laughing.

Smiling a little, Ron shook his head. "You know what they say."

"What do they say?" she asked.

"You can't change a tiger's stripes."

"Nooo, Dad," Jackson chimed in. "You can't teach an old dog new tricks! Hey, can we get a dog?"

· ● · ● · ● ·

A couple of days later, in Phoebe's new hospital room, Isabel came to an appropriate stopping place in her work before standing up to gaze out the window. Though early in the season, snow swirled to the ground, obscuring the earth behind a cloud of white. Isabel could make out little but the shapes of a few evergreens that stood in the distance. It was like being in a dream. She pressed her hand against the glass to feel the cold.

"I want to go home," a voice croaked behind her.

Isabel spun around. Phoebe's eyes were closed. She took hold of her hand. "Sweetheart? Did you just say that?"

Her daughter's eyes opened a fraction, and she nodded her head a little. "Take me home."

"Oh, Phoebe, I will. I will take you home."

"Now, Mommy," she said in a plaintive voice.

Tears gathered in Isabel's eyes and her throat constricted. She squeezed Phoebe's hand, trying to think what to say. "I don't know if you can see it, sweetie, but it's snowing outside. When we go home, I'll make you some hot chocolate, and Jackson will build you a snowman. What do you say to that, my dearest child? Oh,

Phoebe, I love you so much and I'm so sorry—" her voice trailed off. No, now was not the time to get into all that. She'd have time, plenty of time to apologize to her daughter and start anew.

"I *will* take you home, baby, as soon as possible. I promise. With a little more rest you'll be all better and we'll have you back in your own bed. Just hang in there, okay, honey?"

A few weeks later

"Let's see, where shall we begin, Phoebe?" Dr. Sharma said.

It was Phoebe's first face-to-face meeting with Dr. Sharma since her suicide attempt, though they had spoken a couple of times by phone while she was recovering.

"I don't know," Phoebe said, leaning against the back of the beige leather couch with her hands tucked beneath her legs.

"You've been through a lot."

Phoebe nodded. "I have." She gave Dr. Sharma a little smile and studied the woman's kindly face, her lovely complexion, and the slightly sagging skin that was the nicest color. Olive, her mother called it. She wished her coloring were a little more like that. So that her own pale skin could tan, but it was no use, the sun just turned her face bright pink, like her father's.

"We'll talk about whatever you wish. So tell me about today."

"Today was fine, and I hope tomorrow will be too."

"Tell me something that makes you smile?"

"My mother asked me to make her a jean jacket! Can you believe that?" They both burst into laughter.

"Anything else good?"

"Well," she said, her eyes growing wide, "Emma and I are hanging out a lot. You can't believe how hilarious she is! And if you knew her mother, you'd probably be surprised. So that's really cool. And," she elongated the word, "Noah called and asked me out. He did, and I'm going to go." A shy grin crept onto her face.

"Did you know that when I started to wake up in the hospital a few weeks ago, Noah was there? Emma, too. You know Noah? He's the boy I've liked since last year. I mean all through eighth grade. And then things got all messed up, you know, after the Adams Morgan thing."

Dr. Sharma nodded. She sat in a chair opposite Phoebe. A window to Dr. Sharma's right cast a halo of light about her giving her an almost angelic glow. The sight made Phoebe stop speaking for a moment and gaze at the older woman. Then she continued, her eyes rising to the ceiling as the sequence of events spun through her mind, forgetting that she hadn't wanted to talk about the past, but perhaps needing to.

"I couldn't go with Noah to the dance, and then I forgot about Noah because of Shane," she hesitated briefly. "Shane, who turned out not to be a person at all." Phoebe's face puckered, as if she might cry.

"I imagine you must wonder about Mrs. Littleton," Dr. Sharma said. "But you know that her actions had nothing to do with you?"

Phoebe nodded. "I do."

"And that...well, what she did was terribly wrong."

Phoebe nodded again. "What's going to happen to her?"

"I heard she moved away and there might be a legal case against her, I don't know," Dr. Sharma said. "Are you worried she might do something to you?"

"Not really." She paused. "What about Jessie?"

Dr. Sharma tilted her head. "What about Jessie?"

"I've been thinking about her."

"What have you been thinking?"

"That I miss her."

"I'll bet she'd like to talk to you. Perhaps you should call her?"

Phoebe thought about that for a while, imagining what it might be like to have her old friend back. "Maybe I will," she finally said. "Maybe I will."

And a few days later, she did.

THE END

Acknowledgments

Bringing a novel to completion is rarely done alone, and so the list of people I'd like to thank is long. First, thank you, Ann Starr (Upper Hand Press, US) and Joel Richardson (Twenty7 Books, UK), for your excellent suggestions, which made the novel eminently better. I am terribly grateful to both of you for believing in *SAVING PHOEBE MURROW* and bringing it to fruition.

Second, thank you, Emily Williamson, for all your hard work as an agent and also for the many hours you spent reading the manuscript and providing helpful suggestions for improving it.

Third, a huge thank you to the many readers of the manuscript; the list is too long to include everyone, but please know I appreciated your help and encouragement. Special thanks to Reina Brekke, Myra Gossens, Christine Grimaldi, Connie Karageorgis, Katherine Kingsland, Roger Marum, Tricia Paoletta, Kathy Pasley,

Elizabeth Patton, Christine Pride, Darlynn Slosar, Louise Farmer Smith, Joe Vucovich, Rangeley Wallace, and Gail Wilkins.

A heartfelt thanks to my family, Jim, Max and Jack (Feely), my brother (Gary Burbach), my mother and now deceased father (Erna and Fritz Burbach), and my Tante Linde (Weimann) for all your support and encouragement throughout my years of writing.

I am grateful to Dr. Edward Selby for allowing me to use segments of his article, "Cutting to Escape from Emotional Pain;" to Janis Whitlock, Director of the Cornell Research Program on Self-Injury and Recovery, for her insights into the world of self-injury; to Dr. Martin R. Eichelberger and Dr. Brad Chaser for reviewing the medical segments of the story; and for legal aspects to Leslie Harris, Diana Rubin and Gail Wilkins. Obviously, any inaccuracies are mine. And thank you to Tina Meier and her staff at the Megan Meier Foundation for the resources they have provided related to the problem of cyber-bullying.

Finally, I will be forever indebted to the graduate journalism school at UC Berkeley and the masters writing program at Johns Hopkins University. In particular, early encouragement came from Mark Farrington, Margaret Meyers, Elly Williams and Claire Messud. Likewise, I am grateful to the James Jones First Novel Fellowship, the DC Commission on the Arts and Humanities, the Community of Writers at Squaw Valley, the Bread Loaf Writers' Conference and the Iowa Summer Writing Festival, especially Wayne Johnson and Mary Morris.

Cyberbullying Information

The inspiration for *SAVING PHOEBE MURROW* came from an article I read in 2008 about a woman who posed as a 15-year-old boy on a social media site to prey on a vulnerable 13-year-old girl named Megan Meier. In 2006, this woman (Lori Drew) launched a cyber-bullying attack on Megan through MySpace, which resulted in Megan taking her own life.

I was horrified by this report and couldn't understand how a woman, a mother who actually knew Megan and her family, could do such a thing. Over time the fictional characters for my novel emerged. While my characters are nothing like the people involved in the real life incident, my fictional character, Sandy, like Lori Drew, conspires against a young girl, in this case Phoebe Murrow.

I was deeply saddened by Megan's death, and appreciate Tina Meier's efforts to fight cyber-bullying by creating a foundation that honors the memory of her daughter. Not only is this novel written in memory of Megan, but I am also dedicating a portion of the proceeds from this novel to the Megan Meier Foundation. If you'd like to contribute, visit the organization's website: www.meganmeierfoundation.org. The website contains many resources for parents, teachers and teens to deal with cyber-bullying.

Resources to Combat the Problem

Cyber-bullying has become a huge problem, in part because of the ease of social media, texting, and the use of assorted electronic devices. According to the Cyberbullying Research Center, which has reviewed dozens of reports and studies, "it seems safe to conclude that about one out of every four teens has experienced cyber-bullying, and about one out of every six teens has done it to others." With such statistics, clearly something needs to be done.

There are many resources available that can inform you about cyber-bullying, how to combat the problem, and also what legislation exists in your state. Just a few organizations' websites that provide invaluable information include:

- The Megan Meier Foundation:
  http://www.meganmeierfoundation.org
- Cyberbullying Research Center: http://cyberbullying.org
- STOP!T features a cyber-bullying app to report cyber-bullying anonymously: http://stopitcyberbully.com
- The National Suicide Prevention Lifeline:
  1-800-273-TALK (8255) and their website:
  http://www.suicidepreventionlifeline.org
- This website focuses on both bullying and cyber-bullying and contains a variety of information about how to stop bullying, and the policies and laws in each state, information well worth knowing: www.stopbullying.gov

Author Q&A

What prompted you to write this book?

A very troubling article I read about a cyber-bullying incident instigated by a woman posing as a 15-year-old boy on MySpace. I thought that I'd first learned of this in People magazine in 2008, but in fact I must have read about it in the *Washington Post* first because when I looked back at those two articles, The Post piece ran in January 2008 and the People one didn't come out until December of the same year. I saved both articles, read each one once and knew I wanted to write a novel about a similar situation. I simply could not understand how or why a woman could do such a thing to a vulnerable girl she knew.

How closely does your novel follow the actual story?

Not closely at all, except that in both the real incident and in my novel a woman creates a phony teenage guy (on social media) to prey on a 13-year-old girl, her daughter's best friend, or once best friend. In the actual case, the woman (Lori Drew) and her family had even gone on vacation with the girl's family. It's really quite monstrous, and to this day I can't understand someone's motivation.

And yet in your story a woman also does such a thing. How were you able to create her?

Sandy, the character who does this to Phoebe, is damaged, just as I imagine Lori Drew must be. Sandy's backstory, which emerged over time (in my mind), became critical to her present story. I realized that she was damaged by her mother, through neglect and a lack of nurturing. And then she also suffered multiple betrayals. To survive she becomes vengeful. This vengeful side is again stimulated by numerous rejections and public humiliations she receives from Phoebe's mother, Isabel, who it should be noted does not intentionally humiliate her. To get back at Isabel, Sandy decides to strike at Isabel's Achilles' heel – her family.

All of the characters have been hurt in some way and deserve sympathy...but which character do you care about the most, or has the bulk of your sympathy?

Without question, Phoebe is the one I care about most. Hence, the title: *Saving Phoebe Murrow*. But let me add, that I care about all the characters, even Sandy.

There is a lot of love going on in this novel, especially the love between mothers and daughters, as well as between girls. And love gone wrong, and the often poor timing of love between two people. But the publisher felt that title was too evocative of a love story or romance, and this novel certainly isn't about that. *Saving Phoebe Murrow* came about at the very end of the process, when I realized that this story, essentially, is about Phoebe. Everything ties back to her. And we want desperately to save her. But the question always was: can we?

Are you implying that women are mean and cliquish even into adulthood?

I wanted to show the consequences of such behavior. I wanted people to talk about what better choices the women and the girls had, and what it might mean to do the right thing. In the novel, we have one set of actions and reactions. It's stuff you hear and read about, and in some case, what people experience. But how can we rise above the petty differences, the cattiness, and so on. How can we be more loving and accepting toward one another? How can we stop gossiping and putting other girls/women down?

Was there anything in your own childhood that resonated for you as you wrote this novel?

I didn't realize that anything in the novel related to my own life until well after I'd finished the final version of the novel and was discussing it with Emily Williamson. It was then that I realized I too had been bullied as young girl, after coming to the US in second grade. That children had shunned me just as they make fun of Phoebe in the novel. Not for being chubby, but for being

German at a time when Germans were portrayed as Nazis. It was deeply painful, and I guess that emotion has resided there ever since. The emotion being one of non-acceptance, of somehow being ugly and unlovable.

How does the ending of novel differ from the real life event of Megan Meier?

To find this out, you must read the novel.

Discussion Guide

Q: Why does Phoebe decide to defy her mother's restrictions and go to Adams Morgan with her friends? Was it peer pressure or something else? Does she ultimately feel that not telling her parents the truth about it only compounded the problem later on?

Q: Has your child ever been bullied or cyber-bullied? How did you deal with it?

Q: The "mean girl" syndrome is a well-documented behavior among girls. Why do you think girls behave this way?

What about boys? How do they engage in bullying behaviors? Do bullying behaviors vary between genders? If so, why do you think this happens?
(http://girlsleadership.org/blog/what-motivates-mean-girl-behavior/)

Q: Who is a "mean" girl among the adult women in the novel?

Q: As an adult, do you know some "mean girls" among the women in your life or have you ever been the target of a mean girl's bullying? Have you ever been a mean girl yourself?

Q: Whose parenting style do you prefer? Sandy's or Isabel's? Are there elements of both that you identify with or do you feel that neither character is a good mother?

Q: Is Isabel right to say that "trust" is essential in a mother's relationship with her daughter? With her children, male or female?

Q: Isabel once told Phoebe: "There's no point in lying, I'll just find out anyway. Mothers always do." Is this true? Is she talking about intuition or about keeping close tabs on her? Should a parent try to know everything about their child's life, or is that too invasive?

Q: Should girls resolve their own differences without adult interference, as Isabel had tried to do?

Q: Ron chastises Isabel for being overly worried about their daughter. Do you agree with him? Is there such a thing as worrying "too much" about your child?

Q: Ron also feels that Isabel is further alienating Phoebe by punishing her too severely. Is he right? If so, what would be a more appropriate punishment/consequence? What could Ron have done differently?

Q: Do parents tend to take on certain roles, that is, one tends to be stricter and often the disciplinarian, while the other is more passive and/or more lenient?

Q: Isabel questions her own tactics in trying to discipline her daughter. This internal conflict stems, in part, from her fears about Phoebe cutting herself again. How does a parent continue to provide limits and parental supervision when a child exhibits self-destructive behavior?

Q: What does Isabel not understand when she says to Ron that they are being held hostage by Phoebe's cutting?

Q: What do you think about Isabel reversing course and deciding to allow Phoebe to attend the dance after all? Do you agree with her rationale?

Q: Lorraine Blau, Emma's mother, tells Isabel that parents don't really have control over the choices kids make each day once they leave the house. Do you think this is true? What are a parent's obligations to keep a child out of trouble? What responsibility do children have in the choices they make online?

Q: How can one instill good judgment in a child? Does Phoebe have good judgment? What about Emma and Jessie? Would you allow your daughter (or son) to hang out with these two girls, knowing what you know about them?

Q: How should a parent go about discouraging their children from hanging out with unsavory characters? Or with children who they know are a "bad influence"?

Q: It's pretty obvious what Sandy does wrong in the story, but what about the things she does right? Are there any? In what ways is she a sympathetic character?

Some additional questions you might want to ask yourself:

- What are the signs or symptoms of bullying, self-harm, and/or suicidality?
- Are you aware of resources available in your community that can help in case a son or daughter experiences a bullying-related situation? Who can be of help? Who else might have helped Phoebe?
- Why do you think youth are using the Internet to cyberbully?
- As a parent, what is important to know about online social media platforms and networks?
- How do I know if my child is bullying others? What can I do?